REVOLUTIONARY GHOSTS

EDWARD TRIMNELL

PART I

PROLOGUE: 2018

1

I was tying my tie in Dr. Beckman's exam room when I felt the chill. I was alone in the tiny, antiseptic space. The doctor had stepped out to allow me to get dressed.

I took a deep breath. The cool air had a vaguely chemical odor.

There was nothing in here to be afraid of. From where I stood, leaning against the exam table, I could see a sink and counter—spotless and sterile—lined with bottles of hydrogen peroxide and rubbing alcohol. Formica and metal surfaces, gleaming in the bright glare of the overhead florescent light panels.

The tiled floor gleamed, too. Beneath the sink, there was a little rolling stool. (There is one of those in every exam room on the planet, it seems.)

I took a deep breath, and continued tying my double Windsor knot.

There is nothing in here to be afraid of.

Then I saw the closet door, in the corner of the room behind the exam table.

The door was slightly ajar—just a crack.

Had it been closed ten minutes ago, when Dr. Beckman was in

here, prodding me with his stethoscope, tongue depressor, and ear speculum?

I wasn't sure. But after recent events—and after long-ago events—I don't like doors that are slightly ajar, doors that partially reveal dark spaces.

I could feel my skin breaking out in gooseflesh beneath the starched fabric of my white Oxford dress shirt.

The room is chilly by design, I told myself. Someone—I forget who—once told me that temperatures in medical facilities are kept deliberately low, so as to stymie the growth of molds and bacteria.

But what else was growing in here? What was hiding in that closet, that I couldn't see?

I FELT **foolish** for having such thoughts, for even raising such questions. I am not a child. I am a fifty-nine-year-old man, a father and grandfather. I'm a divisional manager at Covington Foods, a large consumer goods company based in Cincinnati, Ohio.

I have investments. Stocks and mutual funds. All the requisite forms of insurance, for a man my age.

No one who knows me would say that I am easily spooked, whimsical, or given to flights of fancy. My wife, in fact, calls me "Steady Steve".

And Steady Steve I am, most of the time.

But this past week, I have not been myself.

FULLY DRESSED NOW, I was trying to decide what to do about that closet door. I was weighing two options.

On one hand, I could walk across the room and push the door shut. That would be the simplest option.

On the other hand, I could pull the door open. Then I would know for sure that there was nothing lurking in that space.

I was still considering these options when I heard a door click open behind me. Not the closet door, but the door of the exam room.

Dr. Beckman was back.

Dr. Beckman is a stoop-shouldered man with a sallow complexion. He is still in his thirties, but his light brown hair is fast receding. He wears thick glasses.

Dr. Beckman has been my family physician for about three years now. My wife, Peggy, and I started seeing him after dear old Dr. Alfieri finally retired at the age of seventy-two.

I greeted Dr. Beckman. I noticed that he was carrying a clipboard.

I was in his office today for the second half of a two-part exam. The first half had been carried out last week.

This was a routine physical, but nevertheless done at the behest of my employer. Covington Foods requires all of its managers to receive a stem-to-stern physical exam every two years.

"We can go over the results of your exam," Dr. Beckman said, "if you're ready. Per the usual procedure, my office will send a copy of the results to the Covington Foods human resources department. We'll also mail a copy to the home address that we have on file for you."

"Please," I said. "Let's go over the results."

Dr. Beckman consulted his clipboard. "The results of the blood work that you had done last week are quite satisfactory. Liver and kidney function look good.

"Same for lipids. We'll have to watch your LDL cholesterol, moving forward. But that's the same for practically everyone. You performed well on your stress test. Not bad at all, for a man your age."

Just then Dr. Beckman stopped himself. "Oh, I'm sorry, Steve. I didn't mean—"

"That's okay, Doc. I'm fifty-nine years old this year. We need not pretend that I'm a spring chicken. But it's good to hear that I shouldn't die in the foreseeable future, just the same."

My last sentence, those words about death, seemed to hang in the air. Was I really certain that I wouldn't die in the foreseeable future? And it wasn't my LDL cholesterol that I was worried about.

I knew, from the events of forty years ago, that there were far worse ways to die.

"Of course not," Dr. Beckman said, with a tight little smile. "I anticipate you'll be coming in for many more biennial exams yet."

The doctor paused, not saying anything for a moment. During my more than thirty years at Covington Foods, I have had literally thousands of encounters with bosses, colleagues, and subordinates. I can always tell when someone has something to say, but doesn't quite know how to broach the topic.

"I sense a 'but' coming here, Doc," I said. "Out with it, whatever 'it' is."

The doctor seemed relieved. "Yes, well, I suppose there is something. I couldn't help noticing that you've displayed signs of acute anxiety this week. I didn't notice that last week, when you came in for the blood work and the stress test."

'Anxiety', Dr. Beckman called it. That was putting the matter lightly. My problems had begun on Tuesday of last week, the day after my visit to Dr. Beckman's office, for the first part of my full-body exam.

But there was no way I could discuss the past week and a half with Dr. Beckman.

"I don't think so," I said, playing dumb. "A little stress at the office maybe. Nothing more."

I could tell that Dr. Beckman didn't believe me. You don't get through medical school without being perceptive.

But in another second my facade would crumble, anyway.

THAT WAS **when I heard** the hoofbeats, thundering down the hallway. I could picture a dark black horse. The animal would be partially rotted from the centuries it had spent in the grave, its muscles and bones exposed here and there. The eyes of the horse would be dead and glassy.

The rider of the horse would be wearing an eighteenth-century military frock coat, also rotted and in tatters, heavy trousers and boots.

The rider would be wearing no hat. Because the rider had no head.

The rider would be wielding a large battlefield sword.

The rider and horse would burst through the door of the exam room. First the Horseman would behead Dr. Beckman. (Dr. Beckman would barely have time to see the blow coming; and he certainly wouldn't have time to save himself.)

Dr. Beckman's head would topple from his body and roll to the floor. Then his body would drop, so much dead weight, his neck spurting blood.

And then the Horseman would take my head, too.

I had evaded him for more than forty years. But I would evade him no longer.

A few more seconds passed, and I realized the nature of my delusion. The hoofbeats in the hallway moved past the closed door of the exam room. Then I realized that they were not hoofbeats at all.

What I had heard was the ruckus of a nurse or orderly pushing a caster-wheeled cart atop the tiled floor of the hallway outside the exam room. A perfectly normal sound in any medical building.

I recovered myself. Dr. Beckman was staring at me with narrowed eyes.

"I'm fine," I said. "I just felt a bit lightheaded for a moment. It's nothing."

Dr. Beckman made not even the slightest pretense of accepting my excuse.

"Steve," he said. "We've got to talk."

DR. BECKMAN DID NOT CONVINCE me quite that easily. As I've said, I'm a divisional manager at Covington Foods. I don't easily budge when I am not of a mind to do so.

"Have you ever heard of cortisol, Steve?" Dr. Beckman asked me.

I was somewhat puzzled by this seemingly off-the-wall question.

"Maybe," I said. "I might have heard of it. One of those hormones, isn't it?"

"Very good," Dr. Beckman said, nodding. "Exactly. Cortisol is your body's main stress hormone. As you might be able to guess, your body secretes cortisol when you are under stress. Part of the body's fight or flight mechanism. A small amount of cortisol is relatively harmless."

"I have a feeling, Dr. Beckman, that you're going to tell me that larger quantities of cortisol are not so harmless."

"Right again, Steve. Over time, large quantities of cortisol can have a myriad of negative effects on your health. And I'm not merely talking about things like a touchy stomach or sleeplessness, though symptoms begin that way. Over time, large amounts of cortisol can lead to autoimmune diseases, heart disease, and even cancer. That's what chronic stress does to your body."

I took a moment to take in what Dr. Beckman had just said. It was a sad irony to think that even if the Horseman hadn't beheaded me forty years ago, the memory of him—these flashbacks—might bring about my death by a thousand proverbial cuts.

In more than forty years, I had told no one about the events that transpired in the summer of 1976. I was the only one left alive who fully remembered them.

Perhaps I had kept my secrets too long. Perhaps I could benefit by opening up, just a little.

Could I tell Dr. Beckman about that horrible summer? No, I didn't think I could. But perhaps I could tell him about the problems that I had been having more recently.

"Okay, doctor. I suppose I get your point. I have been under a more than usual amount of stress lately. Some very unusual things have been occurring."

"Unusual?" Dr. Beckman raised his eyebrows.

"Very unusual," I confirmed.

Dr. Beckman leaned back against the spotless counter where the sink was. He set his clipboard on the counter, near the bottles of rubbing alcohol and hydrogen peroxide.

"By all means, Steve. Do go on. We have some time left in your appointment hour."

I took a deep breath before beginning. "Okay, Doc. It all began with a quarter."

"A *quarter*?"

"Yes. A quarter."

2

There are perks associated with being a divisional manager at Covington Foods. One of these perks is that I have the stereotypical "corner office".

My office is located on the sixth floor of the Covington Foods headquarters building. Two walls of the office are comprised mostly of windows. This affords me a view of the southernmost sector of downtown Cincinnati and the Ohio River. Within sight of my office is also a historic suspension bridge that was built during the American Civil War.

I entered my office last Tuesday a little after ten o'clock in the morning. I had already had two meetings that day, and my mind was awhirl with my usual plateful of deadlines and crises.

It was a gorgeous late October morning, sunny and clear. In general, no one moves to Cincinnati for the weather. The city is characterized by wet, snowy winters, long, rainy springs, and humid summers.

But oh, the autumns. Autumn is the one time of the year when you feel fortunate to be a resident of southern Ohio.

When I walked into my office, I immediately noticed a shiny, metallic object in the middle of my desk blotter. It was glinting in the sun.

I could see that it was a coin. A quarter, in all likelihood.

There is nothing inherently unusual about a quarter, of course (though there would turn out to be much unusual about this one). I knew, however, that it had not been there when I'd left for my a.m. meetings. And very few people have access to my private office.

I sat down at my desk and picked up the coin.

It was indeed a quarter, issued by the U.S. Mint. But this was an unusual twenty-five cent piece—by the standards of 2018, at least.

The quarter in my hand was a Bicentennial quarter. On the heads side of the coin, beneath the usual bust of George Washington, were two dates: 1776 and 1976. On the obverse—tails—side there was an engraving of a Continental Army drummer. Above him was the Torch of Liberty enclosed in a ring of thirteen stars. And beneath that, the Latin inscription, E PLURIBUS UNUM.

Why had someone put a Bicentennial quarter on my desk? The coin was inextricably associated with 1976.

And as I've said, I'm the only one left alive who fully remembers the events of that summer.

1976 U.S. Bicentennial quarter, tails side

"Are you familiar with Bicentennial quarters?" I asked Dr. Beckman.

"Somewhat," Dr. Beckman said. "I was born in the early nineteen-eighties. There weren't many of them around by then."

"No, there weren't," I said. "The U.S. Mint actually produced and circulated one-point-six billion of them. A huge quantity for American coinage in the late middle of the twentieth century. The coins were issued to commemorate the American Bicentennial.

"Anyone who is old enough to remember nineteen seventy-six will certainly remember the Bicentennial celebrations. America had just emerged from Vietnam and Watergate. But the economy was horrible in the nineteen seventies. That was the era of stagflation and never-ending energy crises.

"The Bicentennial celebrations became a forced display of national unity and optimism, even though many people weren't feeling much of either. Both the government and the media made a big deal of the so-called 'Spirit of Seventy-Six.' Bicentennial memorabilia was everywhere. Most of all, those Bicentennial quarters."

"So where did they all go?" Dr. Beckman asked.

"Most of them disappeared into private collections. Everyone was certain that Bicentennial quarters were going to be valuable someday. But do you know how much the average Bicentennial quarter is worth nowadays?"

"No," Dr. Beckman admitted. "Coin collecting isn't exactly an…*avocation* of mine."

"Bicentennial quarters are worth twenty-five cents today," I said, "unless you have an uncirculated proof, or a rare variation.

"But they are still hoarded. Someday, in perhaps forty years, when all the generations that were alive in nineteen seventy-six die off, there will be a flood of Bicentennial coins released into general circulation, I predict. But for now, they're rare, even though they aren't particularly valuable."

"Very interesting," Dr. Beckman said. "But surely you aren't suffering from acute anxiety because you found an unexplained, rare-but-not-particularly-valuable quarter on your desk at Covington Foods."

"Oh," I corrected him. "The presence of the quarter was explained."

"I see," Dr. Beckman said with a little frown. "Do go on, Steve."

A FAMILIAR FEMININE **voice** piped up behind me.

"Oh, Mr. Wagner. You found it."

I swiveled around in my chair and saw Madison Greene. Madison is my student co-op, a marketing major at the University of Cincinnati. She's been assigned to me since August. Madison is a very bright and diligent young woman. She's made a real contribution to our new product marketing campaigns.

Madison has also turned the heads of more than a few males in the office. She's a pretty brunette who wears glasses. I've noticed that the other male co-op students and young male salaried employees take every opportunity to talk to her. But Madison Greene is all business, at least when she's in the office. On more than one occasion, I have seen her dismiss the would-be twentysomething suitor with a frosty look or tone of voice.

And even with me, she's excessively formal. She calls me "Mr. Wagner". I've invited her to call me "Steve" several times. We don't insist on formal modes of address at Covington Foods.

Madison will call me Steve for a day or two, then it's back to "Mr. Wagner". I've given up. Mr. Wagner it is, then.

Madison was holding a manila file folder in her hand. I remembered then that she had promised to drop by my office late in the morning to show me some ad proposals for Ocean Brite Soap, a new product that Covington Foods will launch next year.

But first there was the matter of the observation she had just made. "Found what, Madison?"

"Well, I mean...that quarter, of course. It's a Bicentennial quarter."

"I know. *You* put it on my desk, Madison?"

I was taken aback. This prim-and-proper young woman, who wouldn't even address me by my first name, had found cause to enter my office when I wasn't present, and place a Bicentennial quarter on my desk. Was that what she was saying?

This was an unusual occurrence. I wasn't angry—not by any means—but it probably seemed to Madison that I was.

"I—I found the quarter in my change this morning," she said, "from the coffee kiosk in the first-floor lobby."

"And why did you think that *I* would want it?"

Madison had no way of knowing what I was truly thinking. So, of course, she continued to perceive my reaction as annoyance.

"I—I don't know. I guess I figured that you might want it as a memento."

"A 'memento'?"

"Yes, well—you were alive when it was minted, right? Oh—I didn't mean—"

"Madison," I interrupted. "It's okay. I'm just wondering why you put the quarter on my desk. I've never given you any indication that I'm into coin collecting."

"I don't know," Madison said, flustered. "The truth is—and this will sound silly—but it was like a little voice just told me, *Give this to Mr. Wagner.*"

I don't know if I flinched, but I probably did. Madison wasn't the sort of person whose actions were ruled by "little voices". And where, exactly, had that little voice come from?

Madison Greene would have absolutely no idea of the significance of the year 1976. What that year meant to me.

"Oh!" Madison was visibly shaken now. "I feel like such an idiot. I don't know why I did that!"

I raised my hands in what I intended to be a calming gesture. "Madison. Madison. It's all right. I appreciate the thought. But in case you haven't already guessed, Covington Foods pays me a pretty fair wage for the work I do here. I don't want to become known as the manager who takes money from his student co-ops." I held out the quarter to her. "Please, Madison. Take the quarter back. But thank you, once again, for the thought."

I suppose that I made things worse for her by returning the quarter. But I didn't want to have it in my possession. Even then, before everything else happened.

Madison reached out, and took the quarter from my hand. She dropped it into the right pocket of the skirt of her gray business suit.

"I'm sorry," she said.

I figured that the best thing for me to do now would be to change the subject.

"Nothing to be sorry about, Madison. Anyway, let's move on to the next item. I believe you brought some ad mockups for Ocean Brite Soap…"

Together we went over the ad mockups. Neither one of us mentioned the quarter again.

But there was a palpable air of discomfort in the room between us. Inadvertently, my overreaction to the quarter had caused Madison to feel ashamed.

Now, I knew, she would never address me as Steve. I would be Mr. Wagner for the remainder of her time at Covington Foods.

"A SOMEWHAT UNUSUAL INTERACTION WITH A SUBORDINATE," Dr. Beckman said, when I'd finished. "But I still don't see how any of this is the cause of your anxiety."

"That's not all," I said. "I'm not finished yet."

"You keep mentioning the year nineteen seventy-six. What exactly is it about that year?"

I wasn't yet ready to directly answer Dr. Beckman's question—and I didn't know if I ever would be. But I did have something more to tell him about that day at the office. And it was a lot more disturbing than an unexpected quarter, and an awkward conversation.

The unusual was about to become horrific.

3

As the rest of that morning—and the early afternoon—dragged on, I largely forgot about the unexplained Bicentennial quarter, and my somewhat prickly discussion with Madison.

Perhaps it had been nothing more than a mere coincidence. Madison, moreover, was something of a mystery to me. Bluntly speaking, she was an odd duck. Why else would she doggedly insist on calling me Mr. Wagner, when I had invited her, multiple times, to call me Steve?

I had two meetings after lunch. Nothing unusual about that. Much of my day is consistently filled up with meetings.

I returned to my office in the middle of the afternoon.

There was a shiny object in the middle of my desk blotter. Now it was glinting in the afternoon sun, instead of the morning sun.

I walked over and picked it up. I already knew that it would be a Bicentennial quarter. But I felt a compulsion to confirm that fact.

I turned the quarter over in my hand. I saw the familiar design of all U.S. quarters minted in 1976, to commemorate the American Bicentennial.

I dropped the quarter into my pocket. Then I walked out into the anteroom of my office. My administrative assistant, Loretta Byrd, was busy at work. She was proofreading one of the many reports that my division issues each week.

"Loretta?" I said. "Excuse me."

Loretta lifted her head of platinum blonde hair.

"Yes, Steve. What is it?"

Loretta is about my age, give or take a few years. Unlike Madison, she has no qualms about addressing me by my first name. Loretta has worked at Covington Foods for seventeen years. She has raised two children, and she's coped with two husbands. She outlived the first husband. I expect her to outlive the present one, too.

"Has Madison Greene been in my office since lunch?"

"No," Loretta said. "I've been here the entire time. I would have seen her."

"You're sure?"

"Of course I'm sure. Didn't I just say that I've been here the entire time?"

There was no way I could push the matter further without accusing Loretta of lying.

"Thank you," I said.

"Would you like me to ask Madison to come up here?" Loretta reached for her phone. Madison, we both knew, occupied a cubicle on the fourth floor. Along with most of the other co-ops.

"No," I said hastily. "That won't be necessary."

Loretta leaned slightly forward, and eyed me suspiciously.

"Is something wrong, Steve? Is something going on?"

"No. Thanks again, Loretta." I turned back toward my office.

Something was indeed wrong. Loretta was right about one thing. She would have seen Madison enter my office. So that didn't make sense.

But the idea of Madison dropping the quarter on my desk a second time was equally inexplicable.

Madison Green was a young woman who dotted every "i", and crossed every "t". Placing the quarter on my desk the first time had been a gesture of monumental forwardness for her. Completely out of character, in and of itself.

But for her to place the quarter on my desk again, thereby defying my explicit wishes…?

I took a step inside my office, looked up, and saw what was on my desk.

And then I forgot all about that quarter in my pocket.

MADISON GREENE'S **severed head** was sitting in the middle of my desk blotter, where the quarter had been just a few minutes before.

Her eyes and mouth were both open. *She had not seen the blade coming*, I thought absurdly.

The blotter was soaked with blood, I could see—Madison's blood.

What had happened? I wondered frantically. Apparently there had been much that Loretta hadn't seen, despite her insistence that she'd been stalwartly at her desk.

Then Madison's eyes rolled over in their sockets. Her mouth moved soundlessly. Madison was trying to rebuke me. For what I had brought down upon her with my arrogance.

That may have been the element that knocked me out of my daze. This isn't real, I told myself. There was no way it could be real. It was a deliberately concocted illusion. Or my own hallucination.

But it wasn't real.

I turned around, and walked back into the anteroom. This time Loretta heard me coming.

"Yes, Steve. Are you all right? You look a little pale."

I didn't address her remark. I wasn't at all surprised to hear that I looked a little pale.

"Would you mind coming into my office for a moment, Loretta?"

"Okay," she said with slow emphasis. "May I ask what for? I really need to get these reports done."

"It won't take a minute," I promised her. And it wouldn't. Loretta would either see what I had seen, or she wouldn't.

Loretta let out a sigh, as if to say, *You're the boss. What can I do about it?* Then she stood up and walked around her desk.

"Could you take a look in my office, Loretta, and let me know if you see anything out of place or unusual?"

Loretta gave me a frown.

"What?"

"Please, Loretta. Just humor me."

She let out another sigh. "Oh, all right. Very well."

I stepped aside so that she could enter my office. I remained just outside the threshold, with my back to her.

If she screams, I thought, *then it's real. I'll know in a matter of seconds.*

BUT LORETTA DIDN'T SCREAM. And after another five seconds passed without her screaming, I turned around.

"What? You wanted me to look for 'anything unusual'?"

"That's right," I said.

"Well, other than that pen that's exploded on your desk blotter, I don't see anything unusual."

I was standing beside her now, and I could see the situation that she was referring to: An ink pen was in the middle of my desk blotter. It was the ballpoint pen that the company had given me more than a decade ago, to commemorate my first twenty years of service.

As Loretta had noted, the ink tube inside the pen had indeed ruptured. The pen was sitting in a puddle of its own ink.

Had the pen been there a few minutes ago? I wasn't sure. I did vaguely recall using the pen to write a memo to myself, immediately after lunch.

All that mattered was that it wasn't Madison's head.

I was still breathing heavily, but I willed myself into some kind of composure, a recovery.

"Thank you, Loretta," I said. "That—that will be all."

But Loretta wasn't letting me off the hook that easily.

"'*That will be all*'?" she mimicked. "You still haven't told me what this is about, Steve. You pulled me away from my reports to tell you that a pen was *leaking ink*?"

"It's a market research thing," I told her. "We—we're checking to see how quickly people notice anomalies in their environment. That helps us anticipate the average person's responsiveness to ads. Forgive me for making you a guinea pig, Loretta, but it would have ruined the experiment if I'd explained it to you in advance."

"Okay," Loretta said, grudgingly.

I didn't know if she actually believed my elaborate lie. I only cared, at that moment, that she was willing to drop the matter.

And yes, I did feel guilty for lying to her. But I had to give her some explanation.

"Would you like me to clean up that mess on your desk for you?"

"No, thank you, Loretta. I'll take care of the pen. Sorry to disturb you. I'll let you get back to your reports now."

With that Loretta went back to her desk—and I immediately left the office. Loretta watched me walk out without comment. She was probably fed up with my strangeness, wanted no more part of it.

There was another, related matter that I had to attend to. And I wouldn't be able to focus on anything else until I had seen to it.

I walked down the hallway to the elevators, and rode down to the fourth floor, where the co-op cubicles were located.

I exited the elevator on the fourth floor and walked to the edge of the co-op wing. I didn't want to attract any attention. I didn't want anyone to notice me at all, in fact.

I stood at the edge of the co-op wing and saw Madison Greene seated inside her cubicle. She was typing away at her company-issued laptop.

She was very much alive, and her head was completely intact upon her shoulders. Thankfully, the layout of the cubicles enabled me to see Madison without her seeing me.

I was about to go back to my office. And then I saw *him*.

He was a red-haired young man, with an angular face. Another one of the student co-ops—or rather, that's what he might have been pretending to be.

I don't know how long he'd been with the company, but I'd never noticed him at Covington Foods before. He was sitting a few cubicle rows away from Madison.

He looked up from his computer and smiled at me.

He looked immediately familiar. A red-haired young man I'd encountered decades ago, in the summer of 1976.

I gasped. He saw me gasp, and he smirked. Then he shook his head and returned his attention to his computer.

Before he could look up again, I left the co-op area, boarded the elevator, and returned to my office.

4

I was done now with my telling—or as much as I was going to reveal to Dr. Beckman for the time being.

The doctor paused and glanced at his watch. When I had begun my story, there was still time to spare in my appointment hour.

Now we were about to run over.

"I would say that you've suffered from a mild delusion," Dr. Beckman said. "That's my initial assessment, anyway."

You think? I wanted to say. But I held my tongue. This was no time for sarcasm. Dr. Beckman was trying to help me, after all.

"Your delusions—if you're not offended by that word—"

"It's okay, Doc. I'm not offended. Say whatever words you need to use."

"You have suffered from some delusions, but you aren't *delusional*, if that makes sense. When you saw—*correction*—when you believed you saw—your co-op's severed head atop your desk, you were able to recognize that you were having a hallucination. You were still capable of appealing to logic. And this is important, Steve. Because there is a logical explanation for everything."

The standard retort of the evangelical skeptic, I thought. I was determined not to take an arch tone with Dr. Beckman, but I had to challenge him a little. I knew he wouldn't even consider the notion that my temporary "delusion" of Madison's head on my desk had any cause outside my own mind. But there was objective reality to consider, too.

The quarter. The quarter had returned to my desk. Inexplicably.

When I posed this question to Dr. Beckman, he smiled indulgently.

"Steve, you have to check your premises here. You're making two assumptions. First of all, you're assuming that that student co-op of yours wouldn't defy your orders. Secondly, you're assuming that your administrative assistant was being completely truthful when she assured you that she had been sitting faithfully at her desk the entire afternoon."

I nodded. Those were, indeed, my working assumptions. Based on my experiences with Madison thus far, she would have sooner skipped naked through the halls of Covington Foods than placed the quarter on my desk a second time. And although Loretta could be a bit irascible on occasion, she had never lied to me.

"Have you considered the possibility," Dr. Beckman said, "that you've misjudged both of these individuals? This Madison does seem to have a strong passive-aggressive streak. And your administrative assistant: Is she a smoker, may I ask?"

"Yes. Loretta is a smoker."

"Well, there you have it. Loretta was probably out of the office on an unauthorized smoke break that she didn't want to reveal to you. That gave Madison a window of time in which to enter your office, and place the quarter back on your desk."

I said nothing. I didn't agree with Dr. Beckman's hypothesis, but I couldn't disprove it, either.

"And this thing about the young man in the co-op area. You said you'd had some interaction with this same young man in nineteen seventy-six?"

"Yes. It's been more than forty years, but I'm almost certain I saw him back then."

"Surely you realize that that's impossible, Steve. If he had been a young man in nineteen seventy-six, he'd be in his late fifties—or more likely his *sixties*—today. And if he truly is a young man today, in twenty eighteen, then he hadn't even been born in nineteen seventy-six. He wouldn't be born for around twenty years, in fact."

Once again, I found myself unable to either agree with Dr. Beckman, or to logically refute him.

When I didn't speak, Dr. Beckman glanced at his watch again.

"Steve, we're about out of time, and I have another patient at the top of the hour. But I don't want to let this go. So let me tell you what I want you to do."

"Whatever you say, Doc," I said—though I wasn't quite certain about that.

"As you know," Dr. Beckman began, "I'm just a general practitioner. I'm not a specialist on these matters. But I think I may be able to make an assessment that will tell us if we need to refer you to a specialist."

"You mean a shrink?" I said. "A head doctor?"

"I mean a psychiatrist or a psychologist, Steve. Lots of people see them nowadays. They can often help. But before we get to that, I need more information. I don't believe that we quite got to the source of your trauma in this visit. The root cause."

Yes, that was true. *And you wouldn't believe me if I told you, Doc.*

"I am therefore going to ask you to make a written account of what happened to you—or what you *believe* happened to you. Write it down, Steve. Write it *all* down."

"Excuse me?"

"I've listened to your story, and it's plain that you're harboring a deep trauma related to something that happened in the year nineteen seventy-six. That is a common element throughout everything we've discussed over the last twenty minutes—from the Bicentennial quarter on your desk, to your belief that one of Covington Foods' student co-ops is a young man you knew in that year.

"If we can uncover your trauma from nineteen seventy-six, then we can get to the heart of what ails you...Or, I can refer you to someone who can."

DR. BECKMAN ADDED a final word of explanation—or assurance. "Needless to say, Steve, this matter will remain strictly between us. It won't be part of your Covington Foods physical. Your official biennial exam has already been closed out, and you've passed with flying colors."

Dr. Beckman fixed his gaze on me, doctor-to-patient style: "Will you do this, Steve? Will you write that journal?"

I didn't want to outright lie to him, so I answered as plainly and as honestly as I could: "I'll give it serious consideration, doctor."

"Please do. You can write it in any format. When you're done, send it directly to my attention. You should have my email and my mailing address. If not, you can pick up a calling card at the receptionist's counter on the way out. And don't worry about other eyes reading it. Send your document to my attention, with the designation 'confidential'. My staff won't peak at it. They know better."

"Thanks, Dr. Beckman. Like I said, I'll think about it. Seriously think about it."

"That's all we can ask," Dr. Beckman said.

AS I PREPARED to exit the exam room, a final question occurred to Dr. Beckman.

"Oh," he said. "What did you ever do with that quarter? Did you give it back to Madison?"

"No." I hadn't. I had spoken to Madison numerous times since that day. At no point had she given me any indication that she was expecting a rebuke from me, or further questioning about the quarter.

So I never mentioned the quarter's return. Perhaps Madison was —as Dr. Beckman put it—passive-aggressive. I tended to think, however, that Madison simply didn't know about the quarter's second appearance on my desk.

"Where is the quarter now, then?" Dr. Beckman asked.

I knew exactly where the quarter was. The quarter was in my pocket. I'd been carrying it around with me since that day.

I had my reasons. If I discarded the coin a second time, and it inexplicably returned to me, that might be more than my sanity could handle.

"Actually, doctor, I have the coin right here." I dug into my right pants pocket and pulled out the quarter.

Just then, a somewhat unusual thought occurred to me. But this had been a week for unusual thoughts.

I extended the quarter to Dr. Beckman on my open palm. "Here—take it."

"Me?" Dr. Beckman asked. He nearly drew back. "But—why?"

"Call it a tip for the extra psychological counseling," I said. "Or maybe it would simply be good for me to get rid of it... And there's nothing for you to be afraid of, right? It's just a quarter, after all."

Dr. Beckman caught the implicit challenge in my words, and—to his credit—he rose to meet it.

"All right," he said. A sly smile. "Why not? Maybe this will be one of the rare Bicentennial quarters that's actually worth something."

"If that's the case, Doc, you don't owe me anything."

"Oh, you're right about that," he said. "I plan to research this quarter's value on a numismatic website tonight, and sell it accordingly. In any event, though, I feel quite confident that no harm shall befall me, despite having this cursed, diabolical quarter in my possession."

Dr. Beckman slipped the coin into his pocket.

And then I left. As I headed out, into the waiting room, I said a silent prayer that Dr. Beckman's parting joke didn't take a dark turn.

Now that I thought about it, I had ample reason to believe that the quarter was indeed cursed.

5

I returned to the office. When I walked in, Loretta wryly asked me if the doctor had declared me unfit to work, and thereby ordered an early retirement. *(She knew that I had the second half of my physical this morning.)*

If Madison Greene is too standoffish, then perhaps my administrative assistant is too familiar. But Loretta works like a rower in a Turkish galley.

Speaking of Madison Greene: she came to my office shortly after lunch. More discussions about Ocean Brite Soap.

I wanted to confirm my earlier impressions: I paid close attention to the inflection of every word she said, to every facial expression.

There was no indication that she was hiding anything from me, or waiting for another shoe to drop.

Despite what Dr. Beckman had said, I firmly concluded that she had not returned to my office a second time that day.

On the contrary, she had been eager to put the incident with the quarter behind us. She would not have done anything that might have prolonged the drama, provoked another discussion about that damned Bicentennial coin.

I further speculated that she had barely noticed when the quarter mysteriously disappeared from her possession. She had probably thought (if she noticed at all): *Who cares? It was only twenty-five cents.*

I*T WAS* **late afternoon** when I received a text from Peggy, my wife. I have only recently become comfortable with sending text messages. Peggy, however, was an early adopter—among our generation, that is.

"H*EY*, *Don't forget that Adam and Amy are coming over tonight! Get home as soon as you can. Luv you!!!"*

H*ER WORDS WERE FOLLOWED* by a string of little symbols: hearts and pictorial representations of hugs and kisses. *Emojis*, I believe they're called.

Adam and Amy are our grandchildren, the children of our adult son, Mark. This weekend Mark and his wife, Laura, had planned a "romantic getaway" at a bed-and-breakfast in northern Ohio. They asked Peggy and me if we would be willing to watch our grandchildren over the weekend. Of course Peggy and I were delighted to comply.

"I haven't forgotten," I typed in response to Peggy's message. *"I'll be home as early as I can. I love you too!!"*

I omitted any emojis from my reply, however. To be honest, I don't know how to create them. (I am still finding my way around my iPhone.)

L*EAVING EARLY WAS THE PLAN*, anyway. But as is always the case on Friday afternoon, last-minute emergencies arose. Impossible demands that were incredibly urgent, but which no one had managed to conceive of until the waning hours of the workweek.

As I had told Madison, Covington Foods does pay me a fair wage for the work I do. But there are tradeoffs: Early Friday afternoon departures are a rarity for me. Today was no exception.

I walked out of my office around 5:30 p.m. Loretta had already gone home for the day. As I passed her desk, I wondered if she had forgotten about that strange day last week, when I had called her into my office on that bizarre pretext.

Of course she hadn't forgotten. What was I thinking? I knew Loretta, after all. Oh, well, she would get over it.

While the sunny days in late October in Ohio can be glorious and mild, the cloudy days can be downright gloomy. Today was nothing like that clear day early last week, when I'd found the Bicentennial quarter (not once—but twice!) on my desk. The clouds were low and grey in the sky, threatening rain.

And another thing about late October: As the Winter Solstice begins to approach, the days grow shorter.

By the time I reached the Covington Foods parking garage, the photosensors had already kicked on the security lights. Nevertheless, it would still have been too dark to read a newspaper inside the garage.

My feet echoed on the concrete floor of the garage. Today I'd parked on the third level up from the street. There were few vehicles at this hour on a Friday evening.

I pushed the little unlock button on my key fob, and my Acura honked and clicked open.

I had a sudden feeling of being watched.

Maybe the Horseman was coming for me, after all, I thought. There would be plenty of room here in the garage, for him to ride atop that horrid undead animal of his.

He would behead me right here. I would never arrive home, of course. Peggy would grow worried, and she would call the police.

They would find my headless body right here beside my car.

For the Horseman would have taken my head.

I stopped and listened. I was listening for hoofbeats.

I didn't hear hoofbeats. But I did hear the sound of footsteps.

I turned in the direction of the footfalls. A wiry young man of medium height, with reddish hair, was walking toward his car. It was a little compact machine, probably a hybrid.

I took a closer look: It was the male co-op I had seen that day, when I'd gone to the fourth-floor co-op area to check on Madison.

But he wasn't really a co-op, was he?

He was Banny. Forty-two years had passed. My age had increased from seventeen to fifty-nine. But Banny was still youthful, an early twenty-something.

Both young and very, very old. But then again, that had been the case already, in 1976.

Banny clicked his own key fob, and the little compact/hybrid car beeped and clicked open. Banny was wearing the sort of young man's entry-level suit that is common attire for young men who are trying to appear both professional and stylish.

He was still pretending to be a co-op. But I knew better. I knew who he was.

Banny glanced in my direction as he opened the driver's side door of his car. He obviously recognized me, because he gave me that smirk.

I looked directly at him. I wanted him to know that I wasn't afraid. I might fear the Horseman, and I might fear some of the spirits the Horseman had brought with him.

But Banny I simply despised.

Two hundred and forty years ago, I knew, Banny had worn that same smirk, as he'd ordered men to their deaths. Back then he'd also worn the uniform of the British Legion.

Bloody Ban, they'd called him. The Butcher of Waxhaws.

For now, though, he was wearing his twenty-first century disguise. Banny broke the stare, and slipped into the driver's seat of his little car. The ignition started up, and I watched as the car backed out of its parking space.

The little vehicle chugged toward the exit of the garage. Banny —*Bloody Ban*—was maintaining every pretense of conformity to the present.

. . .

OUR HOUSE IS LOCATED near the end of a long, winding country road. I grew up on the fringes between the suburbs and the country, and I have always preferred to live outside the city.

Tonight, though, I wouldn't have minded living in a neighborhood closer to the center of town.

As I drove through the near darkness, I looked at the lights in the houses on either side of me, somewhat distant from the road.

I felt alone inside my car.

At one point, as I crested a hill where there were no houses, I might have sworn I heard the echo of hoofbeats on the road behind me.

I resisted the temptation to look in my rearview mirror. I turned on the stereo to drown out the faint clatter until I arrived home.

6

I stepped inside my house, and they were waiting for me.

I'm talking about my grandchildren, of course. Adam and Amy.

I may not always be popular at work. (No one in management, in any organization, is popular one hundred percent of the time.) But I'm popular with my grandkids.

"*Grandpa!*" they cried out. And then they came running. I didn't even make it past the foyer.

Adam and Amy are nine and eleven, respectively. They are no longer small enough for me to swoop them up in my arms. I was knocked back a step when they executed their grandpa-tackle. They wrapped me in a joint hug.

I like being a grandfather. No—I love being a grandfather.

"You're finally home," Peggy said. She was walking in from the kitchen, wearing an apron. I could smell one of her meatloaves cooking.

"I got out as soon as I could," I said.

Peggy looked down at Adam and Amy. She leaned over, her hands on her knees.

"Why don't we let Grandpa change out of his work clothes? Then we'll all have some meatloaf, and watch some TV."

"Yay!" they shouted in unison, releasing me.

"Thanks, Peg," I said. "I'll be back in a jiffy."

I watched Adam and Amy run off, back into the living room. I assumed they were playing video games.

Despite everything that had happened over the past week and a half, I was filled with a simple gratitude for my family, my station in life.

And no matter what had happened in the summer of 1976, the last forty years had been good ones.

I was especially grateful for Adam, whom we privately refer to as our "miracle child". For Adam was almost taken from us.

But more about that a bit later.

THE BEDROOM WAS MOSTLY DARK. A bit of light filtered in from the hallway, and through the shutters.

I considered turning on the overhead light. But no—that would be giving in to fear. I wasn't going to go down that road. Not in my own house.

I removed my tie and draped it over one hook on the tie rack that hung behind the bedroom door.

I sat down on the bed, and kicked off my wingtips. I keep a pair of slippers beneath the bed.

I was slipping into the left slipper when I noticed something: The closet door was open—just a smidgen.

That feeling again. The feeling of not being alone, in a space that was supposed to be otherwise empty.

That feeling of being watched.

I slipped into the second slipper. I stood up from the bed. I walked over to the doorway of the bedroom. I could hear my grandchildren laughing at the other end of the house. Peggy's meatloaf wafted down the hall.

I looked at the closet again. The little wedge of absolute blackness, between the door and the doorframe, was completely inscrutable.

But it was also taunting me. This is my house, I reminded myself. It is one thing to be jumpy in Dr. Beckman's exam room. One thing to see things in my office, even.

One thing to see Banny in the parking garage of Covington Foods.

And who knew what might have been behind me on the road this evening?

But not here. Those forces will not be allowed to invade my home.

Rather than continuing out of the bedroom, I walked back to the closet. I ignored my fear, ignored the gooseflesh on my arms and neck.

I pulled open the closet door.

Nothing jumped out at me. Good.

There were clothes, both mine and Peggy's, hanging on the shoulder-high closet rod. I pushed the clothes to one side, and then to the other, so that I could see the back wall of the closet.

If you're there, I thought, *show yourself now!*

But which one of them was I silently speaking to?

In the summer of 1976 there had been far more than one.

At any rate, the closet was empty. I smelled the odor of fabric, the scent of mothballs.

I pushed the closet door shut until it clicked.

PEGGY'S MEATLOAF WAS DELICIOUS, as usual. After dinner, the children preceded us into the living room. The television drew them like a tractor beam. Last year I splurged on a big, 85-inch Sony LED UltraHD television.

Extravagant, yes, I know. A far, far cry from the boxy Zeniths and RCAs of my childhood. But the children love the TV, both for watching and for playing video games.

Peggy and I were just walking into the living room, when Adam's face lit up. He was scrolling through the on-screen channel guide.

"Hey, Grandpa!" he said. "Guess what's on!"

I figured that it would be something involving either superheroes or spaceships. Both Adam and Amy are also ardent fans of those Harry Potter movies, based on the novels of that British author, JK-something-or-other. I've seen a couple of those films, and I couldn't make heads or tales of them. But then, my grandparents would have found the original *Star Trek* equally incomprehensible. Each generation has its proprietary forms of entertainment, I suppose.

"What's on, Adam?" I asked gamely.

"*The Legend of Sleepy Hollow!*" he shouted. "You know: the Headless Horseman!"

I hoped against hope that my horror at Adam's movie selection didn't show.

Peg gave me a funny look.

"Are you all right, Steve?" she asked.

"I'm fine!" I said—though I wasn't fine. There was nothing supernatural about Adam wanting to see a film version of "The Legend of Sleepy Hollow", of course. But how many coincidences did I need, in order to make me accept that something was up? How many coincidences would Dr. Beckman have needed?

I was vaguely aware of a movie rendition of *The Legend of Sleepy Hollow*, made during the 1990s, or thereabouts. Johnny Depp starred in it. Or maybe that had been Sean Penn. (I haven't really been current on my actors since the days when the average new Hollywood release featured some combination of Burt Reynolds, Sally Field, and Clint Eastwood.) I hadn't seen the movie, of course. But I knew that it existed.

"It's a cartoon!" Adam said. "By Disney!"

I was aware of such a cartoon. I had seen it as a child myself, when I was around Adam's age. The cartoon was already at least ten years old then.

"Why, that's a really old one, Adam," I said. "Older than Grandpa!"

"It was made in nineteen forty-nine," Adam provided. He had read about the cartoon on the online guide, obviously.

"Are you sure you'd want to watch something that old?"

"Some old movies are good!" Amy piped up. "Like *The Wizard of Oz*. Did you know that was made in nineteen thirty-nine?"

Where do kids nowadays accumulate so much information? I wondered. On the Internet, no doubt.

"It might be a bit too intense for you," I tried. "*The Legend of Sleepy Hollow* might give you nightmares."

I was hiding behind my grandchildren, of course. I was actually afraid that the old cartoon might give *me* nightmares—or at least contribute to them. (And that is, incidentally, exactly what happened.)

Then Peggy intervened. "It's a Disney animated feature made in nineteen forty-nine, Steve. I think it will be all right. Have you seen some of the things kids see on the Internet nowadays? That old cartoon will be mild by comparison. Heck, I saw it myself when I was about their age. I think everyone did, at one time or another. It's a classic."

The Legend of Sleepy Hollow—a classic? I didn't think so. But I didn't argue my point any further.

I SAT through *The Legend of Sleepy Hollow*. Luckily, it's a short one: about an hour, with commercial breaks.

At several moments in the movie, I found myself flinching at the animated version of the Headless Horseman.

And when I flinched, I noticed Peggy noticing me. From her perspective, my behavior must have seemed odd.

The creators who conceived and made that cartoon seventy years ago had not intended it to be shocking, of course. They had, rather, produced it as light children's entertainment.

But we can safely assume that none of them had ever encountered the real Headless Horseman. To them, *The Legend of Sleepy Hollow* was just that…a legend.

7

Peggy and I were alone in our bedroom, later that night, when she asked me about my reactions to *The Legend of Sleepy Hollow*. Adam and Amy had already been put to bed. Peggy and I were getting into our nightclothes.

"I'm just going to come out and ask you this, Steve. Why were you freaking out over that damn cartoon? Is there something going on here that I should know about?"

In that instant, I briefly considered telling her everything. But how could I, after I had kept my secrets for so long?

Peggy and I have been married for more than thirty years. In that time, I have hidden almost nothing from her. There are no secret bank accounts in the Caymans. There have been no women on the sly. (I haven't even been inside the walls of a gentlemen's club, believe it or not. Why would I go to one of those places?)

But I have never told Peggy about what happened in the summer of 1976. By the time we met, as college students, those traumatic events were over. I was focused on moving on with my life.

And so Peggy—who knew more about me than any living human being—was completely oblivious to that one crucial chapter in my history.

"I've just been stressed at work," I said. I thought of my earlier conversation with Dr. Beckman.

But Peggy knows me better than Dr. Beckman ever will.

"Steve. You've been employed at Covington Foods for thirty years. You've always handled work stress well. I'm thinking that it's something else."

She's guessed it, I thought. *Somehow, Peggy has put the entire story together.*

I was wrong, however. "I think you're worried about Adam," she said.

"Well," I said—and this time I was being completely truthful —"I'm always a little worried about Adam."

I MENTIONED EARLIER that we call Adam our "miracle child". Shortly after Adam was born, the pediatrician—and later a pediatric cardiologist—informed us that Adam had been born with a serious heart defect.

Adam was less than a year old when he underwent open-heart surgery. That's right. The surgeons had to cut him open, and invade his tiny ribcage in order to fix one of his heart valves. There was no other option, they informed us. Without the surgery, Adam would not have seen his first birthday.

Those tense weeks Adam spent in the hospital were, in their own way, almost as jarring as that summer of the Headless Horseman. At several junctures, we almost lost Adam.

To make a long story short, Adam pulled through. But he wasn't completely out of the woods. The doctors said that he would likely need another surgery before he attained full adulthood, possibly before he reached adolescence.

And even with the second surgery, there would be no guarantees. Adam would never be like other children. He would not be like other adults—assuming he lived to become one.

. . .

"I UNDERSTAND **that you're worried** about Adam," Peggy said now. "I am, too. But we have to let Adam be a kid, not just a kid with a heart condition. Mark and Laura understand that. That's why they let him participate in normal activities—within reason…What I'm saying is, Steve, I get that you didn't want Adam to watch that cartoon because you thought it might be too much for his heart. But we can't think that way. We can't shield Adam from everything in the world."

So Peggy thought that my reaction to *The Legend of Sleepy Hollow* was rooted in my usual concern for Adam. I felt a fresh wave of guilt wash over me.

"Adam is going to be fine," I said, with as much bravado as I could muster. In that moment, at least, I was no longer thinking about Bicentennial quarters and ghosts from long ago. I was thinking about my grandson, and the lot that he'd been given in life. "Adam is going to outlive us all."

Peggy put a hand on my cheek. "Steve, we don't know that. Not for sure. We have to be prepared for any eventuality. I mean, we can hope—we can pray—and Mark and Laura are taking Adam to the doctor every two months. But we can never really be sure of what the outcome will be. And we have to get used to that."

"I know," I said. "But it doesn't seem fair."

"No," she agreed. "It isn't. But we both know all too well that life isn't always fair. And if we don't know it by the time we're pushing sixty, then I guess we never will." She smiled and kissed me. "Good old Steady Steve. Anyway, let's call it a day, huh?"

WE HAD BEEN **in bed only a few minutes** when Peggy reached across her space of the bed, and touched me in that way that I have always found to be both arousing and delightfully shocking.

"If you're suffering from stress," she said, "maybe I could help you with that."

"Yes," I said. "Yes, I think I'd like that."

I leaned over and kissed her. One thing led to another, and soon we were both undressed, and I was lying atop her, her legs entwined in mine.

I rubbed against her, our complimentary body parts at the appropriate angles and contact points. This was a maneuver that I knew fondly and very, very well.

I, however, was not responding as I should have—as I *always* had, in thirty-five years of marriage.

I tried to make it happen, rubbing against her more vigorously than normal. I think my extra effort may have done more harm than good.

"What's up?" Peggy finally whispered in my ear.

But the point was—something wasn't up.

"I—I'm just having a little trouble tonight, is all."

"Do you want me to…" she whispered the rest in my ear.

While that sounded quite enticing, I knew that I would only humiliate us both if nothing happened as a result. I rolled off her, as gently as I could, onto my side of the bed.

"I'm sorry," I said.

"Hey, it's all right." She rubbed my chest. "These things happen, you know."

"They've never happened to me in the past—to *us*."

"Well, there was bound to be a first time. Like I said earlier, we're both pushing sixty. We're not the same two horny college kids who met in Intro to Accounting at UC, back in the seventies."

"No, I suppose not. But in any case, I can assure you that this will be temporary. I really am under an unusual amount of stress…at work."

"No worries," she said. I both heard and felt her roll over. "I'm sure that Steady Steve will be back tomorrow night—or the night after."

I AWOKE FROM A HORRIBLE, **incredibly vivid dream.** In the dream I found myself in the middle of a grassy field. The sky was pitch-black, and there were fires burning on the horizon.

In the dream I watched helplessly as a headless man on horseback ran down and murdered the people I love. There were people from both my present and my distant past.

The horse, just like the rider, had obviously been dead for a long time. But still they were up and moving around with lethal efficiency.

My loved ones ran in vain—none of them fast enough to escape the rider and his blade.

I called out in the dream for the creature to stop. I couldn't make my feet move, however.

Then, when the Horseman had killed everyone in sight, when the field was strewn with mutilated corpses and severed heads, he came charging for me.

That was when I woke up.

I awoke with a start; and as is often the case with exceptionally realistic dreams, some time passed before I fully realized that it *had* been a dream.

My back and my chest were moist with a light coating of perspiration. The blanket and sheet on my side of the bed were wrapped around my feet. I must have been thrashing about in the dream.

I turned my head and saw that Peggy was still asleep. Her eyes were closed, and her chest was gently expanding and contracting as she breathed. At least I hadn't woken her up.

I looked over at the digital clock on my nightstand. 3:22 a.m. Too early to get up, but would I be able to get back to sleep...after that dream?

I heard something move on the other side of the room. It might have been the house settling. But it might have been something else.

Even in the darkened bedroom, I could see that the closet door was open—just a crack.

I was certain that I had closed it the previous night, after I had done a full sweep of the contents of the closet. I had closed the closet door until I both heard and felt the tumbler click.

And now the door was ajar again.

There were possible explanations, of course. Peggy might have accessed the closet last night, and left the door partially open.

I didn't think so, though.

I lay awake for a while and thought about Dr. Beckman's advice. *Write it down, Steve. Write it* all *down.*

THE TIME WAS 4:02 A.M. when I slipped out of bed. I was not going back to sleep. Not this morning.

The mattress creaked a little. I was careful to avoid waking Peggy. I stood up on the carpeted floor and looked down at her.

Still sleeping...

I slipped into my shorts and pajamas. (I had discarded them on the floor in our unsuccessful attempt at lovemaking.)

Then I kicked on my slippers. Once again, I was careful not to awaken my wife.

I turned away from the bed and took a step toward the hallway, when I heard it.

The sound of a half-formed word, not quite a breath, and not quite a complete syllable.

The sound had come from the closet.

Perhaps. And perhaps not. The furnace had kicked on around 3:45 a.m., so perhaps I had heard nothing but an anomaly in the normal wheezing of the house's heating system.

I couldn't be sure. I couldn't be sure of much of anything, after the past week and a half.

That was why I needed to carry out the decision I had just made.

I turned away from the closet, and walked quietly out of the bedroom.

8

Now I am sitting in my downstairs den, at the big oak desk I keep in here.

Before I sat down, I checked the closet in the den. There was nothing in there, save some cardboard boxes filled with old books and documents, and an old desktop printer that stopped functioning last year (but which I have neglected to either discard or attempt to fix).

I shut the door of the den's closet. (I heard it click.) Then I placed a spare chair against the door, wedged under the doorknob.

That closet door will not come open. At least not while I'm in here, writing. While I put pen to paper.

Yes, you got that right. I said: *pen to paper*.

Sitting atop the side extension of this desk is an iMac computer, with at least one word processing software package installed.

I also own a laptop computer, and a Samsung tablet. Oh...and an iPhone.

Any number of electronic gadgets that can be used for writing. But I will be employing none of these for the task ahead.

Instead, I have removed a college-ruled Mead notebook from the filing cabinet here in the den. (I recall purchasing the notebook at a clearance sale at the OfficeMax near my house a few years ago.) And I've taken a ballpoint pen from the top drawer of the desk.

These are the tools that I would have used, had I written a document such as this in 1976. In those days, no one had yet heard of Bill Gates. Apple Computer was still a garage project that Steve Jobs and Steve Wozniak were tinkering with. And so people wrote with pen and paper.

We're going to do this old-school, you might say.

I CAN'T GUARANTEE, of course, that my reliance on antiquated tools will give me the full authenticity I am hoping for. After all, a long time has passed between 1976 and today.

In the summer of that year, I was a seventeen year-old boy, still in high school. My whole life was ahead of me, as the saying goes. So much of my future was yet unwritten.

Today I am fifty-nine…not quite elderly, but certainly within sight of that territory. My perspective has changed.

But all the same, there are days when 1976 feels like yesterday. A part of me has never left that long-ago summer. I suppose that is how the Horseman, and all those other *revolutionary ghosts* (as I've come to call them) have begun to find their way back into the present. I've become their conduit.

Yes, I can feel them coming, breaking through into yet another new century. I suppose that's why I finally decided to take the advice of my family physician. I can no longer pretend that the events of the last ten days are a mere fluke, or hallucinations brought on by ordinary stress.

I don't know who you, the reader, are. (For the time being, I will assume that you are Dr. Beckman. It is just barely possible, however, that this story may eventually find its way into other hands.)

I will endeavor to tell the story of what happened that summer as faithfully and as thoroughly as I can. Much of what follows you will find to be fantastical, horrific, and downright unbelievable. I ask only that you withhold judgment till the end, before you dismiss me as a charlatan or a madman.

And without further ado, I begin.

PART II

1976

9

It all started with those hoofprints on the grassy hillside. I wonder, even now, if I could have ignored the hoofprints—if I even had that option.

And if I had ignored them, would things have turned out differently?

I PULLED into the empty parking lot of the Pantry Shelf, a family-run convenience mart in Clermont County, Ohio. It was the first Saturday of June 1976, about midway through the noon hour.

I brought my vehicle to a stop at the edge of the parking lot, where the blacktop met a rising, grass-covered slope. The sun was reflected on the white paint job of my 1968 Bonneville.

I had owned the Bonneville for less than a week. Although the car was used, it was the first car I had ever purchased with my own money. I sat there, listening to the engine for a few seconds before I shut it off. I already knew that there might be a problem beneath the hood...but that explanation can wait.

I stepped out of the Bonneville and onto the blacktop. I squinted against the glare. The smells of pollen and freshly cut grass filled the air. And, of course, the gasoline and oil smells of my car. The humidity of a southern Ohio summer prickled my skin.

The Pantry Shelf occupied a little squarish brick building. A big window, directly behind the cash register, faced the parking lot. From where I stood, I could see Leslie Griffin's blonde hair, and the back of her pink shirt. She was leaning over the sales counter.

Leslie was probably reading a book. She was majoring in English Literature at Ohio State. She was home for the summer, and working at her parents' convenience mart.

I was about to walk toward the store, when I noticed the hoofprints.

THE HOOFPRINTS ASCENDED the adjacent hillside. Although today was clear and sunny, we had had a soaker of an early summer rainstorm only a few days ago. (This accounted for the humidity.) As a result, the top layer of the hillside was still moist and easily disturbed. The hoofprints cut a rutty, muddy path up to the top of the hill.

At the top of the hill was a short plateau. And beyond that, a stand of woods.

From somewhere back in those woods, I heard a cicada chirr.

There were plenty of woods in Clermont County in 1976. The county is located about twenty miles east of downtown Cincinnati. Today western Clermont County has been absorbed into what is called Greater Cincinnati. But in those days, the entire county was rural or semirural, not far from Cincinnati, but basically a place unto itself.

But even here, the presence of the hoofprints was rather unusual. There were many farms in the vicinity; and it wouldn't have been a huge surprise to find some horses among them. But the Pantry Shelf was located along Ohio Pike, the two-lane highway that ran directly into Cincinnati. This was no horse trail.

And why would anyone want to ride a horse up into those woods? There was nothing back there, after all…but even more woods.

I looked back at the Pantry Shelf. Leslie was still leaning over the counter, the very sight of her making my heart ache a little.

Nevertheless, I found myself drawn to the hoofprints. There was something—I couldn't quite say exactly what—strange about them, besides their mere location.

I stepped over to the edge of the blacktop, knelt down, and looked at the hoofprints more closely. They were big.

Almost immediately, a nausea-inducing smell assaulted my nostrils. Then I identified another oddity: Each hoofprint was rimmed with a putrid black gunk. That was the obvious source of the odor.

The smell reminded me of rot and death, of small animals that had been struck by cars, and left to fester alongside the road. Along country roads, there was never any shortage of roadkill—

I asked myself why I was bothering to think about such things, on the first Saturday of the summer before my senior year of high school.

Come to think of it: *Why had I bothered to examine the hoofprints at all?*

Yes, they were a little unusual. Their presence was difficult to explain, and I had no guesses about the black goo around their edges.

But so what? What did those hoofprints have to do with anything? I asked myself.

Absolutely nothing, was the answer that came back.

I stood up, glad to be clear of the noxious smell. And then I saw the missing person's flyer, and the grainy, black-and-white photos of the two young people who were probably already dead.

10

"HAVE YOU SEEN US?" the words at the top of the flyer read, in large black font, and all in caps. Below these words were two black-and-white photos, then more verbiage, in a much smaller print.

The missing persons flyer was tacked to a telephone pole at the other end of the small parking lot. The telephone pole was planted in the patch of grass beside the short access road that connected the Pantry Shelf's parking lot with Ohio Pike.

I was immediately curious. I had to know what this was about before I went inside the store. (I had already delayed my entry into the store over mere hoofprints, after all.) In a small community like Clermont County, a missing person case was a rather big deal.

And this appeared to be a case of *two* people missing.

As I drew closer, the faces in the photos began to take shape. The one on the left was a young man, with dark, longish hair, and the skimpy mustache of a teenage boy. The photo on the right was of a young woman, with shoulder-length blonde or light brown hair.

The photos were obviously mimeographed from the pages of a high school yearbook. I read the captions beneath the pictures. The young man was identified as Robert McMoore. The young woman's name was Donna Seitz.

Beneath their names, their birthdates were also printed. Both of them were born in 1956, which made them twenty years old.

I didn't recognize either Robert McMoore or Donna Seitz, but the three of us may have crossed paths at one time or another. McMoore and Seitz were three years older than me. They might have been seniors at West Clermont High School when I was a freshman. Even if they had attended nearby South Clermont High School, they were well within my extended sphere. I just hadn't met either one of them yet.

And based on the information contained in this flyer, the odds were high that I wasn't ever going to meet them:

"ROBERT MCMOORE AND DONNA SEITZ, *both age 20, have been missing since Saturday, May 22, 1976.*

The pair was last seen departing from the residence of Donna Seitz, at 4573 Cumberland Dr., around 7 PM on May 22, 1976. According to the parents of the missing young people, the two had planned to see a movie at the Eastland Drive-In.

McMoore and Seitz departed in McMoore's vehicle, a blue 1969 Chevrolet Impala, Ohio license plate number 918 QNB.

If you have any information regarding the whereabouts of McMoore and/or Seitz, please contact the Clermont County Sheriff's Department, at the number listed below."

I STOOD THERE LOOKING at the flyer, the noontime sun lightly stinging my face.

It was a lot to take in.

Robert McMoore and Donna Seitz might be found, of course. There might be a perfectly logical explanation for two local young people disappearing into thin air.

But for some reason, I didn't think so.

To the best of my knowledge, no one had ever gone missing in Clermont County before. Not for two weeks, anyway.

Clermont County was no idyllic Mayberry. We had our share of petty crime. There were biker bars, and biker bars brought fights, drugs…the usual problems. Every other year there would be a homicide in Clermont County, usually attributed to a personal feud or a domestic dispute.

Clermont County wasn't, however, a place where you had to worry about serial killers.

And that was the explanation that sprung, unbidden and immediate, into my mind. *A serial killer got them.*

That was the only explanation I could reckon. How else could McMoore's car disappear, too, for two whole weeks?

I had an unwelcome thought: McMoore and Seitz were already underwater. The county contained innumerable farm ponds, and a handful of decent-sized lakes. The Ohio River ran along Clermont County's southern border.

This thought was immediately followed by a sudden, vivid mental image: The bloated bodies of Robert McMoore and Donna Seitz, having been violated in an unspeakable manner by a serial killer, were locked in the trunk of McMoore's Impala, beneath ten or twenty feet of muddy water.

For a brief moment, I could almost see them.

I shook away the image. What was wrong with me today?

This was shaping up to be a dark afternoon, despite the sunny weather.

The hoofprints were a mystery, and the two missing young people represented an unfortunate situation.

But the hoofprints were ultimately irrelevant, and there was nothing I could do for McMoore and Seitz.

It was high time for me to head inside the Pantry Shelf, already.

11

When I walked in the front door, a little bell tinkled overhead. Leslie Griffin looked up from her paperback novel (I had been right about her reading) and pushed a lock of blonde hair off her forehead.

Then she saw that it was only me, and said, "Hey, high school boy."

"Hey, yourself," I said.

Leslie habitually called me *high school boy*, as if to remind me that in her estimation, I was strictly bush league.

Leslie and I had been vaguely acquainted for years, but we weren't exactly friends. She was three years older than me, and we had always moved in different circles. Plus, there was the fact that she was one of the more sought-after young women in the southwestern quadrant of the county. Leslie rationed her attention like a miser.

My parents were friends with Pete and Sandy Griffin, her parents, and the owners of the Pantry Shelf. This bought me a modicum of civility from Leslie, but not much more.

"How's your summer going?" I asked her.

She shrugged. "Okay. Todd—my boyfriend—is staying in

Columbus for the summer. So I won't see him much until September."

This was the first time Leslie had mentioned that she had a boyfriend, but this information wasn't a big surprise.

I loathed Todd, of course, sight unseen. He would be an arrogant, square-jawed football player, or a well-heeled member of one of OSU's most prestigious fraternities. Possibly both.

Leslie returned her attention to her paperback novel.

And that was the way my conversations with Leslie usually went.

THERE WASN'T **much unoccupied space** inside the building. The Pantry Shelf was the kind of family-run convenience store that is almost nonexistent today, in this era of ubiquitous chain stores, and gas stations that double as supermarkets.

The center of the store was dominated by four rows of shelves. These were stocked with dry goods: canned fruits and vegetables, boxed cereals, and a wide assortment of snack chips and pretzels. Along the far wall the freezers were situated. These contained milk, soft drinks, and—needless to say—beer. Cigarettes and smokeless tobacco products were kept behind the counter.

But I was here for the magazine alcove. The Pantry Shelf had an unusually large selection of magazines, for a store its size.

Specifically, I was looking for a copy of *Car and Driver*. I knew next to nothing about cars. My father was a hobbyist mechanic who could complete all but the most complex automotive repairs. I barely knew a spark plug from an oil filter. I was determined to correct this deficiency.

I was stepping past the cash register, and into the magazine alcove, when Leslie looked up from her book.

"Hey, you aren't in here looking for condoms, are you?" she asked.

The question literally stopped me in my tracks.

"What?"

"I think you heard me."

I had heard her. I can't say for certain if I turned beet-red at that moment. But I likely did.

"What would make you ask me a question like that, Leslie?"

"Because," she began, "just the other day, another high school boy, just like yourself, came in here asking where we kept the condoms. I told him that this is a family-run store, and that my parents would never stock items like that. I told him that he'd have to go to Walgreens or Rite Aid if he wanted to buy condoms."

Leslie fixed me with a crooked smile, obviously savoring this moment of watching me squirm. I strongly suspected that the "other high school boy" was a fabrication.

Since coming home for the summer, she had been without her boyfriend (Todd!), and her parents had dragooned her into working the cash register of the family store every day. She was bored, she recognized that she had some leverage over me, and my embarrassment was a brief diversion.

"No, Leslie. I'm not here to buy condoms. I'm here to look at the magazines."

"Well." She looked down at her book again. I could see her trying to control her laughter. "I believe you know where we keep those."

12

I finally made my way into the magazine alcove. It didn't take me long to find a stack of the June issue of *Car and Driver*, directly in front of me at eye level.

The topmost copy of the magazine had a dogeared and creased cover. Someone had read and roughly handled the magazine without buying it. I lifted up that copy, and selected the more pristine one immediately behind it.

I could have simply made my purchase and left then, but this wasn't my day for sticking to plans.

To the right of the stack of *Car and Driver*, there was a single copy of a magazine called, *Spooky American Tales*.

The artwork on the cover was elaborate and gaudy. A full-color illustration of the folklore character known as the Grim Reaper, standing astride a map of the United States. The Grim Reaper was in the act of swinging his scythe from Maine to Texas.

The tagline of the magazine (printed just below the title) was: "*True Ghost Stories from the American Heartland*". Below the blade of the Grim Reaper's scythe were the words, "*Why the Summer of '76 will be Scary as Hell!*"

I was vaguely familiar with *Spooky American Tales*. As the tagline indicated, the publication billed itself as a repository of authentic paranormal reporting, with an exclusive emphasis on ghostly happenings within the United States.

I couldn't remember exactly, but I may have owned a single copy of the magazine in the distant years of my adolescence, when I was eleven or twelve years old.

I was intrigued. It couldn't hurt to take a look.

I picked up *Spooky American Tales*. I turned to the table of contents.

The first item I saw was an article about a haunted silver mine in Nevada. Then there was a story about a Confederate cemetery in rural Georgia, where Dixie's fallen soldiers were not yet at rest.

Then, near the bottom of the table of contents, I saw another article:

"The Headless Horsemen *rides again in 1976, to bring in the American Bicentennial!*"

Once again, I was intrigued. That article began on page 84, near the back of the magazine. I flipped back to it.

The byline of the article was given to a man named Harry Bailey. I skimmed the first paragraphs of Harry Bailey's piece:

"The Headless Horseman *has been known to generations of Americans as the ghostly figure who pursued Ichabod Crane in Washington Irving's classic short horror tale, 'The Legend of Sleepy Hollow'.*

"But every legend—no matter how seemingly outlandish—is based on at least an element of truth.

"That is what the old-timers say. And now it appears that the Headless Horseman is back, to terrorize America in 1976, the year of our Bicentennial..."

. . .

I would have read more of the article right there in the store. But I was interrupted by Leslie Griffin again.

"Hey!" she said. "This is a store. S-t-o-r-e. You know: where people like, *buy* things. This isn't the Griffin Family Library!"

13

"I'm going to buy both of these magazines," I said.

I realized that I had just committed to purchasing not only the *Car and Driver*, but also the copy of *Spooky American Tales*.

"I don't see you doing any buying. All I see you doing is reading. Mom and Dad are always complaining because people come in here and read magazines without buying them. They mess up the covers, and then no one else will buy them."

I thought about the mangled copy of *Car and Driver* that I had bypassed, in order to grab an unsullied one directly behind it. Leslie did have a point, I supposed.

"I'm ready to check out now," I told her.

I walked to the cash register and laid both magazines on the counter. Leslie saw the second one I had picked out, and said, "*Spooky American Tales*? Aren't you a little old for that? Campfire ghost stories?"

I had grown weary of her ridicule. Even where a pretty girl was concerned, I had my limits.

"What's your deal, Leslie? First you give me a hard time because I'm not buying magazines. Now you're giving me a hard time because you don't like the ones I'm buying. I can't win here."

"Yeah, yeah," she said, with a hint of a smile.

Before she rang up the price of *Spooky American Tales*, she did a double take on the cover. "This is the May issue," she said. "If you come back in a few weeks, we'll maybe have the June issue in stock."

"I'll keep that in mind," I said. Leslie wasn't above teasing me about my reading habits. But nor was she above trying to position me for the next sale at her parents' store. I would never figure her out.

Leslie's paperback novel lay on the counter, but the cover was facing downward.

"What are you reading?" I asked.

"*A Garden of Earthly Delights*," she said, "by Joyce Carol Oates."

I admitted that I had heard of neither the book nor the author.

"No," Leslie shot back, "of course you haven't. Joyce Carol Oates writes literary fiction, and you like to read campfire ghost stories."

She pronounced the words "literary fiction" as if they amounted to a sacred incantation.

"That will be two dollars and six cents," she said.

I dug into my back pocket for my wallet, and into my side pocket for some change. Whatever I said, it seemed, Leslie would find a way to turn it around on me.

(I HAVE one note to add to her remark about literary fiction. Some years later, on a whim, I did remember that conversation with Leslie, and I picked up a book by Joyce Carol Oates. I found it to be the most dreary, pretentious stuff I had ever read.

But what do I know? In my adult life, I have read maybe two or three novels per year, on average. These are usually titles by James Patterson, John Grisham, or Stephen King; and they are almost always books that I pick up in the airport bookstore, minutes before I board a flight.)

I HAD **one more card** to play with Leslie before I left.

"Did you see my car?" I asked her. "It's right outside, in the parking lot."

Leslie turned around and gave my Bonneville a pro forma look-see through the window.

"Nice," she said. She pushed back a lock of blonde hair.

I was just about to leave, when her face lit up. A flash of hope. Then she spoke.

"Hey, speaking of cars: Does Jack still have that red Corvair?"

Jack was my older brother. At that point in my life, he was one of my least favorite topics.

"Yeah," I said, as neutrally as possible. "He still has the Corvair."

"I remember that car," Leslie said, smiling now. "He used to drive it through our neighborhood. My friends and I, we were just little girls then. We'd run out into the front yard, and he'd blow the horn and wave at us."

"Great," I said. I couldn't believe it. Leslie had ignored the car that I had purchased less than a week ago, while she was giving Jack credit for an old Corvair that he'd owned for over a decade.

"What's Jack up to nowadays?" she persisted.

"I don't see him much," I said.

"Oh, yeah. I hear that he's been living out in the country, near Goshen Hill Road, in that farmhouse. With a bunch of other people."

"That's right. Jack's hippie commune."

"Hey," Leslie said. "Jack's not a hippie. He's a veteran, don't forget."

"He isn't much of a veteran," I said quickly.

"He went to Vietnam, didn't he?"

"Yeah, for about three weeks."

"Well, there you go," Leslie said, without asking for further elaboration.

That was just as well. The resulting conversation would have been tricky.

In 1976, in certain environments, the appellation "hippie" was regarded as something of an insult. (Clermont County was one such place.)

And as for Jack's brief, ignominious military career: Per my parents' wishes, only a few people outside the family knew the full story about that; and I didn't believe that Leslie was one of those people.

"Thanks for the magazines," I said. It was time for me to leave.

"Thank you for the purchase," Leslie said, adopting her shopkeeper mode. She picked up her book again. "At the Pantry Shelf, we aim to please."

I HEADED BACK OUT into the parking lot, my magazines in hand.

As I approached the Bonneville, I couldn't help noticing the missing persons flyer, tacked to the telephone pole.

Over on the hillside, the hoofprints with the nasty black residue.

I wasn't going to look at either one of them again, I'd decided.

Then I caught a flash of movement from the corner of my eye. Someone was walking down the road that connected the Pantry Shelf to Ohio Pike.

He was a young man of medium height with a wiry build. He was wearing jeans and a white tank top. He was ambling down the road.

The young man's most striking features were his head of thick, reddish hair, his long nose, and his pointed chin.

He saw me looking at him, and he slowed down.

The young man met my eyes. He gave me a smirk—not a kind one—and then he paused there by the edge of the road.

It was as if he was waiting for me to make a move, to start a fight.

Though I was by no means a habitual brawler, I had been in my share of scraps by the age of seventeen. That was an inextricable part of being a teenage boy in a semirural environment in the 1970s. The jostling on the totem pole was constant, and there was always someone looking to knock you down a peg. Sometimes there was no choice but to fight.

Other times, though, you did have a choice. I wasn't afraid of the red-haired young man, even though he looked to be in his early twenties, and even though he looked mean.

But nor was I eager to get into a random fight with some random guy—a fight with an uncertain end. I had no interest here.

I turned away from the young guy with the red hair and the angular face. I climbed into the Bonneville before he could say anything.

In the rearview mirror, I saw him continue his walk. But not before he gave me a final, inexplicably vicious smirk. He apparently knew that I was still watching him.

That was my first encounter with Banny, though I didn't yet know his name.

14

I lived with my parents in a little red brick ranch house in a small suburb. The land on which our house was built had been cleared from farmland in the late 1940s, during the postwar housing boom (which reached even Clermont County).

Our house was about fifteen hundred square feet, no basement. It was the first house my parents ever owned, and—as things turned out—the only one they would ever own.

It was Saturday, so my dad's tan Ford pickup truck was in the driveway. My mom's little Maverick would be in the garage.

My father was a production line manager at one of the Ford plants that used to exist in the Cincinnati area. My parents only purchased Ford Motor Company products. I felt a little guilty for having bought my used Pontiac Bonneville. But since that was a used car, it was technically permissible.

I pulled my car into the little concrete pull-off space on the left side of the driveway. I could still recall the day, the previous September, when my father and I had made the pull-off. We peeled back the turf, and then we mixed, poured, and leveled the concrete. Afterward, we each had a single bottle of beer in the late afternoon heat. Just the two of us.

A pleasant memory to savor, on a day when the unpleasant memories were to begin.

WHEN I WALKED in through the front door, I found my parents both in the living room.

Dad was sitting in his La-Z-boy recliner. He was smoking a cigarette.

My dad was in his mid-fifties, but he still exuded the vibrancy of a relatively young man. He was tall and broad-shouldered. He was a World War II veteran—and not just any World War II veteran. My dad had been among the men of the U.S. Army's 29th Infantry Division, the one that landed on Omaha Beach on June 6, 1944—otherwise known as D-Day.

Although I never would have expressed the idea in so many words, I would have assumed that my dad was going to live forever. His only Achille's heel was his cigarette habit: He went through a whole pack of Pall Malls every day.

Mom was sitting on the couch, working on one of her knitting projects. She had not served in World War II, but her hardscrabble childhood on a Kentucky farm had been filled with manual labor and marginal deprivation. She told stories of raising chickens and selling their eggs to help her parents make ends meet.

No one would have described my brown-haired, grey-eyed mother as beautiful, but she was small, and neat, and somehow dignified. A fifty-four year-old woman who carried every one of her years in the crow's feet and incipient wrinkles that creased her squarish face.

They were both made of a heartier stock than I was made of. But today there was something bothering them, and I could tell as soon as I walked in.

THEY SAID HELLO TO ME, and even made a show of cheerfulness.

Then they grew silent and immediately locked their faces on the television again.

"Everything all right?" I asked.

"We're just watching the news," my mother said.

Even though this was a Saturday, they were watching a news program. Politics, of course. Nineteen seventy-six was an election year. The two major political parties were both holding conventions later in the summer.

The GOP was in disarray. After the resignation of the disgraced Richard Nixon two years earlier, Gerald Ford—an appointee—had assumed the White House. He was widely favored to head the Republican ticket in 1976; but he was facing an insurgent campaign from Ronald Reagan, an ex-actor and former governor of California. The Democratic frontrunner, meanwhile, was Jimmy Carter, an ex-governor of Georgia.

"Election news?" I asked.

"Of course," my mom said. "What else?"

"Neither the Democrats nor the Republicans are worth a damn anymore," my dad grumbled.

My parents had been Democrats for most of their lives. Then the Democratic Party became associated with the chaos of the 1960s student protest movement, and my parents became Republicans.

And then Watergate happened, and the Republicans offered no refuge, either. Like most Americans, my parents were disillusioned with both parties, and pessimistic about the state of the country.

"Everything okay?" I persisted. "Besides the whole world, that is?"

My dad, who usually liked to joke around, merely grunted in response. My mom, too, barely acknowledged my remark.

"Because I get the feeling that something's wrong," I said.

My mom looked across the room at my dad. He shook his head at her implied question. Then she looked down at her knitting again.

"Everything's okay," my dad said.

Yeah, right, I thought.

"I've known both of you for my entire life," I said, "and I can tell that something is up."

My dad took a drag on his cigarette, looked at my mom and shrugged. On the television, a CBS anchorman was talking about Jimmy Carter.

My mom exhaled loudly and dropped her knitting into her lap.

"If you must know," she said, "your brother stopped by earlier."

"Jack," I said. "Of course."

15

"Did he want money again?" I asked.

Of course Jack would have wanted money. That was the only reason my brother ever bothered to drop by the house.

"Let us worry about Jack," my father said.

"It's probably better if you let us handle it," my mother added.

Her words were clipped—not angry, exactly, but peremptory.

They didn't want to discuss Jack with me. They never did. Nor did my World War II hero father, or my world-hardened mother, seem capable of standing up to their elder son.

I was about to say something else, when my words were choked off in my throat.

From where I was standing in the living room, I had a clear view down the main hall of the house, where the bedrooms were located. (As I've mentioned, it was a small house.)

Right outside my bedroom, I saw a grayish, human-sized shape move in the hallway.

It was there, one second; and the next—it was gone. Vanished into thin air.

Or maybe it had been nothing more than a trick of the light. The hallway was filled with sunlight from the windows of the surrounding bedrooms. There were trees outside most of the windows, and they could be easily stirred by the wind. This created shifting patterns of light and shadows. The shadows played on the painted walls and carpeted floor of the hallway, sometimes producing brief optical illusions.

Perhaps that vaguely human shape I had seen had been another one of those shifting patterns.

But it had looked more substantial. For a second, anyway.

My parents both noticed my startled reaction.

"What's the matter son?" my mother asked. "You look like you've just seen a ghost."

A ghost, I thought...

"You did turn pale, all of a sudden," my father agreed. "Are you okay?"

The conversation, I realized, had just been turned around. We weren't talking about Jack anymore. We were talking about me. About what might be wrong with...me.

"I—I think I'll go to my room now," I said. "Do some reading."

Suddenly, I was in no state to make further queries about Jack.

"I see you bought a copy of *Car and Driver*," my dad said approvingly.

The two magazines I'd purchased were tucked underneath one arm. The *Car and Driver* was on top, facing outward.

I wondered: Had that order of placement been deliberate? My parents were regular churchgoers, but they had little interest in—or tolerance for—anything with a New Age or occult vibe. They would probably share Leslie's opinion about *Spooky American Tales*: "campfire ghost stories".

"That's right," I said, composing myself.

I still had plenty of questions about what my brother was up to;

but now I also had questions about what I might have seen in the hallway.

Right outside my bedroom.

A ghost, my own mother had suggested, her distaste for the occult notwithstanding.

16

My bedroom was a small, cramped affair, very typical of secondary bedrooms in postwar tract homes. There was barely enough room for a bed, a desk, a dresser, and a chest of drawers. The one selling point of the bedroom was the window over the bed. It afforded me a view of the big maple tree in the front yard, when I felt like looking at it.

I lay down on my bed and opened *Spooky American Tales*. I briefly considered reading about the Nevada silver mine or the Confederate cemetery in Georgia.

Instead I flipped back to page 84, to Harry Bailey's article about the Headless Horseman.

After the opening paragraphs, Harry Bailey explained the historical background behind the legend of the Headless Horseman. While most everyone knew that the Headless Horseman was associated with the American Revolution, not everyone knew the particulars:

"Is the Headless Horseman a mere tale—a figment of fevered imaginations? Or is there some truth in the legend? Did the ghastly Horseman truly exist?

"And more to the point of our present concerns: Does the Horseman exist even now?

"I'll leave those final judgments to you, my friends.

"What is known for certain is that on October 28, 1776, around three thousand troops of the Continental Army met British and Hessian elements near White Plains, New York, on the field of battle.

"This engagement is known in historical record as the Battle of White Plains. The Continentals were outnumbered nearly two to one. George Washington's boys retreated, but not before they had inflicted an equal number of casualties on their British and Hessian enemies..."

BY THIS POINT in my educational career, I had taken several American history courses. I knew who the Hessians were.

The Hessians were often referred to as mercenaries, and there was an element of truth in that. But they weren't mercenaries, exactly, in the modern usage of that word.

In the 1700s, the country now known as Germany was still the Holy Roman Empire. It consisted of many small, semiautonomous states. In these pre-democratic times, the German states were ruled by princes.

Many of these states had standing professional armies, elite by the standards of the day. The German princes would sometimes lease out their armies to other European powers in order to replenish their royal coffers.

When the American Revolution began, the British government resorted to leased German troops to supplement the overburdened British military presence in North America. Most of the German troops who fought in the American Revolutionary War on the British side came from two German states: Hesse-Kassel and Hesse-Hanau. The Americans would remember them all as Hessians.

The Hessians had a reputation for brutality. It was said that no Continental soldier wanted to be taken prisoner by the German troops. The Continentals loathed and feared the Hessians even more than the British redcoats.

I supposed that Harry Bailey would have known more about the Hessians than I did, from my basic public school history courses. But Harry Bailey wasn't writing an article for a history magazine. The readers of *Spooky American Tales* would be more interested in the ghostly details:

"T*HAT MUCH, my dear readers, is indisputable historical record. Journey to the town of White Plains, New York, today, and you will find monuments that commemorate the battle.*

"*But here is where history takes a decidedly macabre turn, and where believers part ranks with the skeptics. For according to the old legends, one of the enemy dead at the Battle of White Plains would become that hideous ghoul—the Headless Horseman.*

"*A lone Hessian artillery officer was struck, in the thick of battle, by a Continental cannonball. Horrific as it may be to imagine, that American cannonball struck the unlucky Hessian square in the head, thereby decapitating him.*

"*What an affront, from the perspective of a proud German military man! To have one's life taken and one's body mutilated in such a way!*

"*So great was the rage of the dead Hessian, that he would not rest in his grave! He rose from his eternal sleep to take revenge on the young American republic after the conclusion of the American Revolution.*

"*This is the gist of Washington Irving's 1820 short story, 'The Legend of Sleepy Hollow'. The tale is set in the rural New York village of Sleepy Hollow, around the year 1790.*

"*But we have reason to believe that 'The Legend of Sleepy Hollow' was not the last chapter in the story of the Headless Horseman. For according to some eyewitness accounts, that fiendish ghoul has returned again from the depths of hell.*

"*Read on, my friends, for the details!*"

LYING THERE on my bed reading, I rolled my eyes at Harry Bailey's florid prose. He was really laying it on thick. But then, I supposed, that was what the readers of a magazine called *Spooky American Tales* would require.

Then I noticed that the hairs on my arms were standing on end.

My gooseflesh hadn't been caused by the article in *Spooky American Tales*—at least, I didn't think so. I hadn't yet bought into the notion that the legend of the Headless Horseman might be anything more than an old folktale.

Nor was the temperature in my bedroom excessively cold. Three years ago, my parents had invested in a central air conditioning system for the house. They used the air conditioning, but sparingly. It sometimes seemed as if they were afraid that they might break the air conditioning unit if they kept the temperature in the house below 75°F. With the door closed, it was downright stuffy in my bedroom.

I had an unwanted awareness of that bedroom door, and what might be on the other side of it.

The shape I had seen in the hallway.

Then I told myself that I was being foolish.

It was a bright, sunny June day. The walls were thin, and the door of my bedroom was thin. I could hear the muffled murmurs of the television in the living room.

It wasn't as if I was alone in some haunted house from Gothic literature. I was lying atop my own bed, in my own bedroom, in the house where I'd grown up. My parents—both of them—were only a few yards away.

There is nothing out there in the hall, I affirmed.

With that affirmation in mind, I continued reading.

17

The main thrust of Harry Bailey's article was that the Headless Horseman had returned—in 1976. That was the matter he covered next.

"AND NOW, *my friends, we come to the most disturbing aspect of this story. According to various eyewitness accounts, the Headless Horseman is indeed back, in this year of the American Bicentennial.*

"*The Headless Horseman has been seen in New York, New Jersey, and now in various locations in Pennsylvania.*"

HARRY BAILEY then proceeded to give the readers of *Spooky American Tales* the details of some of these "eyewitness accounts". They were all more or less the same. Someone driving alone in rural New England or Pennsylvania had seen the Headless Horseman galloping down some country road.

I noticed, however, that while eyewitnesses were quoted, no names were given. The cited source was always *"a terrified witness in a small New Jersey town"* or *"a stunned believer not far from Philadelphia"*.

Then Harry Bailey raised an issue that did get my attention.

"IF ONLY THE Horseman were content to make these late-night appearances, to simply demonstrate his powers, and spread fear.

"There is evidence, however, that this horrible demon is once again claiming American victims, exactly as described in that classic short story of Washington Irving's.

"This magazine has done some research. There has been a string of unexplained disappearances throughout western New England and Pennsylvania, along the trajectory of these eldritch nighttime sightings.

"All of the missing persons have been young, and all have disappeared from rural or semirural locations along the Horseman's path."

HARRY BAILEY ENUMERATED a list of missing persons cases throughout New England and Pennsylvania. All of the missing were between the ages of sixteen and twenty-four, and all had disappeared since March.

Jennifer Willis, age 18, was last seen driving alone near Harrisburg, Pennsylvania. That was in April. Her parents had reported her missing, but no trace of her had been found.

Howard Thomas, age 22, left his job at a grocery store east of Pittsburgh on the night of March 23, 1976. He, too, was still missing.

I supposed that all of these missing persons cases were, in fact, real. But even at the age of seventeen, I recognized the difference between correlation and causation.

There were plenty of reasons why a young person might disappear. And decapitation by the Headless Horseman was by no means the most obvious one.

That said, for the first time I was forced to explicitly consider a connection between those hoofprints I had seen on the hillside adjacent to the Pantry Shelf, and the missing persons flyer that had been tacked onto the telephone pole.

There might be a connection.

But then again, there probably *wasn't*.

Correlation and causation. They weren't the same thing.

But Harry Bailey's tale was about to become even more outlandish.

18

"Our eyewitnesses have reported much more, as well. When the Headless Horseman arrives at a location, he does not arrive alone. It appears that the Headless Horseman is a magnet for other dark spirits, all of them having their roots in the bloodshed of the American Revolution.

"One of these spirits is the malevolent Marie Trumbull. At the start of the Revolution, Marie Trumbull was a Boston socialite, who was remarked upon for her grace and physical attractiveness.

"But Marie Trumbull was also a dedicated Loyalist who would not embrace the patriot cause. After the start of the war, she enlisted herself as a spy for the British overlords.

"Marie Trumbull's perfidy was exposed, and she was arrested by Continental military authorities. As was customary in cases of spying, she was sentenced to hang.

"But Marie Trumbull cheated the hangman, and American justice. The night before her scheduled execution, one of her confederates arranged to have a sharp-edged knife smuggled into her cell. With this she slit her own throat. Her jailers found her dead at dawn.

"But perhaps Marie Trumbull will yet have her revenge on the land she betrayed. In life, Marie was a dark-haired beauty. Now she appears in the *form of a hideously decayed corpse, often bearing the knife she used to take her own life."*

A CONTEMPORARY PORTRAIT of Marie Trumbull was reproduced just below this paragraph. The reproduction was small, and printed in black-and-white. Marie Trumbull was wearing a dress that exposed her long, graceful neck, and a generous portion of her shoulders.

Assuming that the portrait was accurate, she had indeed been a "dark-haired beauty". And now, according to Harry Bailey she was some kind of undead creature.

But Harry Bailey wasn't quite done:

"NOR HAS the Headless Horsemen returned from those infernal regions without the company of his wartime comrades. There have been sightings along the Horseman's path of Hessian soldiers, risen from the grave to join their headless leader in the reconquest of America. These soldiers appear as skeletal ghouls, as might befit their undead state..."

HARRY BAILEY FINISHED the article with a flourish of armchair philosophizing.

"IT IS REASONABLE TO ASK: Why, after two hundred years, has the Horseman chosen this moment in our history to return, to once again terrorize America?

"The answer, I would submit, is obvious, my friends. Certainly the American Bicentennial is one reason. But this would not be the only one.

"This year of 1976 finds America in a most perilous state. Our country is reeling from a disastrous conflict in Vietnam, the shame of Watergate, and continuing economic stagnation.

"When you consider those factors, is it not reasonable to conclude that this is the most logical time for America's undead enemies to once again *assault her? America, after all, is on the ropes. This is no longer the country where so many of us grew up."*

IN THIS PASSAGE, Harry Bailey reminded me of my father. Dad was always saying more or less the same thing: That the country had seen better days, that the turmoil of the last decade had transformed America into something he no longer recognized.

Harry Bailey's byline in *Spooky American Tales* did not include a photo, nor was there any biographical information. Nevertheless, I was already certain that Harry Bailey would be at least my parents' age, and probably older.

I was about to set *Spooky American Tales* aside and peruse my copy of *Car and Driver*. Then I heard the telephone ring.

19

By the second ring, I had already tossed both magazines aside, and sat up on my bed.

Telephone communications were a completely different thing in 1976, especially if you were a teenager living with your parents.

There were no cell phones, of course. Most homes had only one landline. This meant that at least half of all calls you made or received went through an adult, on one end or the other. (Today's teenage boys know nothing of the awkwardness of asking a young lady's mother or father to summon her to the phone.)

My social life had been barren in recent months. In March, my girlfriend of two years, Julie Idelman, had abruptly informed me that it might be a good idea for us to "see other people".

I soon realized exactly what she meant by "other people". It wasn't long before I saw her standing in the hall with Brad Kemp, a senior (now graduated) member of the West Clermont football team.

I could have used some action on the social front—the female front, specifically. I wasn't expecting a call from the likes of Leslie Griffin, of course. (Despite the eerie feelings of the afternoon, I wasn't *delusional*.) But a call from a girl in my class might not be too much to hope for. Surely many of them knew by now that I was single.

My parents habitually answered the phone when they were home. I sat there on my bed, heard the phone ring once, twice, three times.

I dimly heard footsteps as one of them walked into the kitchen to answer the call on the wall phone in there. There was no fourth ring.

About fifteen seconds later, my mother called out: *"Steve! Telephone!"*

I was up from my bed in an instant. I pulled open the door of my bedroom. I barely thought about the feelings I had experienced a few minutes ago, that sense of something lurking in the hallway.

"I'm here!" I said.

It was a straight line from where I stood in the hallway, down to the place where our living room connected to our kitchen. My mother was standing between the two rooms, holding the handset of the kitchen wall phone. The coiled rubber cord was stretched taught. Her hand was cupped over the receiver.

"For you," she said. "I don't know who it is."

She was frowning. But that might not mean anything.

"I'll take the call in your bedroom, okay?"

There were two telephone units in our household. (This, too, was a fairly common arrangement in the 1970s.) There was the wall phone in the kitchen, and a desk/tabletop phone in my parents' bedroom.

My parents understood my need for privacy. They always allowed me to use the phone in their bedroom, provided I asked for permission first.

"That'll be fine, Stevie."

Why was my mother frowning? I wondered. Why did she have a puzzled expression on her face?

And no, my mother wouldn't have been overly protective about her younger son receiving a call from a girl. Before she discovered Brad Kemp, Julie Idelman used to call our house almost daily.

There was something else going on.

Oh, well, I would know very soon, wouldn't I?

20

My parents' bedroom was familiar territory. At the same time, though, it was distinct from the rest of the household. I didn't go in here very often, not unless I was using the phone, for the most part. On the bureau, there were framed portraits of all four of my grandparents, all four of whom were dead by 1976. The room smelled vaguely of my mother's perfume, my father's after-shave.

I sat down on the tightly made bed and lifted the receiver from the phone on the nightstand.

"Hello?" I said into the receiver. "This is Steve speaking."

I heard a little click as my mother hung up the phone in the kitchen. Another thing about my parents: They didn't spy on me.

"Steve, is it?" said a male voice.

I felt my heartbeat make a little jump. The voice jolted me for several reasons.

First of all, I had been (realistically, I thought) hoping for a phone call from a girl. The voice on the other end of the call was not only male, it was also edged with an unmistakeable overtone of hostility.

And there was something more, besides. Some kind of an accent.

"Who is this?" I asked, setting an edge of confrontation in my own voice.

On the other end of the line: a low, throaty chuckle.

"You niffy-naffy bugger. You'd better watch your step, keep yourself to yourself. Otherwise, one of us is going to run you through!"

I now recognized the accent: British. At that point in my life, I don't believe that I had ever actually met a British person, in the flesh; and there were few foreigners of any variety in the Clermont County of that time. I had heard plenty of British accents on television, though.

I couldn't exactly discern the age of the speaker, but he sounded older than a high school kid, while significantly younger than my parents. Somewhere between the ages of twenty-one and forty, I thought.

And whoever he was, he was threatening me. The entire experience—being threatened out of the blue by an unknown someone with a British accent—was disorienting. But I wasn't going to take it lying down.

"Tell me who the hell you are," I said, raising my voice a notch or two.

Another chuckle. "Say a little prayer you never find out, you yaldson!"

What's a *yaldson*? I wondered. Then I said, "Do I *sound* scared, buddy?"

But I was scared—for some reason I could not quite articulate.

More laughter. "You fopdoodling, goose-saddling imbecile! Don't say you 'aven't been warned!"

And with that, the line when dead. A second later, I heard a dial tone.

I noticed that my hand was shaking as I returned the handset to the cradle.

That had been a strange telephone call, by any standard.

A prank, I decided. It must have been a prank.

Still, I wondered if anyone I knew would be capable of executing such a complex prank. I was no expert judge of accents, but that had sounded like a fairly authentic British accent.

Not to mention the unusual vocabulary. *Niffy-naffy bugger? Goose-saddling imbecile?* (I wondered: *Do British people really talk that way?*)

And what would be the motive? If that had been a mere joke, it had been a very elaborate one, with no clear purpose.

21

When I exited my parents' bedroom, my mother called out to me.

"Is everything okay, Stevie?"

I walked forward to the entrance of the hallway, to the edge of the living room.

What should I tell her? To convey to her—to her and Dad—the gist of the conversation that I had just had would entail an elaborate discussion. Perhaps it was best not to go there.

"Everything's fine, mom."

I wondered if she would ask me who had called. But she didn't.

"It sounded like you were yelling at someone," my father said.

"It was nothing," I said. "You know: just teenage stuff."

"Whoever that was on the phone, he didn't sound like a teenager," my mother said. "He was a little rude, too, I might add."

I was tempted to ask her for more information. Perhaps my mother had caught some clue that would enable me to figure out who the caller had been.

But just then, we were all interrupted.

The phone was ringing again.

"Let me take it," I said. "I have a feeling that it's for me."

My mother and my father exchanged looks.

"All right, Steve," Dad said.

"I'll take this call in your room, too," I said, as I walked back toward my parents bedroom, this new phone call now on its third ring.

I closed the door of my parents' bedroom behind me, and I picked up the phone.

"Yes," I said, somewhat emphatically. I didn't even say hello.

There was some hesitation on the other end.

"This is Steve," I said, even though the caller hadn't yet asked for anyone.

That finally prompted the party to speak.

Once again, my caller was male. This phone call, however, was far less threatening than the last one.

"Steve, buddy," I heard a familiar voice say, "have I got an opportunity for you!"

"Louis," I said, exhaling with relief.

"Yeah, that's right. What's up with you, man? For a moment there, I thought I'd gotten the number wrong."

"I was just—" but then I thought: No, the story would be too complicated— for Louis, as well as for my parents.

And anyway, the incident was over now. *Right?*

"Nothing," I said. "You just kind of caught me off-guard, Louis, that's all."

"Well, now that you're back down to earth, Steve, buddy, let me tell you about the special, exclusive opportunity that I have—especially for you!"

22

Louis Crenshaw was my manager at the McDonald's where I'd worked since the previous February. During the school year, I'd pulled about twenty hours per week at the restaurant. Now that we were into the summer vacation months, I was more or less full-time.

The McDonald's franchise was owned by Ray Smith, a somewhat well-known businessman in the local area. Ray Smith had a reputation for being eccentric and difficult to deal with. Luckily, though, I didn't have to deal with him very often. For the most part, I interfaced with Louis.

And that was just fine with me. Louis was in his early twenties, and he sometimes couldn't decide if he wanted to be another one of the high school kids on the hourly crew, or a full-fledged adult manager. As a result, I had observed that many employees took advantage of his easygoing nature.

"If you have an opportunity for me," I said, "that can only mean one thing. You want me to take an extra shift."

"Steve, buddy. You're a mind reader. How did you guess?"

I grunted in response. "Let me make another guess. Anne Morton called off again."

"Steve, I do believe that you are a genuine *clairvoyant!* Yes, Anne was supposed to work the six to ten shift tonight. But she called off about an hour ago."

Anne Morton was around Louis's age. She was married, with a son who was perhaps two or three years old. When scheduled for the weekday shifts, Anne was reasonably reliable. But her husband was off work on the weekends, and Anne wanted to be off then, too.

"Let me make one more guess," I said. "Something is wrong with her son."

I heard Louis sigh on the other end of the line. "Yep. Ear infection this time."

"And that doesn't strike you as strange? I understand that little kids get sick. But her kid only gets sick between Friday night and Sunday night."

"Steve, buddy, there are many things in this world that strike me as strange. But the fact of the matter is that when Anne Morton was in high school, she babysat for Ray Smith's youngest child. Ray Smith almost considers her another daughter. She's got an in with the man, you might say."

"It's Saturday, Louis," I immediately countered, "and I've worked every night this week."

"So you work another night. What difference does it make? It's not like you have a date or something. You've been living like a monk since that high school girl dropped you. And you're not even Catholic."

"Ouch. Now you're getting personal, Louis."

But Louis had a point. I had been thinking the same thing myself, more or less, when that weird prank phone call had come in.

"Come on. What are you going to do tonight, except sit home and watch Bob Newhart and Carol Burnett with your parents? And besides, you could use the extra money. Am I right?"

Louis had yet another point. Not only did I not have much on my agenda tonight, my bank account had recently taken a major hit. I had just purchased a new car, that already seemed to have a mechanical problem (which my father had warned me about).

Louis was right: I could use the extra money.

"So are you going to be a hero, and help old Louis out?"

"All right," I said, relenting. "I'll be there."

"Excellent! And as it so happens, I have a special surprise for you."

"What? We finally got the Arctic Orange Shakes?"

Louis chuckled. "No, McDonald's hasn't given us the Arctic Orange Shakes yet."

This was a running joke at the restaurant. In the late spring of 1976, McDonald's launched the Arctic Orange Shake with a nationwide advertising campaign. And millions of McDonald's customers around the country eagerly slurped them up.

But not at our McDonald's, they didn't. As of early June, McDonald's corporate had neglected to send the new materials and equipment to Ray Smith's McDonald's franchise in Clermont County, Ohio.

Ray Smith had placed multiple irate phone calls to the McDonald's headquarters in suburban Chicago. Ray claimed that there had been a snafu in the national corporate logistics department, and that McDonald's would soon rectify it. Louis, on the other hand, claimed that the McDonald's people didn't like Ray Smith very much, and someone in corporate had engineered the foul-up just to spite him. Knowing what I did of Ray Smith, I saw both explanations as equally possible.

Either way, those of us who manned the cash registers had to tell customers that no, the much sought-after Arctic Orange Shake was not yet available at our McDonald's. This had become a tiresome daily ritual.

"I believe we are going to be the last franchise in the country to get the Arctic Orange Shake," Louis went on, "if we get it at all, that is. But what I have is a surprise that might be more interesting to you than a new milkshake, given your currently pathetic and celibate state. I hired a new girl the other day to work the cash registers. Like you, she's going to be a senior this year. Do you know a Diane Parker?"

I took a moment and flipped through my mental Rolodex. It

didn't take long. "No, I don't know a Diane Parker." We were coming up on senior year. By this time, I knew everyone in my class at West Clermont, at least by name.

"She must go to South Clermont, then. Anyway, she's cute."

"Really?" I said, revealing perhaps a bit too much eagerness.

"Didn't I just say she was cute? Yeah, really. It's enough to make me wish I was a younger man."

"You're not all that old, Louis," I said." What are you? Twenty-two or twenty-three?"

"Twenty-three," Louis said.

But once again, Louis had a point. The 1970s were a tolerant and freewheeling time, at least compared to our present era. But even then, it wouldn't have been acceptable for a twentysomething restaurant manager to engage in sexual poaching among his teenage staff.

"I guess high school girls would be a little out of bounds for you at this stage," I said.

"Yeah. Cindy Clifford is more my speed."

Cindy Clifford was another young woman who worked the cash registers at Ray Smith's McDonald's. She wasn't too young for Louis. But we both knew that she was way out of Louis's league.

"So I can expect you here at six?" Louis asked.

"I'll be there," I said.

23

I dropped the phone onto its cradle and walked out into the hall.

"Everything okay?" my mom called out.

"Everything's fine, Mom," I said. "It was Louis. I'm going to work an extra shift tonight."

"Good man," my dad said. "Build up that bank account."

Members of my parents' generation saw incessant work as a matter of course. That was what living through the Great Depression and World War II would do, I supposed.

"That's right," I said. I would gain nothing by revealing to either of them that I would have much preferred to have the evening off, even if I'd have done little but watch the boring shows that the three television networks ran on Saturday night.

I walked back into my room. Was there a strange odor in the air? Something sulfurous perhaps, or maybe something rotten?

I put a stop to these thoughts before my imagination could run away with itself—or me. Today had been a strange day thus far. There was no denying that. But there was nothing in my room. I was a teenage boy, and the laundry hamper at the foot of my bed was presently full. If there was a weird smell in here, it was coming from my dirty clothes.

I had no further desire to read—either the *Spooky American Tales* or the *Car and Driver*.

I was hopeful, of course, about the new cashier, Diane Parker. That was as yet a speculative long shot, though.

Mostly I was thinking about the hostile phone call I'd received before Louis's call came in.

Another thing that has changed regarding telephone communications: Nowadays, almost every telephone has some kind of a caller ID function. Not so in the days of analog landlines. Back then, it was technically possible to trace telephone calls, but only with the intervention of the telephone company and the police. The situation had to be outright criminal before this would happen.

Prank calls were therefore common. Most of the perpetrators were bored teens or adolescents.

I recalled one such call that had been made to our landline, a few years prior. The caller had asked if we had Prince Albert in a can. My father hung up before they could deliver the punchline: *Then why don't you let him out?*

But today's call had been no mere random prank call. The call might have been intended as a joke. The words and the tone, however, had been much more along the lines of a threat—British accent and nonstandard vocabulary notwithstanding.

I didn't think that I had many enemies. Perhaps I was being naive. Someone had obviously wanted to rattle my chain.

But the question remained: *Who?*

24

I was halfway to the McDonald's late that afternoon when the Bonneville's dashboard oil light lit up.

My car was leaking oil. I had been in denial about this fact; I'd been putting off the problem. Within the short time that I'd owned the car, however, the oil leak had evolved into a major headache. My first vehicle purchase—my first really big, adult decision—had been fundamentally flawed.

And if I'd only listened to my father, I could have avoided the debacle.

I had found out about the Bonneville through a local "for sale or trade" newspaper. (This was how people commonly disposed of unwanted items before the Internet and Craigslist.) The owner of the car lived just a few miles away from us. I called the number listed for the owner, and made an appointment to look at the car.

I asked my father to accompany me. He knew a lot about cars, after all. But I ignored the basic rule of utilizing the superior knowledge of others: If you borrow or rent someone else's expertise, then listen to what the expert has to say.

I wasn't in a listening mood. The gleaming white paint job of the 1968 Bonneville instantly pulled me in. Also, I had gotten the impression that there weren't many cars for sale in the immediate area. I feared that I might be shopping in a seller's market, with all the disadvantages that entails. I didn't want to miss out.

But a bad deal is a bad deal, even in a seller's market. The Bonneville had a slow oil leak.

This wasn't hard to detect. My father noticed a telltale puddle on the driveway. He was alert to that sort of thing.

When Dad asked the owner about the black puddle, the owner told him—us—that the oil had come from his wife's car (which was conveniently elsewhere at the time).

Dad was openly skeptical of this explanation. For a brief moment, I thought that he was going to outright accuse the owner of lying, and a serious argument (or maybe even a brawl) would result.

In the end, though, Dad let me make my own decision. I wanted the car, and I would buy it with my own money—money I had earned at my McDonald's job, and from various lawn-cutting gigs the year before.

"It's your decision, son," my dad had said. "It's your cash, after all. But I would advise you to hold off."

While the owner of the car stood there scowling at my father, I took less than half a minute to make up my mind.

"I want this car," I said.

And so I bought it.

I NOW KNEW **that my dad** had been right, though. Since I had purchased the Bonneville, I had been refilling the car's oil supply practically every other day.

I had already called the owner and complained that he'd told me a lie and sold me a lemon. The man brusquely informed me that the sale was final, and hung up the phone on me.

Theoretically, I suppose, it would have been possible for me to get my money back through legal channels, but who was going to do that in southern Ohio in 1976, for a used car?

Not many people, I didn't think, and certainly not me.

But now I was on my way to work, and my car needed yet another infusion of 10W-30 from the folks at Pennzoil. There was a Sunoco station on the way to the McDonald's. It was a large station that sold various automotive supplies.

I had left home a few minutes early, and I figured that I had time to stop for a quart of oil without being late for the six o'clock shift at McDonald's.

And besides, what choice did I have?

25

The Sunoco station was a glass-paneled square building on a small parking lot. This was June, and the longest day of the year was fast approaching. At a little after 5:30 p.m., the sun was only beginning to edge toward the horizon. The windowed walls of the Sunoco station were lit up with reflected sunlight.

I parked at the edge of the parking lot, not at the gas pumps. I walked into the station, where a lone man around my father's age was seated on a stool behind the counter. He was the only one minding the station. This he was doing while reading the sports section of the *Cincinnati Enquirer*.

I could only see the balding dome of the clerk's head over the top of his newspaper. He had hair that was going grey, and receding from every possible angle.

The clerk had heard me come in, but he made a point of keeping his newspaper up. Yes, this was an hourly employee who was only putting in time. There were plenty of teenage employees like that, of course; but not every employee with a poor attitude was under the age of twenty-five. (*Same thing now, as then.*)

The store area of the gas station consisted of multiple rows of free-standing metal shelves. There was no signage to indicate what was shelved where. I supposed that I could have started at the front, and worked my way through every aisle and level of shelf. But I didn't have that kind of time.

"Could you tell me where the oil is?" I asked. There might have been an edge to my voice. Maybe just a little one.

"Shelf closest to the window. Near the end of the aisle. Right side. Bottom shelf."

The clerk delivered all of these instructions without looking up from his newspaper.

"Gee, thanks a lot," I said.

The clerk lowered his newspaper for a second. He looked at me over his bifocal reading glasses. He pointedly glared.

Then he raised his newspaper again.

AT LEAST THE **oil** was where he said it would be. The Sunoco station didn't stock Pennzoil, but it did carry Quaker State. Just as good.

The clerk spoke to me as little as possible, and repeatedly glared, as he rang up my purchase and took my money.

What a dick, I thought, heading out to the parking lot, my quart of 10W-30 in hand.

I popped the hood and poured a quart of oil into the Bonneville. It was a maneuver with which I was well familiar by now. I removed a rag that I had placed in the footwell of the rear passenger seat. I used the rag to wipe the dipstick clean, then I checked to make sure that I had enough oil.

I did. For the time being. Luckily, it was a slow leak. I would be okay tonight. Possibly through tomorrow. By Monday I would likely need more oil.

I slammed the hood shut, and I happened to look over at the little patch of grass just beyond the parking lot, to my left.

And I saw the hoofprints.

A LITTLE CHILL **went** up my spine, defying the late-day heat.

The coincidences were stacking up.

I knelt down and examined the hoofprints in detail, just as I had done at the Pantry Shelf.

Once again, the hoofprints were slightly larger than normal. Growing up out on the fringes between the suburbs and the country, I knew what horse hoofprints were supposed to look like.

Not like this.

There was black gunk around the edges of each hoofprint. I could smell the foul odor, redolent of death and decay.

I was grappling with the weight of so many coincidences, trying to find a logical answer.

Maybe someone has been riding a horse, I thought—a normal Quarter Horse or Morgan—in the area.

If only a witness could tell me that he had seen a regular man or woman on horseback, their animal perfectly ordinary and mundane. If someone could tell me that, I could dismiss the black gunk around the edges of the indentations in the mud as unexplained but ignorable phenomena.

Because what was the alternative?

The alternative was that I had to think seriously about Harry Bailey's article. About the Headless Horseman.

According to Harry Bailey's article, the Headless Horseman had recently been seen in Pennsylvania. I knew my American geography, and I knew that Pennsylvania lay directly to the east of Ohio.

If the Headless Horseman had last been seen in Pennsylvania, and he was moving west...

I needed assurance of a logical explanation for the hoofprints.

But who could provide me with such assurance? If that horse was ridden this close to the Sunoco station, who might have seen it, and its perfectly human rider?

Who else, perhaps, but that man behind the counter of the Sunoco station, the man reading the sports section of the *Cincinnati Enquirer*?

26

When I walked back into the Sunoco station, the clerk was still reading his newspaper. Following his now established pattern, he made every effort to avoid acknowledging my presence.

I was in no mood to beat around the bush. Moreover, I would be late for my shift at McDonald's if I dithered much longer.

"Excuse me," I said.

The clerk sighed, as if greatly put upon, and lowered his newspaper.

"What?"

"I know this might sound like a strange question," I said, "but have you seen any horses around here?"

You would have thought that I had just called the clerk a four-letter word, or insulted his wife (assuming he had one).

I watched as a range of emotions crossed the clerk's face. First there was shock, then an attempt at denial.

And finally—rage.

"Get the hell out of here, you little punk!" he erupted.

. . .

"Whoa, whoa," I said, holding up my hands, in an attempt to calm him down.

Maybe I was trying to calm myself down, too. Something strange —something that I couldn't quite identify—was happening here.

"I asked you a question," I said. "I asked you if you'd seen a horse around here. Because I saw hoofprints out there in the grass near the park—"

"What the hell kind of question is that? You're bein' a real smartass! Aren't you?"

"I'm not being a smartass," I fired back. Before I could try to tell him about the hoofprints, he cut me off.

"Sure you are! You had an attitude when you walked in here. *'Gee, thanks a lot!'*" he said in a falsetto voice, throwing my earlier words back at me.

"Okay," I said. "Maybe we got off on the wrong foot, and maybe that was partly my fault. If I offended you, I'm sorry. But there are some very unusual hoofprints in the grass beside the parking lo—"

The clerk stood up suddenly from his stool. He slammed his newspaper down on the counter. *"Damn kids! I see what's going on in the news. Hell, it's been going on for a good ten years now! All you kids are on drugs! You're protesting, and burning the flag, and—!"*

I was taken aback at his sudden ferocity, but I was also determined to defend myself from this barrage of accusations. I stopped him. "Listen, Mister. I've never taken drugs, and I've never taken part in a protest. I was still in grammar school when most of that was going on."

"I said get outa here! You've got your oil. Now go!"

I decided that in this case, discretion was the better part of valor. I might have stood my ground, but my objective in coming back in here had been to gather information. It was obvious that this fellow had absolutely no intention of telling me anything helpful at all.

"All right," I said. "I'll go."

I backed up slowly, the clerk's dagger-tipped stare following me all the way.

When I estimated that I was close to the door, I turned around.

. . .

I slid into the Bonneville and started up the car's ignition. At least the oil light wasn't lit up anymore, but I knew that wouldn't last for long.

I was puzzled, and yes, more than a little troubled, by the clerk's response.

The clerk couldn't have been that mad over the content of anything that I had actually said.

I'd had my share of interactions with adults who believed that all Americans under a certain age were hippies and antiestablishment flag-burners. If the clerk had adopted a condescending tone, and dismissively called me an idiot, I could have squared that reaction with my previous experiences. *(I wouldn't have liked it, mind you, but I could have squared it with past experience.)*

But not that sudden rage. When I'd asked him if he'd seen a horse, I had forced him to think about something that he didn't want to think about.

The clerk had indeed seen something, I concluded. Something that he wanted to forget, something that he wanted to pretend he'd never seen.

27

I made it to the McDonald's on time—barely.
I walked in through the front door. As the six o'clock hour neared, the restaurant was doing a fair amount of business.

This early, it was mostly families. Young parents with small children. McDonald's wouldn't release the Happy Meal for several more years, but the fast food chain was already a hit with children.

When I walked back into the employees area, behind the customer counter, I didn't see any unfamiliar faces—and certainly no one who could be Diane Parker.

I was about to take my place behind the open cash register—the one on the far right. But first I had to clock in. The time clock, with a card for each employee, was mounted on the wall, adjacent to the manager's office. As I stepped past the office door, I saw Louis seated behind the desk. He was smoking a cigarette, as always.

Louis saw me through the window in the center of the top half of the door. He waved me in.

I pantomimed punching my timecard. Louis nodded. I clocked in, so I would get credit for my time. Then I entered the smoke-filled office.

Oh, another thing about 1976: Smoking in public was still more or less acceptable behavior. Most restaurant dining rooms had nonsmoking sections. But smokers lit up without hesitation in the common areas of offices, shopping malls, and bars.

"Shut the door behind you," Louis said.

I complied. The smoke inside the office was so thick it stung my eyes, filled my mouth and nostrils.

I waved my hands about dramatically, as if I could drive the smoke away. "You're going to stunt my growth with that stuff, Louis."

Louis was a tall, gangly young man with black curly hair and a light complexion. He often developed inexplicable red blotches on his cheeks and neck. He wore thick glasses encased in heavy black frames.

Louis smiled impassively at my objection to the smoke. We had had this discussion before.

"How tall are you?" he asked.

"Six-one."

"Well, there you have it. You've already done all of your growing. And look at me: I'm six-three."

"We could both get cancer."

"You won't get cancer. Have a seat, please." He motioned to the visitor's chair on the far side of the desk. "I wanted to go over next week's schedule with you."

I sat down, coughing.

"Quit hamming it up. The smoke will make a man of you."

"If that's the case, then I should have a twelve-incher by the time I walk out of here."

"Hey, I didn't say that smoke is a miracle drug. Think of what you're starting with. Anyway, take a look at the days and shifts I have you signed up for next week. Let me know if there's any problem. But please don't let there be any problems. If I have to redo your schedule, I have to redo everyone else's schedule to fill in the gaps."

He slid the paper across the desk to me and I gave it a quick look. I was scheduled to work almost every evening, as usual.

Ray Smith had a diktat about day shifts: Day shifts were reserved for the older employees, especially the young married women with children. I think Ray Smith believed that he was doing his part to keep at least a handful of the local teenage population out of trouble, by keeping us at work at his restaurant during the witching hours.

"I don't see any problems," I said, sliding the schedule back to him. "That will be fine."

"I saw you looking around when you came in," Louis said. "You were looking for Diane Parker, weren't you?"

"Not really." I said.

"Bullshit. You were rubber-necking like you'd never seen the inside of a McDonald's before. Anyway, Diane Parker is working a half shift tonight. She'll be in at eight. Speaking of schedules: You're good for closing up tonight, right?"

"Closing up" referred to the procedures that we went through after the conclusion of business hours. Some light cleaning, restocking supplies, etc. Everything that needed to be done so that the morning shift didn't walk into a chaotic, messy restaurant.

"Of course," I said dutifully. I would leave the restaurant at 10:30 or 10:45 p.m. tonight, I estimated.

"I guess you can go ahead and get to your cash register." He glanced at his watch. "Did you get here at six?"

"Five minutes early, actually. Then you called me in here to talk."

"Ah. Yes. Well, anyway."

I could sense Louis hemming and hawing around. There was something else he wanted to talk to me about.

"Is **something else** on your mind, Louis?"

After pondering my question for perhaps five seconds, he said, "I'm not sure, really. I've been feeling a little...weird, of late."

"'Weird'? You're always a little weird, Louis."

"Come on. I'm being serious."

"All right. What do you mean by 'weird'? Are you sick?"

"No. I don't mean that there's anything wrong or weird about me. I feel like there's something weird *going on*. Around here, I mean."

It was as if Louis had read my thoughts, been privy to the events of the entire day: the hoofprints at the Pantry Shelf, the missing persons flyer, that shadow I saw in the hallway of my home…and then finally, the second set of hoofprints and the bizarre reaction of the clerk at the Sunoco station.

"What about you, Steve? Have you noticed anything unusual of late?"

I could have confided in him in that moment. I could have told him about everything I had experienced since roughly noon.

Unlike the clerk, Louis was certainly open to a speculative conversation.

But I didn't reveal anything to Louis.

"I haven't noticed anything out of the ordinary," I said. "Not really. Not at all, now that I think of it."

Why didn't I meet Louis halfway, when he was clearly attempting to take me into his confidence?

I wondered to myself—even then.

My reasons had nothing to do with Louis. I don't know if I was still in denial, but I was definitely in a state of resistance. This was the summer before my senior year of high school. I wanted it to be filled with fun. Pleasant memories. Maybe a new girlfriend.

I didn't want to think about young people around my age going missing, possibly the victims of some horrible forces that I could barely imagine existing. I didn't want to consider the notion that Harry Bailey's article in *Spooky American Tales* might be anything more than the sensational ramblings of a pulp journalist. I didn't want to contemplate the possible meaning of those two sets of hoofprints, the nasty gunk around their edges.

"I'd better get to my cash register," I said.

"Yes, I guess you'd better."

I was standing up from the visitor's chair when Louis gave me yet one more thing to think about.

"Oh," Louis said, "if you do happen to hit it off with Diane Parker, I recommend that you don't take too long in making your move. What I mean is: Don't let Keith Conway make his move first. You know how he is, after all."

28

Leaving Louis's office, it occurred to me that I hadn't yet taken Keith Conway into consideration, and that yes, he might be a problem.

But had Keith Conway even noticed Diane Parker?

My answer to that question was not long in coming.

"Hey, Stevie!" I heard someone shout.

Speak of the devil. Or Keith Conway. Scant difference between the two.

Keith worked back in the kitchen area. I could see his tall, broad-shouldered frame between the metal shelves that the kitchen crew used to supply the customer service staff with cooked menu items, almost all of them fried.

Keith's long blond hair was tied back in a hairnet. He was smiling sardonically at me, accenting that dimpled chin of his, which I found ridiculous, but which I had once heard a girl at West Clermont describe as "the likeness of an ancient Greek god."

This same girl was quite intelligent. *(How many high school students, when pushed for a metaphor, go instinctively to classical mythology, after all?)* And I would have thought her amply capable of seeing past Keith Conway's superficial charms. But I still had much to learn—or at least to accept—about such matters.

"Come back here," Keith said, beckoning to me. He was standing over one of the fryers, tending a batch of the uniformly cut, uniformly cooked French fries that have always been a signature staple of McDonald's.

I was torn. I should really have proceeded directly to my cash register. But I also wanted to hear what Keith Conway had to say. Ordinarily, I regarded Keith as a noisome presence to be avoided. But now I was in intelligence-gathering mode.

The other two cashiers on duty had been watching me while I was talking to Louis. They were watching me now, too, as I talked to Keith Conway.

"Hey, *Steve*," Jenny Tierney said, pulling some coins from her register's cash tray to give to a customer. "Come on. We're backing up here."

Jenny had just graduated from South Clermont High School. I didn't know her well, and that was fine with me. Jenny had a reputation for being something of a tattletale, a goody-two-shoes who was always telling other people what to do.

But in this instance she wasn't being unreasonable: I looked out into the dining area and saw that there was, indeed, a line backing up behind both of the two cash registers that were currently in operation.

"I'll be right there," I said. And then I stepped around the shelves and back into the kitchen area.

IN CONTEMPORARY PARLANCE, **Keith and I** were what might be called "frenemies". We had known each other forever, really—ever since our days of elementary school and tee-ball. But we were like oil and water together, and both of us knew it. We had never come to blows; and we maintained an external pretense of civility. We were teenage boys, however, and that pretense of civility occasionally cracked.

As soon as I walked back into the kitchen area, two of Keith's sycophants immediately fixed their attention on me, clearly interested in what was about to happen next. Keith was the unofficial leader of the guys in the kitchen on the night shift.

Jonesey, a seventeen year-old who attended South Clermont, diverted his attention from his fryer to fix his gaze on his leader. Jonesey—whose actual name was Albert Jones—would seemingly miss no opportunity to curry favor with Keith.

The other Keith Conway follower, a chubby West Clermont junior named Scott Thomas, was watching and listening, too. He was chopping unions on a metal table near the fryers, but that work was paused as I stepped back into the kitchen.

"How are you doin', Stevie?" Keith asked.

"Excellent," I said. "Never better."

My mother called me Stevie, and that was fine. But when Keith adopted the diminutive form of my name, it was usually because he was about to annoy me.

"I guess you've seen the new girl," Keith said, jumping right to the heart of the matter. "Diane."

"No," I said. "I haven't seen her." I hadn't yet, after all.

Keith made a noise with his lips that suggested I was lying. Scott Thomas and Jonesey simpered at their master, and sneered at me.

"Don't tell me you don't think she's cute," Keith insisted.

"Have you even heard me, Keith? I just got here. I haven't seen her yet."

"Well, when you do, you're going to think she's cute. And you shouldn't get your hopes up. That girl is sweet on me, I'm telling you. She's going to be taking a ride in the Love Machine any day now."

This prompted much laughter and sniggering from the red-haired Jonesy, as well as the chubby Scott.

Keith drove a black 1971 Trans Am. He constantly referred to it as his "Love Machine".

And not entirely without reason. Plenty of girls found Keith attractive. Not only was he a big blond guy with an attitude. He occupied a niche between jock and outlaw that was uniquely possible in an environment like Clermont County.

Keith played tight end for the West Clermont football team. He was also fond of smoking weed, and binge drinking. Keith had been arrested at least once for drunk driving. He saw no contradiction between these two modes of behavior.

And many girls—*including some otherwise smart ones*—found this combination irresistibly appealing.

"Steve—come *on!*" I heard Jenny Tierney shout from the cashiers' area. "We need some *help* here."

"I've got to get to work, Keith," I said. "Later."

29

About an hour later, both Jenny Tierney and the other cashier were on break.

I was a few minutes away from yet another shock.

For the time being, however, I was reenacting the running joke that Louis and I had discussed earlier in the afternoon, when he'd called me to request that I take the extra shift.

"No," I was telling a thirtyish couple with their grade school-age daughter. "We don't have the Arctic Orange Shakes."

"McDonald's is running ads about the orange shakes nonstop," the man said. "What do we need to do to get one?"

Both the man's wife and his daughter produced disappointed facial expressions. The little girl frowned and stuck out her lower lip.

"To be honest with you," I said, "your best bet would probably be to go to one of the McDonald's locations in Cincinnati. I don't know when we're going to have them here."

The man turned to his wife. "Do you want to go to Burger Chef?" he asked.

"Does Burger Chef have Arctic Orange Shakes?" the little girl chimed in.

"No, but they have their act together, Holly—which is more than I can say for this McDonald's."

"Let's go, Frank," the woman said.

The whole family abruptly gave me their backs and headed toward the exit.

"I'm sorry," I said.

They didn't turn around to reply.

THE RED-HAIRED YOUNG man walked in at almost exactly the same time that the family of three walked out. He might have passed them in the double glass doors.

He was wearing blue jeans and a white tank top.

I recognized him immediately as the same fellow I had seen walking down the access road beside the Pantry Shelf. It had been only a matter of hours since then, after all.

And now he was here. At my workplace.

I didn't believe this was a coincidence. Not after all the weird coincidences I'd already experienced today.

I braced myself. But at the same time, I took pains to remember: There was a chance (even if an increasingly small one), that the red-haired youth was just another customer, that there was a logical explanation for everything I'd seen, heard, and felt today.

As he walked up, he looked directly at me, just as he had on the access road beside the Pantry Shelf.

He was already giving me that smirk.

He had known that I would be here. But how was that possible?

He made a beeline for my cash register. With the other two cashiers still on break, I was the only one present.

I was about to speak, but he beat me to the first word.

"What, are you just going to stand there like a lubberwort?" he asked.

His use of this strange vocabulary (which I was not familiar with, but which I knew to be an insult of some kind) made me instantly certain that he was the one who had called me at home this afternoon, and issued that string of odd invectives.

Also, he spoke with a distinctly *British* accent.

But how was any of that possible? How had he known my phone number? How had he known that I worked at the McDonald's?

"What do you want?" I asked him.

He laughed. It was more of a snort. "Oh, I wants me a lot of things."

"What's your name?" I asked him. "Who are you?"

"You can call me Banny."

At the time, I took his name to be nothing more than some unusual nickname. (But I wasn't totally surprised by this, as I figured that different names were common in the United Kingdom.)

Somewhat later, I would learn his full name.

But right now, I was mostly concerned with meeting his obvious challenge. The challenge had begun at the Pantry Shelf, and continued when he called my house. It was now entering its third phase.

"Did you call me earlier?" I asked.

"And what if I did, plague-sore? What are you going to do about it?"

While so many of the unwanted visitors of that summer inspired fear in me, Banny immediately stoked my anger. (And that was before I even knew who he actually was.)

I took a moment to ponder my next steps. I was seized by a sudden desire to walk around from behind the counter, and give this guy a punch in the nose. At the very least, I would have given him a good shove.

Then I remembered where I was. My role here at Ray Smith's McDonald's.

"Are you going to *order* anything?" I asked. "Would you like an order of fries? A Big Mac, maybe?"

"Are you bleedin' serious? You think I want to *eat* here?"

"Why else would you be here? *Banny*."

"Just remember what I said. Whatever you see, whatever you think you understand, leave it alone. Stay out of it. Otherwise, we'll be makin' you sorry."

He paused and looked me over. "You fopdoodling cow dung," he said. "Best you keep to your place."

Then Banny, just like the family of three, turned and walked away from the counter without ordering anything.

I WANTED to run after him, to knock that smirk off his face.

But he was still a customer of Ray Smith's McDonald's—on some level, at least. If I made a scene, I would risk losing my job.

I wouldn't be able to count on the good offices of Louis. Louis was certainly my benefactor, but even he couldn't excuse me from starting a fight in the dining room of the restaurant.

It was now around seven o'clock. And while the twilight was still a full two hours away, the sun was at a low angle in the sky, and orange light was glinting off every polished and metallic surface in the restaurant.

The restaurant faced west, so that I had to squint against the glare when I looked toward the parking lot.

I watched Banny take a turn toward the twin sets of doors that comprised the main entrance and exit of the restaurant. You've seen them: Every fast food establishment in the world is constructed in the same way. There are two sets of glass doors, with a small foyer in between. This helps keep the warm air in during the winter, and the cool air in during the summer.

But Banny never completed the turn to the first set of double doors. It appeared to me that Banny just…

Faded away.

One moment he was there. And the next he wasn't.

No, I thought. *I did not just see that.*

I blinked, and squinted, and still couldn't see Banny.

"What's up with you?" someone said over my shoulder.

I turned and saw Jenny Tierney and the other cashier, returning from break.

"Nothing," I said. "I'm fine."

"You look a little pale," Jenny said.

"Like I said, I'm fine."

"If you say so, Steve. But you look pale to me."

30

Sometime later...It must have been going for eight o'clock. There was still daylight coming in through the windows of the restaurant, but it now had a much darker hue. The long twilights of June. They can go on forever, it seems.

I was in another lull in customer action, and I was thinking about my interaction with Banny, of course.

Of what I'd seen.

Or what I'd thought I'd seen.

"Steve? Do you have a minute?"

It was Louis who had spoken up behind me.

I turned around, and saw Louis standing there, as expected.

But he wasn't alone.

Standing beside Louis was a girl about my age. She was of medium height, svelte, and she had dark brown hair.

She was wearing a McDonald's uniform.

She had a nice smile. I took in her delicate nose, her dark eyebrows, her brown eyes. All of her.

Diane. Diane Parker. I had been so discombobulated by the visit from "Banny" that I had forgotten all about Diane Parker. The new girl.

"Diane Parker, meet Steve Wagner," Louis said. "Steve Wagner, meet Diane."

I managed to compose myself, to put thoughts of the strange visitor—of everything that had happened today—behind me.

This was the way I wanted the summer to be. I wanted to meet new girls. I wanted the summer to be filled with promise. Not with bizarre and unexplainable phenomena.

"Louis tells me you're his best cashier," Diane said. She gave me another little flash of that smile. There is nothing like being seventeen and having a girl smile at you like that. Nothing.

"I know a thing or two," I said.

"Well," Louis said, "you can show that thing or two to Diane. I've assigned her to work with you, so you can teach her the ropes. Tell her everything there is to know—everything that *you* know—about working a McDonald's cash register."

BY THAT TIME, **the cash register crew** was down to Jenny Tierney, Diane, and me. The other cashier had already left for the evening.

Jenny Tierney didn't pay much attention to us. Jenny had already been introduced to Diane, and she didn't seem very interested in getting to know her. That was just fine with me.

The lull in the customer traffic continued—a small miracle for a Saturday night—and I had the opportunity to talk to Diane about topics that had nothing to do with the nuances of customer service at the Golden Arches.

Diane was, in fact, a senior at South Clermont High School. I asked her about sports and cheerleading, and she mentioned that she didn't participate in any extracurriculars.

"You must study a lot, then," I said.

She shrugged. "I guess so. I'm third in my class now. In academic ranking, that is."

I was taken aback. I had no idea what my class ranking even was. I was no slouch, academically, but nor would anyone have described me as a "brain". I was slightly above average, grade-wise, but nothing to brag about.

"Have you picked out a college yet?" I asked her. In the 1970s, college was by no means the assumed post-high school destination that it would become in later years. If she was third in her class, however, it was probably safe to assume that she'd be going on to college.

"I'm going to UC," she said. (Nationally, "UC" most often refers to the University of California. Everyone in that part of the world, though, understood UC to mean the University of Cincinnati.)

"Me, too," I said. "Have you thought about your major?"

"I'm interested in the medical field," she said.

"Nursing?" I asked, and immediately regretted the assumptions my guess entailed.

"No. I want to go to medical school. What's the matter? You don't think that women can be doctors?"

"Sure," I said. "Of course. I just—"

"You just assumed that since I'm a girl, if I'm interested in something medical, it will be nursing."

I started to fumble out a response, and she laughed. "I'm just messing with you, Steve. I'm not mad. But never assume that girls can only pursue certain careers, and other career paths are reserved for the boys. It's nineteen seventy-six, after all."

WE HIT IT OFF WELL, I would have said. Diane was a fast learner. And although I was indeed something of an expert on the cash register, there turned out to be little for me to show her.

While I was helping Diane figure out one of the few points she hadn't already grasped, I happened to turn halfway around, and I could see Louis standing in the doorway of the manager's office. He was smiling. He gave me a quick wink, and disappeared into the office.

Yeah, Louis was in my corner, all right.

Louis might be twenty-three, but he was by no means oblivious to what was going on with the high school kids. Moreover, he clearly had his preferences among us. Louis didn't want to see the blustering Keith Conway end up with yet another pretty girl.

I was thinking, though, that I might not have so much to worry about. Diane was third in her class. She was going to be a doctor.

Certainly a girl with a resumé like that could see through the superficial charms of Keith Conway, I thought.

31

My fifteen-minute break period arrived some time later, as the twilight was fading into night.

I didn't want to hang out in the dining area, and the hourly employees were actively discouraged from loitering in the front parking lot during our breaks. Ray Smith didn't want his customers to be intimidated by the sight of his employees skulking around outside the front door.

There was an area behind the McDonald's, directly off the kitchen, in the small rear parking lot of the building. Employees could go there to escape the constant gaze of diners during their break periods. It was kind of lonely back there. The rear parking lot wasn't visible from the road, and vice versa.

But I had fifteen minutes to myself, and I wanted to do some thinking. I wanted to think more about Diane Parker, and what possibilities might exist there.

I didn't want to think about everything else that had happened today. I imagined myself clipping out the vast portion of the afternoon: from my visit to the Pantry Shelf around noon, to that visit at the counter from the British-speaking, red-haired Banny.

Banny, who had seemed to disappear into thin air....

My introduction to Diane Parker had been okay, though. I would keep that.

I passed through the kitchen. Keith Conway and his friends were absorbed in their cooking tasks, for once. They either didn't notice me, or decided to save their annoying banter for another time.

The door to the rear parking lot was in the far corner of the kitchen, not far from the freezer. I opened the metal door and slipped outside.

The first thing that struck me was the impending darkness. The rear parking lot ended a stone's throw from the back door. Beyond the parking lot, there was a little rambling field of overgrown grass and weeds. And beyond that, the woods. This late in the day, this close to full darkness, the tree line was black and monolithic, a jagged profile against the purple sky.

The humidity lingered, but it was now at a tolerable level. The restaurant's dumpsters were located back here, too; and they emitted a rancid effluvium. There was nothing even vaguely supernatural or unexplainable about that.

That wasn't the only odor back here, though. I detected the distinct odor of cigarette smoke.

From the lower right corner of my field of vision, I caught the glow of a cigarette's burning ember in the darkness.

"Louis!" I said, startled.

Louis was sitting on an overturned wooden crate between the rear brick wall of the restaurant and the dumpster.

He was smoking, of course.

"Didn't see me, did you?" Louis smiled.

"You're like a cat."

He smiled again and took a drag on his cigarette. "Well, don't be thinking that you're going to put a bell on me. Because that isn't happening."

"You just startled me, was all."

Louis nodded thoughtfully. "You seem to be hitting it off with Diane."

"I think so," I said. "Time will tell."

"Well, don't let too much time tell. Remember your competition."

My earlier interactions with Keith Conway had been grating, as always. My time with Diane, and what seemed to be a genuine rapport between us, had buoyed my outlook concerning my prospects. I was waxing both hopeful and self-assured—maybe a little too hopeful and self-assured, even.

"Diane is too smart for an idiot like Keith Conway," I said. "But don't worry, I won't take too much time."

Louis took another drag on the cigarette and raised one eyebrow at me. "Feeling confident, are we?"

"Like you said, we hit it off."

"Just don't get *over*confident," Louis advised.

Then my boss abruptly changed the subject. He looked back at the tree line. Despite the mugginess of the June night, he visibly shivered.

"I've never been afraid of the woods," he said. "Not in my whole life. But I don't feel comfortable back here now. This is like, a very recent thing. I get the feeling that something's watching, that something's out there."

He paused, and looked up at me. "And I can't explain it. Does that make any sense to you?"

In that moment, I almost told him everything. Today I had seen two sets of very unusual hoofprints (coated with nasty black gunk!) where no hoofprints should be. I had learned that two young people, only two years older than me, had gone missing while on a routine Saturday-night date. I had seen something unusual in the hallway of my home.

And then there was Banny—the disappearing Brit with the strange, nasty vocabulary.

All of this, moreover, might have some connection to that article in *Spooky American Tales*, written by one Harry Bailey.

I was seventeen, though, and I was seized by the conviction—more a general sense of things than an explicit idea—that my willpower could make the world go the way I wanted it to.

And I wanted no part of the things I'd seen today.

"It might just be your imagination, Louis."

"I'm *suggestible*, is that what you're saying?"

I shrugged. "You said it, I didn't."

Louis stood up and dropped his cigarette butt on the ground. He stamped out the butt, and then picked it up, before tossing it over the side of the dumpster. His break had come to an end.

"I'm going back inside," he said. "I'll see you."

"Yep. And Louis—thanks. Thanks again."

He appeared honestly puzzled. "For what?"

"Well, it hasn't escaped my notice that you've kind of put your finger on the scale for me, where Diane is concerned."

"Oh, that. No problem. All I did was put you in front of an opportunity. Making something of it is another matter. That's up to you. Remember: You need to strike while the iron is hot."

"Sure, Louis. Got it."

With that he opened the back door of the restaurant and disappeared inside. The door fell back with a sigh of the overhead pneumatic cylinder, and a sharp click.

I was now alone behind the restaurant.

I stared into that impenetrable tree line. I tried to think pleasant thoughts, about the summer that might be ahead of me.

The summer that would include some predictable unpleasantries, of course. There would be drama at home with Jack, no doubt, but that was nothing new. It was a bad thing, but I had learned how to live with it.

I would spend a lot of hours working at McDonald's. I had already learned, though, that work is life and life is work, and so I accepted that with equanimity. My McDonald's paycheck had paid for my Bonneville, such as it was; and I was socking away money for college next year. My parents had already told me that they would help me out with tuition, but I would have to cover my textbooks and car expenses.

It was also because of my job at McDonald's that I had met Diane Parker. I knew the dangers of counting one's chickens before they're hatched—especially in matters of the heart.

But I had my hopes up. Louis and I had both seen that Diane and I had hit it off.

These were the thoughts I was trying to focus on, as I stood there alone behind the McDonald's, facing the dark woods.

But these thoughts wouldn't stay in my head. I wasn't comfortable, standing there. I had the feeling of being watched. From somewhere back in those woods.

My break wasn't quite over yet, but I decided that I had made myself as refreshed as I was going to be, under the circumstances. I turned around and opened the door to the kitchen.

As I opened the door, I could have sworn that I heard something moving around in the woods.

I didn't turn around to look.

32

Diane, as a new employee in the training phase, wasn't asked to stay for the "closing up" procedures. Jenny Tierney and I had that covered. Two was more than enough for the cashiers' portion of the closing.

We retrieved fresh boxes of condiment packets from the back storage room, and restocked the supply beneath the counter. In the customer dining area, we filled the straw and napkin dispensers.

I walked out at not quite 10:45 p.m. My earlier estimate had been right on target.

When I saw the boys gathered in the parking lot, under one of the big halogen lights, I groaned silently.

I had avoided Keith Conway for the entire evening since our initial conversation. But I was to avoid him no longer.

Keith was there with Jonesey and Scott Thomas. They were smoking a marijuana cigarette, passing the reefer back and forth between them.

They hailed me almost as soon as I came out through the main door.

"Yo! Stevie, buddy! Come here!" Keith Conway, of course.

"Have a good night, Keith," I said, as I approached them. I was about to veer toward the Bonneville. "I'm going home." I nodded curtly at Jonesey and Scott. "I'll see you later."

There was nothing about my response that struck me as humorous, or even mildly ironic. It nevertheless occasioned giggling from Scott and Jonesey. They knew that Keith and I were not exactly best friends, and they saw this as another way to curry favor with him.

"'See us later'?" Keith said. "I was thinking you might want to toke up with us. Come on, Stevie. The Carol Burnett Show is already off the air."

Jonesey and Scott found this hysterically funny. I recalled that Louis had said something similar. Why did everyone seem to think that I watched Carol Burnett?

"I don't think so," I replied. I turned away from them.

"Ah, man. Can't you ever just be one of the guys?" Keith said. "I mean like...for once in your whole life?"

I had no desire to be one of this particular group of guys. Under different circumstances, I would have told them so.

I was in turmoil, however. I couldn't rid my mind of all the unusual events of the day—despite my conscious intention to focus on pleasant summertime thoughts.

It had occurred to me: If Louis has been having strange experiences, too, then it can't be all coincidence.

In the midst of that inner conflict, the needling from these three knuckleheads caused my temper to snap suddenly.

They wanted me to be one of the guys? Fine. I would show them.

I spun on my heels and walked up to them. I saw Keith's body tense. He was likely wondering if I was going to hit him.

And for a second, I was wondering about that, too.

"Here," I said. I snatched the joint from Jonesey's hand. I put it to my lips and inhaled.

I had never smoked marijuana before. I had only smoked regular cigarettes on a handful of occasions, and I hadn't liked the experience. One thing you may have noticed about the children of smokers: They either automatically drift into their parents' tobacco habit, as a matter of course, or they quickly decide that they want nothing to do with the products of RJ Reynolds and Philip Morris. I was firmly in the latter group.

I wanted to cough out the lungful of acrid, oddly sweet marijuana smoke. But that would give them undue satisfaction. They would have themselves a good laugh at my expense.

So I willed myself not to cough. I exhaled the smoke slowly, luxuriantly, as if this was something I did every day.

"Are you happy now?" I said to Keith.

I handed the joint back to Jonesey, and then turned and walked in the direction of my car.

Now I HAD to drive home. I was feeling light-headed.

Surely a single hit from a joint hadn't affected me that strongly, I thought.

Nevertheless, I could see a little field of stars swimming before my eyes. I had experienced this feeling once before, when I'd played touch football, and another kid had tackled me from my blind side.

The placebo effect, I told myself. One hit on a joint is nothing. Keith and his moronic friends, after all, seemed to smoke bales of it. And they somehow managed to drive themselves around.

I started up the Bonneville, backed out of my parking space, and began my journey home. I had a feeling that I hadn't yet exhausted the day's surprises.

And I hadn't—not by a long shot.

33

Most of the route home consisted of secondary two-lane highways that cut through farmland, woods, and open fields. Country roads, in other words.

I passed the Sunoco station where I had stopped for oil. I wondered about the clerk. Was he sitting behind the counter now?

And what had he seen, that provoked such anger in him when I asked him about hoofprints, and seeing a horse?

I rolled down the window on the driver's side. The Bonneville was equipped with an early version of air conditioning; but I didn't want to overly tax the car's capacities until I had the oil leak fixed—another worry on my mind that night.

The wind blowing in through the open window was sharp with the smells of cow pastures and tilled fields. I glanced to my left: I saw a field of early corn, still less than knee-high, and behind that the dark hulk of a wooden barn. There was a three-quarters moon tonight, and I could read the words, CHEW MAIL POUCH TOBACCO painted in white against a black background on the side of the barn that faced the road.

This sure was a lonely spot, I thought. I passed a farmhouse. The little white clapboard structure was at the far end of a long gravel driveway. A single light burned in what appeared to be the kitchen window.

But for all practical purposes, I was alone out here.

When I first heard the distant clatter of hoofbeats, I immediately went into denial mode. I told myself that I was hearing nothing more than the echo of the radial tires against the blacktop.

Then the hoofbeats grew louder.

I pushed down on the accelerator pedal. This two-lane country road was narrow, and the narrow berm left little margin for error. But at least I was on a straightaway.

The hoofbeats faded.

And they grew louder again.

I took a quick look at the speedometer. I was driving 60 mph in a 40 mph zone. If a cop happened by, I would be more than deserving of a speeding ticket.

That would be fine with me. Red flashing lights in the rearview mirror would have been a relief.

But when I looked in the rearview mirror, I was looking for a horse.

Which made absolutely no sense. There was simply no logical explanation for my being pursued by a horse along this road, at 11 p.m. on a Saturday night.

The sound of the inrushing wind was so loud that it wouldn't have been possible for me to converse with a passenger, if I'd had one.

I pushed the accelerator again. 66 mph.

I was almost home. Only a few more miles to go.

I WAS COMING **up on** the secondary road that led to our neighborhood. A sharp left turn.

I could still hear the clattering hoofbeats behind me.

I released the gas and touched the brake—just a little.

I pulled the steering wheel to the left. Hard. Tires squealed on the pavement.

As the Bonneville made the sharp turn, I overshot the far side of the road by a good foot or more.

One of my tires slid on the gravel that covered the berm.

I had only a split second to correct the car's trajectory, lest I take it into the ditch.

My only option was to pull the steering wheel to the left again. But that meant the risk of overshooting the road in the opposite direction.

Somehow, I managed to yank the wheel to the right. But not too far to the right.

The car swerved back and forth for a short distance until I was able to stabilize it.

This road was heavily wooded, and curvy. A speed of 65 mph simply wasn't an option here, no matter what was on the road behind me.

I slowed the car to 25 mph as I neared a sharp curve that sloped upward.

I looked behind me. Nothing in the rearview mirror.

I sighed with relief. I was only a few miles from home now.

And I couldn't hear the hoofbeats anymore.

SOMETHING CAUGHT my attention at the side of the road—to my right.

There was movement in the thick underbrush at the front of the tree line.

I saw manlike shapes, bearing long rifles.

No—*muskets*.

At least, that was what I thought I'd seen. But that wasn't the worst of it.

I thought that I'd seen a flash of the manlike shapes' faces, five or six feet off the ground.

Their faces were a bony, bleached white.

Skulls.

I remembered what Harry Bailey had written, more or less:

"These soldiers appear as skeletal ghouls, as might be consistent with their undead state..."

This could be a dangerous road at night, even at a slow speed. Nevertheless, I felt compelled to look backward, at the spot where I had seen them.

There was nothing back there now.

I looked straight ahead, gripped the steering wheel with both hands, and continued home.

34

My heart was still pounding. But at least I had reached our neighborhood now.

I saw no sign of the skeletal figures that I had seen in the bushes, no sign of anyone on horseback.

I permitted myself to wonder if I had imagined it all—what I had seen and heard on the drive home.

Today had been an emotionally charged day, filled with various circumstantial evidence of the weird and supernatural.

I had foolishly allowed Keith and his friends to goad me into taking a hit on the reefer.

I didn't believe that a single hit of regular marijuana would have altered my senses. But how did I know what was really in that joint? I had heard stories of people lacing ordinary marijuana cigarettes with LSD and hallucinogenic mushrooms.

If that had been the case, then there was, indeed, a logical explanation for that most unusual drive home from McDonald's.

Keith Conway had set me up. Maybe I would deck him the next time I saw him, consequences be damned.

Then our house came into view, and I forgot about Keith Conway and the last five miles I had driven.

. . .

JACK'S RED CORVAIR—THE one that Leslie and her girlhood friends had been so fond of—was sitting in the driveway.

Or to be more precise, Jack's red Corvair was parked in the pull-off space, the one that Dad and I had made—for my car.

I was immediately tense. But tense for an entirely new set of reasons.

I parked on the street. Otherwise, I would have to move the Bonneville again in order for Jack to leave. And I didn't want to delay his departure by even a minute. Hopefully, he would be on his way out already.

BUT JACK WASN'T on his way out. Jack had just arrived, in fact.

My brother was sitting in the spare recliner in the living room. Dad was sitting in his La-Z-Boy, Mom on the couch.

The television screen was dark. In 1976, there wasn't much to watch late at night. Most of the networks signed off around midnight.

And anyway, my parents had a visitor—an unwelcome one, I thought.

Jack was wearing blue jeans and a black tee shirt. He wore his hair and his beard long.

Jack had never been much for cracking the books. But as a high school student during the 1960s, he had been a respectable baseball player. Back then he'd been clean-cut. Now he looked like a cast member of the musical *Hair*.

"Hello, little brother," Jack said.

Jack smiled at me through his dark, heavy beard. I recall thinking that there was something wild and dangerous in my brother's eyes; and that was the impression I had had of him since as far back as I could remember.

Jack had never laid a hand on me—with the exception of some harmless roughhousing during our brief time together in our parents' house. But I was afraid of him, nonetheless.

That might have been the moment I first faced that realization head-on. After a day of so much that was unbelievable, I was facing up to a mundane truth of my childhood, a truth that I had lived with my whole life—and yet—evaded to the best of my ability.

I feared my brother.

And I hated him a little bit, too.

"Hello, Jack," I said.

Jack appeared to be moderately intoxicated. But Jack always seemed to be intoxicated back in those days.

"A little late for a casual visit," I said.

"Really?" he asked, an edge in his voice. "Might I remind you, Steve: I was here ten years before you were. If one of us is the interloper here, it's you."

I felt a tide of rage welling up inside me. I wanted to tell him off, to tell him to leave.

But my father intervened before I could.

"That's enough of that kind of talk," Dad said. "Your brother was out working tonight, Jack, which is more than I can say for you."

"I have been working," Jack said. He looked away from me, dismissively, and back at our father. "I've been working as an assistant at Hal's Body Shop, over in Batavia."

"You've been doing that about five hours per week," Dad scoffed. "You spend the rest of your time screwing around, getting drunk, getting high. Which is why you're twenty-seven years old, and still unable to support yourself."

Although Jack thought nothing of using harsh words with me, he knew better than to attempt a frontal assault on our father. His tactic was always to make some allowances for Dad's criticisms, before attacking stealthily from another angle.

But this time Jack's modus operandi backfired.

"I know I need to do a better job of getting my act together," Jack conceded, with what I took to be contrived humility. "I've been working on myself. Try to have some sympathy, for me, please, Dad. Some understanding. We're both veterans, after all."

I saw the color rise in my Dad's face. My mother's eyes went wide with alarm.

Jack shouldn't have said that.

"Please, Jack," my father said, with an obvious effort to control his sudden anger. "Don't say things like that. I served my country in combat, including D-Day. As you well know. Your time in the military wasn't anything like that."

"I know," Jack said, hanging his head dolefully. "I was just saying—"

"Well, don't say things like that."

Jack raised his head again. "Everything you're saying is true, Dad. Every word of it. I really need to work on myself, like I said. But I'm in a jam. I'm behind on my portion of the rent out at the farmhouse."

This was the living arrangement that Leslie had mentioned, which I had dismissed as a "hippie commune". Jack shared space—probably not much more than a cot and a corner of a room—at a farmhouse farther out in the country. He lived with a group of six or seven other guys, all of them dropouts in one way or another.

"And so now you're here for money," my mother said.

"I'm here with the sincere hope that my parents will be willing to help me out when I'm in need."

"Jack," Dad said, "your mother and I have already given you hand-outs, or 'tide-me-overs' as you like to call them, on numerous occasions."

I had heard versions of this conversation multiple times in the past. Today had been a long day. I was tired and shaken by the events of the day (though partly buoyed, too, by my pleasant interactions with Diane Parker.)

Under ideal circumstances, I would have liked to have talked to my parents about my day, to have made them understand—if it were possible to break through their understandable skepticism—what I had experienced since noon.

I was almost certain that I had seen something in the bushes. Those hoofbeats, moreover, I had heard for at least two miles.

Could all that really have been mere figments of my imagination?

But Jack was here, and so Jack's needs, Jack's deficiencies, Jack's addictions, were going to dominate the conversation.

"Excuse me," I said. "I'm going to head to bed now, if that's okay."

"Of course, Stevie," Mom said.

My father echoed a similar sentiment.

I headed toward my bedroom.

As I was leaving, Jack gave me a sardonic, "Goodnight, little brother."

I didn't answer him.

35

At several points in this narrative, I've alluded to Jack's service in the military—such as it was. Perhaps now would be an opportune juncture to tell you exactly what happened.

Jack was eighteen in 1967, which made him prime draft material. Jack wanted no part of either the military or the war in Vietnam. Despite his lackluster academic performance, he perceived that a student deferment offered him the best chance for avoiding all that.

He could have attended the nearby University of Cincinnati; but he convinced my parents to fund his enrollment at the Ohio State University, located two hours away in the state capital of Columbus.

Jack was no more of a scholar in college than he had been in high school. Freed from all sense of restriction and structure, he was worse, in fact. To make a long story short, my brother required only two semesters to flunk out of OSU.

Jack returned to Cincinnati. He bummed around for a while at odd jobs. Without his student deferment, he knew that he was draft meat. He tried desperately to secure a spot in the Ohio National Guard or the U.S. Army Reserves. (During the Vietnam War—unlike the more recent wars in the Middle East—the National Guard and the reserves were not deployed abroad.)

Finally, Jack decided to take classes at the University of Cincinnati, with the hope of acquiring another student deferment. But by then it was already too late.

There had been complaints throughout the country that the very concept of the student deferment was unfair. The result of the student deferment system was to place the burden of fighting the war disproportionately on lower income youths, while exempting the sons of the wealthy.

In 1969, President Richard Nixon signed legislation that made all incoming male college students eligible for the draft lottery. So Jack couldn't escape the war simply by signing up for classes at UC.

Shortly after that, Jack's draft number was called.

Jack briefly toyed with the idea of going to Canada. But while my father might have been willing to bankroll Jack's abortive attempts at scholarship, there was no way he was going to finance an illegal flight to Canada.

Bowing to the inevitable, Jack enlisted in the U.S. Army. In the days before he left for basic training, Jack seemed to turn over a new leaf.

Maybe he would even like the Army, he said. In a rare moment of self-reflection, he went so far as to say that the discipline might do him good.

That attitude, however, didn't last.

JACK WAS SENT TO VIETNAM. No big surprise there. But he wasn't sent out into the jungles, hunting down Vietcong. Jack had—with uncharacteristic wisdom—selected the Quartermaster Corps, which handles the Army's supply and logistics operations.

The U.S. Army sent Jack to Vietnam to serve as a low-level warehouse clerk in Saigon. He was stationed at Tan Son Nhut Air Base, just outside the capital city of South Vietnam.

The assignment might have afforded Jack an opportunity to serve out his enlistment in relative peace and safety. But this was Jack; and with Jack, things could never be simple or easy.

He became involved in a scheme to export narcotics from Southeast Asia to the United States. By this time, an illegal market for recreational drugs was already booming in the U.S. Jack's role in the Quartermaster Corps placed him in an ideal position to transport the Southeast Asian contraband to U.S. destinations. (Keep in mind, this was before drug-sniffing dogs, and the draconian airport security of the post-9/11 world.)

Jack wasn't the only one involved in the scheme. There were two other conspirators from the Army, and at least two from the Air Force. But this assembly of halfwits didn't equal one full wit, apparently.

Once again, I'll make a long story short: The scheme was exposed before the cabal ever sent a single shipment of hashish, heroin, or other intoxicating substances to a single American port. All of the men were arrested, placed in the stockade, and told to prepare themselves for court martial procedures.

Then someone in the Army hierarchy learned who Jack was. Or rather—who his father was. That changed everything for Jack.

BY THE EARLY 1970s, the nightly news was filled with footage of antiwar protests. Public sentiments about the war in Vietnam had reached a low point. Several incidents, moreover, made the situation even worse.

In 1970, we learned that a rogue group of U.S. Army soldiers had massacred over three hundred Vietnamese civilians in the South Vietnamese village of My Lai in 1968. (We also learned that another group of American soldiers, members of a helicopter crew, intervened on behalf of the villagers. The helicopter crew threatened to turn a machine gun on their fellow countrymen, should they continue to murder civilians.)

That same year, a raucous student protest at Kent State University, in northern Ohio, took a tragic turn when National Guardsmen fired on rock-throwing protestors. Four students were killed and multiple others were wounded.

One of the dead, an ROTC scholarship student from Cincinnati, wasn't even involved in the protest. He was on his way to class when he was killed by a stray bullet.

These were dark days for the American military—for the entire country, for that matter.

But the men who had fought in World War II were still largely revered as heroes. Especially the ones who had participated in the big, historic battles. All of the men in my dad's division had been decorated for their actions on June 6, 1944.

In the atmosphere of the Vietnam era, the last thing the Army needed was a news report of a decorated D-Day veteran's son being court-martialed for engaging in a conspiracy to transport illegal drugs to the United States.

Or that, at least, was the conclusion that the Army brass eventually reached. The Army dropped Jack's court martial and sent him packing with a dishonorable discharge.

This was a mixed outcome for Jack, but it could have been much worse. On the plus side, Jack avoided a lengthy term in the United States Disciplinary Barracks at Fort Leavenworth, Kansas. The Army, meanwhile, avoided yet another lurid public scandal.

But Jack was not truly a veteran, in the sense that my father was a veteran, in the sense that all the other young men returning from Vietnam were veterans. He had been drummed out of the Army under a cloud of disgrace.

Jack returned to Cincinnati. Where else was he going to go?

There were inevitable questions and suspicions about Jack's hasty return from the service. But the story of Jack's debacle never made the papers. We were therefore able to get by with vague explanations. No one outside the family knew the whole story—so far as we knew—but I'm sure that plenty of people suspected something near the truth.

. . .

YOU MIGHT NOW ASK me why my parents didn't simply disown their elder son at this point. Jack had, after all, disgraced them, even if that disgrace never made the news.

I didn't understand their forbearance at the time, but I understand it better now, since I've had children of my own.

My son Mark, and my daughter, Patty, never sold drugs or engaged in other forms of criminal behavior. But they did at times disappoint me, and try my patience in various ways.

Even if they had done worse, though, I don't believe that I could have truly disowned either of them. That is a difficult step for any parent to take.

36

That night, I did manage to go to sleep. For a while, I lay awake in bed, listening to my parents arguing with Jack.

I don't know if they gave him yet another handout that night. Eventually, though, he left. By then I was asleep.

Late that night—or early the next morning, I should say—I awoke from a dream.

The dream itself was routine enough: a mishmash of random scenes and events from my daily life. First I was at home with my parents, then I was going to classes at West Clermont High School. In another segment of the dream, I was working at McDonald's.

The dream was subject to the usual distortions and inconsistencies of the dreamworld, but it contained no content that was especially memorable or disturbing.

And then some force invaded the dream.

The dream images of daily life abruptly dissolved, replaced by total darkness. I was awake now—but not quite awake. Paused on the boundary between sleep and full consciousness.

And I wasn't alone there.

A presence was leaning over my bed.

I dared not open my eyes. As is often the case in this in-between state, however, I was capable of some version of sight, or what I imagined to be sight.

Lying on my back, I could sense the vague shape leaning over me.

It terrified me, whatever it was. It was horrible and seductive at the same time.

The thing was trying to speak to me. But before I could make out the words, I pulled myself out of this in-between state.

FULLY AWAKE NOW, I sat up in bed. Looked around my darkened bedroom.

I was alone. But I noticed something: The door of my bedroom was slightly ajar.

I had closed it when I went to bed, to drown out the sound of Jack's rambling pleas for charity, and my parents' frustrated but half-hearted responses.

But now the door was slightly open.

Not good.

It was just a dream, I told myself. Just a dream.

Another part of me perceived that it hadn't been a dream, though. The scenes of school and home life and McDonald's—yes, those had been dreams. But I had been at least marginally conscious when that thing visited me.

I struggled to figure it out. The thing had appeared as nothing more than a mere shape.

Or no—more than a mere shape. The shape had been distinctly female. But no longer female in the sense that Leslie Griffin and Diane Parker were female.

The shape had *once* been female, it occurred to me. My visitor carried femininity—and humanity—as distant memories. But it was something else now.

Marie Trumbull, were the words that sprang to my mind.

Ridiculous, I told myself. *You were not visited by Marie Trumbull, the executed Loyalist spy. You're letting your imagination get the best of you.*

I lay there, for perhaps an hour or more, before I finally willed myself to go back to sleep.

37

I made it to Sunday morning without any further incidents.
   I wouldn't have described my parents as especially devout, but they were regular churchgoers. In the morning, I accompanied them to services at the small Lutheran church we attended.

I daydreamed through the service. When I left the church, I would not have been able to recount a single sentence from the pastor's sermon to save my life.

My mind was otherwise occupied.

When we arrived home, our Sunday copy of the *Cincinnati Enquirer* had arrived, too. I took my time skimming through the paper, pausing only briefly on stories about the ongoing national headache of stagflation, and the upcoming presidential election.

Then I saw a story that did catch my attention.

"Headless bodies found near Zanesville"

In the wake of several young men going missing in the area, Zanesville authorities made a grisly discovery in a wooded area just beyond the city limits last Thursday.

The partially decomposed, headless bodies of two young men were found in a ravine..."

THE STORY WENT on to include quotes from local law enforcement officials. There were speculations of a serial killer, or perhaps organized crime.

Zanesville was a small city in central Ohio. No more than a few hours from Cincinnati.

How many more coincidences do you need? I asked myself.

"Looks like an article there has your attention," Dad said. Sitting on his La-Z-Boy, he was busy reading the sports section. The Cincinnati Reds were going gangbusters this year. The local sports media was already hyping the possibility of them winning the World Series (which they did, in fact, win in 1976—though I would have little interest in baseball that year).

I told my father the gist of the article. His reaction caught me off guard.

"What else can you expect?" He practically shouted. "With the way so many kids are using those damn drugs today, losing all control, it's no surprise that things like that happen!"

I didn't know quite what to say. We had not discussed Jack's visit the prior night. Nevertheless, no major feat of interpretation was required to discern that my father's words were a reflection of his frustrations and disappointments with Jack.

And I, for my part, was no fan of Jack's lifestyle, for the rest of the hippie drug culture. But I wasn't sure that I could so easily ascribe those headless bodies in Zanesville to the ongoing problem of young people getting high and dropping out.

More and more, I was coming to the conclusion that Harry Bailey's article might have an element of truth to it.

But this was a conclusion that I was still fighting.

My mother had been in the kitchen, making the three of us pancakes, as was our usual after-church Sunday ritual.

She walked out into the living room, drawn by the sound of my father's outburst.

"Is everything okay?" She asked.

My father smiled at her, obviously struggling to calm himself down.

"Everything is just fine, Marge. Steve and I were just talking, that's all."

My mom looked over at me for corroboration.

"Just a disturbing article in the newspaper," I said. "Some young men murdered in Zanesville."

"Do they know who killed them?"

"Not yet."

"Oh," my mother said. "Yes, that is a shame."

My mother didn't bother to ask why such a news report would have provoked my father to shout.

Thanks to Jack, yesterday had been a stressful day for them, as well as me.

38

We finished breakfast without further outbursts. My mother's pancakes were delicious, as always.

As we were all clearing off the table, my father's mood visibly brightened.

"How are things going with the Bonneville, Steve?" he ventured.

I decided that the time had come to eat crow, to come clean.

"Not so well. To tell you the truth, Dad, the car leaks oil, just like you said."

"I have noticed the puddle on the concrete, over where you park," he said. "Tell you what. What say you let me take a look at the situation, then the two of us can head over to Bauer's Auto Parts?"

I felt my own spirits lift along with my father's. I had been at a loss in regard to the Bonneville. And now it seemed that my father was going to bail me out.

"Yes, Dad," I said. "That sounds like a good idea. Please."

We opened the garage door, and Dad and I put the Bonneville up on jacks inside the garage. My dad slid underneath the car on his rolling creeper. He needed only a few minutes underneath the car to diagnose the situation.

"Well, son," he said, as he stood up from the creeper. "You're in luck. The oil pan isn't cracked. That would have been a fairly major repair. What you've got is a leaky gasket. We should be able to get a new gasket at Bauer's Auto Parts."

Once again, I felt the clouds lifting.

They would not remain lifted for long.

WE DROVE over to Bauer's Auto Parts. Much like the Pantry Shelf, Bauer's Otto Parts was an independent store, not affiliated with any national chain. The auto parts store was located inside a long, grey building constructed around the turn of the twentieth century. The building had originally been a small factory or a warehouse.

Otto Bauer was around my father's age. A second-generation American, he was the son of German immigrants. Otto had also served in the Second World War—on our side, of course—as a battlefield interpreter.

Otto was standing behind the counter when we walked in. He hailed my father and me, but he seemed distracted, maybe a little glum.

"Where do you keep the oil pan gaskets?" my dad asked.

Unlike the surly clerk at the Sunoco station, Otto was immediately helpful. He walked us back to the location in the dusty store where the oil pan gaskets were kept.

"You should find what you need here," Otto said. "I'll be waiting for you at the counter. Let me know if you need any further assistance."

As Otto walked back to the front of the store, I turned to my father.

"Something wrong with Otto?" I said in a low voice.

My dad shrugged. "Can't say. Maybe."

Otto also had a ne'er-do-well son, who was a former classmate of my brother. Jack and Dan Bauer had even run around together from time-to-time. Unlike Jack, Dan had managed to avoid military service completely during the Vietnam conflict, by staying enrolled in classes at UC, and keeping his grades barely above the passing level.

Maybe Otto was having similar problems with Dan, I figured.

We—or rather, my dad—selected the particular gasket from the ones hanging from pegs. An oil pan gasket, in case you don't know, is a long, oddly shaped piece of rubber that seals the oil pan to the engine block. On the way over to the auto parts store, my father had explained to me that the gasket currently on the Bonneville was warped and cracked, hence the slow, constant leak.

As we headed toward the counter, I started to remove my wallet from my right rear jeans pocket. My dad put a hand on my arm.

"No, son. This will be my treat."

"Really? Dad, you don't have to—"

"I know I don't have to. But I want to. Next time, though, please take my advice on automotive matters."

"Sure thing, Dad. Thanks."

O‍TTO WAS WAITING for us at the counter, looking sour-faced and distracted as ever.

"Find the one you needed?" he asked.

We both told him that yes, we had, and Otto rang up the purchase on his mechanical cash register.

Now my father had taken notice of his mood, too.

"Anything wrong, Otto?" Dad asked. "You don't seem quite yourself today."

"Yes, now that you mention it," Otto said. "Dan."

I figured that Dan was involved in some kind of predictable trouble. He had been arrested for drunk driving or drug possession, maybe. But that wasn't it.

"Dan's gone missing," Otto said.

"*Missing?*" I said.

"*Ja*," Otto said. Though Otto spoke perfect English, he had grown up speaking German at home. "Dan took off on his motorcycle three days ago," Otto went on, "leaving his girlfriend's house. And he hasn't been seen since."

"You've reported him missing, of course," my father said, more a question than a statement.

"Yes." Otto nodded. "They already have their hands full with another missing persons case. Those two other young people."

"What other young people?" my dad asked. "Someone else is missing?"

"Yes," I inserted. "Two twenty year-olds. Robert McMoore and Donna Seitz." Dad looked at me as if to ask: *How do you know?* "I saw a missing persons flyer," I added.

"Oh," my father said. "So we now have three missing young adults in the area."

Otto paused to think. "I wonder if they're connected. I hope they're not connected. I hope that my Dan has simply gone off on a binge somewhere, and that this McMoore fellow and his girlfriend have eloped. Not an outcome that their parents would like, perhaps, but much better than some of the alternatives."

"I hope so, too," Dad said. "Good luck finding Dan, Otto. We'll keep your family in our thoughts and prayers."

WE WERE DRIVING home in Dad's pickup truck. Otto's bad news had put a damper on my relief at discovering a simple solution to the problem with the Bonneville.

"Now you see, son," Dad said, "you see how much is going wrong with our country. When I was in my early twenties, we had the war, of course; but we didn't have serial killers. Young men weren't found in the woods with their heads cut off; and if young people did go missing, it was almost always temporary, and it was almost always because they'd eloped or just run off. Do you know when those other two were last seen?"

"More than two weeks ago," I said.

"That means they probably didn't elope, then. It also means that there probably isn't going to be a happy ending for them and their families."

39

At least the repair of the Bonneville went smoothly. But something happened immediately afterward.

We drove home and Dad went to work installing the new gasket.

I briefly offered to do the job. But we both knew how that would have gone.

"Better let me do it, son," he said.

I didn't argue. "Yes, Dad, maybe you'd better."

MY DAD, **his tee shirt** stained with grease and oil, slid out from under the car.

I had helped him, for what it was worth, as best I could. I handed him tools when he asked for them.

Only once did I inadvertently hand him the wrong tool.

"You shouldn't have any more oil leaks," Dad said, now that the job was finished.

"Thanks," I said. I had already thanked him multiple times, but I was sincerely grateful.

"Next time, don't let a problem go on like that. Ask for my help when you need it."

"Sure thing, Dad. Thanks again."

We were just about to take the car down from the jacks. My dad was putting his tools away, hanging them on the pegboard above the workbench.

I had the sense of someone watching me. In recent days this feeling had come to me when I was near the woods at night.

I had also felt it while alone in my room.

But now I was standing in our open garage, in the company of my father, in broad daylight, in the middle of a bright summer afternoon.

The most un-spooky setting you could possibly imagine.

Above the sound of my dad clanging tools against the pegboard, I heard the sound of someone whistling.

I looked in the direction of the sound. Standing at the end of our driveway was Banny. Now he was wearing a pair of jeans and a tee shirt; but he also wore his now usual smirk.

He looked at me and waved his hand in a beckoning gesture.

"Come on, you bugger, if you're up to it!"

"Steve?" my dad asked. "Could you help me pull the big toolbox out from underneath the workbench?"

I turned toward my dad. "Sure, Dad. I'll be right there."

He saw me hesitating.

"Anything wrong, son?"

"No, Dad. Nothing's wrong," I lied.

I looked back at Banny.

But Banny was gone.

Just as I had half-expected would be the case.

40

I worked at McDonald's that night. Diane wasn't on duty, and neither was Keith Conway. At the time, I attached no particular significance to this coincidence; I had plenty of other things to think about.

Banny, for one.

Who, exactly, was Banny?

Or more to the point: *What* was Banny?

In some ways he seemed like an ordinary young guy, albeit one with a British accent, an oddball vocabulary, and an extremely insulting manner. There was an aspect of him that was perfectly corporeal and mundane.

At the same time, though, he seemed to possess some extraordinary capabilities. After seeing me once at the Pantry Shelf, he had discovered my name, my phone number, and now, my address.

And most significantly of all: He had disappeared into thin air before my eyes—twice.

Provided I could trust my senses, that was.

. . .

That night I was scheduled for the six to ten shift. Because it was a Sunday night, the flow of customers slowed to a trickle after eight o'clock. Few residents of southwestern Clermont County wanted a Big Mac at nine p.m. on a Sunday night.

Ray Smith occasionally caught some flak for keeping the restaurant open so late on the sabbath day. But he insisted that this was the practice of McDonald's restaurants in cities, including those in Cincinnati. "We can't make special rules just because we're out in the country," Ray Smith was known to say.

We were not, however, completely without customer traffic. I was contemplating my most recent encounter with Banny, and the uncomfortable fact that he knew where I lived, when Tim Schmidt walked in wearing his Clermont County Sheriff's deputy uniform.

Tim had been a classmate of Jack's (and, I suppose, the now missing Dan Bauer). But Tim had pursued a very different path. He had served two tours in Vietnam. During one of these tours, he pulled a wounded comrade to safety during a firefight with the Vietcong. He was subsequently decorated for valor.

From what I had heard, Tim was rapidly becoming the standout deputy of the Clermont County Sheriff's Department. *"That Tim Schmidt is going to be sheriff one day,"* I had heard my father speculate, *"and probably before he turns forty."*

I didn't ascribe any special significance to the presence of the lawman. Tim often came into the restaurant. He routinely ordered a plain hamburger, a small order of fries, and a medium Coke.

There was another cashier on duty, but Tim walked up to my register. He was a big guy, with a trim waistline. He wore his black hair in a buzzcut, as if he were still in the service. I guessed, though, that there wasn't all that much difference between the police and the military, in many aspects.

"You'll have your usual, I assume?" I asked.

Tim nodded. "That's right. Plain hamburger, small fries, medium Coke."

"One of these days you're going to order a cheeseburger, and I'm going to go into shock."

"If I order something different, it's going to be one of those Arctic Orange Shakes. I've seen the commercials on TV."

"Well, we don't have them yet."

"What's up with that?"

"Long story," I said. I recited Tim's order into the microphone, keyed it into the cash register, and told him his total.

Tim reached into his rear pocket for his wallet.

"How's Jack doing?" he asked.

"Same as always," I said. "You know Jack."

Tim laughed knowingly, but not unkindly. "Yeah, I guess I do. But there are lots of people around here of late who have much bigger problems."

"What do you mean?" I said, as I made change for him.

"You know about the missing persons cases, right?"

"I know. I saw one of the flyers about Robert McMoore and Donna Seitz. And I was in Bauer's Auto Parts this morning. Otto Bauer told my dad and me that Dan's missing."

"That's a lot of missing people at one time, and we're only talking about the southwest corner of Clermont County."

"Do you have any leads? I know you're not supposed to talk about ongoing investigations, and everything but, well…you know."

"I can talk about this investigation, because there's nothing to talk about. No, we don't have any leads. That's why we're asking the public to come forward if they see anything or anyone unusual."

I nodded. I had seen plenty unusual in recent days. But how to communicate it to a hard-boiled type like Tim Schmidt?

"Have you seen anything unusual, by chance, Steve?"

"Like what?"

"Well, this isn't rocket science. Any unusual people, or any activity that strikes you as unusual."

I might've told him about Banny. I might have told him about the hoofbeats that I heard driving home from McDonald's the previous night, the ones that had pursued me for a full two miles. I might have told him about what I thought I had seen in the bushes that same night, near our house.

Or about that strange dream I'd had, early this morning. Would Tim want to hear about my dreams? I wondered.

I knew better. If I told him any of that, he would assume that I was being a smart-ass. Or he might decide that I had joined my brother Jack in the abuse of recreational substances.

And there was another factor, as well: I wasn't sure that I had correctly interpreted all of these events. I had traced them all back to that article in *Spooky American Tales*, about the return of the Headless Horseman.

Campfire ghost stories...

A psychologist would have said that I was succumbing to the powers of suggestion, and the overly fertile imagination of a seventeen-year-old boy in the grips of late-stage puberty.

I couldn't have said with absolute certainty that such an assessment would be wrong.

"I haven't seen anything or anyone that I would exactly describe as unusual," I told Tim Schmidt. "But if I do see anyone or anything like that, I'll be sure to let you know."

41

And that very night, during my drive home, I would have my irrefutable proof, a sight that I could no longer deny, or chalk up to a trick of the light.

I left the restaurant around 10:45, as usual, after wiping down the metal customer service counter, and refilling the hoppers and bins with condiments, napkins, and straws.

I stopped by the manager's office on my way out. Louis was tapping away on a desktop calculator. I believe that he was adding up receipts. Or vendor invoices.

He looked up when I came in.

"I'm heading out," I said.

He paused his work, ground his cigarette out in the ashtray.

"Be careful," he told me.

This was an unusual thing for one young guy to say to another. My mother sometimes admonished me to be careful. Once in a while, my father would. Males in my age group didn't often express such an interest in my safety.

"I will," I said. "Why?"

"Why what?"

What makes you tell me to be careful? Do you know something I don't?"

Louis smiled at me. I wonder, even now, how much he had figured out, if he knew that I was holding out on him.

"Just be careful," he said. "It may be a Sunday night, but there are no blue laws in Clermont County. Plenty of bars will be open. Plenty of drunks out on the road."

When I walked outside, the parking lot was desolate. That was typical of post-closing time. Tonight, though, the parking lot looked even more desolate than usual.

I looked up into the big halogen light, where only yesterday I had allowed myself to be provoked into taking the hit off the joint. Keith and his buddies weren't out here smoking weed tonight, at least.

Turning back to the restaurant, I saw the last few lights go off, as Louis was preparing to leave. I couldn't go back in there, so what was I thinking?

There was only one thing for me to do now: and that was to go home.

I was approaching **the big wooden barn** with the CHEW MAIL POUCH TOBACCO sign painted on its side, when I heard the hoofbeats. As before, I was driving with the front driver's side window down.

The hoofbeats grew louder now: *ka-thumpity, ka-thumpity, ka-thumpity...*

They were louder than they had been the last time I'd heard them.

I pushed down on the accelerator.

I didn't want to look in my rearview mirror. That is always a dangerous thing to do late at night, while driving on a country road, at least ten miles per hour above the posted speed limit.

I had to look, though. I really didn't have a choice.

I glanced up at the rearview mirror. What I saw in the little rectangular frame of glass was impossible—but at the same time, undeniable.

I could see a horse and rider in the ambient moonlight. The horse was large. Even my brief glance, however, told me that there was something unnatural about the animal—the angle at which it held its head was all wrong. While the horse was galloping at a rapid pace, fast closing the distance between us, its movements were jerky, and unlike any motion that I had ever seen from others of its species, either in real life or on television.

More mind-bending, though, was the rider.

The man atop the horse was clad in dark-colored, heavy riding clothes that struck me as vaguely military—but not the military of the present century.

The military of several hundred years ago.

One of his gloved hands was gripping the reins of his mount.

The other hand was holding a large sword.

Something else about the rider:

He had no head.

THE HORSEMAN RAISED his sword high in the air, and I turned back around to face the road.

I knew instantly that I would need all of my wits in order to survive.

It was obvious: what the figure on horseback behind me intended. As impossible as it might seem, I was being pursued by the Headless Horseman, the monster that Washington Irving had described in his short tale of terror, "The Legend of Sleepy Hollow".

But I didn't have time to process that now, to even attempt to process it.

I kept my eyes on the road, and I gunned the accelerator.

I thought I had a plan of escape.

A *temporary* escape, that was.

42

Some instinct told me that supernatural entities are selective when it comes to revealing themselves.

I don't know how I knew this, exactly. Perhaps it was a basic human instinct. Hundreds of thousands of years ago, prehistoric humans were hunkering over fires on the African savanna. At that time, when there was no reading or writing, and the only source of acquired knowledge was oral tradition, we must have relied largely on our innate senses of the world...and the otherworld, too.

At the rate at which the Horseman was gaining on me, I would not have had time to make a run for my house.

Better, I thought, to go to the nearest place where I could find people—*living* people.

I knew of such a place, barely a quarter-mile down the road.

But it was less than ideal.

THE SAWMILL WAS one of the more active biker bars in Clermont County. The bar was housed inside an old cinderblock building that had—until only four or five years prior—been an auto body repair shop.

Although I continued to hear the clatter of hoofbeats, I resisted the temptation to look in the rearview mirror again. I drove until I reached the gravel parking lot of the bar.

I pulled into the parking lot going way too fast. Pebbles clattered against the undercarriage of the Bonneville. I swerved, and narrowly avoided hitting a chopper that was parked directly in my path.

I slammed on the brakes. My car came to a stop.

I allowed myself to turn around now, and look back at the road. I half expected that my instincts had been faulty, that I would see the Horseman, sword aloft, bearing down on me.

My instincts had been right, though. There was nothing on the road. No sign that the Headless Horseman had ever been there at all.

I took a moment to examine my surroundings. The cinderblock walls of the Sawmill were painted a dirty white. There were small windows of opaque glass through which a grainy light could be seen.

I could hear the sound of loud rock music thumping away inside. Something by Ted Nugent, I believed.

Mine was the only four-wheeled vehicle in the parking lot. Big surprise at a biker bar. Moreover, I was a high school kid at a rough-and-tumble hangout for adults. I would inevitably attract attention if I stayed here.

I killed the Bonneville's engine. An idling car would be more likely to draw notice.

I didn't plan to stay here long, though—only long enough to regain my composure, to complete the rest of the drive home.

Would the Horseman make another appearance before I arrived home? That was anyone's guess. I knew, however, that I couldn't stay here long. And I didn't want to have any interactions with any of the patrons of the Sawmill. These could only be problematic.

But I was about to have such an interaction. Directly in front of me, the front door of the bar edged open.

THE MUSIC BECAME MOMENTARILY LOUDER as three patrons of the Sawmill—one man and two women—walked out.

The man was in his early to mid-thirties. He had long black hair, possibly going to salt-and-pepper, and a shaggy beard. His two female companions might have been a tad younger, but they were both a good ten years older than me.

All of them were wearing standard biker bar attire: The male patron was wearing jeans, and a denim vest with various patches affixed. He wore a black tee shirt bearing a skull-and-crossbones logo.

The women were wearing jeans and tee shirts. They were shapely, and had a worldly air about them. One was blonde, the other brunette.

The two women were walking on either side of the man, each holding one of his hands. I wasn't sure if this was horseplay, drunks supporting each other, or some sign of a tridirectional romantic arrangement. I didn't care, either. I only wanted them to pass by without taking note of me.

But of course that didn't happen.

The blonde woman noticed me first, almost as if she had been actively looking for me.

"Hey, Carlos, Kitty—look! A high school boy! Sitting in a car. And it looks like he's wearing a…McDonald's uniform!"

Carlos and Kitty glanced in my direction, and showed about as much interest in me as they would a random fencepost.

"Okay, Sally," the man—Carlos, apparently—said. "A high school kid who works at McDonald's. Ain't exactly Bigfoot or the Loch Ness Monster, is it?"

That might have been the end of it. But the blonde, Sally, was determined not to let the matter go.

"Let's go over and talk to him," she said in a slurry voice. "See if he needs help."

Carlos was about to protest, but Sally was already dragging them toward my car.

Three sets of feet scuffed through the gravel. I tried to ignore them, knowing that it wasn't going to be as simple as that.

A few seconds later, Sally was leaning down, looking into the Bonneville. Carlos and Kitty were standing right behind her.

"What's your name?" she asked. "You work at McDonald's? Can you order us all some Big Macs and fries?"

In the common manner of drunks, Sally found her own banal humor irresistibly funny. She fell into a fit of giggles.

The brunette, Kitty, found the joke a bit humorous, too. Carlos was simply annoyed.

"Come on," he said, pulling her away. "Git over by the bikes."

"Hey," Sally said, affronted. "You never trust me to drive the bike."

"I didn't tell you to start it up or drive it. I told you to go over and stand beside it. Kitty—you too. Git."

"But—"

"I said, *git*."

Carlos glowered at them in a way that brooked no argument. Although I hadn't fully grasped the group dynamic of this trio, Carlos was clearly the leader.

Carlos shooed the two women away from my car, presumably in the direction of their motorcycles.

Carlos might have been a little tipsy, but the two women were both sozzled. Neither one of them looked fit to ride a motorcycle.

As the women walked away, Carlos paused and took the measure of me. He smiled, not unkindly, really—but as if I were some kind of probably harmless alien who had landed in his world. In a manner of speaking, I suppose, that's exactly what I was.

"What are you doin' here?" he asked. There was no malice in his words that I could detect. And it wasn't an unreasonable question, all in all.

So I decided to try honesty, laying my cards out on the table.

"I—I saw something," I said.

"*Something?*" he asked. "That really narrows it down."

"It might have been only my imagination," I said.

Did I really believe that? Could I even think that?

"It was...disturbing," I added. Understatement of the year.

I looked at my hands. For the first time, I realized that I was gripping the steering wheel of the Bonneville, white-knuckled, even though the car was parked, the engine turned off.

"Okay," Carlos nodded. "My advice to you is to go ahead and get out of here, assuming that car of yours is roadworthy." He gestured in the direction of the bar. "Not everyone in there is friendly,"—a toothy smile—"as you might have guessed."

"Sure," I said. "I plan to get back on the road right away."

"Best you do that," Carlos said. "And best you watch yourself out on those roads. Lots of dangerous and beautiful things on the roads around here lately. They're dark things, some of them. You have to be careful."

"Thanks," I gulped. "I—I'll keep that in mind."

With that, Carlos turned and took his leave of me.

I could hear the loudmouthed Sally, calling at him to *Come on, already*.

I wondered what Carlos had meant by "dangerous and beautiful things" on the roads. Surely he wasn't talking about the Horseman?

But I didn't have the mental bandwidth to overly interpret the words of a biker bar patron. I was merely thankful that Carlos had decided not to make sport of me. My encounter with the patrons of the Sawmill could have been far worse.

I PULLED out of the lot of the Sawmill and drove home.

I drove a little faster than usual.

All the way, I kept looking in my rearview mirror. I strained my ears for the faintest clatter of hoofbeats.

I neither saw nor heard any sign of continued pursuit.

I arrived home at almost the standard time—a little after 11:15 p.m. Although it had been unnerving, my terrifying experience—including my detour into the parking lot of the biker bar—hadn't added more than a few minutes onto my drive.

My parents were already asleep. I took pains not to wake them.

It could be a hormone thing, I thought—not for the first time—as I undressed for bed.

Once I had seen a documentary about adolescents who, during the emotional turmoil of puberty, had experienced dreadful hallucinations. According to the documentary, their visions were quite disturbing and extremely realistic. But in the final analysis, their visions were nothing but brief, passing delusions.

At seventeen I should have been past all that (if such things were even possible). But I was eager to believe that the aberrations of the past two days had had a logical, organic cause.

You might think that sleep would be the last thing on my mind, after that drive home. You'd be wrong.

Even though I was still in a mild state of shock, even though I was still terrified, I was also exhausted.

But I was not to sleep through that night unmolested.

43

I awoke several hours later. For a moment I wondered: Had I merely dreamt of being chased by the Horseman? The patrons of the Sawmill—Carlos, Sally, and Kitty—had they been part of the same dream?

Then I realized that no, that had not been a dream. Whether I could believe what I had seen behind me on the road or not, I had been fully awake when it happened.

And now I was awake again.

I had not been dreaming, to the best of my knowledge.

So what had woken me up?

I looked around my room, alert to any signs of a hostile presence.

Nothing that I could see.

Then I heard a voice—not in my room, but from another part of the house.

Lying perfectly still, I strained my ears to listen.

"Come here..."

The sound had come from the living room, I thought.

Did I really hear that?

"Come here, boy," the voice said again. *"I fancy you."*

Now I faced a choice. I figured that I had three options.

One, I could ignore the voice, and try to go back to sleep.

Two, I could awaken my parents.

Three, I could go out into the living room and confront whatever was there.

You might think that my first impulse would be to awaken my parents. Believe me—I thought about it. But I wasn't sure that would be a good idea.

Whatever these forces were, they had so far left my parents alone. I wanted to keep it that way.

Recall what I said about my parents being part of that no-nonsense generation that went through the Great Depression and World War II. My parents would be even more skeptical of these phenomena than I was.

And if the phenomena were real—if the powers behind them had any toehold in reality—then my parents' skepticism would make them more vulnerable.

You can't fight what you don't even believe in, right?

But did *I* believe?

Well, I was getting there…

"Boy, are you going to come out and see me, or am I going to have to come in there after you?"

So much for the option of ignoring the summons, and trying to go back to sleep.

"Come out here…!"

There was an edge to the command now. Gone was any attempt to appeal to persuasion.

The voice sounded quasi-female. It was the presence that had been in my room just the other night. I was sure of it.

Marie Trumbull.

That was crazy, of course. But then, I had been pursued by the Headless Horseman during my drive home that night.

I slid out of bed. I was already shaking, but I willed myself to be brave—as brave as I could be, under the circumstances.

I walked over to the door of my bedroom and gently pulled it open.

My parents' room was just down the hall. I didn't hear them stir. They hadn't been awakened by the strange sounds coming from the living room.

Because they hadn't heard them. The summons hadn't been intended for them.

I turned away from my parents' bedroom, toward the living room. It was a short walk.

I STEPPED **into** the living room. She was sitting there on the sofa.

She might have materialized from Harry Bailey's article in *Spooky American Tales*. Marie Trumbull was wearing a whitish crinoline dress. Or the dress had originally been white. It was stained with dirt, mold, and torn to tatters in places.

Marie's face was nearly skeletal. Bits of dried flesh still clung to her, like an Egyptian mummy. But unlike a mummy, Marie's eyes were open. And there was a cold understanding in those glassy eyes.

She tilted her head, and grimaced at me, revealing a mouth that was missing half its teeth.

Her stringy hair—what was left of it—might have been black once. Now it was a color between white and grey.

In her lap, I noticed, she was holding something. The object reflected back the small amount of ambient light in the darkened living room.

A knife. This detail, too, I remembered from Harry Bailey's article. This was the knife that Marie had used the night before her scheduled execution. The blade that some sympathizer had smuggled into her cell.

She held up the knife in one clawlike hand.

"Come here, boy," she croaked. "I have something for you."

I don't have to play her game, I thought.

No, I replied in my thoughts—speaking to her with my mind rather than my voice. (I still did not want to wake my parents.) *I don't have to play your game. Go away. You aren't welcome in this house. You have to leave.*

She said something else, but I forced myself not to hear her. I imagined, for a moment, that perhaps I could will her out of our living room, will her back to the place where she had come from.

I turned around, and headed back toward my bedroom.

I heard one of my parents—my mother, I believe, roll over in bed.

You can't stop me, I thought. *You can't take any more power from me than I allow you.*

But it wasn't going to be that simple.

JUST PAST MY BEDROOM, Marie Trumbull was standing in the hallway —or maybe, hovering is a better word.

I held up my hand—a universal gesture meaning, *back off, go away.*

Marie drifted back perhaps a foot or two. She brandished her knife.

I had a sudden, spiking pain in my forehead.

Go away!

Before Marie Trumbull could move toward me again, I took a lateral step into my bedroom.

Stay out!

I shut the door of my bedroom. As I closed the door, I saw a bony, skinless hand skitter across the space between the door and the wall.

The door closed with a soft click.

There were scratching sounds on the other side of the door. I heard Marie uttering throaty curses at me.

Not unlike Banny. She was speaking English, but some archaic, profane version of it.

She can't come in here, I thought. There are limits to her power. By closing the door on her, I created a barrier of some kind.

But how?

How? How was any of this possible?

I returned to my bed. There was nothing else for me to do now.

Once again, to my surprise, I felt exhausted, when sleep should have been the farthest thing from my mind.

44

You might think that after the terrifying experiences of Sunday night, I would have forgotten about everything else.

Let me be clear: My nighttime flight from the Horseman certainly did occupy my mind, as did the terrible visitor of early Monday morning.

When we are young, however, our sense of reality is not as hardened as it becomes in later years. It can bend without breaking, you might say.

We also have less experience in this plane of existence. We therefore have fewer, softer preconceptions about what the nature of things is supposed to be.

That, at least, is the way I remember it—and those are the conclusions I've drawn in the intervening years.

When I went into work Monday evening, I was still thinking about the Horseman and Marie Trumbull.

But I was also thinking of Diane Parker. And she was about to give me a shock, too, albeit it of a wholly different kind.

. . .

I HAD NOT SEEN **Diane** since that night when Louis had introduced us.

I had not seen Keith Conway, either.

But apparently the two of them had been seeing each other, or at least communicating.

Diane and I were scheduled to work together on the six to ten shift. She was friendly enough with me, but I immediately saw that she was distracted.

Throughout the shift, Diane kept smiling at Keith Conway. When he handed her an order from the kitchen, they exchanged knowing glances, laughed at inside jokes that I wasn't privy to.

It was almost as if…

They were an item.

But that wasn't possible. Diane had just started working here a few days ago.

And I had concluded that a girl who was third in her class at South Clermont would be impervious to Keith Conway's cheesy, superficial charms.

Right?

I TRIED **throughout** the shift to make conversation with Diane.

She talked to me; but her mind was constantly elsewhere. The easy rapport that I had sensed between us that first night seemed to have vanished. I was just a guy she worked with now.

Just another guy.

The shift eventually ended. Jenny Tierney, Diane, and I completed the close-up procedures. Before long, we were done.

I looked around for Diane, trying not to be too obvious about it.

I couldn't find her.

I knew that there was something desperate about my attitude at this point. What had I been expecting? I had just met the girl, after all.

I was standing in the darkened dining room of the restaurant, just beyond the counter. The dining room was empty. Louis was finishing up in the manager's office. Jenny Tierney had already left for the night.

Where was Diane?

And equally important—where was Keith Conway?

Then I happened to glance out the front window of the restaurant, into the parking lot.

DIANE PARKER AND KEITH CONWAY were walking—unmistakably together—toward the latter's Trans Am.

The Love Machine, Keith called it.

Diane opened the passenger side door of the Trans Am and slipped inside.

I couldn't believe it: Had Keith driven her to work, too?

And where were they going now—together?

Keith opened the driver's side door. Just before he lowered himself into the seat, he looked in the direction of the restaurant.

It seemed to me that Keith saw me, standing there forlorn, like a complete loser, in the middle of the dining room. I might have been wrong about that. But for an instant there, Keith appeared to see me and to mock me.

The Trans Am's engine rumbled to life. The taillights lit up as Keith backed the car out of the parking space.

I caught a flash of Diane in the passenger's seat, laughing at something that Keith had just said.

Maybe he had just made a joke about me...

Under the circumstances, that was entirely possible.

I was feeling like a laughingstock, after all.

I KNEW that I was making an even bigger loser of myself, but I couldn't resist. As Keith's Trans Am headed for the exit of the parking lot, I walked over to one of the front windows.

What was I expecting to see? I couldn't have given you a sound explanation.

Keith pulled the Trans Am out onto the main road. From inside the McDonald's, I could hear the Firebird's eight-cylinder engine rev up.

The car accelerated suddenly, and the taillights receded into the darkness.

I let out a long sigh.

I TURNED AROUND, and immediately cried out in surprise. Someone was standing right behind me.

"Louis! What are you doing? Sneaking up on me like that."

"I'm sorry," Louis said. He had watched Keith and Diane drive away, too.

"I don't care," I said.

"Yes," Louis replied. "Yes, you do."

I sighed. "Okay, Louis, so I do care. But there isn't much I can do about it, can I?"

"No. Not now."

"Then why should I worry about it?" This question was addressed more to myself than to Louis.

"I told you to make your move quickly," Louis said.

"I know you did. But jeez—I just met Diane the other day."

Louis shook his head. "You should have moved faster. You know how Keith Conway is, after all."

45

Less than five minutes after that conversation with Louis, I was pulling out of the McDonald's parking lot in my own car. But I was going in the opposite direction—toward home.

I wasn't even thinking about the Horseman.

But the Horseman, apparently, had not forgotten about me.

AT ABOUT THE same place in my drive home, I heard the galloping hoofbeats on the road behind me.

Ka-thumpity, ka-thumpity.

I was on a straightaway section of the road, so I turned around to look out the back window.

The Headless Horseman was riding down the center of the two-lane highway, maybe a quarter-mile back. He was holding his sword aloft.

His undead horse was thundering down the asphalt, running on bones and muscles that should have decayed years ago. Centuries ago.

For a brief second, I contemplated the idea of stopping once again at the Sawmill.

I knew, however, that I had pushed my luck there the first time. It was not a place where I was welcome, where I would find refuge or succor.

Nor, moreover, did I have a desire for another meeting with Carlos, Kitty, and Sally.

I thought about what Carlos had said, about "dangerous and beautiful" forces out there on the roads.

I stepped on the accelerator of the Bonneville. I felt the car surge forward. The scenery on either side of me became an amorphous blur.

I thought it best not to look at the speedometer.

Going this fast on the narrow two-lane highway, I was taking a risk that was almost as great as the one behind me.

I was familiar with the basics of the plot of "The Legend of Sleepy Hollow". Ichabod Crane had fled through the woods of rural New York, in a desperate effort to escape the Headless Horsemen.

I accelerated more. Now I didn't even consider a glance at the speedometer.

I did, however, feel compelled to look in the rearview mirror. Briefly.

The Horseman was receding behind me, into the distance.

The road that would take me directly into our neighborhood was in sight now. This time, it seemed, I had outrun him.

This time.

And then another thought occurred to me: I had become Ichabod Crane.

46

When I arrived home, the house was dark. As usual, my parents had already gone to bed. I let myself in with my key.

The living room was dark. I looked over at the sofa, half expecting to see Marie Trumbull waiting for me there.

The sofa was empty.

I had a feeling that I had not seen the last of Marie Trumbull. She would be back. When she came at me again, though, she would attempt a different tactic. I had beaten her once—or at least it could be said that I had *escaped* her once.

I padded down the hall. I heard the house's central air conditioning kick on.

I walked into my bedroom and closed the door. I turned around. I almost cried aloud at what I saw on my bed.

The bodies of Robert McMoore and Donna Seitz were draped across my bed, left there for me as grizzly trophies.

Both of their heads had been removed.

I was about to scream. Then I did a double take.

There were no headless corpses on my bed. What I saw was my bedclothes, and several pieces of laundry. In the moonlight that filtered through the slats of the shutters of the window above my bed, the configuration had created a brief optical illusion.

This time, I really could be certain that my imagination had gotten the best of me.

I sat down on my bed, and untied my shoes. I had a lot to think about.

My first impulse was to wallow in my disappointment over Diane. (How could a girl like Diane Parker go for a guy like Keith Conway?) But as Louis and I had discussed, there was nothing I could do about it. Diane had made her decision, and that was that. By hanging on like a lovesick puppy, I would only make myself look more pathetic.

I made a decision: I was going to forget about Diane Parker.

But what about these other things? I would have liked to have forgotten about them, but they seemed intent on making me constantly aware of their presence. And they were becoming more real—and more threatening—by the hour.

I was out of my depth here. I knew nothing about the paranormal or the supernatural. My practical knowledge of such things was limited to urban legends, and "campfire ghost stories", as Leslie Griffin would say.

I needed help. If this were an earthly problem, my first instinct would have been to talk to Mom and Dad. But I had already decided that it would be impossible for me to even explain all of this to them, let alone convince them that there was any truth behind it.

I needed to talk to someone else: not my parents, but someone who was older and more knowledgeable on these matters.

And I knew exactly who that someone would be.

47

It took me some effort, but not too much, to find Harry Bailey's phone number.

I began by reading the brief biography of him listed in the back of *Spooky American Tales*. According to the magazine, Harry Bailey was a freelance writer who was a regular contributor to the publication. Per the biography, Harry Bailey lived and wrote from his home in Detroit, Michigan. That narrowed things down somewhat.

In the pre-Internet days, there were two basic methods of acquiring an unknown residential phone number. If it was a local number, you could usually get it from your local white pages directory. For a number outside your area, you had to call the operator.

I called the operator, and got no fewer than a dozen numbers belonging to individuals named Harry Bailey who lived in the Detroit area. I had no idea which one of them (if any of them) might be the man who had written the article about the Headless Horsemen.

So I started calling them, one by one.

This being early on a weekday, no one picked up the line at at least half of the numbers. At one number, the phone was answered by the wife of a man named Harry Bailey. When I explained to her my objective, I think she suspected that I was making her the butt of an elaborate prank. Nevertheless, she patiently explained to me that her Harry Bailey was a high school history teacher at a public school in Detroit, who had no connection to *Spooky American Tales*.

I was near the end of the list when I finally hit pay dirt.

Sort of.

"HELLO?" **the man on** the other end of the line said. The gruff, phlegmy voice suggested a man in his early- to mid-sixties. Even before I explained myself, I was fairly certain that he would be the Harry Bailey I was looking for.

This Harry Bailey did confirm that he was the writer for *Spooky American Tales*. But he stopped me before I had gotten too far into my spiel.

"If you have any questions or feedback about an article in the magazine," he said, "you should direct that to the editorial offices in Hartford, Connecticut. The address is listed in the front of the magazine, just below the masthead."

I made another observation regarding Harry Bailey, this far into our conversation—which would turn out to be quite brief. Although it was only about ten o'clock in the morning, Harry Bailey had already consumed several drinks. (My long experience with Jack had given me an acute awareness of levels of intoxication. I knew that I was talking to a man who was mildly intoxicated.)

"But you don't understand, Mr. Bailey. I'm not a fan. I mean, I *am* a fan. But I have something very important to discuss with you. The things you wrote about: the Headless Horsemen, Marie Trumbull, and even the Hessian soldiers—I've been seeing them. Near my house. Here in Ohio. Just outside Cincinnati."

Harry Bailey exhaled in a long, exasperated manner. It was clear that I was inconveniencing him, or at least that was his perspective.

"If you have an idea for an upcoming article, or you would like to contribute an eyewitness account to an upcoming article, you are asked to direct such correspondence, in writing, to the editorial offices of the magazine in Hartford. As I have tried to explain to you, this information is readily available in the front of the magazine, just below the masthead."

It had occurred to me by now, of course, that Harry Bailey was simply blowing me off. He was a pompous ass, and possibly a bit of a drunk.

But there was another factor here to consider, as well. A man who wrote articles for *Spooky American Tales*, a magazine devoted to aficionados of the paranormal, probably fielded any number of claims like this in any given week.

I had called Harry Bailey at his private residence, out of the blue, without any introduction. Whatever my opinion of the man might be, he probably believed that I was some random kook.

"Mr. Bailey," I tried, "I understand how this must look from your position. I apologize, calling you at home like this, but I'm telling you the truth about...about seeing these things."

I might just as well have been speaking Greek. "Please direct your feedback and correspondence to the editorial offices in Hartford," Bailey said.

"Mr. Bailey," I said, insistently, raising my volume a notch. *"Please."*

A second later I heard a dial tone. Harry Bailey had hung up on me.

48

I worked at McDonald's again, the evening shift. Neither Keith nor Diane worked that night.

I figured that the two of them were out doing something together. Then I reminded myself that I had resolved not to think about that—to forget about Diane Parker.

Midway through the shift, Jenny Tierney and the other cashier went on break. Two cashiers technically weren't supposed to go on break together, thereby leaving only one person to handle the counter. But we didn't have too many customers that night, so I didn't object when they walked away and left me to fend for myself.

Besides, I was in the mood for solitude tonight.

I wiped down the counter, and I mentally reran my earlier conversation with Harry Bailey. The more I thought about it, the more annoyed I became.

The guy might have been a real help to me. Instead, he had chosen to be an impenetrable wall. Then he had hung up on me.

What an SOB, I thought.

Then I saw someone enter the McDonald's who was even more distraught than I was.

. . .

I watched her enter the McDonald's—a lone woman, maybe thirty-five years old. Pleasantly pretty, maybe with a few extra pounds.

Jenny Tierney and the other cashier would be back any minute. But it was still just me for now.

Working the cash register of a McDonald's is, in some ways, a bit like being a bartender. You interact with people who are in all varieties of moods. Many of them are quite pleasant to deal with. Others, not so much. You like to be prepared, when a potentially touchy customer walks up to your station. Therefore, you develop the habit of carefully observing customers as they walk in, assessing their moods.

This woman's mood was easy enough to assess. She was terrified. When I first saw her face, my first thought was: She's just come out of a war zone.

But that, of course, was impossible. There was no war in Clermont County.

I stood up straight and waited for her as she approached.

"Could I have a small coffee?" she said.

"Certainly. That will be thirty-five cents."

She began to dig into her purse for change. Her hands were shaking so badly, she nearly dropped the purse before she managed to produce a quarter and two nickels.

"Ma'am," I said. "Are you okay?"

She didn't directly answer my question. But she did make a revelation.

"Something horrible," she said vaguely. She was still shaking like a leaf. "Something horrible out on the road."

That was the only clue I needed. I was certain that she had seen the Horseman, too, or perhaps those Hessian soldiers. Maybe she had seen Marie Trumbull or a group of the Hessians at the side of the road—literal hitchhikers from Hell.

"*What* did you see?" I leaned forward over the counter. "Did you see…?"

She shook her head. "I'd rather not talk about it."

"Was it...?" I spoke in a whisper.

She waved away my question, frowned.

"I don't want to say..."

Don't want to say? I thought. Or *can't* say?

As an employee of Ray Smith's McDonald's, I was supposed to focus on customer service. The first rule of customer service (or one of them, anyway,) is that you don't do anything to disturb or rile up the customer.

But this was too important. This woman had, perhaps, seen some of the things that I had seen. She might be able to corroborate my interpretation of events, and thereby prove that all of this was real, not simply my self-induced hallucination or delusion.

"Please, ma'am. If you've seen something, tell me. I—I might be able to help."

"I said I don't want to talk about it." She was more insistent this time. "Please, just give me my order."

"All right," I said, exasperated but resigned. "All right."

I GAVE **the woman** her coffee, and asked her no more about what she might have seen out on the road that evening.

She took the steaming cup to a small table at the edge of the smoking section. I wondered why anyone would want to order coffee on a hot night in June.

After that, another group of customers came into the restaurant. I caught glimpses of the woman, sitting alone with her coffee, mostly just looking down into the cup without drinking.

Jenny Tierney and the other cashier returned. I looked over to where the distraught woman had been sitting, and saw that she was gone.

49

We were busier when Banny slipped into the line. I didn't even see him until he was directly upon me. He was the last of four or five customers.

Or maybe he had simply appeared there—just like he had disappeared.

"Hello," he said. A sneer.

I felt a surge of fear and rage.

"What do you want?"

I glanced over at Jenny Tierney and the other cashier on duty. They were both absorbed in taking customer orders. They hadn't taken note of Banny.

No one else sees him, I thought.

"What do you want?" I asked.

Banny didn't respond directly. But his next words took a far more dangerous turn.

"Your parents," he said, "they look kind of fragile to me. What's that about your father? A war hero, is he? I've seen war myself. And let me tell you, to be a man of war you've got to know how to use a sword. You've got to know how to run a man through with the sword. You've got to do it without hesitation. You must be merciless."

"You're bullshitting me," I said. "You can't be older than twenty-one or twenty-two. No way you were in Vietnam."

Banny laughed. "No, you're right about that. My war was a little earlier than that."

"That makes no sense. No sense at all."

Did it, though? What was the truth here that I was trying to evade? I knew, didn't I? Banny obviously wasn't talking about the Vietnam War.

Somehow, Banny was one of them. He was one of the revolutionary ghosts—in league with the Headless Horseman and Marie Trumbull.

But Banny didn't look like a ghost. He looked like an obnoxious, vindictive young man in his early twenties.

He leered at me. "Really?" He winked. "Are you sure about that? But let's talk more about your parents. I could run them through, just as easily as I could run you through."

"You come near my family," I said, in a level tone, "and I'll fucking kill you."

Banny laughed. "If you really understood things as well as you seem to think you do, you would know damn well that that's not exactly possible."

"*Steve?*" Jenny Tierney said, to my immediately left.

"What?" I turned to her. My tone was a little sharp.

"Who are you talking to, Steve?"

Jenny's last customer had departed. She had been watching me and listening to my argument with....

But Banny was gone.

JENNY TIERNEY THOUGHT that I was weird, of course. But Jenny Tierney had probably thought that I was weird anyway, even before she'd seen me threatening the blank space directly in front of my cash register. Throughout the rest of the shift, I caught her watching me, waiting for more weirdness, no doubt.

I, meanwhile, scanned the face of every customer with tense

apprehension. Whenever I had more than two customers in line, I involuntarily leaned to one side, to look at the back of the line. Banny might not be done with me for one night.

Banny didn't reappear, however.

As we were finishing up the closing, Jenny Tierney remarked, "Don't feel bad, Steve. I talk to myself sometimes, too. When I'm alone, that is."

50

The following evening, I had a rare night off McDonald's.

But as Louis might have reminded me, it wasn't as if I had a date or something. I therefore spent the evening watching sitcoms with my parents.

I was staring at the television screen, but mostly I was thinking. I had to puzzle this out.

Provided that I accepted all of this as real, I was quite certain of the origins of the Headless Horseman and Marie Trumbull.

But what about Banny? There were no clues about him in Harry Bailey's article. Banny seemed frustratingly corporeal, even if there were aspects about him that defied easy explanation.

Perhaps I needed to extrapolate.

The Headless Horseman was the vengeful spirit of a Hessian artillery officer who had been killed at the Battle of White Plains. Was Banny some incarnation of a Hessian, too?

I was pretty certain, however, that Banny's accent was British—not German.

So Banny was the ghost of a British soldier, perhaps? Maybe. But Banny didn't strike me as the military type.

I was lost in these contemplations when my father stood up from his easy chair and announced, "I think I'm going to head to the Pantry Shelf for cigarettes."

This was a ritual that my father had repeated hundreds, perhaps thousands of times that I could remember. Sometimes of an evening he would get restless. He would burn these excess bursts of energy by hopping in his truck and driving the three or four miles to the Pantry Shelf. He would always buy cigarettes. Sometimes he would also pick up a gallon of milk or a dozen eggs at my mother's request.

Ordinarily, I would not have regarded this as a cause for any concern. My father was a good driver, after all. And it was only a few miles.

But I couldn't stop thinking about what Banny had said—his not-so-veiled threats against my parents.

As my father prepared to leave, he noticed the sudden alarm on my face.

"Anything wrong, Steve?"

Yes, everything's wrong, I wanted to say. What I actually said was: "Maybe it would be better if you didn't go for cigarettes."

"What?"

What could I tell him? I certainly couldn't reveal that this fellow named Banny, who was possibly a supernatural being and possibly wasn't, had made a threat against his life. I therefore opted for another angle.

"Smoking is bad for you, Dad. Remember what the Surgeon General has said."

By the 1970s, the Surgeon General had already begun warning people about the dangers of cigarette smoking. Many people, especially of the older generations, ignored this advice.

My father had once told me that during the war, the Army had issued packs of cigarettes with each soldier's regular rations. In the middle of the twentieth century, cigarette smoking was simply a part of the American way of life.

"I've heard the warnings," my father said now. "And I believe we've had this discussion before."

We had, indeed, had versions of this discussion before. During my grade school years, I had gone through a phase in which I was certain that my father was going to die of lung cancer. (This was immediately after we had learned about the dangers of smoking in health class.) I had come home from school practically hysterical one day, pleading with my father to throw away his cigarettes.

My dad, who was by then well into his forties, tenderly put my fears to rest with well-intentioned but ultimately flawed logic.

"Think about all I've survived, Stevie," he said. "I survived the war. I've told you about what D-Day was like, right? And I'm already more than forty years old. Do you really think that your dad can be harmed by these little sticks of tobacco?"

In the intervening years, with the improved rhetorical skills of adolescence, I had occasionally broached the issue of smoking's harmful side effects with my dad. He made clear that while he appreciated my filial concern, he had no desire for unsolicited advice from his adolescent son. He had survived the war, after all.

"I'll be back in a jiffy," he said, putting an effective end to our discussion.

I WAITED **on pins and needles** until my father returned, fidgeting in front of the television set.

I was certain that Banny was going to make good on his threat. I was certain that my father would not return home. Perhaps an hour or two later, Tim Schmidt would stop by the house, and inform us that my dad had been murdered on his way home from the Pantry Shelf.

"Stevie, are you okay?" my mother asked me.

"I'm fine," I lied. "Really. I just think it would be a good idea for dad to back off on the cigarettes."

"Well, maybe he will someday. Don't worry about it in the meantime, though."

MY WORST FEARS **didn't materialize**, at least not that night. Less than thirty minutes after he'd left, my dad walked in the front door with a fresh pack of Pall Malls and a half-gallon of milk.

When he walked in, the fact that I had been worrying about his safety was not lost on him.

He smiled at me, but I'm sure he was baffled (and perhaps a little disappointed) at my apparent fragility. My father had come from a generation in which men didn't worry, not even about the welfare of their parents.

"You see, Steve? I'm back. Nothing to be concerned about. I might not live forever, but I plan to be around for a long, long time yet."

"Sure, Dad," I said.

I honestly wondered, though.

51

The next night I was scheduled to work at McDonald's again. I had checked the schedule posted outside the manager's office, and I had seen that Keith and Diane were both scheduled to work, too.

Great.

Then I remembered my determination to forget about Diane Parker.

Even by this stage in life, I had witnessed the sorry spectacle of guys who became hopelessly infatuated with girls who had no interest in them. I didn't want to be one of those losers. I didn't kid myself regarding my degree of disappointment; but I had resolved not to show it.

I therefore greeted Diane with a cool "hello" when I saw her at her cash register. She returned my greeting with equal coolness.

That wasn't all, though.

Something was off about her mood. Or perhaps she had simply decided that now that she was going with Keith, I was no longer worth her time, even for casual conversation.

Perhaps Keith had spent their recent evening together running me down. Perhaps Diane now shared Keith's opinion of me.

Oh well, I thought. If that's the way she wants to play it, then to hell with her.

A LITTLE WHILE LATER, Diane turned around to grab a Big Mac and fries from the polished aluminum shelves between the cashiers' area and the kitchen. I saw Keith slide the sandwich and the little cardboard container of fries forward.

I wanted to look away, so I wouldn't have to watch the two of them make lovey-dovey. But something—I suppose it was the masochistic side of my personality—forced me to watch.

Diane didn't make lovey-dovey, though. When her eyes met Keith's, she gave him a neutral expression that was anything but pleasant.

I would have called it a frown, in fact.

And Keith, for his part, didn't flash Diane the cockeyed grin that he usually reserved for girls.

He looked away from Diane.

Diane took the Big Mac and fries, loaded them onto a tray, and walked them back to the customer service counter without even a word to Keith.

Then I understood: Diane wasn't angry at or disdainful of *me*.

Something had happened between her and Keith. And it hadn't been something good, from the perspective of either of them.

I saw them repeat this frosty exchange several times. There could be no mistaking the situation. If Diane and Keith had been an item, they weren't any longer.

I KNEW **the basics of** girl-guy romantic strategy. (Or, at least, I thought I did.)

The strategic thing for me to do now would be to wait a few days, to bide my time. Then, at the opportune moment, I could casually ask Diane out.

But I also remembered how I had lost Diane in the first place. Another competitor had been faster, more nimble, and less hesitant.

Maybe I should strike while the iron was hot. For all I knew, another Keith Conway might be waiting in the wings.

I waited until the customer flow thinned out a bit. It was near the end of the shift, when the third cashier was on break, and Diane and I finally had a few minutes alone.

Then I made my move.

I didn't waste any time once I had an opening. I just threw it out there.

"Diane, I was wondering if you would like to go out with me on our next night off?"

Diane didn't answer at first. She was clearly surprised. After all, I had greeted her in a less than friendly manner when we started our shift; and I had spoken to her since then no more than was absolutely necessary.

I could sense her mental wheels turning. Finally she figured it out. (Like I said, Diane was third in her class at South Clermont.)

Her puzzled expression broke into a smile. Like the smiles that she had given me when Louis first introduced us.

"Sure, Steve," she said. "I'd love to."

52

We decided to go see a movie. This still left a few choices to be made.

First of all: the drive-in or the cinema?

In the 1970s, drive-ins—outdoor venues in which patrons watched movies from their cars on a giant screen at the front of a vast gravel parking lot—were still quite common. (According to the missing persons flyer, Robert McMoore and Donna Seitz had been planning to see a movie at the Eastland Drive-In on the night they disappeared.)

Drive-ins were also popular make-out spots. Keith had probably taken Diane to a drive-in, I figured.

But that hadn't gone so well, apparently.

I would get to that stage with her. But I didn't want to rush things, to make Diane think that I was only interested in one thing.

Diane seemed innocent—or at least that was what I told myself at the time.

Moreover, when I checked the local paper, I saw that the movie selection at the Eastland Drive-In was fairly lame: mostly spaghetti westerns that everyone had already seen.

There was a new cinema nearby, that had been built and opened only a few years ago. I saw that two newly released movies were playing there. The first of these was *All the President's Men*, a docudrama about the Watergate scandal, starring Robert Redford and Dustin Hoffman.

The second one was *The Omen*, a horror film that would become wildly popular that year and beyond, spawning multiple sequels throughout the 1970s and 1980s.

I called Diane and asked her which movie she would prefer.

"Let's see *The Omen*," she said. "I've already heard enough about Watergate. Nixon was guilty. The end."

The Omen it was to be, then. I hung up the telephone, thinking that maybe—just maybe—life was returning to normal. Better than normal, perhaps.

You might think that given recent events, I would be squeamish about watching a horror movie.

Quite the opposite, in fact. Once you've experienced the real thing, you'll find that supernatural terrors on the screen pale in comparison.

As Diane and I sat together in the darkened cinema, I wasn't thinking about the supernatural.

I was watching the movie, wondering if I should put my arm around Diane. I decided that now would be premature. Diane wouldn't be ready for that. Not yet.

I happened to turn around, to see how alone the two of us were (always an important factor when deciding whether or not to make a move of some kind). This was a weeknight; and I had noticed that there weren't too many moviegoers.

There was one, though, that I hadn't anticipated. But maybe I should have.

Two rows up from us, I saw him leering in the darkness: Banny. He was sitting in the seat nearest the aisle.

Curiously, no other moviegoers has chosen to sit near him.

I turned back to the screen again.

"What's wrong?" Diane asked, frowning a little.

"Nothing," I whispered.

I glanced around again.

"Something's up," she said. "What?"

"Nothing's up," I insisted.

What could I have told her, that would make any sense whatsoever?

I turned around yet again. Banny cocked a thumb at me, and stood, to indicate that I should follow him out into the lobby.

I didn't want to go, of course. I also figured that I had no choice. If I didn't go, he would escalate things, right there in the cinema.

"I'll be right back," I told my date.

"Okay," Diane whispered in the darkness, clearly a little puzzled.

Diane and I were sitting near the aisle, too, me in the seat at the end of the row. I stood up without disturbing anyone else, and began to walk toward the lobby.

I could see Banny walking ahead of me. He turned around and winked.

I'm going to kill him, I thought. What I was also thinking, though, was: *I'm going to touch him. I'm going to prove to myself that he's real, made of flesh and bone. Not a ghost.*

Banny reached the end of the main aisle.

He opened the door and—

No, he didn't open the door. I stopped and blinked in the darkness. Behind me, I could hear a jump-scare scene of *The Omen* taking place.

Banny had simply passed through the wooden double doors that connected the theater with the lobby, without opening either of them.

I, on the other hand, had to open one of the doors to walk out into the lobby. I stepped out, ready to confront Banny.

But Banny was nowhere to be seen.

. . .

The lobby of the cinema was a lonely place on that weekday night, with all of the movies running.

This was not the main lobby, where the main entrance, the ticket booth, and the concession stands were located. This was the wing that provided access to the individual theaters. This section of the lobby was decorated with movie posters for coming attractions. The overhead lights were dimmed, and the floor was covered with carpet, to keep the noise levels low.

I heard the sound of someone whistling.

I looked down toward the entrance of the men's room.

I had just found Banny.

There was no wood or metal door to the men's room. It was separated from the lobby area by the "L" configuration of its entrance.

I walked into a brightly lit public restroom of white tile and mirrors. There was a row of urinals directly ahead of me. To one side, a counter containing five or six faucets and sinks—

"So you come, eh?" Banny said. He was standing at the far end of the sinks. "I wouldn't be thinkin' you had the guts."

I noticed that Banny was dressed differently this time. He was wearing knee-length white trousers, high black boots, a white blouse of some kind, and a green frock coat.

Not the clothing of a young American—or British—male in the middle of the twentieth century.

"What do you want, Banny?" I shouted. "And who are you? Tell me."

But Banny had already proven that he wouldn't answer questions he didn't want to answer.

"What about that girl you're with, eh? Not a bad little doxy, she ain't."

"Stay away from her," I said, taking a step closer to him.

He showed no fear of me, but no sign of attacking me, either.

"I've had some girls in my time," he said. "That looks like a nice one. I wouldn't mind giving her a go."

I lunged at him. Banny darted skillfully out of my way, as if he had been trained in some form of Far Eastern jujitsu.

"Is there a problem here?" I heard a distinctly adult voice say.

I turned and found that a security guard had observed our altercation.

"WE WERE JUST HAVING A DISCUSSION," I said. "But it's over now."

"We?" The security guard said. "Who the hell is 'we'? You're the only one I see here. Yelling and jumping around in the men's room."

I looked back at Banny. But before I even completed the turn, I extrapolated what the result would be.

Banny was gone. Vanished into thin air.

The security guard hitched up his belt over his considerable girth. He gave me an unfriendly stare. "Say, you haven't been smoking anything, have you? Do we need to take you into the police station, get you a drug test?"

I had no idea if a cinema security guard even had such authority. But this was my first date with Diane, and I didn't want it to turn into a disaster. Me getting arrested for public intoxication, when I hadn't even had a Coke from the concession stand, would qualify as a disaster.

"I'm okay," I said, "there's no problem here."

The security guard raised his eyebrows. "Are you sure about that, son?"

"Yes, I'm sure," I replied, politely but firmly.

The guard didn't believe me. I could tell that he was deciding which option would likely entail the greater hassle for him: letting me go—and accepting the risk that I would cause some real trouble —or detaining me, and turning me over to the police.

"All right," he said. "But I don't want to see or hear from you again. Get back into your movie."

"Yes, sir," I said.

The guard shook his head at me and left.

. . .

I waited in the restroom for a few seconds before leaving. I half-expected Banny to make a sudden return.

He didn't, though. Nothing.

I couldn't linger here. For all I knew, the security guard was standing directly outside the restroom, waiting to see if I'd make good on my promise.

And then there was the not-so-minor consideration that Diane would be wondering about me by now.

I hurried out of the restroom. The security guard, thankfully, had gone. As I walked back to the theater where *The Omen* was playing, I continued to look around for Banny.

Banny stayed gone.

I opened the door of the theater—near total darkness again—and headed toward my seat.

I felt a sudden chill. Then I heard a hissing sound.

I looked in the direction of the sound.

Marie Trumbull, sitting in an empty row of seats. The light from the movie screen reflected on her dead eyes, her mummy-like skin.

They aren't real, I told myself. *Keep walking.*

I kept walking. When I arrived at my seat, Diane gave me a questioning look. I smiled and shrugged. She smiled and shrugged back.

Then we both continued watching the movie.

I resisted the temptation to turn around, to see if Marie Trumbull was still there.

I also resisted the temptation to turn around and see if Marie Trumbull had moved any closer. I imagined her sitting directly behind Diane and me. Any moment, I feared, I would feel her cold, bony hand on my shoulder.

Or perhaps I would feel the cold, rusty blade of her knife against my neck.

I had just told myself that neither Banny nor Marie Trumbull was real. But I knew that wasn't entirely accurate.

They might not be completely real, in the sense that Diane and I, and the other living moviegoers in the cinema were real. But some aspect of both Banny and Marie Trumbull had to be real. They had punched their way through to my reality, after all.

And they showed no sign of going back to where they came from.

53

Diane was gracious enough not to interrogate me any further about my peculiar behavior during the movie.

We drove back to her house in relative silence. She mentioned that she had found *The Omen* darker than she'd expected. I could barely remember any of the movie. My attention had been completely diverted by those two ghoulish moviegoers, Banny and Marie Trumbull.

Her house was a nice place in one of the new neighborhoods in this part of the county. Diane's dad, I knew, was a CPA. My father made a respectable income at the Ford plant, but Diane's dad did a lot better.

I stopped the car in her driveway and killed the engine.

Kiss her now, I thought.

Then I reminded myself that Keith Conway's ambitions with Diane had probably been derailed by very similar impulses. The evening had been ruined for me—but not because of anything that Diane had said or done. She was pretty, yes; but more than that, I enjoyed her company.

I liked her a lot, in fact.

"Well," I said, opening the driver's side door.

"Well." She opened the passenger's side door.

There was a winding, ascending cobblestone walkway between the driveway and the front porch. Diane's house was a split-level—a common suburban home design in the 1960s and 1970s—and the driveway was located downhill from most of the house.

We were climbing the path, me directly behind Diane. About halfway up, she suddenly stumbled.

From what I could see, she hadn't tripped on one of the stones. (And the stones were well-laid, anyway, deeply embedded into the soil.)

Her body, rather, had simply gone slack. Almost as if Diane had fallen asleep for a moment.

"Are you all right?" I said. I reached out and grabbed her arm. For a second there, I was certain that she was going to fall onto the cobblestone walkway.

She didn't fall, though. I wasn't sure how much my steadying grip had to do with that, but she seemed grateful for my immediate concern.

Nevertheless, I released her arm.

"I'm fine," she said. "It's just that...I've been getting these dizzy spells of late."

"Really?"

"Yeah. They just started a few weeks ago. I've been getting them several times per day, in fact. Sometimes I get these little headaches with them, too."

Now that I thought about it, I had noticed something like that, the night that she had had the fight with Keith at McDonald's. The night I'd asked her out. Diane's face had suddenly gone slack, and a little pale. She had paused her work, and steadied herself with both hands on the counter.

I hadn't thought much of it at the time. I was still resentful over losing her to Keith.

I knew that there were any number of ways in which chronic dizzy spells could be dangerous. While driving a car, for example.

"You should see a doctor about that," I said.

"I have an appointment," she said. "Thanks, Dad." She gave me a little hint of a smile. I felt a warmth flood through me.

"Hey, now. I'm not your dad."

We made it to the front porch. Her parents had left the porch light on for her, but all the windows were dark. Mr. and Mrs. Parker seemed to be in bed.

I was grateful for that.

We stood on the front porch. It was now or never.

"I think you're supposed to kiss me now," she said.

As I've likely made clear, when it came to moments like this, I wasn't overly aggressive, as guys go. But nor was it necessary for me to be asked twice, when a girl invited me to kiss her.

I leaned forward and pressed my lips against hers. The warmth flooded through me again—only much stronger this time.

I started to pull away, ever conscious of the dangers of moving too fast for her.

She reached up and grabbed my shoulders, and pulled me back to her.

"Goodnight," she said, finally, turning toward the front door of her house.

"I'd like to take you out again," I said.

"You'd better, buster."

She slipped inside her house—but not before the two of us came together for one more kiss. It wasn't me initiating it, or her initiating it. We just—spontaneously met each other's mouths again.

I RESISTED **the urge** to skip down the driveway. Despite the appearances of Banny and Marie Trumbull in the cinema, my first date with Diane had gone well.

Very well, in fact.

I opened the door of the Bonneville. I had a sudden premonition —that Banny and Marie Trumbull would be in the back seat, unwanted passengers for the ride home.

When I looked in back seat, however, I saw nothing but the vinyl upholstery.

I drove home without any further visits from Banny or Marie Trumbull. Nor did I hear any hoofbeats on the road that night.

54

I never did find out exactly what happened between Keith and Diane, that sent their incipient relationship spiraling downward so abruptly.

"Keith believed he was...entitled to certain things," was all Diane ever said about it.

I felt no need to push the matter further. Whatever had happened between Keith and Diane, she was with me now, and he was on the outs.

So much for the Love Machine, I thought. I realized that I was being petty—at least within the confines of my own thoughts—but I couldn't help myself.

Keith was no rocket scientist, but he wasn't a complete idiot, either. I don't know if Diane told him about us. My guess is that she didn't. One way or another, though, he found out.

I could tell, based on some of the dirty looks he gave me. Gone was the half-friendly, half-challenging jesting of our previous interactions, him calling me Stevie, and whatnot. He was serious about this now. An adolescent rivalry had been replaced by real enmity—at least on his part.

Go ahead and scowl, I thought smugly.

Revolutionary Ghosts

I didn't yet know what would happen to Keith Conway— within a few short weeks—or how Keith's fate would intersect with those forces detailed in Harry Bailey's article.

I WAS SOON **to find out,** though, that Diane was no prude. She simply didn't want a guy to assume that he was… "entitled", to use her word.

For our next date, we'd planned a meal at Luigi's—a local Italian restaurant—and then another movie. We had tentatively decided to see *All the President's Men* this time, even though neither one of us was very interested in a Watergate docudrama.

After dinner, though, Diane suggested that we go parking instead.

And once again, I didn't have to be asked twice.

I drove the Bonneville out to Coleman's Pond. This was a little body of water not far from the Pantry Shelf. The site was secluded— but not too secluded. I had not forgotten about the Horseman. About Marie Trumbull and Banny, about those ghastly Hessians that I'd glimpsed at the edge of the woods that night.

TEN MINUTES **after** I'd turned the engine off, I slipped my hand inside Diane's bra, and cupped my palm around one of her breasts.

My body felt like something I might have built with my childhood erector set, all tense and stiff and unyielding. Suffice it to say that I was feeling the full rush of my seventeen-year-old hormones.

Julie Idelman and I had never "done it". (She had insisted that she was saving her virginity for her wedding night.) But in the more than two years we had gone out, she had done various things to relieve that all-consuming pressure that every young man is all too familiar with. I won't tell you the details; I'm sure you're capable of figuring them out for yourself.

I was about to try my luck with the front snap of Diane's jeans, to see if she would let me go that far, when I heard a sound that put an instant chill on my passions, like cold water.

The unmistakable, but unnatural whinnying of a horse. A horse that had been long dead. And atop that horse, I knew, would be a rider who had no head.

I knew because I had seen him. There could be no doubt of that—not anymore.

The whinnying had come from some distance away. But if the Horseman was out and about tonight, then we couldn't stay at Coleman's Pond.

I removed my hand from Diane's shirt, and sat up in the backseat.

"What's wrong?" she asked.

"That sound," I said. "Did you hear it?"

She nodded and sat up in the back seat.

"I heard it," she said.

"And do you know what it is?"

"No," she admitted. "But I know it's something…bad. This isn't the first time I've heard it."

She looked away from me, out the back window of the Bonneville. We could see the moon from where we sat. "I've seen some things, too. At least—I think I have. But I was never sure." She faced me again. "What about you? Do you know something about this—"

We were interrupted by whinnying again. Only closer this time.

"I do know something about it," I said. "I'll tell you, but—not here. I think we should leave."

Diane nodded. We both got out of the car, so that we could move into the front seat. As I stepped out into the warm night air, I heard something shift in the nearby woods.

I stood up in a defensive posture, suddenly protective of Diane.

"What is it?" she asked.

"Nothing," I said, after pausing for a few more seconds to make sure it really had been nothing.

Despite all of the horrible things that had appeared of late, the woods in Clermont County were still filled with plenty of perfectly mundane nocturnal creatures: raccoons and foxes among them.

"Let's get out of here," I said.

55

It was too late to follow up on our original plans of catching another movie. We briefly thought about going to Ray Smith's McDonald's, but then nixed that idea. We wanted to be alone and anonymous for the discussion that lay before us.

We headed over to the Frisch's Big Boy restaurant on Ohio Pike. Even late at night, the Big Boy was clean and well-lighted. Exactly what we needed, given the conversation ahead of us.

I ordered a large vanilla Coke. Diane ordered a cup of Sanka.

"Tell me," she said. "Tell me everything you know."

And so I told her. I told her everything, basically—from my discovery of the hoof prints and Harry Bailey's article in *Spooky American Tales*, to my horrific encounters with Marie Trumbull, my glimpse of the undead Hessians.

Throughout my explanation, Diane occasionally asked for clarifications. But she never challenged the basic truth of what I was explaining to her.

"I've seen that woman," Diane said, referring to Marie Trumbull. "She was—in our back yard a few nights ago. I looked out my bedroom window, and there she was."

"What did you do?"

Diane shrugged. "What could I do? I went back to bed. In the morning, I told myself that it had been nothing more than a dream."

"But she never came inside your house?"

Diane shook her head. "No. Not yet, at least."

I wondered why Marie Trumbull had invaded my home, while she had been content to linger outside Diane's house. Another mystery.

I told Diane about Banny, too.

"He's the only one I can't figure out," I said.

Then I noticed that Diane had just shuddered.

"What's wrong?" I asked, "other than all these crazy things we're talking about?"

"That British guy," Diane said. "He showed up at McDonald's the other night. You weren't working that night. He came up to my counter, and he leered at me. I challenged him, and he said a number of rude things."

"You saw Banny?" I asked, leaning forward over the table.

"Yes. I—I didn't know who he was, of course. But I remember him as you described him. Reddish hair, about twenty-one years old, a British accent. And a very foul, nasty mouth."

"That bastard," I said. I noticed then, how Banny made me more angry than scared, even though I was quite certain he was a ghost. "What, exactly, did he say to you?"

"Never mind. I'm sure you can guess. He used some words that were unfamiliar to me, but I could figure out their meanings based on context."

"Did you recognize what he was?" I asked. "I mean...a ghost?"

She shook her head. "No. I did think that there was a lot unusual about him. It isn't every day that you meet a foul-mouthed Brit in Cincinnati, let alone in Clermont County. But no, I didn't think he was a ghost."

"Well, he is," I said.

"Are you sure? He seems almost...normal," Diane countered.

I reminded Diane how Banny had disappeared on me—multiple times.

"No," I concluded. "Banny is a ghost. I'm just not sure who he was when he was alive."

56

The next night I pulled cashier duty with Jenny Tierney again. I also had another surprise visitor—but I was quite sure that this visitor wasn't a ghost.

I was finishing up a customer order when Jenny returned from the front of the restaurant, obviously eager to talk about something. She had been rubbernecking out the front window. A disturbance or spectacle in the parking lot had drawn her attention.

Ordinarily, gossiping with Jenny Tierney would have been the last thing on my mind. Recently, though, I was in a state of high alert, and more attentive than usual to everything in my environment.

This was especially true after my conversation with Diane. She had not only corroborated my experiences (which I had half-thought, half-hoped, to be mere hallucinations). Diane had also agreed to help me find more information.

"Research," Diane had said, "that's what we need to do."

I wasn't quite sure what Diane had meant by that—not yet.

For now, though, I glanced up at Jenny as she hustled back to her place behind her register.

"What?" I asked her. The question seemed incumbent on me.

"There's a man out in the parking lot," Jenny said. "He seems to be drunk or high, and he's harassing the customers."

I had a bad feeling about that, but there was nothing supernatural about my feeling.

At that moment, a young couple came in through the main entrance. They were obviously distraught over something that had just happened immediately outside the restaurant.

I stepped out from behind the counter, walked forward a few paces, and looked out into the parking lot.

There was indeed a very human figure out there: a tall, burly young man with dark hair and a beard. He was waving his arms wildly about, like a mad prophet from the Old Testament.

"You see?" Jenny said. "That guy's a nut case."

"He sure is," I said.

I recognized the man in the parking lot.

He was my brother, Jack.

Louis, perhaps drawn by the commotion, perhaps drawn by some sixth sense that all fast food shift managers possess, appeared behind the counter.

"What's going on?" he asked.

"Louis," I said. "We need to talk." Without looking at Jenny Tierney, but acutely aware of her hovering presence, I added, "in private."

"In private?"

"Yes, in private."

"Okay," Louis said.

I pulled Louis aside and told him who the man in the parking lot was. Louis was surprised—but not exactly shocked. I had long ago given him the scoop on Jack, in broad outlines.

"Let me talk to him," I said. "I can talk some sense into him."

But could I, really? Even my World War II hero father usually failed at talking sense into Jack.

"Okay," Louis said. "But I'm going with you."

"But—"

"No buts," Louis said.

57

I headed out into the parking lot, Louis trailing behind me.

Jenny Tierney asked what was up. Louis waved her to silence.

"Man the cash register, please," Louis told her. "Steve and I will be right back."

As we passed between the two sets of double doors leading outside, Louis briefly stopped me to deliver a proviso regarding our little mission.

"Listen, Steve," Louis said. "I want to cut you some slack here. I understand that you've had some problems with your brother, and I don't want to create any more."

"And?" I said. I knew that Louis was leading up to something else.

"And I'll give you a chance to convince him to leave. Hopefully that will work. If it doesn't, though, I'll have no choice but to call the police."

I groaned inwardly. I could imagine the scene that would unfold then. Tim Schmidt, or perhaps one of the other deputies, would arrive at the restaurant with flashing lights. Then Jack would be handcuffed, and loaded into the police car. Then my mom, my dad, or possibly both of them, would have to drive to the county jail, and bail him out.

Or maybe they would just leave him there.

No, I knew my parents. They would bail Jack out.

"Thanks," I said. "I think I can convince him to leave peacefully."

Louis nodded at me. I could tell that he had his doubts.

"Okay, Steve. Give it a try."

When we made it outside, Jack was standing there in the muggy twilight. He was swaying on his feet. He looked ready to topple over at any moment.

"Jack," I said. "What the hell are you doing here?"

Jack looked up and recognized me. I couldn't discern how surprised he was by my sudden appearance. Surely he knew that I would be here. He knew that I worked at the McDonald's. Had he come here with the specific motive of drawing me out?

Possibly.

Jack replied with a glassy smile. "What am *I* doing? What are *you* doing?"

"I work here." Then I added, "*Big brother.*" I recalled Jack's use of the familial nomenclature the other night, when he'd dropped by the house. "You need to go home, Jack, sleep it off. Whatever you've been into."

"I don' wanna," he slurred.

"And why is that?" I asked.

"Because I'm afraid," he answered at length.

58

"Afraid?" I asked. In all the years I had known Jack—my whole life—I had heard him make all manner of wild claims.

But he had never claimed to be afraid.

"What are you afraid of, Jack?"

Jack didn't answer me, though. He threw me a question instead.

"I know, Steve. I know that you know a lot more about these things than you're telling. You've been keeping secrets, haven't you?"

I took a step toward him.

"Jack. What do *you* know? What have *you* seen?"

From behind me, Louis cleared his throat. "Let's not forget our objective here, Steve. We're trying to get him to *vacate the premises*."

"Right," I said. Then, to Jack, "Jack, you need to leave. If you don't leave, then my boss, Louis over here, will have to call the police. You'll spend the night in jail. You don't want that, do you?"

Jack paused, and assessed the situation. Louis wasn't an intrinsically intimidating character, but he was displaying his best no-nonsense expression.

"You have to leave, sir," Louis said. "You're disrupting our business."

Another pair of customers approached from a few rows up in the parking lot. They gave the three of us curious looks. Louis smiled at them, as if to say, "nothing wrong here". But clearly there *was* something wrong, with two uniformed McDonald's employees confronting an intoxicated man in the parking lot.

"Jack, you need to get out of here," I said.

"Okay," Jack said. He nodded slowly. He looked at Louis again. "Okay," he repeated.

"Okay, then," Louis replied.

Louis looked at me, I looked at Jack. What now, now that he'd agreed to go?

Jack's shoulders drooped. For a moment there, my older brother looked like the most pathetic member of the human race. His usual swagger was completely gone.

And why had Jack challenged me, about what I knew and what I had seen?

What was Jack afraid of?

I already knew the answer to that question, didn't I?

Jack began a shaky walk over to his Corvair. It was parked near the car of the customers who had just walked in. I hadn't noticed the Corvair parked there until now.

I had mixed feelings about sending him away. While I was relieved to be rid of him, I knew that he would pose a potential hazard out on the roads, both to himself and to others.

"What do you think?" Louis asked—an obvious reference to Jack's inebriated state. "Will he be okay?"

I sighed. "He's driven while intoxicated before. And besides, what choice do we have?"

Louis slowly shook his head. "None, I guess."

Jack opened the door of the Corvair and lowered himself inside. Louis and I watched as he fumbled around for his keys and then started the engine. We watched him drive to the edge of the parking lot, and then pull out onto the main road.

I noted that at least he wasn't driving at a very high speed. Jack was familiar with the local roads. If he continued to drive slowly, and as carefully as his incapacitated condition demanded, then perhaps he would make it home okay.

If he doesn't encounter the Horseman, I thought.

As we walked back inside, Louis asked me: "When your brother asked you about keeping secrets, what did he mean?"

After a pause that went on too long, I said, "Nothing."

"Really? There seemed to be *something* there. You challenged him back, after all. You asked him what he knew, and what he'd seen."

"Family matters," I said.

Louis took a few seconds to contemplate this. We were inside the restaurant now, and Jenny Tierney was watching us from behind the counter.

"Oh," Louis nodded. But Louis perceived more than he was letting on, I was certain.

59

Diane didn't waste any time taking charge of the research. I was over at her house the next afternoon. Both of her parents were gone.

We were standing in the kitchen, and I was kissing her. Diane was pretty permissive by this point, about letting my hands roam. But she still shook her head slowly and removed my hand when I tried to undo the clasp of her jeans.

"Not yet," she said. "Besides, we've got work to do."

"Work?"

"Uh-huh. Research. I've already done a lot of it. Over here. Look."

She had a stack of books on the kitchen table. She also had an open notebook. Diane had been doing research, all right.

"Where did you get the books?" I asked.

"Where do you think, silly? The library."

"The library," I said.

"They have lots of books there, you know."

I stepped over to the kitchen table, and examined the titles. Diane must have done some real digging, to find these books at our local library branch:

A Survey of Paranormal Phenomena...

Ghostly Legends of Early America...

Another one was titled, *Witches, Demons & Fairies: the Evidence for the Supernatural.*

"This makes sense," I said. "After all, I put the pieces together after reading that magazine article."

"Oh, yes, *Spooky American Tales*. Maybe the magazine could help us? The writer of that article, maybe?"

I made a short, bitter laugh.

"What was that about?"

I told Diane about calling Harry Bailey, about how he had been completely dismissive of me.

"Perhaps you didn't go about it right," she suggested.

"He hung up on me," I said.

"Still, it might be worthwhile to try another approach. Maybe this situation needs a woman's touch."

"*You* want to call Harry Bailey?"

She shrugged. "I might. What is there to lose? Do you have his number handy?"

"I do," I said. I wrote Harry Bailey's phone number on a page of Diane's notebook. I had been carrying the number around in my wallet, jotted down on a slip of paper.

"Sit down," she said. "And I'll tell you what I've discovered."

DIANE THEN PROCEEDED to give me a crash-course in the paranormal, as it applied to our present situation.

"I'd say that what we're dealing with here is a spirit group," Diane said. "In a spirit group, there is usually one, especially powerful spirit that is the anchor."

"The Headless Horseman," I said.

Diane nodded. "And there's more."

She explained that there were various ways to banish evil spirits, at least temporarily.

"Salt often works, according to the books."

"*Salt?*" I asked. I had never ascribed any special significance to salt.

"Salt has long been believed to have powers of spiritual purification. There are references to the spiritual powers of salt in the Old Testament, in the Sermon on the Mount, even in the Muslim Koran. Hindus and Buddhists use it to ward off evil spirits, too, as do practitioners of the Japanese animist religion, Shinto."

"'Animist'?"

"Animism is the belief in the spiritual powers of ordinary objects and places. It's the oldest form of religion, and the basis for many folk religions. But let's not get off the subject. Evil spirits can also be repelled by holy water. That should be easy enough to get. But you aren't Catholic, are you?"

"No," I said.

Diane had already told me that her parents were more or less agnostic. She had memories of them taking her to a Presbyterian church on occasion during her early years. But the Parker family—which consisted only of Diane and her parents—had no regular religious practice.

"But I do know where I can get some," I added.

"Well, if you can, then it might not be a bad idea."

"I'll do it," I said.

Diane was wearing a clingy tee shirt bearing the logo of the Cincinnati Reds. It was more than enough to distract me. I reached for her hand, leaned over and kissed her.

She kissed me back. But when my hand moved to her breasts, she gently pushed it away.

"Now now," she said. "There's something else. And it's very important."

"Okay," I said. I was a seventeen year-old boy, and at that moment there didn't seem to be anything more important than kissing Diane, exploring her lips and mouth, and the rest of her body.

Forty-two years later, though, I know better. Diane had been right; and I was being short-sighted.

"Trust me, Steve, you're going to want to see this."

60

Diane opened another library book, bearing the title, *A Student's Guide to the American Revolution*. I hadn't noticed it amid the other, more sensational titles.

This was not a book on the occult, but rather a book about the American Colonial period and the Revolutionary War—as was suggested.

"I thought it would be a good idea to brush up on the history of the American Revolution," she said. "After all, that is where all of these ghosts are coming from, right? I thought I might even get lucky, and find a clue in here. And boy, did I."

"Something about the Headless Horseman?" I asked. "Or Marie Trumbull?"

"There is only one brief mention of the Headless Horseman in the book," Diane said. "And there's a reproduction of this nineteenth-century painting."

Diane turned to a page that she had bookmarked with a slip of paper. There was a painting called, *The Headless Horseman Pursuing Ichabod Crane*, by a nineteenth-century American painter named John Quidor.

The Headless Horseman Pursuing Ichabod Crane, *by John Quidor*

"The text doesn't tell us anything that we don't already know," Diane said. "The Headless Horseman is believed to be the restless spirit of a Hessian artillery officer who was beheaded by an American cannonball at the Battle of White Plains, New York, in 1776. The book, of course, takes the position that the Legend of Sleepy Hollow is nothing but a legend."

"Of course," I said.

"But this is the big thing. Brace yourself."

"Okay," I said.

Diane turned to another bookmarked page. I was expecting something gruesome. What I saw was a portrait of a young man in a green military frock coat with white breeches, and knee-high boots. He was wearing a leather helmet with a bill and a large, ostentatious, fur plume. Behind him was a montage of smoke, cannons, and horses —the standard imagery of eighteenth-century warfare.

Then I took a closer look, and realized that I recognized the face in the portrait.

Banastre Tarleton

"Banny," I said aloud.

"I know," she said. "That's the guy who came into the McDonald's that night, the one who made the crude remarks."

I was surprised. But then, I should have known: I should have known that Banny would eventually be traced to something—someone—from long ago.

"Who was he?" I asked.

"Banastre Tarleton," Diane said. "He was British, and he was sent to America during the Revolutionary War to command the Loyalist forces." She read the next few paragraphs, then summarized. "On several occasions, he bayoneted and shot Continental troops who had already surrendered. One of these incidents occurred at the Battle of Waxhaws, in South Carolina. Banastre Tarleton was subsequently given the nicknames, "Bloody Ban" and "The Butcher of Waxhaws.""

I wasn't surprised to hear that Banny—Banastre—could be capable of cruelty. But I did have another observation.

"He was kind of young to be leading troops, wasn't he?"

"He reached the rank of colonel while he was still in his twenties," Diane explained. "He was only twenty-one when the American Revolution began."

"How did he die?"

Diane scanned the text. She had already read through it once, of course.

"Banastre Tarleton survived the war. He returned to England. He had a lengthy affair with a woman named Mary Robinson, a popular actress of the period, and the ex-mistress of the Prince of Wales, the future King George IV. Tarleton had seduced her on a bet."

"Nice guy," I said.

"He was later elected to the British Parliament. Tarleton was a strong advocate of the slave trade, at a time when other members of the British Parliament were working to abolish it. He was known for his habit of publicly mocking abolitionists."

"A *really* nice guy," I added. "So how did he die?"

"Peacefully in his bed, from what I can tell," Diane said. She looked up at me. Banastre Tarleton didn't die until 1833. He lived until the ripe old age of seventy-eight. Quite a feat for that time, I'd imagine."

Yes, indeed, it was. So why had Tarleton—Banny—shown up here, among the restless spirits of the American Revolution? By the time of his death, the American Revolution was already two generations in the past, after all.

Perhaps Tarleton had relished the violence and the power that his military command had brought him. The battlefield, with its opportunities for maiming and killing, were his true element.

I tried to think of Banny as an elderly man of seventy-eight, and I couldn't. But it was easy enough to imagine him advocating for the slave trade. What else would one expect of *the Butcher of Waxhaws*?

"What about Marie Trumbull? Is she in this book, too?"

"No," Diane said. "Not that I could find, anyway."

That would figure, too. Marie Trumbull had been a minor Loyalist spy. Banny had been a colonel in the British army, a future member of Parliament.

"Wow," I said, impressed with her research. "But let me ask you this. I'm guessing that a little salt and holy water isn't going to be enough to put an end to all of this, I mean—for good. Have you found…"

"Have I found the solution, you mean."

"Yeah."

"No. But that's why I have the books. Sit down and open one of them. We need to keep looking."

61

We didn't find the final solution to our problems—at least not during that session.

I did learn some interesting facts about ghosts, fairies, and other supernatural beings. There was nothing, though, that told us how we might send the Horseman, Marie Trumbull, Banny, and the others back to the spirit world.

Meanwhile, I decided to get busy with the acquisition of the holy water.

St. Andrew's was the local Catholic church. Even though I wasn't a Catholic, I had been inside the church a few times—once to attend a wedding, another time to attend the funeral of a neighbor's elderly mother.

As I recalled, there was a holy water font in the vestibule of St. Andrew's.

The Catholic Church was an institution that had preferred to endure the Protestant Reformation rather than give in to the forces of change. I therefore figured that the layout of St. Andrew's hadn't changed, since my last visit there.

I knew that Catholic masses might be held on any day of the week, but usually the mass was celebrated either in the morning or in the evening. With that in mind, I dropped by St. Andrew's in the middle of the afternoon. If I was lucky, I might be able to complete my task without being seen by anyone.

St. Andrew's was a large church, even by Catholic church standards. The parish served the entire southwestern quadrant of the county. I parked the Bonneville in a far corner of the mostly empty parking lot.

While still in my car, I took a look around.

No one had noticed me so far.

In my pockets I had three small bottles. My mother never threw away a jar or a bottle. She washed out and reused ketchup bottles, pickle jars, and the little vials in which vanilla and hot sauce were packaged. As a result, there was no shortage of glass containers in our kitchen pantry.

I walked up the cement steps of St. Andrew's and entered the airy foyer. The holy water font, carved from marble, was located beside the entrance to the nave, just as I'd remembered.

I got to work quickly. I walked over to the font, removed the first bottle from my pocket, and unscrewed the lid.

I immersed the bottle in the holy water. Little bubbles gurgled from the mouth of the bottle as liquid filled the vessel.

When the first bottle was full, I capped it, stuck it in my pocket, and started on the next one.

By the time I had capped the second bottle and started on the third, I was convinced that I was going to be able to finish this without anyone questioning me.

I was wrong about that, too.

62

I heard footsteps behind me on the marble floor. I looked up from the holy water font.

Father Malloy, the pastor of St. Andrew's Catholic Church, was standing there. He was wearing his priestly vestments.

I was familiar with the priest, but we were not personally acquainted. Father Malloy was perhaps sixty years old in 1976. He was a tall, thin, gentle-looking man who most people in the area seemed to like, regardless of their religious affiliation.

"You have a use for holy water?" Father Malloy asked. An obvious question.

I didn't want Father Malloy to think that I was involved in some kind of a prank, some act of sacrilege. With this risk in mind, I answered the priest in the most earnest tone I could muster.

"Yes, Father. Yes, I do."

"I see. Are you a—Catholic—may I ask?"

"No," I answered honestly. "I'm not Catholic."

"I didn't think that I recognized you from Sunday mass."

"We're Lutherans. My parents and me, I mean."

"I see. I know plenty of Lutherans. Good people, most of them."

I could feel my face turning red. "Thank you."

"So what brings you here? And what use do you have for holy water?"

His questions did not come out as challenges or interrogations, but as simple, matter-of-fact inquiries. Nor were these questions unreasonable, considering that I was standing in the vestibule of his church, collecting holy water.

"I've heard that holy water has certain... powers," I said.

"Powers?" The priest said, raising his eyebrows. "If you're hoping that holy water will help you get a date with some special girl, or give you a good grade on a calculus test this fall, you may be disappointed." The priest finished this remark with the slightest hint of a smile.

"No. I'm talking about power over...evil things."

I threw that out there, to see what he would do with it.

"Evil things," he repeated. "There are many evil things in this world. There is crime, there are drugs, broken homes—"

"I'm talking about a different kind of evil," I said. "Something very dark and very powerful. Its been around here these past few weeks."

Father Malloy thought about that for moment. "Yes, I have sensed that something around here is not quite right of late. I don't know exactly what is going on, but I think I have some idea of what you're talking about."

"Oh," I said. "Have you seen..."

"I haven't seen anything," the priest said. "I have heard about the disappearances, though."

"Oh."

"What is your name, if I may ask?"

"Steve," I said. "Steve Wagner."

"No, I haven't seen anything, Steve Wagner. It is, rather, a sense I get. A feeling that when I'm sitting alone in the rectory at night, that there might be something watching me from a nearby window." Father Malloy made another ironic smile, and shook his head at the revelation he had just made. "Does that sound strange to you?"

"Father, I'm the one stockpiling holy water," I said. I smiled, despite my discomfort at being caught.

The priest laughed. "Yes, it appears that you are. Well, whether you're a Roman Catholic or not, feel free to take as much as you need." He winked. "We can always make more."

With that, Father Malloy nodded one last time at me. Then he turned around to go back the way he had come.

I stood there for a moment, listening to his footsteps echo on the marble floor.

I began to fill the last of my bottles with holy water.

63

Even with everything that was going on, Diane and I still found time to go on dates.

We still found time to go parking, too. But now we avoided remote locations.

Diane and I were in the back seat of the Bonneville the night after I acquired the holy water. I'd parked the Bonneville at the edge of the parking lot of the cinema. We had seen another movie that night, a comedy this time: *Monty Python and the Holy Grail.*

The spot was secluded enough that no one was likely to walk past the car, but not so secluded that we couldn't make a fast return to electric lights and human activity, should we hear the whinnying of a horse.

Once again my hand moved to the front snap of Diane's jeans. Once again she pushed it away.

"I want to..." I said.

"I know what you want," she said. "And that will come. In time."

"Really?" I asked.

I hoped that I didn't sound too eager. But I knew that I was very, very eager, indeed.

"Yes, really. Just give me some time, okay?"

I thought about Keith Conway, who had felt "entitled". I was determined that I would not repeat his mistakes.

I also told myself that that could never happen, because I was nothing like Keith Conway.

Was I being a little smug, though? Perhaps all guys were like Keith Conway, to one degree or another. Only some were naturally better at it than others.

SPEAKING OF KEITH CONWAY, the other night he had seen Diane and me walking out of the McDonald's hand-in-hand.

What had happened next told me that there might be more trouble from him.

I had expected Keith to smirk when he saw us, to pretend that his loss was no big deal. Keith was always one to play it cool.

But not this time.

Keith glared at us—particularly at me—with daggers. He still hadn't gotten over the reality of losing Diane to me. Keith considered me to be his inferior—at least where girl issues were concerned.

What I wondered was: What did Keith plan to do about it?

AT A CERTAIN POINT THAT NIGHT, Diane and I both agreed that the hour had grown too late. I had to take her home. Diane's parents typically didn't wait up for her when we were out on dates. But if one of them happened to awaken after midnight and she wasn't in her room, her absence would become an immediate cause for worry. In that time before cell phones—before any form of digital communications—there was no way to contact a teenager who wasn't near a known landline.

Diane and I were walking up the little cobblestone path to her front door, hand-in-hand.

Suddenly her face went slack. Her eyes rolled back in their sockets, and then closed.

I moved quickly to prevent her from falling.

This time there was no question about whether or not my help was necessary. Had I not been there, Diane would have gone face-down on one of the hard stones.

She recovered as I held her, supporting most of her own weight. Her eyes fluttered open. I could feel the load lighten even more, as she regained full control of her legs, and braced herself.

"Are you okay?" I asked.

"I—I'm fine. I just—had another dizzy spell. That was all."

I hadn't thought too much about the dizzy spells until that night. But this had been her most serious spell since I had first noticed them.

"You almost passed out and fell," I said.

"Well, I didn't. Thanks to you," she added.

I knew that the last thing any girl wants is a boyfriend who is a worrywart. But I couldn't help expressing a bit of concern.

"Diane, you really need to get this looked at."

"I already have."

"And?"

"And our family doctor has referred me to a specialist. But don't you worry, Steve." She stood on her tiptoes and kissed me. "I'm going to be just fine. Our family doctor says that it might be nothing more than an iron deficiency. An acute iron deficiency can give you bouts of anemia—and light-headedness. If that turns out to be the case, then I'll be able to fix the whole problem by taking iron supplements. But the doctor wants to be sure. That's why he's sending me to the specialist."

"A specialist?" I said.

"Yes. A pediatric neurologist."

As I started the drive home from Diane's house, I kept mentally repeating that phrase in my mind: *pediatric neurologist*.

64

I was a few miles from home, driving down a stretch of two-lane rural highway. Not far from where I'd both seen and heard the Horseman.

Both of the front windows were open. I heard a rumbling on the road behind me.

I was on-guard, but not exactly frightened. This was a distinctly mechanical sound. Nothing otherworldly about it.

Then there was a sudden glare in the rearview mirror. Electric, battery-powered lights. More non-supernatural phenomena.

I now realized that a group of motorcycles was coming up from behind. I was well ahead of them for now. But they were traveling faster than I was.

My thoughts, somewhat naturally, turned to that night at the Sawmill, the less-than-friendly reception I'd received there.

That had not been my first or only experience with bikers, however. Living in Clermont County in the mid-1970s, the heyday of the outlaw bikers, one encountered them all the time. You learned to respect them, to give them a wide berth. But you couldn't run scared every time you saw a group of them. Most of the time, they didn't cause you trouble.

The bikers on the road behind me were certainly aware of my presence by now. If I attempted to outrun them, they might perceive that as a challenge. And that might goad them into giving chase.

On the other hand, if I maintained my present speed, then—if I was lucky—they would simply drive past me, without any significant interaction.

An optimistic assessment, to be sure. But it was the only real option I had.

Less than a minute later the bikers overtook me. Rather than driving by me, though, they enveloped me.

Two bikes took up positions on the road directly in front of the Bonneville. At least three hemmed me in from behind.

I dropped my speed. If I hit one of them, it would be a disaster in any number of ways.

A biker rode up alongside me, so close that he could have reached inside the car. He whistled to get my attention. Then he made an emphatic arm gesture that embodied a very clear command.

Pull over and stop the car.

So I stopped. What choice did I have?

I brought the Bonneville to a stop. I didn't turn off the engine, though. If this situation got ugly (and it was already kind of ugly, really), then I might make a run for home, after all. Consequences be damned.

The night air was filled with the sound of rumbling engines. I could now see that I was surrounded by perhaps ten motorcycles.

One of the bikes that had been behind me rolled forward, to the lane beside my stationary, idling car. The bike was a chopper. It had a long front end, the front wheel attached to the bike on an extended fork.

I recognized the man riding the chopper as Carlos, whom I had seen with Kitty and Sally that night in the parking lot of the Sawmill.

He recognized me, too.

"You again," he said.

"That's right," I said. "Me again. You again, too."

He smiled. I couldn't tell if the smile contained friendliness, or something devilish. Carlos was among his fellow bikers now. And they had made a point of stopping me, when I was going about my business peacefully. What did they want?

"Kind of late for a high school kid to be out," Carlos observed. Several of his companions laughed at the observation.

"I had a date," I said.

This revelation occasioned even more laughter. There were sidebar speculations about whether or not I'd gotten laid. The consensus seemed to be that in all likelihood, I hadn't.

Then Carlos became serious.

"Remember what I told you last time? About those dangerous and beautiful things out on the road? We've been spending some time with them, man."

Carlos fixed his gaze on me, and gave me a wide, toothy grin. There was a glassy film over his eyes. It was as if he had slipped into a trance.

I said nothing, waited for him to say more.

"I'll just go ahead and say it, man," he began. "I'm talking about the *headless one*. We've been partying with him, you see. He's a wonderful, amazing dude, if you're only willing to follow his rules."

The headless one. Carlos had to be talking about the Headless Horsemen. There was no other possibility.

A lot of people were aware of the recent supernatural events in the area, then. I wasn't the only one. These included Diane, Louis, Father Malloy, and that woman who had come into the McDonald's that night, frightened over something that she dared not name.

These bikers, too. They were aware.

From what I could tell, every person who noticed what was going on was aware of it to different degrees. This might depend on their age, temperament, and innate degree of skepticism.

Most everyone found the Headless Horseman and the others in his spirit group horrifying.

These men, on the other hand, were apparently drawn to the darkness. They embraced it, in fact.

"*His* rules," Carlos repeated again. He turned to the other bikers. "Come on, boys! Tonight we ride with the headless one!"

They all howled in response. Several looked up at the moon, and yipped as if they were wolves or coyotes. Carlos slipped his chopper into gear, and began to roll forward. The other bikers followed his lead.

The volume of noise around me increased, as one by one, the bikes roared away.

When I could see nothing but their taillights, I permitted myself a sigh of relief.

I sat there watching them disappear into the night.

When I could no longer hear their engines, I continued my drive home.

65

Within days, I was disturbed by something else. Something that I would not have expected.

Diane had stopped initiating telephone calls. She also stopped returning my phone calls.

Very abruptly.

At first I feared that there had been an accident, or some other emergency. Even with all these extraordinary events, the comparatively mundane but tragic automobile accident was still a possibility.

But a phone call confirmed that no one was dead or in the hospital. I called the Parkers' residence, and I left a message with Diane's mother.

A simple enough message: *Please ask Diane to call me.*

Mrs. Parker replied with a curt, clipped tone. She was pointedly noncommittal about Diane returning my call.

Mrs. Parker barely acknowledged me, in fact.

At this stage in our relationship, I had met Diane's parents several times, but only briefly. I didn't know what they really thought of me.

Apparently not much, if my telephone interaction with Mrs. Parker was any indication.

I didn't know what to think. Since we had started dating, Diane and I had talked every day, and most days we had gotten together in person. The sudden silence was completely unprecedented.

But then, only a few weeks had passed since I had first met Diane…since I had seen her leave work with Keith that night…since the unexpected turnaround.

Perhaps this was just another turnaround.

From the very beginning, Diane had been full of surprises. She had thrown me off guard with her academic accomplishments and her subtle but insistent feminism. She had surprised me by going out with Keith Conway, then surprised me again by breaking up with him, and accepting my on-the-spot invitation to a date.

The truth was: I hadn't really known Diane that long, and she had been constantly unpredictable.

Maybe she had planned it this way all along. Maybe she had found yet another new boyfriend. The possibilities were endless.

In any event, though, I wasn't going to make myself look pathetic. Nor was I about to turn into a stalker. (Stalking—and sexual harassment—hadn't been defined yet as explicit concepts in 1976; but everyone knew what an overly aggressive suitor looked like.)

I decided to bide my time. If nothing else, our paths would cross at work again. Then I would have a better indication of what was going on.

That was what I thought, anyway.

66

Diane and I had been scheduled to work the evening shift together the very next night.

When I came in, though, another cashier—I no longer recall who—was manning Diane's assigned register.

I had made up my mind to play this cooly and casually. But cool and casual are sometimes difficult when you're a teenager—when your mind and body are swirls of unignorable emotions.

I walked into the manager's office. Louis was sitting behind the desk, busy with paperwork. I was so distraught that I barely noticed the usual haze of cigarette smoke.

"What?" he asked, looking up.

"Where's Diane? She was supposed to work one of the cash registers tonight. I saw the schedule."

Louis's sympathetic frown suggested (yet again) that he knew more than I was giving him credit for.

"You're right," he said. "She was on the schedule. But an employee is no longer on any schedule once she quits her job."

"What?"

"Diane called in this afternoon and said that she's quitting her job here, effective immediately," Louis said. "I had to scramble to find a replacement on such short notice."

I was unconcerned, in that moment, about how difficult it might have been to find a fill-in cashier on short notice.

"But, *why*?" I asked. "*Why* did she quit?"

"She didn't say, exactly. All she said was that she was quitting for 'personal reasons'."

I took a step backward from the desk and let that sink in.

Personal reasons. Diane had wanted to break up with me, but she hadn't wanted to face me again.

So she had simply stopped returning my calls. Then she quit her job at McDonald's, where she knew that we would eventually see each other.

Standing there before Louis, I was filled with a mixture of hurt, and not a little bit of resentment. Even Julie Idelman had had the decency to tell me that she wanted to end our relationship.

Diane, on the other hand, had chosen to simply pretend that our relationship had never existed in the first place.

"So what's going on with you two?" Louis said. "But I think I have some idea already."

"She hasn't been returning my phone calls," I admitted.

"I'm sorry," Louis said. He leaned back in his chair. "I know this is the second time that you've gotten your hopes up about Diane, only to have them disappointed. If it's any consolation, you're not the only guy in the world who has ever gone through something like this. Women have strange ways sometimes."

"You can say that again."

"I'll let you know, Steve, if I hear from her again. But I don't expect I will. Okay?"

"Okay. Thanks, Louis."

So that was that. Come September, Diane would be starting her senior year at South Clermont High School, while I would be going to West Clermont. Southwestern Clermont County wasn't a big place, but the odds were high that I would never see her again—especially if she was going out of her way to avoid me.

I left the manager's office and headed to my cash register, feeling more forlorn than ever.

Not only had I apparently lost Diane (twice!—as Louis had reminded me), I had also lost an ally in my effort to understand—and perhaps combat—the disturbing phenomena of recent weeks.

As I was confirming that my cash register had a full load of quarters, nickels, dimes, and pennies, I happened to glance up. Near the entrance to the restaurant, silhouetted by the twilight-filled window, was Banny—whom I now knew to be Banastre Tarleton, the young, sadistic British officer whom the Colonials had dubbed, "the Butcher of Waxhaws".

Banny was now wearing the clothes he had worn when he'd posed for that long-ago portrait: high boots and white breeches. A green frock coat, and a leather helmet adorned with a large, dark fur plume.

After she showed me the portrait, Diane had subsequently mentioned that that leather helmet—based on an old design for an equestrian's helmet—had been specified by the precocious Banastre Tarleton himself. For years the headgear had been known by the designation *Tarleton helmet*.

Banny acknowledged me with an impudent sneer.

I looked away, and when I looked back—Banny was gone.

I knew, however, that I hadn't seen the last of him, or of the Horseman, or of Marie Trumbull. Even if I had seen the last of Diane.

67

The next night. Still no call from Diane.
Another evening shift at McDonald's.
I was near the end of the shift when Tim Schmidt came in.

He was visibly agitated. As he walked up to the counter, his eyes darted from side to side—as if he was anticipating some threat, here inside Ray Smith's McDonald's.

Keep in mind: Tim Schmidt was not only a local lawman, he had done two tours in Vietnam. He was not a man who would be easily rattled. Or so you would think.

Schmidt might have been agitated over something that had happened on the job—a particularly gruesome automobile accident, a near fatal brush with a felon. But if that were the case, he probably wouldn't be in McDonald's right now, would he?

No. Tim Schmidt was agitated over something else. Maybe the same thing that had distressed that woman who came in here the other night.

The same things that had distressed me of late.

I tried to play it cool. I was on friendly enough terms with Tim; but we weren't exactly pals. He was a decade older than me, one of that cohort of young men who had served in Vietnam (or not, as in the cases of Dan Bauer and my brother).

But most of all, Tim was *the police*. Familiar or not, I knew that he wouldn't react favorably to an interrogation.

So I interrogated him only about his order, for the time being.

"The usual?" I asked. "Plain burger, small fries, medium Coke?"

"Sure," Tim said. He dug into his rear pocket for his wallet. I was suddenly aware of his official uniform and the accoutrements on his leather utility belt. In those days the police didn't carry tasers. But he had a radio, handcuffs, a baton, and his sidearm. The gun was a .357 magnum—a powerful weapon.

I spoke his order into the microphone. I had it ready almost immediately. I drew his drink from the dispenser. I placed the sandwich and fries inside a to-go bag, and slid both items across the counter. I handed him his change.

"Something is not right," he said. "Something is not right around here."

Well, that was pretty out-of-the-blue. Maybe Tim could be persuaded to talk, after all.

"What do you mean, Tim? Are you talking about the disappearances?"

It was a reasonable question. Tim Schmidt was a member of law enforcement. He would know the statuses of the various investigations.

Tim didn't answer. I had the impression that he wanted me to say more.

So I did.

"Listen Tim," I said. "I think I know what's going on."

"Really?" he replied flatly.

He either knows or he doesn't, I thought. If he already knows, then little explanation will be required.

"I think that the problem might be a...ghost. A group of them, actually."

Tim paused for a few beats before replying. In that brief time, his fear visibly dissipated—almost as if I had snapped him out of the trance by naming what we'd both been thinking about.

"*Are you kidding me?*" he asked. "*A ghost?*"

"A group of them," I repeated. "Not only one."

Tim shook his head in disgust. "I can't believe this. People are disappearing around here—people are dead, probably—and you're talking about *ghosts*."

"You said yourself," I replied defensively, "you said yourself that there is something wrong around here."

"There *is* something wrong around here. We've got three disappearances. One of them is a classmate of your brother and me. Wouldn't you call that *something wrong*? What does that have to do with ghosts?"

"I—I thought—"

Tim had caught me off-guard, almost as much as I'd caught him off-guard.

"What's the matter with you, Steve? Is this your idea of a joke?"

"Hey," I said, "I'm sorry. Forget I said anything. Okay?"

"Yes, let's forget you said anything. That sounds like a *great* idea." He picked up his to-go bag and drink. "Thanks for the grub," he said.

Tim gave me one final, disapproving shake of his head, and then turned to walk out.

The sheriff's deputy hadn't fooled me, though.

Tim Schmidt had seen something, too—just like me, just like Diane. Just like Carlos.

But Tim Schmidt was still in denial.

68

You may have heard that old adage: about bad things coming in clusters. The day after that strange discussion with Tim Schmidt, it was something else—something much worse.

I was trying to put a brave face on a bad situation. My parents, however, noticed something amiss with me.

"I'm okay," I lied, when my father asked me how I was doing, as I was leaving for work.

"Really?" he asked, not entirely believing me. (My father, like Louis, had a way of seeing through my B.S.) "What about that girlfriend of yours, Diane?"

My parents had met Diane on one occasion—just a brief introduction when I'd brought her by the house.

"Oh. That. That didn't really work out," I told my dad.

"I see." My father didn't say anything more.

I noticed that his face looked a little pale. At the time, I assumed it was because he was worried about me.

I was wrong about that, too.

69

That night, I came home late from my shift at McDonald's.

I was almost an hour later than usual. I had been driving around aimlessly, thinking—and tempting fate.

I brought the Bonneville to a stop in the spot that had become such an eventful place over the past few weeks: This was the spot where I had first seen the Horseman. It was also the spot where the motorcycle gang had briefly detained me, just a few nights ago.

I stepped outside the car, with the motor idling.

"I'm here!" I shouted into the night. *"You want me? Come and get me!"*

Who was I talking to? Carlos and his biker friends? The Horseman?

Keith Conway, perhaps?

But a full minute or so elapsed, and no one came. Tonight, at least, there were no predators afoot.

I stepped back inside the Bonneville, and drove the rest of the way home.

WHEN I DID ARRIVE HOME, I hoped that my parents would be long asleep, that neither of them would notice my unusually late arrival. It was nearly midnight.

I walked into the house and immediately observed something strange: One of the lights in the kitchen had been left on: the overhead light above the sink.

Most unusual. My parents turned off all the lights when they headed to bed. I always came home to a dark house.

They had been worried about me, after all. They were waiting up for me.

"Mom? Dad?" I called out. If the light in the kitchen was on, then they hadn't gone to bed yet, right?

Or they had gone to bed, and then had gotten up again.

Given that the house was so small, I had a clear view of the kitchen and living room directly from the foyer.

I didn't see either my mom or my dad. Nor did anyone answer me.

I walked down the hallway to their bedroom.

Their bed was empty. Still made. I turned on the lights.

"Mom? Dad?"

I stepped into the little bathroom immediately off the master bedroom.

"Mom?... Dad?"

That room was empty, too.

They had gone somewhere, obviously.

Or someone had taken them, perhaps?

No, I would allow myself to think that way.

Not yet.

70

I walked back out into the living room. I needed time to formulate my next steps.

Perhaps they had gone looking for me. (I didn't think this was very likely. But I had to at least consider that possibility, given the circumstances.)

If they had done that, they would have left me a note. My mother would have thought of that, I was certain.

I searched the front end of the house, looking on all the obvious surfaces: the kitchen table, the counter beside the sink. The refrigerator.

No note.

So now what?

Then the silence was broken by the sound of the landline ringing.

I answered the phone in the kitchen on the second ring.

"*Steve!*" It was my mother's voice. "*Thank goodness!* I called the McDonald's, and I spoke to Louis. But he told me that you'd already left. I would've expected you home much earlier."

"I—I went for drive. I'm sorry that I worried you guys, that you went out looking for me, but—"

"We didn't go out looking for you," she said.

"What, then?" I asked.

I could feel a pool of dread, rising in my chest.

"Are you sitting down, Steve?"

"No, mom. I'm not sitting down. I'm standing in the kitchen. But tell me what's going on."

Maybe I knew already. Why wasn't my father on the line, too?

"Is it something with dad?"

"Your father had a heart attack this evening," my mother said. "Around ten o'clock p.m."

"Oh my God," I said. "Is he—" I didn't want to say the word that I was thinking. The obvious word.

"No," Mom said. "Your father is in intensive care, but he's stabilized."

I wasn't sure how relieved I should be at that. At the age of seventeen, I knew mercifully little about the details of hospital visits and death. Even then, though, I knew that my dad was in trouble if he was in an intensive care unit with a heart attack—even if he was "stabilized".

"The doctor says that in time, he should be able to make a full recovery. But he will have to make some significant lifestyle changes."

Like giving up those damn cigarettes, I thought, but did not say. I knew that now wasn't the time.

"Are you in Clermont Mercy?" I asked. That was the only hospital in the immediate area in those years. The next closest hospitals were all in Cincinnati.

"Yes, but you should just go to bed—"

"I'll be right there."

"Stevie, there's nothing you can do for your dad tonight."

"Mom, I'm not going to argue about it," I said. "I'll be right there."

71

My mother was waiting for me in the waiting room beside the ICU. From there she led me past the nurses' reception counter, to the little room where my father lay in "stable" condition. The room, like all rooms in the ICU, was glass-walled, so that the nurses could always see inside.

My dad was asleep in the little hospital bed. He looked helpless in that space. The oxygen mask over his face made him look gravely ill, on the edge of death.

As if to allay my fears, my father opened his eyes about halfway. He couldn't quite open them fully. This, in itself, was no particular cause for worry. On the way to his room, my mother had told me that his doctor had given him a sedative.

He lifted his hand and I took it. He made an effort to squeeze my hand, but it was a weak squeeze.

My father's nurse entered the room. She was a youngish woman, maybe thirty-one or thirty-two years old, with platinum blonde hair. She and my mother were already on a first-name basis, apparently. Her name tag identified her as Cheryl.

"So this is your son," Cheryl said. She smiled and extended her hand. I shook it briefly. Then, to my mother, Cheryl said, "We should really let your husband sleep, Mrs. Wagner. He's stabilized, and we have your contact information. But you can have a final word with Dr. Phillips if you'd like, before you leave."

"Please," Mom said. "Yes."

"I'll take you two to a consultation room, and then I'll summon Dr. Phillips."

We said goodnight to my dad—and I silently prayed that it would not be our last goodnight. He acknowledged us with a weak nod.

My dad was indeed a war hero. I knew what he had done that day at Omaha Beach, all those years ago, fifteen years before I'd even been born. And yet here he was now, entirely dependent on nurses like Cheryl, all because something had gone wrong inside his body.

We were all vulnerable, I concluded. All of us. All the time.

72

Ten minutes later, Mom and I were sitting in a little consultation room with Dr. Phillips. The room contained two upholstered chairs, a plain dark wood coffee table, and a sofa. A homey atmosphere, in the middle of an otherwise clinical environment. I assumed that this was intended to impart comfort to the loved ones of the hospital's patients in difficult times.

"Your husband should be able to make a full recovery," Dr. Phillips was saying, addressing my mother. "In time. But he has to make some serious changes. Starting with the cigarettes. Those have got to go."

I thought about the past conversations my dad and I had had about the cigarettes, how he'd chided me for my worrying. My mother hadn't exactly taken his side in regard to the smoking, but she hadn't exactly been my partisan, either.

But it never pays to tell a parent, "I told you so"—especially when one of them is lying in the ICU.

I was soon to find that my mother had come around to my way of thinking, though. "Of course," she said now. "By the time he goes home, there won't be a cigarette left in the house. You have my personal guarantee on that one, doctor."

I noted the set expression of my mother's face. There was an unusual level of resolve in her voice. I knew that she wasn't speaking idly.

Dr. Phillips went over some more details with us, then he finally suggested that we both call it a night.

The time was 1:32 a.m., after all.

"There's nothing more that either of you can do for your husband —" he looked at me, "—your father—tonight. What both of you should do, quite frankly, is go home and get some sleep. Come back in the morning, after eight a.m. By then, the doctors and nurses will have made their early morning rounds. You'll be able to spend some time with Harold, and get an update on his condition."

WE WERE HEADING **out** of the ICU wing when I turned to my mother. For the first time, it occurred to me that only one of Harold Wagner's two sons was present.

"Where's Jack?" I asked. "You called him, right?"

"I tried," my mother said. "But there was no answer out at that farmhouse where he's been living. Please, Stevie, let's not talk about Jack tonight. Okay? It's been a stressful enough night as it is."

"Okay," I agreed.

Inwardly, though, I was seething at my brother Jack's failure to show up—or even to be found.

73

My mother and I had arrived separately at the hospital; and so we were to drive home separately, too. I let her walk out ahead of me. After a full shift at the McDonald's, a late-night drive, and my time at the hospital, I was both starving and parched, I realized.

It was too late (too early now, really) to eat anything. But a can of soda would be okay. Before I headed out, I stopped by one of the first-floor lobby vending machines, and dropped a quarter in the slot. I removed an ice-cold can of Dr. Pepper from the bottom of the chute.

I finished the can of Dr. Pepper before I'd even made it out of the hospital.

The Clermont Mercy Hospital was located in a remote area to begin with, and the parking lot was deserted now, long after midnight. There were few cars, and no people—at least that I could see. The parking lot was lit only by two halogen lights, fixed atop steel poles.

I was halfway across the parking lot when my nostrils were struck by a foul odor.

Then I heard the whinnying.

I looked in the direction of the sound. At the edge of the parking lot, on the fringe of a meadow overgrown with midsummer grass and weeds, the Horseman sat atop his undead animal—the probable source of the smell.

I was relieved, at least, that my mother was already on her way home.

I heard the sound of old steel sliding against rotted leather.

The Horseman withdrew a long sword from his scabbard.

I should have run, I suppose. I was within sprinting distance of my car.

But something possessed me just then. Maybe it was my fear for my father, my agony at seeing him lying there helpless in a hospital bed, an oxygen mask over his face.

Maybe it was my churning hunger for Diane, a hunger that had been unexpectedly frustrated.

Maybe it was both. Perhaps I had decided that if this was the way it was to end, then so be it. I knew that seventeen years didn't constitute a very long life. But in that moment, at least, my rage overtook my fear.

I took a step toward the Horseman.

"You want me?" I said in a voice loud enough to carry across the parking lot. I held both of my hands open, and to either side of me, as if to show him—absurdly—that I wasn't holding any weapons. "Come and get me!"

Just then, something about the horse caught my attention.

The animal was looking at me with a certain intelligence. As crazy as this sounds, the animal seemed to have grasped the gist of my challenge.

The horse, then, was not merely a reanimated horse. There was some evil spirit inside that undead animal, another member of the spirit group that traveled with the Horseman.

The horse moved forward at a walking pace, lining itself up with me. The Horseman angled his blade in my direction.

The old steel caught a glint of moonlight.

"I've met your friends!" I shouted to him. "That bitch, Marie Trumbull! And Banny, too! Banastre Tarleton."

I stood there, waiting for the horse and rider to do their worst.

But we were interrupted.

There were footsteps behind me. And very human voices, expressing obvious concern.

I turned around. A couple—a man and a woman—maybe in their early forties. They were well-dressed, but like me, they showed the weariness of their circumstances. No one who finds himself in a hospital parking lot in the wee hours of the morning is happy to be there.

I looked at them, and wondered what I should say.

A quick glance over my shoulder, at the now empty meadow, confirmed what I already knew. Both the undead horse and its undead rider were gone.

"Are you all right?" The male half of the couple asked me.

"I'm fine," I fumbled. "I just—I just had a stressful night, is all."

"Most people are having stressful nights, when they're at the hospital this late at night," the woman said. "Or this early in the morning, I should say."

"My father had a heart attack," I explained. "The doctor says he's going to be fine. As long as he stops smoking, improves his diet, and starts getting regular exercise, that is."

The woman stepped forward and laid a hand on my shoulder. It was an almost maternal gesture.

"I hope your father does make a full recovery," she said. "I'm sure he will."

"Thank you," I said.

"You should go home now."

"Yes. Yes, you're right."

She *was* right. If nothing else, my mother would be almost home by now. She would be waiting for me, expecting me to pull into the driveway shortly after her. Tonight, of all nights, I didn't want to cause her any unnecessary worry.

"Good night," I said.

As I was about to head toward my car, the woman spoke to me again.

"What you were speaking to just a moment ago," she said. "I—I saw something. In that meadow over there."

The man—her husband, I assumed—put a protective arm around her. "Judy, there was nothing in that meadow," he said.

"There was, Henry," she insisted. "I couldn't see it clearly, but I saw the outlines of...something."

I didn't say anything. But I couldn't bring myself to deny it, either.

"There was nothing," Henry said.

They stood before me, a skeptic, and a half-believer. Had Henry seen nothing, truly? Or had he seen something that he was trying desperately to deny? I didn't know.

"This isn't the first time I've seen it, Henry," Judy said. Then, to me, "So tell me: Is it real, then? Is it true?"

"Yes," I said. "Yes, I'm afraid it is."

"May God help us all, then," she said. "What's your name?"

"Steve. Steve Wagner."

"Be careful driving home, Steve Wagner. Because whatever that thing is, I don't think that there's anything alive that can stop it."

74

My life now underwent yet another shift.

With my dad at the hospital, Mom and I made daily visits to see him. Usually, in fact, we went twice per day.

This new routine required me to miss some shifts at the McDonald's. Louis was appropriately understanding.

"Do what you need to do for your mom and dad," he said. "Ray Smith's McDonald's will still be here when your dad is out of the hospital. I'll find people to cover for you in the meantime."

"Thanks, Louis," I said. "The doctors said he should come home next week."

"However long you need," Louis said. His words were solicitous, but there was something about his manner that was distracted.

"What about you, Louis?" I asked. "Everything okay with you? You seem a little...nervous."

Louis made an uneasy smile. "Like you keep telling me, Steve: There's nothing going on around here to be nervous about. Get out of here. Take care of your dad."

I knew that I owed him more. I owed him the explanation that he had been hinting at—over the course of multiple conversations.

But I didn't have the strength for that right now.

I also remembered how I had confided in Tim Schmidt, only to have him turn it around on me.

Louis wasn't the police, true; but he was my boss. And I didn't owe him anything right now, except gratitude for his understanding about the situation with my father.

"Thanks again, Louis," I said. "I'll be back on the job as soon as my dad gets over the hump."

75

One morning—a few days after I had that conversation with Louis—I awoke earlier than usual. My bedroom door was open.

I wasn't alone. I knew that before I was fully awake.

Marie Trumbull was standing there in the hallway. One of her rotted, skeletal hands held that knife of hers.

By some fortunate accident, I had managed to bar her access to my room. She was therefore waiting for me to step out into the hallway.

I was no longer dating Diane; but I remembered all the research she had done. I remembered what Diane had told me about the powers of salt and holy water.

I had started to sleep with a little plastic bag of Morton salt beneath the covers.

I sat halfway up in bed. Marie made a hideous grimace.

"Come out here, boy....Play with me..."

I slipped to the edge of the bed.

"Yes, yes," she said eagerly. A gurgling voice that was there and not quite there. An older version of American English. British, but not quite British.

I flung a handful of salt on her.

Marie Trumbull hissed as if scalded.

"You bloody bastard!" she said. *"I'll carve your eyes out. Cut your ears off..."*

Then she vanished into a wisp of acrid smoke. A wretched, sulfurous smell filled the air of my bedroom.

"Steve?" I heard my mother call out, from my parents' bedroom. My parents had been sharing a bed for thirty years. With Dad in the hospital, her sleep had been troubled and uneven.

"Everything's fine, Mom," I called back to her.

"I thought I heard something."

"I—I had to go to the bathroom," I said. "I'm going back to bed now."

"Okay, Stevie." I could hear her yawn from the other room. "Good night."

76

Early that evening, my mother and I were riding back from the hospital.

Things were looking up. My father was coming along, and he'd agreed to stop smoking. Mom and I were both tentatively optimistic.

"Everything okay with you, Stevie?" my mom said, out of the blue. We were in her car. She was driving and I was in the front passenger seat.

"What do you mean, Mom?"

"I mean, you've seemed...not yourself lately. I know you're concerned about your father. And my mother's intuition tells me that your relationship with that Diane didn't exactly work out—as you'd planned. I believe your father talked to you about it."

"Mom, I'd rather not talk about Diane, if it's okay."

"Suit yourself. I know that teenagers don't like talking about affairs of the heart with their parents."

She was right about that. I was practically squirming in my seat.

"But what I'm wondering is," she ventured, "is there anything else bothering you? Like I said, you just don't seem yourself of late. You haven't for a while now, in fact."

This was my opening, I supposed. If I was ever going to confide in either of my parents—about the Horseman, about Marie Trumbull, about Banny, and the rest of them—this was the moment.

I decided to test the waters a bit, to see if my mother would even be open to the possibility of such things.

So I responded to her with a question. "What do you believe, Mom, about what happens to us after we die? I'm not just talking about heaven and hell. Do you believe it's possible that there's some—state in between life and death—where some souls can get trapped? Or maybe that's where they want to get trapped...?"

Now it was my mother's turn to squirm.

"What are you talking about, Stevie?" she asked, frowning.

In that moment, I almost told her everything. Fortunately, though, I was perceptive enough to gage her reaction.

"I'm not a mind-reader, Steve," she went on. There was the slightest edge to her voice now. "I don't know what to make of—what you've just said."

Of course she didn't. My parents had lived their lives preoccupied with earthly matters, some mundane, some urgent: the Depression, the war, working hard to provide for Jack and me. Neither one of them, I reminded myself, had ever displayed any interest in (or even a tolerance for) paranormal speculation.

What I had been about to tell her—she could never have accepted that.

Then I recalled that there were times when I had had trouble accepting it myself.

"It's nothing, Mom," I said "I'm just worried about Dad. That's all."

"Oh," she said. And for the umpteenth time that summer, I had the feeling that one of my facile lies was not completely believed. "That's understandable. But really, Stevie, your father is going to be just fine. As long as he lays off the cigarettes, that is."

77

Later that week, I did take a swing shift at the McDonald's, from 4 p.m. to 8:30 p.m. Dad was doing better. He would be discharged any day now.

When I arrived home, my mother wasn't there. This didn't alarm me, as she had told me that she might stay late at the hospital that night.

I went into my room, and changed into a pair of jeans and a tee shirt.

Stepping out of my room, I felt a little chill in the hallway. But then, the air conditioning had just kicked on.

Everything is okay, I told myself. Marie Trumbull had not paid me any more late-night visits since I'd banished her with salt.

Something was off, though...I knew it.

Out in the living room, I opened the drapes that covered the window above the television set. I looked out into our front yard. I could see virtually nothing in the near total darkness.

This is the time when evil things come out...

I closed the drapes again.

Don't spook yourself, I thought.

Nevertheless, I walked around the living room and turned on every light in sight. This was a childish reaction, I knew.

I was about to turn on the television set, too. I hadn't watched much TV these past weeks; I didn't even know which programs were on tonight. I might be able to find something decent if I channel-surfed, which—in that era before remotes—basically meant turning a mechanical dial to four or five different stations. I spotted that week's copy of *TV Guide* atop the television set. As I reached for the on-off knob, I figured that I would check the listings, anyway.

Then I stopped, my fingers around the on-off knob.

I heard sounds of movement out in the front yard, just outside the living room window. Clicking, dragging noises.

And some kind of high-pitched chatter.

What the—?

That didn't fit the pattern for the Horseman, Marie Trumbull, or Banny.

Something new, then.

There would be no television for me tonight, I realized.

I wanted to open the drapes again. I had been reminded, however, that nothing is visible when you stare into the darkness of night from a lighted room.

I quickly walked around the living room and turned off all of the lights I had just turned on.

The living room was completely dark now. I tiptoed over to the front window.

I pulled back the drapes.

I stared into the rotted face of a Hessian soldier.

78

The Hessian soldier was not alone. I looked past the one immediately before the window. There were several of them out there.

Waiting inside the house for the creatures to go away wasn't really an option. My mother would be coming home soon.

A few days ago I had almost told her about the revolutionary ghosts, as I collectively described them to myself. I had balked, fearing that she would never believe me.

What would my mother do, when she came home, and found herself surrounded by a horde of undead Hessians?

I needed to do something.

I had driven Marie Trumbull away with salt. But that wasn't going to do the trick with an entire squad of the armed undead, I figured.

What could I do?

I had a sudden burst of inspiration.

I walked out to the garage, which was connected to our house via the kitchen. In the rear corner of the garage, behind my father's workbench, was an item from my earlier childhood years: my old Louisville Slugger wooden baseball bat.

I removed the bat from its place against the wall. I had used it for little league. Realistically speaking, I knew that I was never going to play baseball again. Luckily, though, the bat hadn't been thrown away. My father didn't keep any guns in the house. I suppose he regarded the bat as a last-ditch tool of household protection.

That was, indeed, the purpose it was going to serve—though not in a way that my father could have ever imagined.

I brought the bat in from the garage and carried it into my bedroom.

Outside, I heard more clicking noises, more sounds of movement.

Something metallic tapping against the window. A sword, perhaps. Or maybe a bayonet.

I opened the top drawer of my bedroom bureau, where I had stowed the three bottles of holy water from St. Andrew's.

I opened one of the bottles and poured it over the wood of the baseball bat.

Then I headed for the front door of our house.

79

I stepped outside onto our front porch. I closed the front door behind me.

Now would be a good time for some neighbors to appear. Preferably a neighbor with a large-caliber firearm.

The neighborhood was eerily quiet, though—especially for just after dark on a summer night. I looked at the house across the street. There were lights on in what would be the living room window, but the curtains were drawn.

I felt a sudden certainty that no one was coming to my aid.

From the far end of our front yard, I heard a clicking sound.

Three Hessians were gathered around the maple tree outside my bedroom window, the one that I liked to look at sometimes. Two of them were holding muskets tipped with bayonets. The third had no musket, but a scabbard containing a sword.

Two grenadiers and an officer, I thought.

Their decayed faces were mummified, little more than bare skulls.

I didn't know if their muskets were operational. If they were capable of shooting at me, then I would be dead within a matter of seconds.

Then I saw that it wasn't going to be like that. These were undead soldiers. Their weapons were relics that had long since fallen into disrepair. The Hessian without the musket—the one I guessed to be an officer—moved toward me first. He drew his sword from a scabbard that was little more than a few dangling strips of leather.

He was walking on legs that were stiff with death. His boots were as decayed as the rest of him. I saw a phalanx bone poking through the top of one boot.

I ran at him with the bat raised.

I swung the bat just as the Hessian swung the sword. Wood soaked with holy water connected with the ancient metal.

I heard a loud pop, like a tiny sonic boom.

The sword shattered like dried clay. The momentum from my swing drove the bat into the Hessian's skull.

That shattered like clay, too.

The other two Hessians started walking. They held their muskets out in front of them, leading with their bayonets.

I swung at the first of the two remaining Hessians. When the holy water-soaked bat struck him, I heard another loud pop!

The ghoul collapsed in a pile of bones and rotting fabric.

The last remaining Hessian raised his bayonet-tipped musket.

First I struck the weapon. I flinched as it exploded, more or less, in a cloud of sawdust and rusted steel.

Then I struck the Hessian himself.

I knocked him down as if he were made of papier-mâché.

I smelled something foul. What was left of the three Hessians was dissolving into little clouds of smoke on my front lawn.

Holy water is more powerful than salt, I reasoned. I vowed that henceforth, I would never be without a bottle of it on my person.

I was just about to relax. (As relaxed as I could be, after an experience like that.) The three Hessians were gone. I had killed—or (they had already been dead, after all)—destroyed them.

The front yard was briefly lit up with headlights, as my mother's car pulled into the driveway.

She stopped her car directly behind dad's truck.

From inside the car, Mom gave me a questioning look. She must have wondered what the heck I was doing.

At that moment my immediate concern was: How was I going to explain my stalking around the front yard with my childhood baseball bat? From Mom's perspective, it would appear eccentric, at the very least.

Then I saw flashes of movement on the far side of the driveway.

More Hessians.

80

"Mom! stay in the car!" I shouted.

I motioned in the direction of the Hessians. My mother turned her head, then she looked back at me. Her eyes were wide.

She didn't see the Hessians, I assumed; but she was apparently alarmed at my behavior.

How could I blame her?

There were three of the undead creatures approaching her car. They were entering our yard from the yard of our next-door neighbors.

I ran at them, going behind my mother's parked car.

One of the Hessians was wielding a sword. He made a perfunctory swing in my direction, which I easily deflected.

Then I shattered him with the baseball bat. As he hit the ground, I was vaguely aware that he was already dissolving. I could smell the putrid smoke above the ordinary pollen and grass smells of the summer night.

The other two Hessians came at me with bayonet-tipped rifles.

I went at them in return. I swung the bat twice, in quick succession.

Crunch. Crunch. Down they went.

I looked around, ready for more of them. These three seemed to be all there were.

As I watched these three Hessians begin to dissolve, I realized that this had been almost too easy.

The Hessians were the least intelligent of all the entities I had encountered this summer. *They're little more than mindless zombies,* I thought. They were just going through the motions. The echoes of some distant battlefield memory, perhaps. No wonder I was able to defeat them so easily.

I looked around our yard, then our neighbor's yard. I didn't see any other threats.

My mother was still in the car. I couldn't make her sit there all night. I motioned for her to get out.

She stepped out of her car.

All three Hessians had dissolved by now. But their stench lingered in the air.

"Do you smell that?" I asked my mom.

She wrinkled up her nose.

"There does seem to be something foul afoot," she said.

"But did you see?" I asked my mother. "Did you see what I was fighting with?"

I didn't need to say more. If she had seen, she would already have been asking me for a detailed explanation. Then I would complete the conversation that I had almost begun the other day, as we were driving back from the hospital.

"I didn't see anything," she said. "All I saw was you, waving the bat around."

Really? My mother seemed rather frightened for someone who had seen nothing.

Maybe she *sensed* something, I thought.

"Well, *I* saw something," I said. "A rabid dog."

"A rabid dog," she repeated.

"Yes. But it's gone now."

I walked back to the front door with her, walking on the outside, with her closer to the house. As she opened the front door, I ventured one last look over my shoulder, into the yard.

Nothing else that I could see.

I followed her inside the house, and closed the door quickly behind me.

"So tell me, how is Dad doing?" I asked. I placed the bat against the wall near the front door.

"He should be able to come home at the end of the week."

"Good."

My mother looked around suddenly.

"What?"

"I left my purse inside the car, Stevie." Reluctantly, she added, "I'd better go—"

"No, Mom. I'll get it."

As I walked back out the front door, she reminded me to take the bat with me.

"Just in case, Stevie. Just in case that rabid dog you saw comes back."

I RETRIEVED **my mother's purse** without incident. I saw a flash of relief cross her face when I walked back inside.

I had the feeling that she was withholding something from me, but I didn't press the issue. We were both exhausted, and I had way too much on my mind.

81

The next afternoon I went to the hospital to visit my father.

Jack had shown up. Finally. He was standing on one side of our father's bed, our mother on the other.

When I walked in the room, Jack shot me a defiant look, as if daring me to say something.

I immediately laid into him.

"Where have you been, Jack?"

"What do you mean, 'where have I been'?"

"What do I mean? Dad has been in the hospital for days, and you're just now showing up. 'What do I mean?'" I shook my head in disgust, as if I were Jack's father rather than his little brother.

"What I've been doing, where I've been—that's none of your business." He took a step closer to me. "You want to go at it right here and now? Huh, little brother? Is that what you want?"

"Please!" our mother said. "Remember where you are. Both of you. You're in your father's hospital room."

I raised my hands in surrender. "You're right, Mom. I'm sorry."

"You should be. What got into you, Steve? I would expect this kind of thing out of Jack, but—"

"*What?*" Jack interjected. "So you're blaming *me*, for something he started?" Jack jerked a thumb in my direction.

"Well, Jack, your brother does have a point." She frowned at me. "Even if he doesn't have a great sense of timing or propriety. Your father has been in the hospital for days, and we haven't been able to get ahold of you."

This provoked Jack to become even more defensive.

"I'm outta here," Jack said. "Dad, I'm glad to see you're out of the woods. I'll drop by the house sometime soon to see you."

After Jack had left, my father asked for a word with me—alone.

"Marge, honey, why don't you give Steve and me a few minutes to talk." He winked at her. "Father-son stuff."

"All right," my mother said. "I could use a cup of coffee, anyway. Can I get anything for either of you while I'm in the cafeteria?"

Neither of us wanted anything from the hospital cafeteria.

My father motioned for me to sit beside him on the bed. I did as he asked.

I figured that I was in for a gentle scolding about my ongoing resentment of Jack. My father was going to tell me to cool it, in so many words.

That wasn't what he said, however.

"Steve. I know that your mom and I don't always say this, but we're both so proud of you. We recognize that…you've always tried to be good, to give us no trouble."

My father took a moment to gather his strength.

"It's okay, Dad," I said. "Maybe I should leave, so you can rest."

"No, Steve," he said. "I need to tell you this—all of it. What I'm saying is, Jack is our son. We'll always love him, no matter what he does."

"Of course," I said.

"But your mother and I recognize that you're nothing like Jack. And we're grateful for that. We—we *appreciate* it, is what I'm trying to say."

Now I was feeling vaguely uncomfortable. I appreciated this heart-to-heart, but it was out of character for my dad, who rarely, if ever, spoke directly of his emotions.

"I know you think that we should simply turn our backs on Jack," Dad went on. Before I could protest, he stopped me. "No, I know. That's what you think. And not unreasonably. Jack has more than given us cause. But the thing is, son: We can't turn our backs on him. He's our son, and we can't simply give up on him. Someday you'll have children of your own, and you'll understand."

"Sure, Dad."

"But you need to know that your mother and I recognize the difference between the two of you."

"Okay, Dad. Thanks."

He reached across the bed and patted my hand.

After that, I quickly changed the subject. I asked him about the rehab that the hospital was putting him through.

When my mother returned, we talked more about my dad's treatment, about his imminent release. The subject of Jack didn't come up again.

82

My dad came home from the hospital, and I was able to return to my normal work schedule at McDonald's.

Still no communication from Diane.

I was getting antsy about that situation. I had stopped calling her house. Several times I had considered something more assertive—an impromptu visit—and each time I had decided against it.

We were at the end of our shift at McDonald's, closing up for the night, when Louis called me into his office.

I could see dark circles under my manager's eyes. Louis hadn't been sleeping.

Well, join the club, I thought.

"Everything okay, Louis?" I asked.

"I don't know," he said. "I honestly don't."

"And?"

There was a long, pregnant silence. It was another one of those moments in which I might have confided in Louis, might have told him everything I knew.

And Louis said as much himself.

"If you've got some inkling of what's going on," Louis said, "I wish you would share."

I thought about that for a moment: I had shared my discoveries—my experiences—with Diane. What had it gotten me?

I had tried to confide in Tim Schmidt, and he had turned the conversation around on me, essentially accused me of making light of the recent disappearances in the area.

I had tried to tell my mother, and the resulting conversation had been, well, embarrassing.

I should have told Louis. But I wasn't ready to open up to another person. Not yet.

"Please," Louis said. "Quite frankly, I'm a little frightened of late."

I owed Louis a straight answer—I knew that. He had always been an understanding and accommodating boss. He had pulled strings to help me win over Diane—even if I'd lost her in the end. And after my father had the heart attack, Louis had rearranged the work schedule so that I could have all the time off I needed, so I could be at my dad's side.

I wasn't ready to reveal my secrets to another person yet. But I didn't want to tell Louis no, either.

"Tomorrow," I said. "We'll talk tomorrow. Okay?"

"I really wish you would talk to me *now*, Steve."

"One more day," I said. "One day can't possibly make that much of a difference."

83

But I was to find out that sometimes, a single day does make a huge difference.

When I walked into the McDonald's at around 5:45 the next evening, the customer dinner crowd was light.

The restaurant seemed subdued.

I saw a familiar, grandmotherly woman sitting morosely by herself at one table. I had seen her in the restaurant many times before, even though I didn't know her name. She was friendly with Louis, who often came out of the manager's office to chat with her. (Louis was gregarious with the customers, and many of them were fond of him.)

The woman was—*crying? Could that be what I saw?*

Yes, she was definitely crying.

Could be anything, I thought. *I hope it's nothing too bad, though.* I had the impression that the woman was already a widow. Perhaps one of her children had died?

Then I headed back toward the kitchen and cash registers.

I was immediately struck by a peculiar silence in the employees' area. The fryers were running, and there was the clatter of the normal kitchen activity in the back. But there was none of the usual teenage banter.

I caught a glimpse of Scott Thomas back in the kitchen. The chubby boy, whose default mood was a kind of challenging sarcasm, looked both sad and...*awestruck*.

The cashiers were sad and awestruck, too. Jenny Tierney was crying. So was Anne Morton, the young wife and mother who routinely called off work on the weekends, so she could spend time with her husband and child.

"What's wrong?" I asked. But none of them seemed to hear me.

I decided that I would ask Louis. He would tell me.

I turned toward the open door of the manager's office, where I could see that the light was on. I stepped into the doorway.

I didn't see Louis, however. Ray Smith was sitting behind the desk.

This was most unusual. Ray Smith occasionally visited the McDonald's during business hours, but not often. He usually entrusted things to Louis, and two other managers on his payroll.

If Ray Smith was here, there was a specific reason for it. And probably not a good one.

Why were all the girls and women in the restaurant crying? Why did Scott Thomas look so sad?

I was about to find out.

84

"Ah," Ray Smith said, appraising me from behind the desk. "Come on in. And close the door behind you."

On the few occasions when I had met Ray Smith, he had carried himself with a certain bluster. That was gone now.

In fact, Ray Smith looked ready to cry, too.

I did as he told me.

The franchise owner stood up from the desk. Ray Smith was a big man in his late prime, perhaps fifty years of age. Louis had once told me that Smith had been an athlete of some renown in his younger years, a moderately successful linebacker on a college football team somewhere.

Those days were long gone, but Smith was still a big man. He had broad shoulders, and a waistline that showed the evidence of too many rich meals. Ray Smith had brown hair that was going to grey, and long sideburns, which were fashionable at that time.

He was wearing a plaid blazer, a wide-collared dress shirt and no tie, a pair of polyester dress slacks. All very common attire for a locally successful tycoon in the mid-1970s.

"Steve, isn't it?" Smith said.

"Yes sir," I replied. "Steve Wagner."

"Well, Steve, why don't you have a seat. We've got to have ourselves a talk, and I'm afraid it isn't going to be a pleasant one."

Once again, I did as asked. Smith sat down behind the desk—in what I customarily thought of as Louis's chair.

"Well, Steve," Smith began, "there is no easy or gentle way for me to tell this to you, so I'm just going to come right out and say it. Your boss, Louis Crenshaw, was killed last night. He died in a car accident."

"*What?*" I leaned forward in my chair. "*What happened?*"

No—I thought. *This can't be happening.*

"No one is exactly sure," Smith said. "It was a one-car crash. Louis drove his vehicle off the road, and crashed directly into a tree trunk. He was killed instantly, from what I understand."

I wasn't sure if this last detail brought me any comfort or not. At least Smith didn't try to console me with the speculation that Louis "didn't suffer". That's the sort of thing you say when someone passes away at eighty or ninety, after a long, full life. But Louis was dead at twenty-three.

I leaned back against the back of the chair, and tried to take in the enormity of what Ray Smith had just told me. Of everything he had told me.

I struggled to string my thoughts—and words—together.

"Last night the weather was clear," I said. "There was considerable moonlight. But you said he was killed in a one-car accident."

"That's right. It's something of a mystery. I don't believe that Louis Crenshaw was the type to use recreational drugs, or to abuse alcohol. And although he is originally from Pennsylvania, Louis has lived in this area for several years. He's very familiar with the roads around here."

"Yes. Yes, he is."

Smith paused. "Are you okay, Steve? Can I go on?"

"Yes. Please—go on."

"As I mentioned, Louis was originally from Pennsylvania, from the Pittsburgh area. His parents have been notified, and they're arranging to have his body transported back home. This means that the funeral will be held in Pittsburgh, not here. I understand that he'll be buried in the same cemetery where his grandparents are buried."

I mentally replayed my last conversation with Louis: Last night Louis had been especially distraught. He had told me that something was frightening him. Like father Malloy, like Diane in the beginning, like Jack and Carlos, Louis had some grasp of what was going on.

But he hadn't perceived the situation as clearly as I had. He hadn't read Harry Bailey's article in *Spooky American Tales*.

Some perception, some instinct, had told Louis that I was privy to more information. That made sense, in a way. Hadn't I often had the feeling that Louis was reading my hidden thoughts and intentions?

He had asked me to talk to him. He had asked me repeatedly.

And each time, I had turned him down, overly absorbed in my own troubles, or my petty aspirations for the last summer of my high school years.

And now Louis was dead.

Could I have given him any information that might have saved his life?

I supposed that I would never know the answer to that question. What was certain was that I had let him down. And now there was nothing that I, or anyone else, could do for Louis Crenshaw.

Louis Crenshaw had also been pursued by the Headless Horseman—just as I had been. But unlike me, he had had no concrete understanding of what he was dealing with.

And so, overwhelmed, he had completely lost it. He ran his car off the road, and into a tree.

Ray Smith stood up, signifying that our painful meeting had come to an end. I stood, too.

"I'll have to make some decisions regarding how to replace Louis from a work standpoint," Smith said. "Needless to say, I wasn't planning for this, and I've only just started to think about it. You, and the rest of the regular night shift employees, will be informed as soon as I've reached a decision."

He leaned across the desk and gave me an avuncular pat on the shoulder. I was certain that I saw tears in the corners of his eyes.

"I'm awfully sorry about this, Steve," he said.

85

The next day I ended my stalemate with Diane. Maybe it was Louis's death that pushed me over the edge. I felt as if I had nothing to lose.

I would accept Diane's answer—whatever it might be—but I was going to put an end to the mystery.

As I should have put an end to the mystery for Louis, I thought, while driving toward her house.

I rang the doorbell of the Parkers' house, and Diane's mother came to the door.

She didn't look pleased to see me.

"Hello, Steve." Her greeting was guarded and perfunctory.

"I want to talk to Diane," I blurted out. "If she doesn't want to see me again, that's fine. I'll accept that. But I want to hear it from her."

I heard footsteps behind Mrs. Parker. Diane appeared beside her in the semi-darkness of their house.

She was wearing a pair of blue jean cutoffs and a tee shirt. My heart ached, but I held back the expression of any further emotion.

"Okay, Steve," Diane said. "Let's go for a walk."

Mrs. Parker started to object, but Diane cut her off.

"It's okay, Mom," she said. "I'm going to step out for a while. Steve and I need to talk."

"But—"

"*But* it will be okay. Steve—Steve has a right to know."

Know what? I thought. *What did I have a right to know?*

Diane stepped outside, and stood within a foot of me. I wanted to take her into my arms; but I knew that wouldn't be appropriate, under the current circumstances.

I reached into my pocket for my car keys. Even though Diane had just suggested that we go for a walk, I assumed by default that we would go for a drive in my car. That was what we had always done, after all.

"No," Diane said. "Let's not go for a drive. Let's just go for a walk."

86

I considered this a little strange—though no stranger than her behavior in recent days. The silent treatment. The sudden and unexplained resignation from her job at McDonald's.

But if she wanted to go for a walk now, I was willing to play along.

It was early morning, and the heat of the day was just starting to come on in full force. In the distance I could hear the sound of a lawnmower.

"Come on," she said, motioning toward the street.

She made no sign of wanting to hold hands, to embrace me. That hurt.

She really had dumped me, then.

We were at the end of her driveway when I spoke.

"Listen," I began, "if you've decided that you want some other guy, I can deal with that. What I can't deal with is not knowing."

Then Diane surprised me yet again.

She leaned forward and kissed me, though only briefly.

I wanted more. I reached for her, but she gently pushed me away.

"Come on now," she said, "let's get away from my house. My mother will be watching."

"All right," I said, more confused than ever.

. . .

We were probably **two houses** down the street when Diane finally spoke.

"My dizzy spells," she said, "they aren't caused by an iron deficiency."

"What then?" I asked. Before she could answer, I added another question: "So this is it? You broke up with me because you're sick? Did you think that would make any difference to me?"

At this stage in my life, I had scant experience with illness. As I've previously mentioned, all four of my grandparents were dead by 1976.

Two of them had died from lingering illnesses. The process of their dying, however, had in both cases been hidden away from me. My parents had dealt with the doctors and nursing home officials, and then the clergymen and the funeral directors.

Besides. It wasn't as if Diane was going to—

She was, like me, only seventeen. Seventeen year-olds weren't immortal, I knew. They occasionally died in automobile accidents. But seventeen year-olds didn't die from illness.

I knew that. Everyone knew that.

What was going on, then?

"Something is really, really wrong with me," Diane said. Now I could see, for the first time, the fear in Diane's face.

I was suddenly afraid, too.

"It's called a glioblastoma," she said.

I repeated the unfamiliar term as best I could. I had no idea what a glioblastoma might be. But it sounded ominous. And, as I was about to learn, it was.

"A glioblastoma is a brain tumor," she said.

"A brain tumor?"

"Yes. That's what I just said."

"How—?"

"There is no 'how' with brain tumors. With any kind of cancer. It just happens."

I felt suddenly dizzy. This couldn't be real. Could it?

"But—but they're fixing it, *treating* it. Right, Diane? They're going to make you better."

Diane slowly shook her head. "No. It's—inoperable and untreatable."

I didn't want to ask the next question, but I couldn't not ask it, either.

"So what happens, then?"

"So the doctors tell me that I have six months, maybe a year at the outside. And then..."

Diane didn't have to complete the sentence. I knew exactly what she was getting at.

I COULDN'T ACCEPT THIS, though. I could accept the idea of the Headless Horseman returned from the dead to terrorize America in 1976. I could accept the idea that the spirit of a condemned Loyalist spy was making appearances in my house. I could accept my encounters with the Hessians.

I could even accept my father's heart attack. He was a man in his fifties, and a lifelong smoker. And he was recuperating, after all.

But I could not accept what Diane was telling me now.

"You're going to get better," I said.

"Steve, don't," she said.

"No, Diane. Don't you see? Think about everything that has happened this summer. This is a summer of, well—miracles. Many of them have been dark miracles."

I thought about the death of Louis Crenshaw which Diane probably didn't know about yet. All of this summer's miracles had been dark ones, really.

"No, Steve," she said. "Don't talk like that. Don't make this any harder on you—and on me—than it has to be."

I took both of her hands in mine.

"Diane—I don't want this to change anything between us. Do you think this changes my feelings for you?"

"Steve," she said. "I may seem normal to you now. But this tumor is going to change me. It isn't going to be pleasant."

"It won't make any difference to me."

Diane disentangled her hands from mine. Then she spoke slowly but firmly. "No, Steve. I don't want to become your project—your charity case—and I won't accept it."

"But, Diane," I said. "I—I love you."

I had never said that to a girl before. Not even to Julie Idelman. And I'll admit that it sounded a little ridiculous now. My feelings were insignificant, really, in the face of what Diane had just told me.

"You don't love me," she said. "We haven't even been going out for an entire month. You like me a lot, and I've liked you, too. If things had turned out differently, who knows what might have happened? But things are what they are."

"You're going to get better, Diane," I said. "I can feel it."

Tears were streaming down her cheeks now. "Steve, you're already making this harder on me. Please. Stop. I've been seen by three doctors, including two neurologists. They're unanimous on the diagnosis."

She wiped the tears from her face with the back of one hand. "What you need to do, Steve, is get on with your life. Forget about me."

"I can't forget about you, Diane."

"Maybe not. But you can move on. You have to move on. You don't have any choice. And it's what I want you to do."

"But—"

"No buts, Steve. Please. Let's change the subject."

"Okay."

"How's the restaurant?" she said. "How's Louis?"

Now it was my turn to deliver a bombshell. I told Diane what had happened to Louis, and the tentative conclusions I had reached regarding his death.

"I should have told him," I said.

"Maybe," Diane said. "And maybe it wouldn't have made any difference. You can never be sure about those things."

We turned around and walked back toward Diane's house. I wanted to ask her more details about her condition. But I could see that she didn't want to discuss that.

So instead I told her more about what had been going on with me—including my father's heart attack and convalescence.

"Thank God he's okay," Diane said. "And I'm sorry that I couldn't have been there for you during all that. But as you can probably understand, I was going through some difficulties of my own."

"Of course."

We reached her house again all too quickly. There was so much I wanted to say to her. I simply couldn't contain it all.

"Don't you see?" I said. "All of this stuff that's been happening of late—the Headless Horseman, and those other horrible things—they're signs that we don't really understand reality."

"Some reality we don't understand," Diane said. "But some of it we do. Louis might have been killed because he was pursued by the Headless Horseman. But based on what you've told me, his immediate cause of death was the collision of his car into a tree. So you see, Steve: Just because some aspects of reality—or what we understand to be reality—go on vacation, that doesn't mean that *everything* changes. There can be ghosts and unnatural things in this world, and people can still die from natural causes."

"I still say you're going to get better."

"Please, Steve," she said. She stood on her tiptoes and kissed me. "Please don't try to contact me again. And have a good life."

Before I could say anything in rebuttal, Diane opened the front door of her house and disappeared inside.

All things considered, there was nothing for me to do but drive home.

87

I spent the next few days trying to recover from Diane's revelation, and her instructions never to contact her again.

Could I really abide by that?

I supposed that I didn't have much of a choice. My impromptu, unsolicited visit to Diane's house had been partly spurred by my heightened emotional state. All things being equal, I wasn't one to tread where I wasn't wanted.

More than that, though, I fully believed that Diane would get better.

Diane—dying from a brain tumor, of all things?

It just didn't seem possible.

She'll get better, I told myself, *and then we'll start over.*

Sure we will...

MEANWHILE, **at the restaurant,** everyone continued to mourn Louis, even as the business of Ray Smith's McDonald's went on.

Ray Smith named an interim night shift manager, Wanda Nead. Previously Wanda had been one of the kitchen assistant managers. Wanda was about the same age as Louis had been, but she might as well have been forty. She was resolutely serious, all business, all the time.

I had never loved my job at McDonald's. (Who, in the history of humankind, has ever "loved" working at a fast food restaurant?) But I hadn't minded it, either.

Now, though, that was soured, too. Walking into McDonald's meant constant reminders of my losses: Louis and Diane.

Keith Conway continued to cast hostile stares in my direction. Did he know that Diane and I weren't even dating anymore? Did he know about Diane's illness? Probably not.

AT HOME, my father continued his convalescence. His doctors told him that he could resume his duties at the Ford plant in two weeks, provided that his health was still improving.

To the relief of Mom and me, he seemed to have ditched his cigarettes for good—though he now chewed an excessive amount of Wrigley's spearmint chewing gum in their place.

"I suppose I've had about enough cigarettes to make one life complete," he said stoically one evening. "I did enjoy my smokes; but I'm done with them, forever." He patted me on the shoulder. "I guess you were right about that one, too, son."

I responded with a statement of satisfaction at the improvement in his health. I had no desire to play a game of one-upmanship with my dad.

I might have been right about the cigarettes, but he was still the one who had waded ashore on Omaha Beach.

IT WASN'T LONG, though, before my thoughts were drawn back to that summer's unwelcome visitors from the world beyond. (And I had been on the verge of believing that it might be over.)

88

If Harry Bailey wouldn't talk to me, I decided, then perhaps I could avail myself of his subsequent writings about the Headless Horseman, and those other revolutionary ghosts.

As Leslie had pointed out, I had the May issue of *Spooky American Tales*, which wasn't the most current issue of the magazine. She had implied that the June issue would be in stock soon. With that in mind, I made another trip to the Pantry Shelf.

Leslie was behind the counter of her parents' store, as expected. But there was something "off" about her.

Her appearance, to begin with.

Leslie looked as if she had spent the past several weeks on a desert island. She was still pretty, but her appearance was haggard.

There were dark circles beneath Leslie's eyes.

I walked in, and she didn't say anything, didn't react. She hadn't even turned her head in the direction of the bell above the door.

"Leslie?" I ventured.

Finally she looked at me.

"Oh. Hi."

Under different circumstances, I might have interpreted her reply as one of arrogance or indifference. That wasn't it, though. Leslie appeared to lack the physical and mental reserves necessary to poke fun at me.

"You remember me, right? High school boy."

I waited for her to pick up the thread of her own joke.

She nodded catatonically.

I felt as if I was no longer the same person whom Leslie had teased a few weeks ago. Nevertheless, I had been prepared to gamely endure her banter.

But this new Leslie was in no mood for joking. Not only did she look exhausted, but gone, too, was her swagger, her bluster.

"What's wrong, Leslie?"

"I—I haven't been sleeping," she said. "I've been—scared."

"Scared?"

She leaned over the counter, and motioned for me to come closer. Then she looked from side to side conspiratorially, even though we were the only living souls in the Pantry Shelf.

"There's a man on a horse," she said, in a low voice. "He rides by here sometimes at night. There—there's something wrong about him. I can't say what it is."

I would have been able to tell her exactly what it was, that was wrong with the man: He had been dead for two hundred years, and he had no head.

Leslie beckoned me to step closer. I did.

"And there's this horrible woman," she said. "She comes around at night, and taps on the window. And she's—she's carrying this knife."

Marie Trumbull, of course.

"Do you believe me?" Leslie asked. "Do you believe me?"

Then Leslie did something quite unexpected. She reached forward and grabbed my wrist.

A short while ago, I would have been delighted to have Leslie touch me in any manner. But that was before I had encountered the entities that Leslie was referring to. That was before my father's heart attack, the death of Louis Crenshaw, and Diane's horrible news.

I involuntarily recoiled, twisting out of Leslie's grasp.

"The last time I was in here, Leslie, I purchased a copy of a magazine called *Spooky American Tales*. The most recent issue you had was the May issue. You told me that you might have the June issue in soon."

"Oh," Leslie continued to speak in that blank, half-asleep tone. She shook her head slowly. "No," she said, "not yet, anyway. Maybe next week—when the truck comes in."

I didn't want to wait until next week. I wanted the magazine now.

"And you don't know for sure if there will even be copies of the June issue of *Spooky American Tales* on the truck, right?"

She shook her head. "No. I'm sorry."

This was the first time that Leslie had ever apologized to me. But I was in no mood to savor that minor triumph.

"Okay. Thank you, Leslie. I guess I'll have to do without it."

I was about to go. Then she stopped me.

"Wait! There's another store that sells magazines, not far from here," she said. "Have you ever been to Clark's Convenience Mart?"

"Never heard of it," I said.

"They have a lot of magazines, but not as many as we do."

"Can you tell me how to get there?"

"Yes, I can."

Leslie gave me brief directions to the other store. Although I had not heard of the store, I was familiar with the roads she mentioned.

I thanked her. Then I gave her one final warning. "Be careful, Leslie," I said. "Be careful of that man on horseback. He isn't a man at all. And don't get near that woman, either."

Her eyes went wide. "How do *you* know about them?"

"It doesn't matter. But I'm telling you the truth. Anyway, thanks for your help. I have to be going."

"Steve—?"

I paused in the doorway. "What?"

"Do you think it will stop soon? It can't go on forever, right?"

I had no good answer for her. So I gave the most honest answer I could.

"I don't know, Leslie. I just don't know."

89

I followed Leslie's directions. But I couldn't find Clark's Convenience Mart.

Driving down one of Clermont County's endless country roads, I was concerned that perhaps I had misunderstood her. Or perhaps she had inadvertently bungled the directions. Leslie hadn't been herself today, after all.

Then I came to a store. But it wasn't Clark's Convenience Mart.

The building was old, constructed of white cinderblock. The face of the one-story structure was dirty. It needed a good cleaning, and probably a new paint job.

Nevertheless, this had to be it. I had driven for miles now, and encountered nothing but empty fields and acres of woods.

I slowed down and flicked on my turn signal.

The plank wood sign above the door read:

"Ye Olde Store. John André, Proprietor"

. . .

Maybe Clark's Convenience Mart has changed names, I thought optimistically.

I brought the Bonneville to a stop in the weed-choked gravel parking lot. In the middle of the parking lot, a small dead apple tree leaned toward the front door, an immediate and unmissable eyesore.

I silently remarked that whoever owned Ye Olde Store—this John André—really ought to clean the place up.

I was mildly suspicious of the name of the store, of course. *Ye Olde Store*. But there were plenty of business establishments that were branded with old-fashioned, or early American themes. This was especially true in 1976, that year of the Bicentennial.

Still, I should have known better, you might reasonably say.

And you'd be right—in retrospect.

I stepped out of the car and approached the front door. The windows, I saw, were darkened with something that resembled soot.

There's something unusual about this place, I thought. I shouldn't go in.

Then I noticed the little sign pasted in the adjacent, blackened window. The sign was made of plain white paper (parchment?) and handwritten in an ornate style:

"Y E O LDE S TORE caters to readers! We stock many of the latest magazines and periodicals!"

All right. This fit Leslie's description.

I decided to go in.

The door was made of wood, with a little half-window that was also blackened with soot. I pushed open the door and stepped inside a large, musty room.

I wouldn't have described the air inside as putrid, but it was stale. The place was dimly lit, too. Some sunlight did filter in through a set of windows on the far wall, but there wasn't nearly enough light.

I did see lots of shelves, though. This was obviously a store, though it seemed like more of a second-hand shop or a pawnshop than a convenience store.

I became aware of someone watching me. A clerk standing behind a counter, at the back of the little room.

The clerk didn't look exactly normal, but he wasn't Banny, the Headless Horseman, or Marie Trumbull, either. A compact man of medium height, perhaps thirty years old.

"You have magazines, right?" I asked.

The clerk nodded, and pointed me toward the far end of the store.

"Thank you." I walked in the direction that he had indicated.

Along the way, I passed through an aisle of shelves. There were no canned goods that I could see. There were pewter dishes, and what appeared to be burlap sacks of flour.

Nothing modern. Nothing from the middle-late twentieth century.

And where were the refrigeration units? The cold drinks?

I should have walked out right then, and I was about to do just that. Then I saw the shelves that bore the magazines and periodicals, all facing outward.

They were magazines and periodicals, all right, but I didn't recognize any of the titles. All were printed on plain, off-white paper. Without lifting it from the shelf, I read the front page of the first one I came to:

COMMON SENSE;

addressed to the

INHABITANTS

of

AMERICA,

On the following interesting
SUBJECTS

1. Of the Origin and Design of Government in general, with concise Remarks on the English Constitution.
2. Of Monarchy and Hereditary Succession
3. Thoughts on the present State of American Affairs
4. Of the present Ability of America, with some miscellaneous Reflections

Written by an ENGLISHMAN

I HEARD a footstep just behind me. I started and turned around.

The clerk was standing at my side now.

He was a good-looking fellow, I noticed. Fine features. Although he was completely different from Keith Conway (shorter, and far more delicate) he probably had a similar success with women.

I now took in the clerk's attire: a white shirt, knee breeches.

Plain leather shoes with a single buckle each.

Long hair tied back with a ribbon.

I had made a mistake, coming in here. Hadn't I?

The clerk gestured to the document I had been looking at: *Common Sense*. Then he spoke.

"That author wasn't an Englishman, let me tell you. I'm talking about Thomas Paine, of course, the man who wrote that seditious screed you're looking at."

I felt a chill go up my spine.

The clerk had spoken with a British accent.

Another one of them, I realized. Another *revolutionary ghost*.

But this one was different. In response to the alarm that must have been showing on my face, he smiled disarmingly—almost warmly.

"Oh, I know what you're thinking. You're thinking that I'm one of them."

"Yes," I said, in all frankness. "That's exactly what I'm thinking."

The clerk brought his hand up to his clean-shaven chin, and began rubbing it. "Hmmm," he said. "I suppose I am, in a way. But I'm nothing like that Tarleton. He's a rather crude fellow, you know."

Speaking of Banny, I did notice some differences between Banny and this one—whoever this one was.

Banny had been hostile from the get-go. But this man—he was almost...well, charming. Despite my alarm, I couldn't help liking him, in a way.

"I'm a bit of a writer myself, you know. And I do a bit of drawing from time to time, too."

He brought his hand down from his chin. I caught a glimpse of his palm. The hand was now covered in a greenish mold—graveyard mold.

He saw what I saw. He lowered the hand to the level of his waist.

"Well, what do you expect?" He was still speaking with an air of urbanity. But now there was an edge to his voice. "What do you expect, under the circumstances?" He chuckled, but the laugh didn't sound right.

Now I looked at his face again. It was the face of a corpse. Not quite as decayed as Marie Trumbull, but moving in that direction.

"Thanks," I said, trying to play it cool. "Thanks for your help. But I think I'll go now."

I stepped around him and started down the aisle.

I walked quickly—not quite running. Now I took a closer look at the items on the old-style, wooden shelves. On one of the shelves, I saw a pile of eighteenth-century bayonets. They were encrusted with blood. Beside the bayonets were what looked like a man's severed hand.

I needed to get out of there. Dropping all pretense of normalcy, I broke into a run.

Wooden shoe soles clattered behind me on the plain concrete floor.

I was opening the door when I felt one of the clerk's dry, desiccated hands graze my shoulder.

I pushed the door open. I practically leaped outside into the sunlight.

When I was a safe distance past the doorway, when I could feel the full warmth of the sun, I looked back.

The clerk stood in the doorway. I sensed that he wanted to come after me, but couldn't. He was prohibited from stepping beyond the confines of the store, perhaps.

What remained of the clerk's skin was as white as parchment. His eyes bulged from sunken sockets.

He wasn't such a good-looking fellow anymore. As with Marie Trumbull, time and death had taken away his good looks and his charms.

"Goddamn bloody rebels!" he shouted. "I'll tell you what the rebels did to me! They caught me spying, they did. And so they hung me by the neck! Even though I, as an officer and a gentleman, was entitled to a firing squad!"

I had no idea what the clerk was talking about, beyond the superficial content of his words.

"Washington himself was in on it!" he croaked. "George bloody Washington!"

"Who—who are you?" I asked.

"I'll tell you who I am! John André, is who!"

The name meant nothing to me. Then I remembered having seen the name on the sign above the door.

The clerk stepped back inside the store and closed the door behind him. I was relieved, at least, that he was unable to give chase.

Got to get out of here, I thought. That was my only concern. I was momentarily safe—or so it appeared. But who could say how long that might last?

Behind the wheel of the Bonneville now, I started the engine. I looked up and saw the changes that were already taking place:

Ye Olde Store was no more. The sign was gone, and replaced by a large FOR SALE sign, which included the name and phone number of the real estate company that was brokering the property.

The windows were still blackened with soot. The sign that I had read as an invitation to readers was now a simple, modern "NO TRESPASSING" sign, with orange letters against a black background.

From behind that very same window, I detected a trace of movement. John André was still inside the building.

I pulled out of the parking lot without looking back again.

I DROVE BACK **the way** I had come. Rattled from my most recent experience, I had no intention of driving farther into the countryside.

About midway through my return trip, yet another strange thing happened: I saw Clark's Convenience Mart. Leslie hadn't told me wrong, after all.

There was a large sign at the edge of the road that indicated the name of the store. How could I have missed it?

Then I realized: Something had wanted me to miss it.

I almost didn't stop. I wanted to drive home, to get as far away as possible from that store-not-a-store, from the vengeful spirit of John André—whoever he was. I recalled what he had said about George Washington being personally involved in his death. What was that all about?

But I also wanted to get my hands on the June issue of *Spooky*

American Tales. I had no way of knowing if Harry Bailey had written more about the Headless Horseman and the other entities in the June issue. But I was grasping at straws at this point.

I was relieved to find that Clark's Convenience Mart was a perfectly normal store, with nary a hint of anything supernatural. The woman working behind the counter had dyed black hair, and she appeared to be smoking one cigarette after another as she sat behind the counter. (This was evidenced by the overflowing ashtray beside the cash register.)

She definitely wasn't a ghost.

I walked over to the magazine rack. As Leslie had promised, it was a large selection by Clermont County standards, though not as plentiful as what was on offer at the Pantry Shelf.

I spent a few minutes looking for *Spooky American Tales* before becoming frustrated. I called out to the woman behind the counter.

"Excuse me, do you carry a magazine called *Spooky American Tales*?" I asked.

She gave me a puzzled look. "*Spooky American Tales*? Nope. Never even heard of that one. We do carry *True Detective*, though."

This response made me even more frustrated, but I held my temper in check. She probably thought that I was simply looking for any magazine that was entertaining in a sensational way.

"Thanks anyway," I said, already walking out.

When I opened the door of the Bonneville, I immediately noticed something lying on the front seat.

A sheet of old, yellowed paper. The front page of Thomas Paine's *Common Sense*.

I reached down and swept the paper off the upholstery and into the parking lot. Then I drove home, while constantly checking my rearview mirror.

90

That evening I had a rare night off from the McDonald's.—a much-needed rest, after the afternoon's events.

I watched TV with my parents, all the while thinking about my encounter with the ghoulish John André.

Who was John André? His name sounded vaguely familiar, but I couldn't place him.

Something to do with Benedict Arnold, maybe? *(André had mentioned that he had been caught spying. And hadn't Benedict Arnold been a traitor-spy on the American side?)*

I wasn't sure. Diane would have known, or she would have been able to find out. But that was a moot point now.

After watching several sitcoms, my father announced that he wanted to get out of the house for a while.

"No farther than the back yard," he promised. "I'm sure you both understand. After so many days cooped up in that hospital, I miss being outside."

I heard him step out the kitchen door, which opened into our back yard.

I knew where he would go next—where I would find him perched.

"I'm going to join dad outside," I told my mother, who was working on her needlepoint. "I could use some air, too."

I followed Dad outside, and my predictions were proven correct. Since returning from the hospital, it had become his habit to sit atop the little wooden picnic table behind our house.

We had owned the picnic table for as long as I could remember. I had childhood memories of backyard barbecues, my dad working the grill, my mother serving Jack and me burgers and hot dogs. That was before Jack had devolved into a total dead-ender.

"How are you doing, Dad?" I asked him. Despite everything else that had happened (so far) this summer, I hadn't lost sight of the fact that I had almost lost my dad, too.

"Pretty good, son," he said. "I've been taking walks down the street. I've been riding that bike, too."

My dad was referring to the flywheel stationary bike that he'd purchased from Sears Roebuck, almost immediately after his discharge. He was riding the bike every day, in order rebuild his cardiovascular capacity. Dr. Phillips had said that this was a good idea, so long as he didn't overdo it.

"Sorry again to hear about what happened to your boss," he said. "I know you liked Louis."

My dad made a quick, fidgety glance toward the field and the woods behind our house, where the shadows were lengthening. Speaking of Louis, the present scene reminded me of that night behind the McDonald's with Louis—when he had tried to get me to open up.

"This is going to sound crazy, son," Dad said now, "but I could have sworn that I heard a horse back there."

"Back there in the woods?" I asked.

"Yes."

"A *horse*?"

"Are you hard of hearing tonight, Steve?" He patted me good-naturedly on the shoulder. "Yes, a horse."

"There shouldn't be any horses back there," I said—wishing I could fully believe that.

"No, there shouldn't be," my dad agreed. "There are horses in Clermont County. But I've never seen or heard one here—this close to our neighborhood."

That was alarming. The Horseman had never directly approached my home before. Banny and Marie Trumbull, yes—but not the man with the sword, the man who beheaded people.

Worse yet, my father had been aware of his presence.

This could only mean that the Horseman was growing stronger, punching further into this world.

How long before he rode right up to our house, swinging that sword of his?

Beheading me—or beheading my parents?

"I believe I've had about enough of the night air," my dad said. He began to lift himself off the picnic table. "Let's go back inside, and watch television with your mother."

91

Driving home from McDonald's the next night, the sum of a complex set of realizations occurred to me:

The Horseman had killed many people since his return, if all the details of Harry Bailey's article could be believed. *(And after everything that had happened, I had to assume that all of the article was accurate, including the reports of the missing persons.)*

Closer to home, there had been the beheadings in Zanesville, the disappearances of Robert McMoore and Donna Seitz, and Dan Bauer.

The Horseman had almost certainly been responsible for all of those occurrences.

And yet, the Horseman had so far declined to take *my* head.

It wasn't as if there hadn't been the opportunity. I had been in his path any number of times.

But he had not taken my head.

Why?

Perhaps, I thought, I was the target of something far more complex and cruel than a simple murder.

I recalled the losses I had endured: the death of Louis, the impending death of Diane (though I hadn't yet fully accepted her diagnosis as the truth.)

The near-death of my father.

It might be that the Horseman's intention was to destroy my life by degrees, to drive me to the brink of madness.

And then, finally, he would take my life, too. He would take my head, specifically.

That was a disturbing thought. But there was another side to it, as well...

Maybe—just maybe—I would be afforded enough time and space to defeat the Horseman.

But how could I do that alone?

I had appealed to both Harry Bailey and Diane for help. Harry had refused me outright, and Diane had helped me for a short while, only to desert me.

I was jolted from these thoughts then. Something was happening to the Bonneville.

I WAS DRIVING **in that spot,** that area along my drive home where so many bad things had happened—where I'd first been pursued by the Horseman, where I'd encountered Carlos and his motorcycle-riding pals.

I felt a force like a gust of headwind jolt the Bonneville.

This didn't make sense. It was a hot, still, midsummer night.

Then I noticed that the farmland on either side of me wasn't rushing by so quickly as it had been a few seconds ago.

The car was slowing down, even though I hadn't tapped the brakes, or relaxed my pressure on the gas pedal.

I immediately knew that it wasn't ordinary engine trouble. There was no sputtering, no knocking of the engine.

The car was just...slowing down, as if a giant hand were holding it back.

I finally rolled to a full stop. Now I was sitting there, stuck in the middle of my lane. Yet the Bonneville was still in drive, and the engine continued to run as normal.

As an experiment, I depressed the gas pedal, the engine RPMs increased, but the Bonneville didn't budge.

This far into that strange summer, I knew better than to believe that something this unusual was a coincidence.

Everything was interconnected. Even car trouble. It had all been woven together by some malevolent intelligence.

I put the Bonneville in park and turned off the engine.

The next questions were: *Why exactly was I stopped here?*

And: *What did those dark powers have in store for me tonight?*

92

I saw my answer—or the beginning of my answer—in the adjacent pasture to my right.

A black archway, somewhat like a dark rainbow, dominated the far end of the grassy field. It rose high into the air.

Beneath the archway was a dark, kaleidoscopic swirl of black, brown, and purple mist.

I could see indistinct shadows moving in and behind the mist. I got the sense that this new addition to the landscape was a portal of some kind.

So now what?

My car wasn't going anywhere.

Perhaps I should investigate.

Perhaps I had no choice.

I stepped out of the Bonneville, and closed the door behind me.

I kept my eyes on the portal, waiting for the Horseman or some other horror to charge out of there. Whatever was back there, though, it didn't seem inclined to cross over to this side of that swirling mist.

I leapt across the ditch on the right side of the road. There was no fence to bar my access to the pasture. This land belonged to someone, obviously; but there was no house, nor any barns or other buildings, in the immediate vicinity.

I climbed up the little slope to the beginning of the level ground. My feet swished through the long grass.

Nothing to do now but walk to it.

When I was about halfway across the pasture, I heard a series of sounds from within the portal. Inhuman, unearthly sounds.

Those sounds almost sent me back where I came from. I could have gone back, I supposed. It was clear to me, however, that whatever forces had brought me here wanted me to pass through this gateway.

I had a bottle of holy water in my pocket, but it might or might not work against whatever awaited me on the other side of that misty barrier.

I kept walking.

As I walked, I became ever more aware of the size of the portal. It was immense, looming over me.

I caught another flash of movement on the other side of the mist. The mist, I discerned, comprised a limited depth around the entrance.

I continued walking. Now I could hear a series of what sounded like—

Human screams.

Finally I was so close that I had to make an irrevocable decision: Enter or turn back.

I entered.

Then things got really strange.

The mist was cold and moist against my skin, and it had an acidic feel. I closed my eyes against a mild acrid sting.

Keep walking, I told myself.

After a few steps, I no longer felt the mist. I opened my eyes slowly. It took a few seconds for my vision to clear.

Even before my eyes fully adjusted, though, I became aware that I had shifted to some other place.

The ground beneath my feet was no longer the grassy, spongy

texture of the pasture. It was hard-packed earth. I glanced down into the dirt and saw the outlines of horses' hoofprints—normal hoofprints. I was in the middle of a dirt roadway that was a center for traffic—not of cars, but of horses.

The air around me had an unfamiliar smell. It wasn't unpleasant, exactly—just different.

Then, up ahead of me, I saw the outlines of a town.

I had grown up in this section of Clermont County. I had driven down the country road that connected to this pasture more times than I could count.

I knew quite well that there was no town around here.

I wasn't in Ohio anymore. And I probably wasn't in 1976 anymore, either.

93

I was walking toward the town.
It would be better described as a little settlement. It looked like something that would have been found on the American frontier...Or maybe in the New England countryside, around the time of the American Revolution.

The settlement appeared to be deserted. Presumably I was now in a time before electric lights. But I didn't see any sign of candle- or lantern light, either.

"Steve!" someone said, to my immediate left.

It took me only a split second to identify the voice. It was—

No, it couldn't be.

Louis Crenshaw's body, I knew, was now embalmed and lying beneath six feet of ground in a graveyard near Pittsburgh. *Buried near his grandparents*, Ray Smith had said.

Louis was dead.

But not here, he wasn't. Not in this version of reality.

Louis Crenshaw was standing about ten feet away from me. He didn't look ghoulish, or disfigured from his fatal accident. He looked perfectly normal, perfectly solid and alive. He was wearing his McDonald's uniform—the only thing I ever saw him wear.

And he was smoking a cigarette.

Just like Louis.

"Louis!" I said.

He took a drag on his cigarette and nodded.

"I would say 'in the flesh'," he said, "but I'm not sure that's entirely accurate."

"You can smoke here?" I blurted out.

"Yes," Louis said. "And no. The fuzzy point here is the difference between what is, and what you see. You remember me as a chain smoker, always with a cigarette in my hand, so that's how I'm revealed to you now. Does that make sense?"

I didn't know how to respond. None of this made sense, in conventional terms.

"I don't know what to say," I said honestly. "What are you doing here?"

"Let's just say that I have a bit more—mobility—now. The important question isn't what am *I* doing here. The important question is: What are *you* doing here? You shouldn't be here, buddy. This is a dangerous place."

"Is it more dangerous than it is out there?" I asked, pointing back the way I had come. "With that damn Horseman running around? And all those other things, too?"

"Yes," Louis answered. "Back there, those things are out of their element. Sometimes, you might even have the upper hand on them. But here, you're in *their* element, and they're way more powerful. Understand?"

I nodded. I thought about how I had banished Marie Trumbull with salt, and destroyed the Hessian soldiers with my Louisville Slugger.

In the "real" world, they were like aquatic predators on land. Still dangerous—but disadvantaged.

"I'm sorry, Louis," I said. "I'm sorry I didn't tell you everything I knew—before."

Louis shrugged. "Water under the bridge. Don't worry about it, Steve. Worry about your own situation. You've come in to kind of a bad place here."

My surprise at seeing Louis, at seeing him (apparently) alive, had caused me to momentarily forget about my present predicament. I had, after all, wandered across a field at night, and passed into what appeared to be another dimension of space and time.

And based on what Louis had just said, a *dangerous* dimension of space and time.

Then something started happening to Louis.

He no longer looked solid. He took on the appearance of a hologram.

Then he started to break up, like an image on a screen that was slowly fading to black.

"Louis—what's happening to you?"

Louis seemed far less alarmed than I was.

"The problem is," he said, "that I don't belong in this place any more than you do. I can't stay here, Steve. I'm sorry."

"Should I go back, then?"

"No," Louis said sympathetically. "You don't have that option. You can't go back the way you came. You can only go forward, and find your way through to the other side."

I had no idea what he might mean by that. I needed more information.

"Louis! Wait!"

Louis didn't wait, though, and perhaps he was unable to. I watched helplessly as a Louis gradually dissolved into nothing.

What had I expected? Louis was dead, after all.

And I had other things to worry about.

Plenty of other things.

94

I heard a commotion to one side of me. The sounds of cannon and musket fire. Men fighting and dying, crying out in agony.

I looked in the direction of the noise. To my left, down a hillside, I stared into a long, wide valley. A nighttime battle was taking place there. Although the valley was dark, there was a glow from the flames of warfare.

There were men wearing blue uniforms, and men wearing the red of the British Empire. Another group of men was wearing uniforms that might have been blue or green. These men were fighting alongside the British.

Hessians.

Then I saw a familiar menace, adding even more destruction to the scene.

I could see the figure of the Headless Horseman riding among the Colonial ranks. He was swinging his sword, decapitating the rebel soldiers.

I was pretty certain that what I was seeing here was not the American Revolutionary War that I'd learned about in school. I was no historian; but even I knew that there had been no such battle as this

—an engagement in which an undead Hessian officer played a decisive role.

And yet, at the same time—I *was* watching a scene from the American Revolutionary War. This was some version of it that was playing out in an alternate reality.

I looked over my shoulder, in the direction from which I had entered this strange netherworld. If the portal was still there, I couldn't see it. I saw what looked to be a continuation of the primeval forest of eighteenth-century America.

I remembered what Louis had said: *"You can't go back the way you came, you can only go forward, and find your way through to the other side."*

I supposed that I would have to go through, then. There didn't seem to be much in this town to go through, though.

And down below me in the valley, that horrible battle.

I hoped Louis didn't mean to say that I had to go through *that*.

"*Hey, you!*" I heard someone call out.

Several things I noticed immediately about the young male voice: It sounded nonthreatening—concerned for my welfare, even—and it was characterized by an early American, quasi-British accent.

"*Hey, you!*" he said again. "*Yer going to get yerself kilt!*"

I scanned the town, to try to locate the source of the voice.

A young boy, perhaps nine or ten years old, was peering out at me from behind the edge of one of the town's no-frills wooden buildings.

I acknowledged him with a wave.

"*Well, don't just stand there!*" he said, dispelling any doubt I might have harbored about him addressing me. "Wot do you think this is? The May Day festival? You'd better git out of the middle of the road, or that headless bugger with the sword is goin' to come up here and lop yours off, lemme tell you!"

I took another look down the long hillside into the valley.

Men were still fighting and dying. I heard the distinct, loud boom of a cannon.

But the Headless Horseman wasn't there anymore.

Could that mean that he was coming up here?

"Come on!" the boy repeated. "Whatsamatter? You got cotton in yer ears?" He waved me toward him.

I had no other options. I ran in his direction.

95

I met him at the side of that roughly constructed, wooden building. It might have been a private residence or a small warehouse. I couldn't be sure. It was too dark to make out many details.

He barely waited for me to arrive to where he stood. Then he said, *"Come on! We got to take cover!"*

I followed him. (Again, what other option did I have?) He was leading me down a narrow dirt and mud street. Obviously he had a safe destination in mind.

Hopefully he had a safe destination in mind.

"Who are you?" I ventured.

"I'm Giles," he said impatiently.

"Do you live around here, Giles?"

Giles didn't answer me directly.

"I be around here," he said.

A vague answer, with various interpretations.

"I'm Steve," I said.

Giles stopped and turned around.

"Very good, Steve! I be very glad to meet you! But we ain't got time for pleasantries right now. Come on! We can't stay here—out in the open. It isn't safe!"

Having thus scolded me, the boy Giles whirled back around and kept walking.

"*Walk fast!*" he said. "*Keep up!*"

We made several turns at right angles through the narrow streets.

Finally Giles ducked into the doorway of another unpainted wooden structure. It was little more than a log cabin, really. The door of the cabin was nothing more than a large sheet of moldy canvas, suspended from the top of the doorframe.

I followed him inside, pushing the canvas out of my way.

Once inside the poorly lit interior, the first thing that struck me was the smell of cooking. I saw a stone hearth. A large black pot was suspended over a low-grade fire. That fire was the only source of illumination in here.

Stew. Someone was making stew.

I had never been inside an ordinary, Colonial American dwelling, of course. But if I would have imagined what one might look like, this would be it. In addition to the hearth and the cooking fire, I saw an obviously handmade table and three chairs (made of wood, of course); and on the far wall a musket and a powder horn hung from pegs.

The next thing I noticed was that Giles and I weren't alone in the little cabin.

There were two adults, who—based on the circumstances—I assumed to be a married couple. The man and the woman both appeared to be somewhere in that indeterminate country of middle age.

They were both the products of a hard life, too. The woman was a bit chubby and rosy-cheeked. She wore a simple homespun dress. The man was thin, and he had a long, dour face. He was wearing a simple white blouse and brown trousers—also homespun, from what I could tell.

"Are these your parents?" I asked Giles.

The woman answered for him. "No, we ain't his parents. But Giles, he's a right fine boy, and me and me husband, Joby, here, we takes care of him." She looked in the direction of the far-off tumult of battle, which carried through the walls of the little house. There was another loud cannon blast.

"Giles," the woman said, assessing me. "Who's this?"

"I'm Steve," I said. "I'm not from around here."

"Ain't none of us from around here, originally," the man said.

I would have liked to have drawn the man out on that point. But we all heard the sound of approaching hoofbeats.

"It's that headless bugger!" the man said, his face suddenly darkening with anger. He turned and lifted the musket and powder horn off the wall. From another peg he plucked a tricorn hat.

"No!" Giles said. "You can't stop 'im with a musket!"

"There ain't no choice!" the older man said. "If I don't face 'im, he'll come in here and kill us all!"

96

Giles and I followed his surrogate father out into the street. By this time he had put on his tricorn hat. He had also loaded his musket. This was a complicated procedure involving a paper cartridge and a ramrod. I couldn't make heads or tails of the process, but it was obviously second-nature to this fellow.

The woman called out from the doorway, *"Be careful, Joby!"*

I thought: Joby—I knew his name now—was about to confront the Headless Horseman with a musket. How can one do that carefully?

Joby looked at me. "I'll distract the bloody bugger, and Giles here will show you the way out."

I could see tears streaming down Giles's face. "Be careful, Joby!"

The clattering hoofbeats suddenly increased in volume. The Headless Horseman was upon us. We just hadn't seen him yet.

"You two get goin'!" Joby said, addressing Giles and me.

There was a sudden chill in the air. We all looked toward the nearest intersection. The Headless Horseman had arrived, seated atop his undead horse.

The animal looked at me just then. I could have sworn I saw recognition in those glassy dead eyes.

"Come on!" Giles yanked my arm.

The Horseman turned in his saddle, toward Giles and me.

He was about to give chase.

Then a shot rang out.

I saw a tiny explosion in the center of the Horseman's chest.

Joby had shot him with the musket.

The Horseman turned away from the two of us. His horse reared up in the air.

"Run, you two!" I heard Joby shout.

"Come on!" Giles yanked my arm again. And he took off running.

I followed him.

97

We were at the opposite edge of the town. Giles held up his hand for me to stop.

I wondered about Joby, and if he had escaped the Horseman.

I wondered about a lot of things.

"Who are you, Giles?" I asked. "I mean, who are you, really?"

Without turning around, the boy said, "You ask too many questions. Come on! I'm trying to get you out of here alive. If that whapper on the horse catches you, he'll carve you up into little pieces. Won't even be nothing left o' you to put into an eternity box."

I almost asked him for a translation but stopped myself. I didn't know what a "whapper" was, but I could grasp the gist of what Giles had said. "Eternity box" referred to a coffin, no doubt.

Giles scanned the distance, peering into the darkness.

"What are you looking for?" I asked.

"The gate. Help me look, why dontcha?"

I joined him in gazing into the darkness beyond the town.

I heard the whinnying of a horse from far behind us.

Another shot from a musket.

Good. That was a sign that Joby was still alive (whatever "alive" meant in this place). But for how long?

"There!" Giles said. "See it?"

"No."

"Look again!"

I looked again, and I saw it: A curtain-like, purplish cloud. A small version of an aurora borealis.

"That there is the boundary," the boy said. "Make it through there, and you'll get back...to wherever it is you came from."

"All I have to do is pass through there?"

"That's right. At least—I think so."

"You think so."

"Enough with your questions, already! Git goin'!"

"Okay. I'm going."

I started forward. I took off in a run, in fact.

I was halfway to the portal. I could feel traces of that cold, acrid mist on my skin already, carried on the light breeze.

I could also hear a sucking sound, like rushing air being drawn into a vacuum.

Suddenly, I heard Giles cry out: *"Wait!"*

I paused, and looked back at him.

"What?"

"Watch out for the bloody imps!" he said.

"Imps?" I asked.

What were imps? Elves, maybe?

I could see Giles struggling to formulate a concise explanation. Then the boy shook his head in frustration.

"Never mind!," he said. *"No—don't come back! There's no time to explain. Maybe you won't even see 'em. Just be careful. That's all!"*

"All right," I shouted. I was dubious. I suspected that he had left out an important, possibly life-or-death detail. At that moment, though, I wanted nothing more than to get out of that horrible netherworld, where some spectral version of the American Revolution never ceased.

"Oh!" Giles called out. "There's one other thing!"

"What?" I shouted back. "What now?"

This close to the portal, my transition from one world to the next was already underway. Giles was fading away now. I could still see him, but he was indistinct, like a hologram. The outlines of the town were starting to fade, too.

"When he tries to take it back, don't give it to 'im!" Giles shouted.

"Take what back?" I called out. "Who?"

Giles cried out an answer, but I didn't hear it. The boy faded into a cloudlike shape. Behind him, the town dissolved into the nighttime darkness.

"Whatever it was," I said aloud to myself, "hopefully it wasn't too important."

98

I made my final dash for the portal. But I wasn't alone.

A cluster of shadowy figures was barring my way. They were roughly human in shape, but much smaller: no taller than two feet.

At first I mistook them for small trees or shrubs.

Then they started moving.

I recalled Giles's parting words: *Watch out for the bloody imps!*

These were the imps, apparently. I had found them—or they had found me.

There was nothing for me to do but attempt to move through them. As Louis had said, I couldn't go back, I could only go forward. Going forward, moreover, was the only course that would take me out of this horrific place.

As I ran toward the imps, their twisted, misshapen faces—part reptilian, part humanoid—came into focus. Their hands were like claws, with sharp talons at the fingertips.

One of the imps opened its mouth and made a blood-curdling, high-pitched scream. The cry was vaguely avian. Inside its mouth, I could see rows of razor-sharp teeth.

I was directly upon them now. They didn't scatter as I had half-hoped would be the case.

Instead, they leapt at me. I felt tiny claws digging into the fabric of my jeans. Then there was an additional, oppressive weight on my body that momentarily stopped me in my tracks.

They were attempting a group tackle, I realized.

I let out a battle cry of my own. Then I persisted, powered by fear, rage, and adrenalin. If I allowed myself to be tackled, I would be entirely at the mercy of those sharp teeth and claws.

I was playing a high-stakes game here. The imps would rip me apart, disemboweling me while I was still alive.

Two of the imps were yet clinging to me—one on each side. I swung my right fist and connected solidly with a hard, scaly forehead. That imp screeched in anger, and fell to the ground.

Then I felt a sudden, sharp pain in my abdomen.

The other imp was biting me.

"You little—!" I shouted. I squirmed desperately to dislodge the other imp.

This slowed me down. While I was doing that, the others began to swarm upon me again.

I felt another sharp bite. I twisted my body around so that I could punch the clinging imp with my right fist.

I knocked it off.

I delivered kicks to the others. But not before they delivered more bites.

The portal was only a few yards away from me now.

I summoned all of my strength and made the final dash.

As I did, another imp leapt onto my back.

A sharp pain in my shoulder. I didn't cry out. Instead, I hit the thing with my right elbow.

It fell off.

I sprinted into the layer of mist.

The screeching of the imps died out behind me.

99

I half-ran, half-limped back toward my car. I could feel bites all over my body.

The pain from the imps' bites dispelled any suspicions I might have had about the netherworld having been some kind of a dream or illusion—or "virtual reality" to use a term that wasn't yet common in 1976.

The imps had been real. *All* of it had been real.

But I couldn't have proven that to anyone on the Ohio, 1976 side of the portal. When I judged myself a safe distance from the portal, curiosity compelled me to turn around and look. (I also wanted to make sure that none of the imps had followed me across the boundary.)

I breathed a sigh of relief when I noted that there were no scaly, chittering imps chasing me across the meadow.

The portal was also gone. There was nothing where it had been. I could see all the way to the wooded hillside at the end of the meadow. The same scenery that had always been there.

I resumed the walk back to my car.

. . .

But I wasn't the only one who had sought out the Bonneville that night.

I was on the far side of the drainage ditch beside the road before I noticed: Marie Trumbull was in the back seat of my car, leering at me with a desiccated smile, a mouth half-empty of teeth.

I had not seen her since that morning she appeared in the hallway outside my bedroom, since I'd flung the salt at her.

For the umpteenth time this night, I had no choice but to take some kind of action. I was too far from home to walk. I would need to drive. Nor could I in good conscience abandon my car to this monstrosity.

Which meant that I had to get her out of my car.

I walked up to the Bonneville.

"Get out!" I shouted at her, through the glass.

Marie pointed the tip of her rusty knife at me. Her dead mouth opened. I could hear her speak, even though she could barely move the dried husk of her face.

"How about you come in here, boy?"

"How about you come out and get me?" I countered.

I flung open the back door, as if inviting her out. Then I took a few steps backward, beyond lunging distance.

She made a little hissing sound.

"What's the matter?" I challenged her. "Are you afraid of me? Come on out!"

Her reply was not long in coming. A voice in my head.

"You bloody little bastard! I'll slice off your jewels and feed 'em to the hogs."

"Let's just see you try that, bitch. I'm right here. But you have to come out to get me."

Without being too conspicuous, I slipped the little bottle of holy water out of my jeans pocket. I silently prayed that Father Malloy hadn't forgotten to bless this batch.

Marie's body rose out of the backseat of my car. She stood directly before me in the road.

The blade of Marie's suicide knife glinted in the moonlight. Marie

Trumbull might be a ghost, but that knife of hers was very real. Marie, moreover, was not one of the zombie-like Hessians. She was an intelligent spirt, and one with malevolent intentions.

"*Now let's hear you boast, you little bastard rebel boy!*" she said.

In two quick motions, I unscrewed the lid of the little jar, and I threw the holy water at her. At first nothing happened.

Please, please, please, I thought.

Then something happened. There was a sound of something sizzling, a foul smell that forced me to take yet another step backward.

Marie's body began to split apart, as if it were being ripped by giant, unseen hands. The fabric of her dress was shorn apart and dissolved into faint traces of dust. Her chest crumbled inward.

In a rapidly accelerated process of decomposition, what remained of her face shriveled away and fell off. Her remaining hair fell out.

Her eyes retracted inward and shrunk to nothing, leaving only black sockets. Her jaw fell open.

I heard her knife fall to the pavement. Then her rapidly disappearing corpse fell, too.

She had a final menace in store for me: One skeletal hand detached itself from the rest of her, and took on a brief life of its own. Marie Trumbull's hand skittered across the pavement, seeking me.

I jumped aside. The hand stopped at the edge of the road. It broke up into its constituent bones: phalanges, carpals, and metacarpals.

Then those broke apart, too, and dissolved themselves into indistinguishable piles of dust.

100

After I drove home, I stripped before the mirror in our hall bathroom, and looked at the reflection of my body—at the bite marks from the imps.

I had a series of welts on my back, flank, and legs.

Now a new worry came to mind: Would the bites become infected?

I knew that this problem was outside the bounds of conventional medical knowledge. I would gain nothing by worrying.

So I did the only thing I could do: I washed the welts with soap and water. Then I applied a generous coating of mercurochrome to each one.

I would either get some horrible disease from the bites, or I wouldn't, I decided.

After treating my wounds, I went directly to my bedroom and went to sleep.

After work the following night, Keith Conway finally brought the simmering confrontation between us to a head.

Since the reversal that sent Diane in my direction (for a short while, at least), there had been an end to Keith's banter. This had been replaced by glares, as I have mentioned. Other than that, though, I had the impression that he was avoiding me.

But not tonight.

I walked out of the McDonald's at 10:45 p.m., and Keith Conway and his friends were smoking a joint beneath the glow of the halogen lights. Just like that night a few weeks ago, when I'd first heard the hoofbeats on the country road.

As I entered the parking lot, Keith made eye contact with me. I stared right back at him. Then he turned to his friends. But rather than egging them into some ridicule of me, he gestured for them to take off.

That told me that Keith was serious about this. Whatever he had planned, he didn't want an audience. Very unusual for Keith Conway.

When I was a young boy dealing with my first playground scraps, my father had once told me, "Son, never let a bully chase you. But it is perfectly all right to avoid him. You can walk away, but never run."

With those words in mind, I made a beeline for the Bonneville. I walked slowly but deliberately.

Keith had other ideas, though. He stepped directly in front of me.

"It's time for you and me to have a talk," he said.

"Really"? I asked, as slowly and as calmly as I could. "I doubt that. What could you and I possibly have to talk about, Keith?"

"Diane, for one thing."

"You don't know anything about Diane," I said.

I might have had a window of opportunity, just then, to defuse the situation. But I wasn't in a defusing mood.

"It's no wonder she dumped you," I added. "You're such an idiot. A complete loser."

A guy like Keith Conway wouldn't necessarily like being called an idiot. But "loser" was a true fighting word, and Keith Conway did indeed, come at me ready to fight.

Most of my brawls up till now had occurred in childhood or early adolescence, against opponents who were also children or adolescents. This fight was going to be more dangerous, because Keith had the size and strength of a grown man.

But I was committed now.

"You son-of-a-bitch!" he growled, coming for me.

I swung my fist in the general direction of Keith's face. He was a more experienced fighter than me, and he had a longer reach. Keith easily parried my blow with his left forearm.

He swung for my stomach. His fist connected.

Keith's punch landed like a sledgehammer.

I felt like my stomach had just been ripped out. I struggled not to double over. If I lost my upright stance, I knew, it would be all over.

But I did take a step backward, a deliberate feint.

Keith came after me, but he momentarily let his guard down.

I saw my opening, and I swung. This time my haymaker connected. I felt my knuckles strike Keith on one temple.

"*Oof!*"

He stumbled backward.

I came after him, and jabbed him in the stomach, just as he had done to me.

"*Ugh!*"

Was I winning this fight? I wondered vaguely.

Not exactly, I figured. But I was holding my own, at least.

Then we were interrupted.

"*Stop it, you two! Keith! Steve!*"

It was Wanda Nead, the interim manager whom Ray Smith had named to replace Louis for the time being.

Keith and I separated. Maybe we were both feeling chastened. And maybe we both had the sense that one of us was going to get hurt, if this went on much longer.

Wanda was not the least bit intimidated by two large teenage boys, nor by our testosterone-charged violence. She marched out, and stood between us.

"What the hell's going on?" she demanded

"This son-of-a-bitch attacked me!" Keith said. "That's what happened."

I was flabbergasted. After playing the tough guy, and after more or less waylaying me, Keith was now turning tattletale.

"I don't care which one of you started it," Wanda said. "From what I could see, you were both going at it. You're both guilty, so far as I'm concerned."

Neither Keith nor I had anything to say to that.

"Go home now, both of you!" she shouted. "And don't come back until you're ready to act like civilized human beings, instead of two wild animals."

"All right," I said. I started toward my car. "All I wanted was to go home and be left alone, anyway. In peace."

Before he headed for his Trans Am, the no longer quite so glorious "love machine", Keith Conway said to me, "Enjoy your peace while you've got it, Wagner."

"Keith, go home now, while you still have a job here!" Wanda said. "Because you're skating on thin ice right now."

I left it at that. I could practically feel Keith's angry stare following me, all the way to my car.

This isn't the end of this, I thought, as I slid into the front seat of the Bonneville.

I was right about that—but I had no idea, at the moment, how things would end with Keith.

101

The following morning I awoke feeling a little sore.

The injuries I had sustained in that netherworld—the bites from the imps—still smarted. But at least they didn't seem to be infected. I continued the treatments with mercurochrome.

Meanwhile, overnight my abdomen had blossomed into a Rorschach pattern of black and purple bruises—the results of my scuffle with Keith.

I spent the day recuperating, loafing around the house.

I wasn't scheduled to work that night at McDonald's. That was just as well. I wondered if Wanda Nead was going to write Keith and me up, if another shoe was going to drop there.

A disciplinary write-up at my part-time McDonald's job. If only that had been the only shoe that was about to fall.

THAT EVENING, as twilight was settling in, I walked out into the back yard, and found my father sitting on the picnic table again.

He was staring back into the wooded, overgrown area behind our back yard, where he had recently heard the sound of a horse whinnying. The untamed woods and field were separated from our property with a simple fence of log posts and steel wire.

Dad was staring into those woods, as if transfixed by something.

My dad heard me coming.

"Hi, Steve," he said.

"Hi, Dad."

There was something about my father's demeanor that struck me as a little "off".

"Everything okay, Dad?"

My father's heart attack had been a real setback for him, and a scare for us; but he remained the man who was larger than life in my estimation. That would never change.

In this moment, however, he looked…rather scared himself.

"To tell you the truth, son, I'm feeling a little nervous."

"Nervous?"

I didn't believe that my father had ever been nervous, not in his entire life. I waited for him to go on.

"I—I don't know what it is," he said. "It's probably just a feeling that lingers from my time in the hospital. Sometimes I would get little attacks of the heebie-jeebies at night there, you know. I had bad dreams."

"Dreams? About what?"

He shook his head. "You would think it's silly."

"Try me."

My father spoke shakily. "I had dreams about this woman. She was—horrible. She was a monster. And she—she carried a knife."

A horrible woman who carried a knife? I knew exactly who my father was talking about. He was talking about Marie Trumbull.

As I was contemplating this latest revelation from my father, I heard something in the wooded area behind our house.

The whinnying of a horse. An undead horse reanimated by something evil. It had been unmistakable.

Dad made no reaction, though. Hadn't he heard it, too?

"I dreamt about that woman almost every night I was in the hospital," my father went on. "Strange. You would think, after all the horrible experiences I had during the war, I would get flashbacks about that. But instead I dreamt about that woman." He paused and shook his head. "I have no idea where she came from."

I momentarily looked away from my father. I had heard the sounds of movement in the high weeds and foliage on the other side of the fence.

The Headless Horseman, sitting atop that horrible mount of his, was moving slowly out of the woods and into the pasture.

He was approaching the edge of our backyard.

He drew his sword from the scabbard.

"Go inside," I told my dad.

"What?" Dad asked. "Why?"

I looked back at the Headless Horseman again. It was almost full dark, but I could see that long beheading sword of his in full detail. I could make out the rotting fabric of his military frock coat.

He couldn't move into our yard. Not yet. But every day, the boundary was growing thinner. He was getting closer.

In a few more days—possibly as soon as tomorrow, in fact—he would be able to ride right up to our house.

And then he would be able to kill my father with that sword.

Or maybe I was wrong about that, too. Maybe the Headless Horseman was already capable of crossing the boundary.

"Dad," I said. "You're going to have to trust me. There's something back there, just past our back yard."

"What are you talking about, son?" Dad said. I noticed, however, that he did not do the obvious thing: He did not look where I was looking.

It was as if he knew that the Horseman was there, but he was refusing to look. Refusing to accept the reality that he could not reconcile with his beliefs about the nature of things.

"I don't have time to explain, Dad. Let's just say that it has something to do with that woman you dreamt about."

Ordinarily, my father would have immediately lost patience with this kind of cryptic talk from me. As I mentioned, he wasn't a man given to philosophical and metaphysical speculations.

But now, he did as I had told him to do. He gently eased himself off the picnic table, and followed me inside the house.

Once we were inside the house, I gave my father another set of instructions. I knew that I was pushing my luck here; but I had no choice.

"Dad, it would be best to avoid sitting back there on that picnic table. At least in the evenings."

Dad nodded slowly as he eased himself into his beloved La-Z-Boy recliner.

"I didn't see anything out there son," Dad said. "But all right. If you say so, Steve."

102

After that evening in the backyard, I was once again acutely aware of how overwhelmed—how out of my depth—I was. I needed help. I needed help from someone who understood these things better than I did.

I decided to give Harry Bailey one more try.

I still had his number. I waited until the middle of the morning the next day, as I had previously caught Bailey at home at that hour. I was careful not to call too early. Harry Bailey had sounded tipsy the first time I'd called. A man with such habits would probably not be an early riser.

I dialed the Detroit phone number, held my breath, and hoped for the best.

The phone stopped ringing after four rings. I heard a click. I waited for Harry Bailey's phlegmatic "Hello" over the line. What I got instead, though, was a burst of static, followed by the following recording, in Harry Bailey's voice:

"I'm not available at the moment. Please leave your name, number, and a brief message. I'll call you back as soon as possible."

Today there is scarcely a phone on the planet—digital or analog—that doesn't have voicemail functionality. In 1976, though, voicemail was cutting-edge technology. A few companies sold large, clunky answering machines that could be hooked up to a landline. These machines recorded both the outgoing greeting and incoming messages via cassette tape.

I had never left a voicemail message before. (Once again, not an unusual thing in 1976.) I started speaking, feeling awkward and self-conscious as I addressed the machine.

"Mr. Bailey. This is Steve Wagner from Ohio, calling you again."

Now what? I wondered. I had anticipated an interactive conversation. I hadn't anticipated that I would essentially have to deliver a monologue.

"Mr. Bailey," I went on. "I know you don't want to talk to me. I know you think that I'm some kind of a crank, or attention-seeker. But I'm telling you the truth: I've had direct, personal experiences with the things you've been writing about. I have seen the Headless Horseman. I've seen Marie Trumbull."

I paused for a moment, before adding, "I think I destroyed Marie Trumbull, in fact. Or I sent her back to where she came from. Maybe. I'm not sure.

"But I'm in real trouble now. The Headless Horseman has been appearing near my house. And I think he intends to kill my parents.

"I need your help, Mr. Bailey. I have no idea what I'm doing here. It's been a horrible summer for me, so far."

I thought about that statement for a moment. It *had* been a horrible summer. Louis was dead, and Diane insisted that she was going to die. My father had made it through his heart attack, but now he faced a new threat. The threat that he would not accept, and that I could neither banish nor explain to him.

"Please, Mr. Bailey. Please help me."

With that I hung up the phone. Based on my previous conversation with the magazine writer, I did not expect any reply.

103

Two nights later, I was working the cash register at McDonald's, when Wanda Nead interrupted me.

Wanda was still angry at me over my fisticuffs with Keith. I supposed that I couldn't blame her. If you had told me two months ago that I would be involved in a fistfight in the parking lot of McDonald's, I would have called you crazy.

But so much had changed since then.

"You have a guest waiting for you in the dining room," Wanda said. "An older man. A chainsmoker and a coffee drinker."

"Do you know who he is?" I asked.

"He didn't give his name. All he said was that he was here to see Steve Wagner."

I was puzzled. Who would come to see me here at McDonald's? I knew immediately that it wouldn't be my father, as he would have approached me directly at the counter.

Dad, moreover, was no longer a smoker.

"You can take your break now," Wanda said, "and go talk to him. He seems harmless enough, if a tad eccentric."

. . .

Since Wanda had made a point of mentioning that my unannounced guest was a chain smoker, I headed directly for the smoking section of the dining room. It didn't take me long to spot my visitor.

He was a man of medium height, with white hair, a florid complexion, and a mustache that needed trimming. I could see sweat stains in the armpits of his short-sleeved white dress shirt. The shirt could have used a good ironing. He wore a plain brown tie, wide in the style of the times.

And he was indeed drinking a large coffee. He was also smoking a cigarette, while he was reviewing some papers that he had brought with him in a manila file folder. I noticed an attache case on the floor beside him.

I also noticed that there were two spent cigarette butts in the aluminum ashtray on his table. He was presently smoking a third cigarette. Wanda hadn't lied about him being a chainsmoker, either.

"Excuse me," I said. "My name is Steve Wagner. My manager said you were here to see me."

The man looked up from his papers and gave me a brief assessment. He nodded, and smiled. His teeth were tobacco-stained.

"So you're Steve Wagner."

In that instant, it all became clear. I didn't know how Harry Bailey had found out that I worked here at the McDonald's, or why he had chosen to approach me here. But I recognized his voice, from our first conversation, and from the outgoing message on his answering machine.

He stood and proffered his hand.

"Harry Bailey," he said.

"You—you came!" I said, astounded. "You got my second phone call!"

I shook his hand, and he sat back down. Then Harry took a long, leisurely drag on his cigarette.

"I did indeed get your second phone call," he said, with a tight smile. "But that wasn't what finally prodded me into taking a drive down here to pay you a visit. It was the little lady who convinced me."

"*Little lady*'...?" I said.

Harry glanced at his watch. "Speaking of which: She should be along any minute now. I'm talking about that Diane, of course. Nice girl, from what I can tell."

Now I remembered: I had told Diane about my first unfruitful conversation with Harry Bailey. She had suggested that I give her his phone number. I had written the number down in her notebook, but I had thought no more of it since then.

"Steve."

It was Diane.

Without thinking, I moved forward to embrace her. I gave her a quick kiss, not overdoing it, as we were in the dining room of the McDonald's.

She didn't pull away. When we broke the kiss, Harry Bailey was looking at us, with raised eyebrows.

"Well, well," he said. "I suppose I should have expected as much." He smiled approvingly. "But anyway, Steve, I'm here to discuss the matters to which you alluded in your two telephone calls to my residence. Diane here assures me that it's the real deal."

"It is the real deal," I insisted. "I—we—have so much to tell you about. But—" I hesitated.

"But what?"

"I—I need to get back to my cash register," I said. "I'm in the middle of my shift."

"That's quite all right," Harry said. "I'm going to be in town for a couple of days. Based on the testimony of Miss Parker, I do believe the two of you are really on to something."

"We'll be glad to tell you all about it," I said. "But tell me, is there anything you can do to help us get rid of it?"

Harry Bailey gave me another tobacco-stained smile, and patted the pile of papers atop the table. "I can make no guarantees," he said. "But I just might have some information here that can help you out."

"Great!" I said. "When do we get started?"

"Let's waste no time," Harry said. "How about tomorrow morning? I'm rather fond of McDonald's coffee, so we could convene right here. Let's meet at an early, but civilized hour. What say nine o'clock?"

"Nine o'clock works for me. What about you, Diane?"

"I can be here at nine o'clock," she said. "My mom can drop me off."

It occurred to me that given her condition, Diane was no longer driving.

"I can pick you up," I said.

"It's okay. My mom will drop me off."

I decided that it was best not to push this point. I nodded. "Okay."

"In fact, my mom is waiting for me in the parking lot. I have to get going. But I wanted to meet you, Mr. Bailey. Thank you so much for coming." She gave me a meaningful look, the exact nature and subtleties of which I could not fathom. "And it's good to see you again, too, Steve. Anyway, tomorrow morning at nine o'clock."

She walked out. I watched her go. Then I said to Harry: "Thank you for coming, Mr. Bailey. I promise you, what Diane and I have told you about is real. It's been happening."

Harry Bailey snuffed out his third cigarette. "Oh, I believe you, Steve. And I also believe that we have the trials of hell before us. I want you to prepare yourself. Whatever else you've been through this summer, it wasn't as bad as what lies ahead."

104

We met the next morning as planned, at nine o'clock in the McDonald's. Diane and I both joined Harry in drinking coffee. He was the only one who smoked, of course.

"I'd like to begin," Harry said, "with the two of you telling me everything that has happened to you this summer." He had brought a blank yellow legal pad with him, and he had a ballpoint pen ready. "Tell me everything. Don't leave anything out."

And so Diane and I told him everything. My portion was longer, of course.

Most of what I had to tell him correlated directly with his article in *Spooky American Tales*. His article had not mentioned Banastre Tarleton, but Diane had unraveled that mystery for us.

I had no idea, though, who John André might be. The initially charming—then frightening—clerk at Ye Olde Store, the one who had raved about his execution, claiming that George Washington himself was ultimately responsible for his fate.

"Do you have any idea who he is?" I asked Harry.

Harry nodded. "Major John André. He was a British officer and spymaster. André was involved in the defection of Benedict Arnold to the British side.

"André was caught behind the American lines with incriminating papers that were written in Arnold's hand. Because André wasn't wearing his British uniform at the time, he was technically a spy. This entitled the Americans to execute him, according to the established rules of war.

"John André, according to all of the historical accounts, was a man of considerable personal charm and refined tastes. Women loved him, and men admired him. It is said that after he was hanged for treason, he was mourned by both sides."

"And he blamed George Washington for his execution?" I asked.

"Quite possibly he did," Harry said. "George Washington appointed the board of officers that condemned André to hang. Washington also refused to pardon André, though he did offer to exchange André for Benedict Arnold, who had by then escaped over the British lines. But the British declined to send Arnold back. Washington also refused to spare André the fate of hanging by the neck, like a common criminal. André, as an officer and a gentleman, would have preferred the firing squad. That was considered a more noble form of death."

Harry shook his head, and flashed a wily, ironic smile.

"John Andre," he said. "One of the more interesting characters of the American Revolution. In a way, you should feel honored to have met him, even under those circumstances."

105

After Diane and I had finished telling Harry Bailey everything we knew, he announced: "And now, my two young friends, I have some information for *you*."

Harry Bailey pulled a stack of loose mimeographed pages from his attache case.

I could tell from the uneven coloring of the copies that the original, source documents were very old. Also, the copied pages were handwritten, in the florid, blotchy script that is characteristic of writing done with ink and quill.

"These are copies only, obviously," Harry said. "I obtained them by mail, from the Harvard University library." He winked. "One of the librarians there owes me some favors."

The front page of the stack bore a title: "The Diary of Giles Wade".

Harry began his explanation: "Giles Wade experienced the American Revolution firsthand. He was therefore alive when the events that are now causing us so much trouble actually occurred.

"Giles Wade was born in 1755, near Braintree, Massachusetts. By all accounts, he was an eager patriot who joined the Continental

Army almost as soon as the shooting started. He was assigned to an artillery crew.

"Wade fought at the Battle of White Plains. According to his diary, he witnessed the decapitation of the Hessian officer who would become the Headless Horseman. But there's a twist: According to Wade, the Hessian wasn't decapitated with a cannonball."

"How—how did it happen, then?" Diane asked.

"If we can trust the narrative of Giles Wade, then the Hessian officer was not killed in combat it all. He was *captured* in battle. Later, he was beheaded in cold blood by vengeful Continentals. The Continentals loathed the British redcoats, of course. But they especially despised the Hessians. The Hessians were here as mercenaries, after all. Moreover, the Hessians were involved in numerous atrocities against Americans, both on and off the battlefield."

"So the beheading was done as a form of retribution, then?" Diane asked.

"It would seem so," Harry said. "An eye for an eye. The cycle of violence. The oldest story in the world. The Continentals lopped off the captured Hessian's head. They buried the head in an iron trunk. Why, I don't know. Perhaps to add insult to injury, as if it were some grisly trophy. The headless body they threw into the mass grave of the battlefield."

"Does that apparently cold-blooded killing have anything to do with the Headless Horseman's return from the grave?" I asked.

Harry Bailey grinned. "We're getting into the realm of extreme speculation here, but it very well might. You will recall that John André was especially incensed at being hanged by the neck like a common criminal. The Headless Horseman, in life, had been a proud German officer. A mercenary, yes, but a professional man-at-arms. He would have regarded his hasty and impromptu execution at the hands of the Colonials, without even so much as a hearing or trial, as a grave offense. A violation of the rules of war."

"But the Hessians were also guilty of violating the rules of war," I protested.

Harry shrugged. "I'm not making excuses for the other side. I'm only telling you that there *was* another side. At any rate, though, it was because of that beheading, and Giles Wades's witnessing of it, that the next part of the story takes place.

"Giles Wade does not seem to have been directly involved in the execution of that now infamous Hessian officer. Nevertheless, he obviously felt a connection to the event, and the supernatural terror that followed, in the period immediately after the American Revolution.

"I'm sure the two of you have read that story by Washington Irving, 'The Legend of Sleepy Hollow'. Although the story itself is fiction, it is based on eyewitness accounts of residents of rural New York during the seventeen nineties. Apparently things got very bad for a while. Giles Wade, as a resident of the rural district just outside New York City, would have heard the stories. He might even have seen the Headless Horseman himself."

Harry Bailey patted the stack of mimeographed papers.

"Giles Wade, however, was in a position to take action. He had seen the execution. He knew where the head was buried."

"After the war, former Continental Army soldiers had dibs on land titles in the Northwest Territory. That was basically the land to the immediate north and west of the Ohio River, comprising the present-day U.S. states of Ohio, Indiana, Illinois, and Wisconsin, with a little corner of Minnesota thrown in for good measure.

"Giles Wade acquired a deed on a patch of land just north of the Ohio River. About twenty miles east of a small settlement called Cincinnati."

"Right here," Diane said. "What you mean is that Giles Wade settled right here, in Clermont County."

"It would seem so," Harry said. But when he hauled stakes for the Ohio Territory, he brought an unusual object with him. As his final service to the Revolution, he decided to take that buried strongbox with him. I'm talking, of course, about the chest that contained the Headless Horseman's head."

"*That's* why the Horseman has come here!" I said, understanding now. "He wants to retrieve the head."

Harry Bailey smiled grimly and nodded. "Isn't that what the Headless Horseman is supposed to be looking for, in all the old stories? That's a recurrent theme in all of them, including the most famous one of all."

"The Legend of Sleepy Hollow," Diane said.

"That's right," Harry Bailey replied. "Penned by Washington Irving, and published in the year eighteen twenty. Not based on facts, but based on truth. There is sometimes some daylight between facts and truth, as paradoxical as that sounds. Giles Wade settled in this very county of yours. Just a few miles from where we now sit, in fact. It was there that he buried the head of the Headless Horseman—the object of that spirit's murderous quest."

"And so...?" Diane asked.

"And so," Harry Bailey said. "All we have to do is dig up the head."

I wanted to know more—much more—about what Harry Bailey had in mind. But I could no longer contain a new question that had suddenly occurred to me.

Had I already met *Giles Wade?*

I had already told Diane and Harry about my trip into the netherworld. My interaction with the young boy named Giles.

"Was that Giles Wade?" I asked now. "The young boy I met in that netherworld?"

Harry took a moment to ponder this. "Could be," he said at length. "In life he challenged the Horseman, and the evil the Horseman inflicted. Perhaps Giles Wade decided to challenge him in death, as well. If that is the case, then he could very well be your Giles. But you'll probably never know the answer to that question."

What was **before us was an** unusual mission: We would have to dig up the grisly contents of a two-hundred year-old chest.

The head of the dead Hessian would be nothing more than a skull by now, I assumed, if it hadn't already decomposed into dust. But that was a mere technicality for the moment.

"Retrieving the head is the thing," Harry said. "But after we do that, we have a decision to make."

"And what would that be?" I asked.

"Isn't it obvious? We have to decide what to do with it."

"And do you have any ideas there?" Diane asked.

Harry nodded slowly. "According to the legend, we have the option of giving it back to him. That's why he's returned from the dead, after all—to retrieve his head. So once he gets the head back, he'll go back to where he came from."

Harry paused for a moment. "Hopefully," he added.

"What other options are there?" I asked.

Harry shrugged. "Beats me, we're officially in unchartered territory here."

WE MADE plans to travel out to the exact location of Giles Wades's former cabin. Harry had the exact longitude and latitude.

According to the diary, Giles Wade had built a cabin with a stone foundation. If that was true, then traces of it—a stone outline at least should still be visible. The diary further specified that Giles Wade had buried the head forty paces beyond the back door of the cabin, which faced due west.

Harry Bailey seemed to have everything worked out.

"We'll go out there tonight," Harry said. "I know it's sudden, but I don't think we have any time to waste."

Diane and I both indicated that we would be able to go that night.

"We'll meet here, in the McDonald's parking lot, at seven p.m., then," Harry said. "In the meantime, I suggest that both of you rest up, and prepare yourselves spiritually, whatever that might mean, according to your own individual beliefs and traditions. What awaits us tonight will surely be a trial."

"I don't understand," I said. "What do you mean by that?"

"The head of the dead Hessian has immense spiritual power," Harry explained. "Dark power. It acts like a magnet for evil forces. We're sure to encounter some of them tonight. Like I said, be ready."

I wanted to ask more questions, but I figured that even Harry Bailey wouldn't be able to tell me exactly what to expect tonight.

"All right," I said.

Little did I know that another trial—of a very different nature—awaited me that same morning.

106

I was driving home from our morning meeting at McDonald's.

I had wanted to take Diane home, but her mother was already waiting for her in the McDonald's parking lot.

I wanted to be alone with her—*needed* to be alone with her—but she was obviously resisting that.

Or her mother was resisting for her. I couldn't be sure.

I was about halfway home—in that spot along the country route where so much had occurred   but this time I was driving in broad daylight. There was nothing to worry about, I figured. The Headless Horseman wouldn't appear now, in the pre-noon hours. And as for Carlos and the motorcycle gang, they probably weren't out of bed yet.

Before I left the McDonald's, I had asked Harry Bailey why our clandestine mission had to take place at night.

"Because the head can only be returned to the Horseman during the nocturnal hours," Bailey had explained.

I was contemplating this explanation when I became aware that I was being followed. But not by the Headless Horseman, or Carlos and his friends.

There was a Clermont County Sheriff's Department patrol car behind me. Its rooftop lights were flashing.

I immediately slowed down, clicked on my right turn signal, and pulled over.

I was concerned (who isn't, when stopped by the police?); but I was by no means panicked. I figured that I was guilty of some mild infraction: an expired license sticker, or a speed a few miles over the limit. (I had been driving a little on the fast side, now that I thought about it.)

Stopped now, I watched Tim Schmidt exit the patrol car.

His right hand was near his sidearm.

This wasn't good. Not good at all.

He walked up alongside the Bonneville. He looked down at me, with an expression that was all business.

I recalled our conversation the other night, when I had brought up the subject of ghosts, in an attempt to bring him into my confidence. I recalled how that had backfired.

"Hi, Tim. Listen, if you're still mad about the other night—"

"This has nothing to do with that," Tim cut me off. "Please step out of the vehicle."

"Why? What's going on?"

Tim brought his hand to his sidearm.

"Please step out of the vehicle," he said. "Slowly. Don't make any sudden moves. And keep your hands in plain view, where I can see them."

"Can I shut off the car?" I asked.

"Yes. Then step out of the vehicle. Please don't make me ask you again."

I did as Tim had told me.

"What is this about?" I said.

"You're wanted for questioning, in the murder of Keith Conway."

107

"What? What are you talking about?"

"If you're guilty, then you already know," Tim said. "Keith Conway was found murdered last night, in a most horrific manner."

"Are you telling me that he was beheaded?" I blurted out, without thinking.

"Yes, that's exactly what I'm telling you. And how are you aware of that? The details haven't been released to the press yet. Turn around, and put your hands behind your back."

"What?"

Tim put his hand on the grip of his .357 Magnum.

"Okay, okay," I said.

Tim handcuffed me and drove me to the sheriff's department.

I was locked in a little interrogation room, still handcuffed. Tim made me sit, with my back to the wall, at a little table. Then he left the room for a while.

Tim entered again with another man, perhaps forty-five years old, who was wearing a tie and jacket. He was bald, and he had a sandy-brown mustache with flecks of grey. The bald dome of his head gleamed in the overhead lights. He was carrying a legal pad.

"I'm detective John Hale," the man in the suit said. "Deputy Schmidt here says that you have some information about the murder of Keith Conway."

Detective? I hadn't even known that the Clermont County Sheriff's Department had a detective.

Detective John Hale sat down across from me at the little table. He laid the legal pad on the surface of the table. Tim Schmidt remained standing.

"Now," Hale began. "Why don't you tell me how you're privy to so much information about the murder of Keith Conway, if you had nothing to do with it?"

"I didn't know that Keith Conway was murdered until Tim—Deputy Schmidt—told me about it."

"But you knew that he was beheaded," Detective Hale said. "That's pretty specific."

"It was a lucky guess—or no—not a lucky guess. Deputy Schmidt said that Keith Conway was murdered 'in a most horrific manner'. I recently read the stories about the young men up in Zanesville being beheaded, and their bodies being left in the woods. I put two and two together. That was all. So yes, it was kind of a guess. But an educated guess."

Detective Hale looked up at Tim.

"Is that true, Deputy Schmidt?"

Tim allowed that yes, what I was saying was true. He had mentioned to me that Keith Conway was murdered 'in a most horrific manner'.

"Shouldn't my parents be here?" I asked. "I'm under eighteen, you know. And shouldn't I have a lawyer present?"

"Only guilty people need lawyers when they talk to the police," Detective Hale said. "Are you guilty of the murder of Keith Conway?"

"Of course not!" I said.

"That's good to hear," the detective said. "But for the record, it's your right to have an attorney present. Of course, if you do that, things could get a lot more complicated. Is that what you want?"

I was out of my depth here. This Detective Hale was older and more experienced than me, and he was obviously trying to trick me into entrapping myself.

"I didn't kill Keith Conway."

"So you've said."

"What about my parents?"

"You look old enough to have a friendly little chat without your mommy and daddy present," Hale said. "But if you want us to call them, we can do that. Is that what you want?"

I thought about that for a moment. My father was still recovering from a heart attack. My mother had been under a lot of stress lately.

"No. That's not what I want."

"All right. This is why you're here. You were seen fighting with the deceased victim in the parking lot of the restaurant where you both work," Detective Hale said. "The McDonald's owned by Ray Smith. Do you admit to this?"

"It was over—a girl," I said. "High school stuff. Keith Conway was dating her for a while, and then I was."

"I see," Detective Hale said. His tone suggested that I had just admitted my guilt in the death of Keith Conway. "And this girl—are you still dating her?"

"No," I said.

Detective Hale raised his eyebrows. "I see." He picked up the legal pad. He tossed the pad across the table to me. "Write down this girl's name, address, and phone number. We'll need to talk to her, too."

There was an obvious problem here. I was still handcuffed.

Detective Hale motioned for Tim to uncuff me, which he did. He returned the handcuffs to his belt.

I wrote down Diane's information. What would she think, when the police came to question her? Would she think that I had murdered my rival?

Detective Hale engaged in some more verbal jiujutsu with me, asking me for an accounting of every place I'd been over the last forty-eight hours, etc.

It became clear to me that this was a fishing expedition. They had no evidence against me. I hadn't killed Keith Conway, after all. I had done nothing but engage in a minor fisticuffs with him in the McDonald's parking lot. And I had merely been defending myself.

"Am I under arrest?" I finally asked.

"Not at this time," Detective Hale said.

"Then I want to leave. Now."

"You can leave," Hale said. "But we don't want you leaving the area in the immediate future. Do you have any trips planned?"

"No," I said.

"Duly noted," Detective Hale said. He scrawled something on his legal pad. "Deputy Schmidt here will drive you back to your car."

Tim Schmidt, as promised, drove me back to the Bonneville. A few minutes into the drive, he attempted a half-hearted reconciliation.

"Sorry about putting the cuffs on you," Tim said, "but I had no other choice."

"Fuck you," I said.

I saw Tim redden. He stopped the car. "Listen to me, Steve. We might have jumped the gun a little, but if you think that you can—"

"Just take me back to my car, please. Like Detective Hale said."

Tim Schmidt clenched his teeth. But he took his foot off the brake, and continued the drive back to my waiting car.

The Bonneville was still there, unmolested. Without saying a word to Tim Schmidt, I exited the patrol car, got into the Bonneville, and drove home.

108

Diane had to know what had happened. I owed her an advance warning. The police were going to call on her, after all.

And what would she think when she learned that Keith Conway had been killed—beheaded?

She might have decided that Keith Conway was a jerk—*entitled*, to use her words—but that didn't mean she wouldn't be shocked and horrified by what had happened to him.

Come to think of it, I was feeling shocked and horrified myself. I had never liked Keith Conway. For as long as I could remember, his presence had been an albatross around my neck.

I would have liked to have been rid of him—as in seeing him move to Kansas City or Seattle.

I hadn't wanted this.

Driving to Diane's house, I found myself doing something that I would never have imagined: I was mourning Keith Conway.

I ARRIVED at Diane's house in the early afternoon. I was relieved to find her alone.

She answered the door wearing shorts and a tee shirt. She still looked so normal. I still couldn't fully believe that she was under a death sentence—that the clock was ticking against her.

"What's up?" she said. She was understandably surprised to see me. We had been together only a few hours ago at the McDonald's, and we would see each other again at seven o'clock that evening.

"I have to come in," I said.

She barely hesitated. "Okay. Come on in."

'Where's your mother?'

"She's gone shopping with a friend. She'll be back in a few hours. She's agreed to drop me off at the McDonald's tonight. I—I made something up. I said I'm going to a movie with some girlfriends. I hated lying to her; but how could I explain the truth? Anyway, what's up Steve? Or maybe I should say—what else is up?"

It occurred to me that I hadn't thanked her for calling Harry Bailey, for applying that "woman's touch" that convinced Bailey to—on the word of two teenagers—make a five-hour drive from Detroit to southern Ohio.

But there was no time for even that, now.

"There's no easy way to say this, Diane, so I'm just going to come out with it."

I told her what had happened to Keith.

"How?" she asked. *"Where?"*

"I don't know the full details." Then I told her about the police questioning me.

"Why did they question *you*?"

"Keith and I got into a fight the other night," I said.

"Over me?"

"Yeah, I guess you could say that."

"Oh, no—!" Diane said.

She threw herself into my arms. I held her while she cried.

Somehow, her mouth found mine. We started kissing.

My hand moved to her breast.

There had been so much death recently, and I wanted her so badly.

"I want you, Diane. I don't know what's ahead of us tonight. Who knows what will happen? Who knows how much time either one of us has?"

I expected her to protest. But instead she took my hand and guided me up to the second floor of the Parker house, toward her bedroom.

"Wait," she said. We were standing in the doorway of her bedroom now.

"This might—only make things worse for you, later on, I mean."

I thought about what Diane had just suggested. She was right. But I was in this far already. I was in love with her—I could no longer deny that.

"It doesn't matter," I said. "I mean—it does. But there's no perfect choice here."

No perfect choice. Only a few weeks ago, the old Steve Wagner would have clung to the idea that there were perfect choices for every dilemma in this world.

Now, however, I knew better.

109

I pulled into the parking lot of the McDonald's a few minutes before seven o'clock that night.

As the evening drew on, the weather had taken a turn for the worse. The skies were grey, with low-hanging iron clouds. The wind was picking up, and there was a threat of rain in the air.

I wasn't on the work schedule at the restaurant that night. Stepping into the dining room, I caught a glimpse of Wanda Nead behind the counter. As soon as she saw me, she turned away.

I wondered: Had she fingered me to the Clermont County Sheriff's Department? Did she actually believe that I was responsible for Keith Conway's death?

Those were questions that I would have to think about later. I didn't have time to think about them now.

Harry and Diane were already there. They were sitting together at a table in the smoking section. Harry was sipping a coffee and smoking a cigarette.

As soon as he saw me, he snuffed out the cigarette and took a final drink of his coffee. He stood up and said, "Are you ready, Steve?"

"I'm as ready as I'll ever be." I looked from Harry to Diane. "How about you two?"

They both affirmed that they were ready.

When I saw Diane, the events of the afternoon came flooding back to me. I knew, though, that I would have to put those feelings aside, place them in a box in the back of my mind. Otherwise, I would easily become distracted tonight, with possibly disastrous consequences for all of us.

"Who should drive?" Harry asked, reaching into his pocket for his keys.

"I'll drive," I said. "I know the roads."

NEVERTHELESS, we needed some essential items that Harry had brought in his car—a sky blue Cadillac. He opened the trunk, so we could see what he had prepared.

Harry had a map of the local roads. Using the compass headings in Giles Wades's diary, he had indicated our destination with a red felt-tip marker.

"Do you know this spot?" he asked me, holding up the map. He had to grasp the map with two hands, as the wind was now picking up.

"That's a place off Goshen Hill Road," I said. The area around Goshen Hill Road was mostly virgin woods and meadows in 1976. It was in this general vicinity that Jack and his "commune" lived in their rented farmhouse.

"All right then," Harry said. "If you can get us to that spot, we should be able to locate the foundation of Giles Wades's cabin. And from there, we can find the buried head—assuming it's still there, that is."

Harry had also brought some digging equipment: "A shovel and a pickaxe," he said. "Steve, I think you are going to be our default digger. I'm sure you wouldn't think of making the little lady here dig, and I'm a man well over sixty."

110

Diane sat in the front seat of the Bonneville, and Harry sat in the middle of the back seat, while I drove.

We were all somewhat concerned about the weather situation. We could hear thunder rumbling in the distance. Now and then, a lightning bolt lit up the sky.

"Very strange," Harry said from the back seat. "The local weather channel was calling for heat, humidity, and clear skies this evening."

I had seen the same weather report. "Maybe we're dealing with something other than normal weather here," I suggested.

"Yes," Harry said. "You may very well be right about that."

Despite the name, Goshen Hill Road was actually rather flat. It was a very narrow, two-lane rural route that ran through the middle of nowhere. I have repeatedly described the farm pastures I drove by almost daily, on my way home from McDonald's. Out here, there weren't even any farms. We were surrounded on both sides by thick woods.

"Did you see that?" Diane said suddenly.

I put on the brakes. Diane was looking at the section of trees to the immediate right of the car.

"What is it, Diane? What did you see?"

"I saw something moving in the woods," she said.

"You mean the Horseman?"

"No, something much bigger than that."

"We might see a lot of strange things before the night is over," Harry said. "Steve, you better get going. Whatever Diane saw, it probably isn't anything friendly. No sense in hanging around here, making ourselves a target."

What Harry had just said sounded ominous. But I knew that now wasn't the time to ask for elaboration. I lifted my foot off the brake, stepped on the gas, and continued forward again.

A FEW MILES BEYOND THAT, Goshen Hill Road became a gravel path. The ride became bumpy, and we could hear little stones pinging against the undercarriage of the Bonneville.

"Let's hope that rain holds off for a while," Harry said. "A road like this could get soupy when wet."

I was about to comment on that, when I saw another vehicle sitting in the middle of the road, just ahead of us.

It was Jack's red Corvair.

111

I put on the brakes and put the Bonneville in park. I had no choice. Jack's Corvair was blocking the entire road.

As soon as I stopped, Jack opened the front door of his car. He stepped out into the rising wind.

"I'll take care of this," I said.

"Who is that?" Harry asked.

I stepped out of the car without answering him. There was no time now to explain.

During our conversations with Harry, I had neglected to tell him anything about my brother. Although Jack had apparently had some interaction with the wayward spirits that had been in the area of late, I hadn't thought him a relevant topic during my conversations with the magazine writer.

My impression had been that Jack was so disorganized and incompetent, that he would be incapable of influencing anything, one way or the other. Moreover, I hadn't seen Jack since that day at the hospital, when we had our altercation over his failure to visit our convalescent father.

Without hesitation, I walked up to Jack and stood a few feet from him.

"Jack! What are you doing? You're blocking the way! Let us pass!"

Jack looked at me through half-lidded eyes. There was a feral quality to his expression.

"You shouldn't be out here, little brother. It's not what he wants."

"What do you mean by 'he'?"

Jack flashed me a cold smile. "It's just you and me here now, Steve. You don't need to pretend. You know exactly who I'm talking about. I'm talking about the headless one."

The headless one. The exact language that Carlos had used.

I was still angry at Jack, not just for his presence here in the middle of the road, and not just for his lackadaisical approach to visiting our father in the hospital. I was angry at him for years of turmoil that he had brought to my otherwise happy home life.

Nevertheless, I decided to try to reason with him. If that was even possible.

"Jack. I'm out here tonight to do something very important. This stuff that's been happening of late. It's very bad. People are dying. More people will die if it isn't stopped." Then I added: "Our dad might die. That one you call *the headless one*, I've seen him near our house."

But Jack was implacable. "I can't let you do that, little brother. Now get back in your car, turn around, and go back to where you came from. And take those friends of yours with you."

That was it, the final straw. All of my resentment toward Jack suddenly welled up and came to a head.

I closed the short distance between us, and grabbed him by the collar. I brought my face to within inches of his.

"You've been nothing but a drain on everyone around you, Jack!" I shouted. "For your whole miserable life!"

Jack's eyes went wide. I don't know if I had merely jolted him out of the trance he was in, or if he simply couldn't process what was happening—his little brother standing up to him, without any regard for the possible consequences.

And I wasn't even done yet.

"You want to take a swing at me, Jack? Like you were going to do in Dad's hospital room? Well, here I am!"

I shoved him backward, toward the Corvair. For a second, it seemed, he was ready to fight me.

But Jack's mind was a maelstrom of confusion in that moment. His constantly intoxicated state had made him easy prey for the influence of the Headless Horseman. And now the real world had come at him with another development that he could not cope with.

"You're a disgrace, Jack. You should be ashamed of yourself. Get out of here."

Jack hung his head, and walked back to his Corvair. I watched as he started the engine. He put the car in drive, and I stepped aside so he could drive past me.

When he came to the Bonneville, he gave my car a wide berth, driving half in the grass as he went by.

And then Jack was gone.

I returned to the Bonneville.

"We can continue now," I told Harry and Diane.

"Who was that?" Harry asked, repeating his earlier question.

"That," I said, "was my brother."

"Oh," Harry Bailey said, after a considerable pause. "I somehow have the feeling that there's quite a story there. And I'd love to hear it. But—" He looked out the window of the Bonneville, at the dark, swirling sky. "I think we should delay the telling of that—until after we're done with this."

112

As we drew closer to the spot where the cabin should be, I asked Harry to hand me the map.

The twilight was coming on now, and the cloud cover had grown thicker. The wind remained strong, and there were occasional flashes of lightening. But the rain held off—for now, at least.

"This is it," I said, "based on the spot you've indicated on the map."

We had stopped beside a flat clearing in the woods. This would be the logical place to build a cabin. But the cabin had been built almost two hundred years ago. Who knew how much the landscape might have changed since then?

"We'd better get going," Harry said. "The weather is not on our side. And we might have... other visitors, as well."

"You keep saying that," I said, getting out of the car. "Exactly what do you mean?"

"I believe I already told you," Harry replied, as he stepped out into the wind. He raised his voice to finish. "The head is an object with intense, dark spiritual powers. It will draw other entities to it. But if you're looking for a list, an exact taxonomy, I don't have it."

I now noticed that Harry was carrying a little leather-bound book. "What is that?" I asked.

"*What?*" he called out over the wind.

"Never mind." If the book was important, I figured, I would find out soon enough.

Diane got out of the car, too. I turned away from Harry and called out to her.

"Diane, are you sure you're up for this?"

"I'm up for it!" she replied. "And what's the worst that can happen? It will cut my life short?"

I didn't find her attempt at gallows humor the least bit amusing. But nor could I bring myself to scold her.

I opened the trunk, and removed the pickaxe and shovel that Harry had brought with him from Detroit.

"How do we proceed?" I asked.

"I think," Harry said, "that our best course would be to simply walk out across this field, and look for anything that resembles an old foundation."

I nodded. This was not exactly a novel plan, but it made sense.

The three of us trekked through the high grass, me carrying the two digging tools. Harry trudged along by my side. I got the impression that he didn't do a lot of walking.

Diane ran ahead of Harry and me. I wanted to tell her to slow down, to be careful.

Be careful of what, exactly? Diane had made a valid point a moment ago. The greatest danger to her life, at present, was the time bomb ticking inside her own body.

Diane ran through the high grass, as if she knew exactly where she was going. She stopped in a spot in the middle of the weed-infested clearing. She looked down at her feet. Then she turned back to Harry and me.

"I think I've found the foundation!" she called out.

113

Harry and I followed. When we reached the spot where Diane was standing, we looked down. There was indeed a broken, uneven line of mortared stones. If you hadn't been looking for the stones, you might have missed them. But the stones were laid out in a straight line—a pattern that rarely occurs by chance in nature.

"Let's see," Harry said. "West is that way." He pointed to the west. Then he followed the line of stones, until they made a right angle. He walked a few more paces.

"This is where the back door would have been," he said. "So forty steps beyond this point is where Giles Wade buried the head."

From there, Harry started walking, and I could see him counting his steps under his breath.

I heard something screech from back in the adjacent woods.

Diane and I both looked. Harry did not. We followed along behind him.

"Right here," Harry said. He stamped his right foot on the grassy earth. "Right here is where you need to start digging."

"Are you sure about that?" I asked. "You make it seem so simple but—"

Another inhuman screech arose from the woods to our left.

"Something else seems to believe that we've found the right spot," Harry said. "Come on, Steve. We don't have time to argue. We might not have very much time at all. Start digging!"

I began with the pickaxe. I raised the double-edged tool high in the air, and brought it down on the spot that Harry had indicated, throwing all of my weight into it.

A clod of earth came free. I raised the pickaxe again and repeated the procedure.

"Very good!" Harry said. "When you remove the top layer of sod, you can go to work with the shovel."

Under different circumstances, I might have made an arch remark about Harry's casual approach to my labor. As things stood, however, I decided to play the situation straight.

But I was still curious about the leather-bound book.

"What is that?" I asked again.

"It's a book of various prayers and recitations," he said. "Christian, Muslim, Jewish, and others. Multi-denominational, you might say. Now, keep digging!"

It took me only a few more swings to remove all the grass and roots. I dropped the pickaxe onto the ground, and picked up the shovel. I placed the tip of the shovel into the exposed topsoil, dug in with my foot, and removed a shovelful of dirt.

"Good!" Harry said. "Keep it up!"

Above the sounds of the impending storm, I could hear another set of noises from back in the woods, on the far side of the cabin's foundation.

Trees cracking and breaking, as if something big were moving through the forest—in our direction.

When I paused my digging to look, Harry shouted at me.

"*Dig!*" Harry said.

"Harry," I said. "What is that? Tell me!" The magazine writer looked frightened—but not especially surprised. Something told me (yet again) that Harry had information that he wasn't sharing.

Diane appeared to be frightened now, too.

"What is that, coming toward us?" I demanded. "Tell me!"

"If you must know," Harry Bailey said, "that is the guardian of the head. I think. That's my best guess, anyway. Remember what I've been telling you: The head of the Headless Horseman has potent dark powers, just like the Horseman himself. This burial site has therefore attracted formidable entities."

"And is this a particularly formidable entity?"

"If this is the guardian, then its mission is to keep the head from being disturbed. Now, Steve, get back to your digging!"

I tried. But I couldn't ignore the cracking sounds from back in the woods. Something was drawing near us.

Harry couldn't ignore it, either.

The magazine writer began to recite words from the book. I didn't understand them. I can't say for certain, after all these years, but I believe that Harry Bailey was speaking in Latin—or his best version of it.

Then a distinct shape appeared between two large hickory trees at the main tree line. The shape was vaguely humanoid, but much, much larger than any man.

The creature that Harry called 'the guardian' was at least as tall as a two-story house. Its head was porcine, with a long snout, a broad face, and eyes positioned on either side of the head. Two long tusks protruded from its gaping mouth.

Harry shouted something else—once again, I'm pretty sure it was in Latin.

The guardian growled. Harry had done something to hold the beast in that spot. Otherwise, it would have come forward and killed all of us by now.

"*Steve! I need you to dig!*" he said. "*I don't know how long I can keep this thing at bay!*"

"*Steve, hurry!*" Diane shouted.

That got me going. What else could I do? I did my best to ignore the creature at the edge of the woods.

And I continued to dig.

· · ·

MAYBE FIVE—MAYBE ten—minutes later, my shovel struck something solid.

I knew immediately what it was: It was the top of an iron-plated strong box.

"Did you find it?" Harry shouted back at me.

The guardian was twisting its piglike head back and forth. It was as if the beast were caught in a giant fence—an invisible fence that Harry had erected with his incantation.

"I found it!" I replied. "But I'm going to need a few more minutes to dig it out!"

"Hurry, Steve! For heaven's sake, hurry!"

Above our heads another bolt of lightning lit up the sky.

I LAY DOWN **flat** on the damp ground to lift the strongbox out of the hole. I grabbed it with both hands. The surface of the box was cold, and covered with grit and rust.

There was a thump as something shifted inside the box.

"Don't be surprised," Harry said. "What you've just dug up is no ordinary skull." He had momentarily diverted his attention from the guardian to check my progress.

"I think that was just the shifting of the weight," I said.

But the skull seemed heavier—more substantial—than a two hundred year-old skull should be.

I lifted the box out of the hole, pulling it through roots, and at least a few earthworms.

Another thump inside the strongbox, as the skull shifted to one side.

I stood up, and dropped the strongbox onto the ground.

Just then, something happened to the guardian.

It shrank back into the woods. Withdrew. But not before it gave us a final, baleful growl.

Harry exhaled in relief.

"We've won!" he said. "The guardian's mission was to protect the head. But since you've pulled the head from its burial place, the guardian's mission is revoked!"

We've won? I thought.

I figured we still had a ways to go before we would be able to claim victory.

And I was right about that.

114

"Look!" Diane shouted. We all looked in the direction she was pointing.

The Headless Horseman stood at the edge of the clearing.

He had come. Of course he had come.

All I had to do now, according to the legend, was to give him back his head.

That might very well be the easiest way out of this. But was it the best decision?

I RECALLED **the words** of Giles, the boy whom I had met in the netherworld that night. I was now almost certain that he was some version of Giles Wade, the long-dead American patriot whose journal had inspired our mission tonight.

"WHEN HE TRIES *to take it back, don't give it to 'im!*"

. . .

MAYBE GILES KNEW something that I didn't. The Headless Horseman was already a powerful, malevolent entity. How much stronger would he be, when reunited with the object in this little trunk?

We all looked down. There was the sound of movement within the trunk.

The head was coming back to life.

I addressed Harry. "Do you have something in that book that can keep the Horseman at bay for a minute or two?"

"I suppose so," Harry said. He suddenly looked very old and very tired. "But I don't know for how long."

"Try," I said. "Give me a few minutes."

Harry opened his little leather-bound book, and started reading.

I RAISED the pickaxe and brought it down on the main hasp of the strongbox.

The hasp easily separated from the body of the trunk. I kicked the lid free. Then, using one foot, I pushed the strongbox over on its side.

The head rolled onto the ground.

The head looked mummified and ancient. But I had figured that after two hundred years, it would be nothing but dust and bone fragments. Something else had worked to preserve it—the same powers that had brought about the return of the Horseman, Marie Trumbull, and all the others.

Impossibly, the eyes of the head opened.

They were, just as impossibly, very much alive.

The eyes fixed on mine.

I was looking into the face of the Headless Horseman, or what was left of it.

I raised the pickaxe above my head.

"Steve!" Harry Bailey called out. *"What are you doing?"*

I didn't answer him. Instead I brought the pickaxe down on the hideous thing on the ground.

"Steve! Why—!"

. . .

The wind swept **Harry's book** from his hand, even as he was still reading from it—wearily now. He made a perfunctory move to pick the book up from the ground, and then stopped. He paused to rest, bent over, his hands braced just above his knees.

The magazine writer was spent. He would utter no more incantations this night.

That meant that nothing was holding the Horseman at bay.

The Headless Horseman raised his sword, and prepared to charge.

On the ground at my feet, the fragments of the shattered head began to smolder. It was dissolving. An accelerated process of entropy was transforming the head back into dust.

I didn't have a detailed knowledge of the Bible. But I vaguely recalled some words that I had absorbed by osmosis, during one of those Lutheran services I had attended with my parents:

"For you were made *from dust, and to dust you will return....*"

Now I was struck by a new sensation: The ground beneath my feet was rumbling. A low-grade earthquake.

There was only one problem with that: Earthquakes are extremely rare in Ohio.

I felt Diane grab my arm.

"Hold on," I told her.

The earthquake continued. But as I had suspected, this was no ordinary earthquake.

Farther back in the clearing, toward the surrounding woods, I watched in disbelief (even after all the events of that summer) as the ground began to fall away. A large hole opened up.

The hole seemed to go on forever.

There was activity inside the hole. Voices and moans. Inhuman sounds. There were things squirming in the pit, things like the guardian, only even more vile.

"Don't look!" Harry said. "Do you know what that is?"

"No," I said, dumbfounded. "What is it?"

"I can't be one hundred percent certain," Harry said. "But I'm pretty sure that that is a glimpse into Hell itself."

We weren't the only ones who took notice of the pit. The opening of the hole in the earth had an immediate effect on the Horseman, and that horrible undead animal he rode.

The two of them suddenly became indistinct, not entirely solid. Like a single mass of thick black smoke.

Then there was the sound of a huge vacuum coming from the pit.

The mass of black smoke that had previously been the Horseman and his animal thinned into a long, dark tendril. All that was left of the Horseman and his infernal horse were drawn into that giant, gaping crater.

We watched, the three of us momentarily speechless, as that tendril of black smoke elongated and vanished into the crater.

Another series of rumbles. Diane, Harry, and I continued to stare as the pit closed back up. Weeds and topsoil were pushed back into place by some process that I could not possibly begin to fathom.

When it was over, Harry clapped me on the back. He now realized why I had destroyed the head.

"You've done it!" he said. "You broke the curse! You destroyed the head, and you sent the Headless Horseman back to Hell—where he belongs!"

I didn't know quite what to say about that. But I did have a question.

"What should I do with *that*?" I asked. I indicated the pile of dust that had been the Horseman's head, now completely unrecognizable. There were also fragments of the strongbox.

"Push the whole mess back into that hole and cover it up again," Harry said. "It can't hurt anyone now, probably; but it belongs in the ground. Forever."

115

After it was done, I drove us back the way we had come.

There was now some sporadic rain: just a few large drops here and there, blown by the wind. The sky continued to swirl with black clouds. It was now almost full dark. There was more thunder, more lightning. Some of the lightning bolts, I noticed, were tinged with unusual colors: red and green and purple.

"Is it over yet?" I called out to Harry in the back seat. "Finally?"

"Who can say for sure?" Harry said. "You may have ended the curse of the Headless Horseman. But in doing so, you stirred up some other, equally powerful forces. They may not be done with us yet."

"Look!" Diane called out. She was pointing at the road ahead of us. We were still on the gravel section of Goshen Hill Road.

I expected to see yet another supernatural monstrosity. What I saw, though, was the glare of multiple single headlights.

Motorcycles.

The motorcycles were stretched across our path. There was no way to avoid them. And despite everything that I had been through, I didn't quite have the nerve to play chicken with them.

I put the Bonneville in park and waited for them to reach us, and say their piece.

Soon we were surrounded by rumbling, clattering bikes. The noise was loud, even over the wind and the continuing thunder.

I recognized them as the gang that had stopped me on the road that night.

Then I saw Carlos.

Carlos drove up to the driver's side window. I rolled down the window so I could talk to him.

Carlos looked very upset. Very angry.

But I was in no mood to be trifled with, either.

"What do you want, Carlos?" I asked.

"The headless one!" Carlos said. "He's gone! I can feel it."

"You're damn right, he's gone," I said. "And good riddance to him, too."

"And did you have something to do with that? You and your friends here?"

"What if we did?"

Carlos looked slowly around the circle of his confederates. All of their faces held the same expression of low-grade outrage.

"If you did," Carlos said, "then there's going to be hell to pay."

Hell to pay. I considered the irony of that expression, in light of what had just happened back in the clearing.

Then another sound rose above the wind, the intermittent thunder, and the rumbling of the motorcycles.

The sound of a police siren.

In the distance ahead of us, I could see the red flashing lights of a police car cutting through the semidarkness.

After my experience with Tim Schmidt and Detective Hale that afternoon, I wouldn't have expected that I'd have been happy to see a police car. But everything is relative, right? The police might have humiliated me, roughed me up a little, but Carlos and his gang were certainly capable of giving me far worse.

"You'd better get out of here," I told Carlos. "The headless one is behind us. If you go now, you might be able to catch up with him. And I know you don't want to tangle with the cops."

I'm not sure if I was convincing, or if Carlos was merely in a suggestible state. After thinking briefly about what I had said, though, he called out to his fellows:

"Come on, boys! We're going after the headless one!"

116

Now we had another problem, though.

I had expected the police car to swerve around the Bonneville and pursue the motorcycle riders.

Instead it stopped directly in front of us.

I hadn't forgotten the afternoon's encounter with the police, of course. I wondered: Had they found some piece of evidence that could plausibly link me to the murder of Keith Conway?

I knew that I had had no part in the grisly murder of my former romantic rival. But what difference would that make? The Clermont County Sheriff's Department was under pressure to solve the recent string of disappearances.

Perhaps they had chosen me to be their scapegoat.

I waited breathlessly as the front driver's side door of the patrol car opened.

"What the devil?" Harry said from the back seat. I didn't answer him. Although I had told Diane about the time I'd spent with the sheriff's department this afternoon, I hadn't yet informed Harry.

I watched in dismay as Tim Schmidt stepped out of the car. He walked over to talk to me.

"Listen, Tim," I began. "I'm sorry about what I said to you this afternoon. It was a bad time for me."

"What are you talking about?" Tim said.

Then I noticed that something was different about him. He was in a daze.

He was in… shock, I guess.

"Have you seen the things that have been running around out here?" He asked. "They're horrible. Like nothing I've ever seen. Not even in Vietnam."

"I think they're gone now, Tim," I said. "But you should go back to town. It's dangerous out here."

"I'm the police," Tim said. "It's my job to face the things that are dangerous. So law-abiding citizens won't have to."

I started to argue more with him. But he turned away, and went back to his car.

We all sat there, speechless in the Bonneville, as Tim steered the black-and-white patrol car around us, and continued in the direction from which we had come…where Carlos and the other motorcycle riders had gone.

I looked back as he drove away.

"Do you think he'll be okay?" I asked Harry.

Harry shrugged. "Who can say?"

I heard Diane gasp. Then I saw her eyes widen.

"Look!" She said. She was pointing at the left side of the road, over my shoulder.

I turned and looked, too.

We weren't done with the guardian of the head, after all.

117

The porcine head of the guardian was tilted down at us through the trees. The mouth opened, revealing teeth the size of butcher knives.

I looked up, dumbstruck for a moment.

The beast was so large. But was it truly real, or just an optical illusion?

That question was answered barely a second later, when the creature broke a large branch off a tree and flung it down onto the hood of the Bonneville.

"Get out of here!" Harry shouted, frantic now. "That thing is more than capable of flipping over the car. Get us out of here, already!"

I threw the car into gear and pressed down on the accelerator.

The Bonneville spun out at first in the gravel. Then the rear wheels finally found traction, and the car started moving forward.

In my rearview mirror, I saw the massive, roughly human-shaped body of the guardian fill the visible space in the road behind us.

I looked at the speedometer. We were going thirty-five miles per hour.

"Hurry!" Diane was turned around in her seat, looking at it, too.

I could hear the sounds of the guardian's running footsteps. *Boom! Boom! Boom!*

The speedometer crept up to forty-five.

"It's gaining on us, Steve!" Harry said.

We reached the paved section of Goshen Hill Road.

Our speed rose to fifty-five miles per hour.

Then sixty.

Sixty-five.

We were on a straightaway section of country road. Even though it was dark now, I risked a look in the rearview mirror.

I could no longer see the guardian.

"You lost him," Harry said, turning back around. His face seemed as white as his hair. "Or it. Or whatever. But keep driving. Get us out of this place."

118

We made it back to the McDonald's late, but well before closing time.

The storm—if that was indeed what it was—had passed. The air was now thick, muggy, and still, in accordance with the forecasts.

Harry's sky-blue Cadillac was parked where he had left it. I pulled into the empty parking space beside the Cadillac, so that I could transfer the pickaxe and the shovel from my trunk to his.

I never wanted to dig another hole again. Ever.

I noticed Diane looking wistfully into the lighted McDonald's dining room through the windows. There was a moderate crowd this evening. Diane no longer worked there, of course. But she hadn't forgotten about the place.

"I wonder if Banastre Tarleton will be making any more trips to McDonald's," she said.

"Banny," I said. "Let's hope not."

Harry informed us that Tarleton had likely made his last appearance in our lives.

"You probably won't hear from those others anymore, either," Harry said. "Banastre Tarleton, Marie Trumbull, those damn

Hessians—without the Horseman, they have no ability to manifest themselves in this world."

Then he added, "Not for very long, at least. And if they do ever come back, they'll be shadows of their former selves, phantoms that you can disperse with a strong word or mere intention."

I thought about what Harry had said: *Not for very long, at least...*

That seemed to imply that I might very well see at least some of them again, someday. This wasn't a possibility that I wanted to consider for the moment.

And so I didn't. When you're seventeen, the distant future is almost incomprehensible. You see yourself as existing in an eternal now, without time, change, or death.

Those illusions had been partially stripped from me already. But I was determined to hold on to them for as long as I could.

I shook hands with Harry as we all stood beside his Cadillac. "So I guess this is goodbye," I said.

The magazine writer shook my hand. "In a way, yes. But I'll want to talk to you—both of you—as I prepare my follow-up story. I'll be calling you both to make sure our stories jibe. This is going to be the biggest scoop that *Spooky American Tales* has ever had."

"Your editors will be thrilled," Diane said.

Harry winked at her. "Hell, after this, they might just name me editor-in-chief."

"You have a hotel room, right?" I asked.

Harry nodded. "I do. But I won't be sleeping there. I'm too keyed-up. I'm going to swing by and check out, and then I'm driving back to Detroit. A nice long drive should clear my head."

"Be careful," I said.

"Oh, don't you worry. I'll be wide awake."

"Goodbye, then." Diane began to extend her hand to the magazine writer. But after a brief hesitation, she instead threw her arms around Harry Bailey, hugging him.

"There, there, little lady," Harry said, patting her back.

"We couldn't have done this without you!" she said, finally pulling away.

"Maybe," he said. "And maybe not. At any rate, though, I'm sorry I doubted you, Steve. I should have been more receptive when you called me the first time."

"Bygones," I said. "Think nothing of it."

"Well, then."

Harry got into his car, and Diane and I stood back and watched him back out of the parking space.

Before he drove away, he called out the driver's side window.

"I'll call you, Steve! Diane! Early next week!"

He honked his horn and drove away.

But those phone calls would never come. Neither of us would ever talk to—or see—Harry Bailey again.

I WAS GRATIFIED that Diane consented to let me drive her home.

If the Horseman and the other revolutionary ghosts were truly gone now, I thought, maybe I could anticipate other miracles.

Why not? Nothing that had happened that summer had conformed to conventional expectations.

When we reached her house, I leaned across the seat and kissed her. She didn't protest.

"We have a future," I told her. "You and me."

There were tears in her eyes. "Steve—don't."

"Let's take it one day at a time. Now, go in and get a good night's sleep. I'll call you in a few days. If you decide you want to see me, I'll be here. I'm not going anywhere."

Diane slid out of the car and walked up to her front door in the darkness.

As I watched her go, I spoke to myself, in a low voice that she couldn't possibly have heard: "And you're not going anywhere, either, Diane. You're going to be okay. That is what I truly believe."

And in that moment, at least, I did.

119

And that was the end of the revolutionary ghosts—for a long, long time, at least.

Or mostly it was the end. One of them did make a surprise appearance, a short while later, when I was least expecting it.

I HAD MOVED ON, as young people tend to do. I completed my senior year at West Clermont, graduating in the spring of 1977.

By the next spring, I was completing my first year as a student at the University of Cincinnati. I hadn't forgotten about the summer of 1976; but with the innate forward-thinking and resilience of youth on my side, I was starting to put it behind me, at least.

I would never be the scholar that Diane Parker had been, but I liked college well enough. My ultimate path was still undecided, but I had tentatively declared a major in marketing.

My personal life was thriving again, too. Diane, as it turned out, broke my heart one final time (though by no fault of her own). Although that pain was still with me, I had recently started dating a young coed named Peggy Mullins. Peggy and I really dug each other, as we used to say back in the age of disco.

My heart was not only healing; something new and life-giving was growing in the soil of my old pain. This Peggy, I sensed, might stick around for a while. She was a keeper.

One day in the spring of 1978, I was sitting in a study area inside one of the massive concrete and glass buildings where classes were held at the University of Cincinnati. Located in the inner city, there was—and is—nothing quaint or picturesque about the UC campus.

This building, like all the others at UC, might have been better suited to an airport or a factory. But the carpeted study area, located away from the building's flow of foot traffic, was a little oasis of quiet, with comfortable chairs, and a convenient proximity to restrooms and vending machines.

When I arrived at my usual spot that day, I saw that I wasn't alone. Another guy, perhaps my age—or maybe a little bit older—was sitting in one of the other chairs.

He didn't appear to be studying anything. He was just sitting there.

Probably got shellshocked from a test, I thought. I sat down without noting the stranger's hairstyle or clothing. And I certainly made no attempt to strike up a conversation with him. Why would I?

Some time—perhaps ten minutes—later, I looked up from my accounting textbook and saw that the stranger was still there.

And he was looking at me.

I somehow had a feeling that he'd been looking at me the entire time I'd been there.

So I took a closer look at him.

He wore his hair a little on the long side, but that was nothing unusual on a college campus, circa 1978.

Then I saw that he'd tied his hair back in a short ponytail, in the common style of the 1700s.

You're just spooking yourself, I thought. Since that final night—the night of my mission with Harry Bailey and Diane—I had seen no more of the Horseman, Marie Trumbull, or the Hessians.

He was wearing a white, button-up shirt. From my vantage point, I couldn't see either his shoes or his trousers.

I gave him a frown. Then I heard laughter.

Two coeds, pretty young women wearing jeans and tie-dyed tee shirts, entered the study area. It was clear, though, that they wouldn't be there for long. They were chatting about non-academic matters.

"—and so I told him, if you don't want to go to Florida for spring break, then I'll just go without you!"

"What did he say then?"

"He said, 'If you go to Florida by yourself, you'll end up hanging around with strange guys, and no way I'm letting that happen, and—"

This went on for perhaps five minutes. I was glad to hear one of them suggest that they head over to the university center for an early lunch.

I looked up from the chapter I'd been reading about cash flow statements. Out of the corner of one eye, I watched the young man with the ponytail wait until the two coeds were out of earshot.

Then he spoke to me, for the very first time.

"I been meanin' to talk to you," he said.

The accent was unmistakably British, and it instantly rattled me. During my freshman year at UC, I had taken a political science course that was taught by a visiting professor from London. It had taken me several weeks of attending lectures before I fully convinced myself that the professor wasn't one of them—another revolutionary ghost.

But this young man was no visiting professor. Nor was this encounter a random one.

"To me?" I asked, on guard now.

"That's right. To you."

"Do we know each other?" I challenged him.

"Well." The young man smiled. "To say that we know each other might be a bit of an overstatement. Let's just say that we've *met*. Anyway, you did a good thing that day. You know what I mean, don't you? You didn't give it back to 'im. Just like I told you."

This jogged my memory. ("*When he tries to take it back, don't give it to 'im!*")

I now recognized this stranger from my trip into the netherworld. He was the young boy, Giles.

But he was all grown up now.

"Giles Wade," I said.

He nodded. "That's right. In the flesh—well, not really in the flesh, but close enough, I suppose."

I was about to start asking him questions. He sensed this, and he held up a hand: "One thing that I remember about you, is that you're full of questions. I can't give you all the answers you want. That's the way it works, you see. You don't get all the answers exactly when you want them. You get them when you're ready for them."

"Yes, but—"

"Hey, man, who you talkin' to?" I heard someone else say.

Another student had just entered the study area. He had long hair, but his hair wasn't tied back in a ponytail. And I was quite certain that he wasn't a ghost. He was wearing a UC Bearcats tee shirt. In one hand he was holding what looked like a mathematics textbook. In his other hand he held a sweating can of Mountain Dew.

"I'm talking to —."

When I gestured toward the seat where Giles had been sitting, Giles was gone.

I was actually surprised. In about two years, I had almost forgotten how that worked. How the ghosts disappeared whenever they wanted to—or when you drove them away.

"Man, there's nobody *there*. You were talking to empty space. You haven't been dropping acid, have you?" He gave me a lopsided grin. He looked like the kind of guy who would drop acid himself.

Annoyed at this second stranger's intrusion, and a little embarrassed, too, I stood up from my chair and closed my accounting textbook. I walked away without saying anything more to him.

There was nothing I could have said to him, anyway, that would have remotely made sense, that would have made him understand.

PART III

EPILOGUE: 2018

120

Well, Dr. Beckman (I am going to address you directly as I finish up), the story of what happened to me—and to others—in the summer of 1976 is almost over.

Not quite, though. There are a few loose ends that I need to tie up for you.

A WEEK PASSED, and neither Diane nor I received the promised phone calls from Harry Bailey.

We briefly debated calling the police in the Detroit area, but that seemed premature. We told ourselves that Harry Bailey was an independent spirit who walked to the beat of his own drummer. He didn't keep schedules in the way that ordinary working folks did. He would call us in his own good time.

Then another week passed.

Now I was a little worried.

I had no idea how to contact the police in Detroit, nor did I know if they would even talk to me. So instead I called the editorial office of *Spooky American Tales*, in Hartford, Connecticut.

At first my call was bounced around between several secretaries. Finally I was connected to a woman named Doris Poole. She said that she had been Harry Bailey's managing editor at the magazine.

'Had been?'

Harry Bailey, Ms. Poole told me, had never made it home from his journey to southern Ohio. He had stopped at an interstate rest area near the Ohio-Michigan border. Whether he ever made it into the building that contained the rest area's vending machines and restrooms is unknown. He was found in the driver's seat of his Cadillac, there in the parking lot, early the next morning. He had suffered a massive heart attack.

"Oh," I said stupidly, not knowing what else to say. I was already choking back tears. "Did he leave any—survivors?"

"No," Doris said. "Harry Bailey was a bachelor. He was in his sixties, and both of his parents were long dead. He did have one older sister. I happen to know that she passed away several years ago."

"Harry never got to file his story," I said, without thinking.

"He told us that he had gone to Ohio," Doris Poole said. "He claimed to be working on 'something big.'"

"He was," I said. "He was working on something big."

Now it was Doris Poole's turn to ask questions. "You obviously know something about this," she said. "Were you with Harry Bailey that day—before he died?"

Perhaps I should have told her. But what could I have said, really, that would have been believable—even to an editor at *Spooky American Tales*?

I hung up the phone without uttering another word.

DIANE PARKER DIED one Saturday afternoon in January 1977.

Her illness proceeded more or less as she had said it would. On that day that Diane, Harry, and I journeyed out to Goshen Hill Road to send the Headless Horseman away forever, Diane was still a basically normal seventeen year-old girl who suffered from dizzy spells.

Her condition deteriorated rapidly once the autumn wore on. She tried to attend school, but finally that became too difficult. She attended classes at West Clermont High School for the last time in October 1976.

By Thanksgiving, she was no longer able to leave her house.

By Christmas, she was permanently hospitalized.

I won't describe all the changes she underwent. (Given your background, Dr. Beckman, you are more than capable of imagining them for yourself.) I'll just say that they disturbed me more than anything that happened that year.

Diane had been so alive, so quick-witted. So beautiful. I never would have guessed that anything could slow her down, let alone stop her.

Until something did.

I continued to visit her in the hospital, even though she told me that I should stop, that I should go away, and forget about her already.

I wasn't present when she died, but I was there a few minutes later. I had left home that Saturday morning, a cold one, I remember, and driven to the hospital.

By this time, Diane's parents—both her mother and her father—saw me in a different light. Like me, they didn't want to accept the inevitable, I suppose that drew us together.

When I walked into her room, she was gone. I could tell.

Diane was motionless in the bed. All the color was gone from her face, but there was more to it than that.

Diane wasn't there anymore.

"It's over," Mrs. Parker said. There were tears streaming down her cheeks. She was holding Diane's lifeless hand.

I knew that I couldn't stay in that room. I didn't want to see her this way—to remember her like this.

I walked out, and started down the hall.

My father was there, bundled up in his winter overcoat.

"Mr. Parker called the house," Dad explained. "The doctors said she was starting to go, and—he wanted to tell you. Mr. Parker said that you'd been so faithful, coming here practically everyday, that maybe you'd want to—"

I couldn't speak. I walked over to my dad, and I pressed my face into the shoulder of his overcoat and cried.

The two of us stood there—a father comforting his grieving son—for quite some time.

I WAS CLEARED of all suspicions in the death of Keith Conway.

The murder was never solved, exactly. Nor were the disappearances of Dan Bauer, Robert McMoore, and Donna Seitz. To the best of my knowledge, those cases remain open to this day.

Nevertheless, the police soon regretted their treatment of me on that summer day. They had had no evidence against me, except a report of a high school fisticuffs in the parking lot of Ray Smith's McDonald's.

I believed then—and I still believe—that Wanda Nead fingered me to the police, made my fight with Keith Conway seem more than it was.

When he finally declared me exonerated, Detective Hale was actually somewhat apologetic.

"You understand, don't you, why we had to question you that way?" he said.

I didn't understand. It seemed to me then (and now, too) that the Clermont County Sheriff's Department had tried to railroad me into making a false confession. It should have been clear to anyone that I was not responsible for the gruesome murder of Keith Conway, nor for any of the other disappearances in the area.

Tim Schmidt and I never spoke again of that day, of what I had said to him as he dropped me off at my car. We also never spoke of our second meeting that night—out on the gravel section of Goshen Hill Road.

I don't know what ultimately happened to Detective Hale. Tim

Schmidt, though, continued his career in law enforcement. He was elected county sheriff in 1982. He occupied that position for more than thirty years, before his retirement in 2013. Today he lives in Bradenton, Florida.

I sometimes wonder if his sleep is peaceful, if he ever dreams of the events of the summer of 1976, of the things he saw out on the nighttime roads of Clermont County. The things that he dared not admit seeing—neither to himself nor to me.

I HAD LONG BELIEVED that my parents perceived nothing—save the barest impressions—of the supernatural events of that summer. But I was wrong about that, too.

My mother was on her deathbed when she told me otherwise. She was ninety years old.

My father had passed on two years earlier, at the ripe old age of eighty-nine. After his brush with death in 1976, Dad did indeed turn over a new leaf, healthwise. But even he was not immortal, that man who had stormed Omaha Beach on D-Day, that man who I looked up to in so many ways.

Mom had been in and out of the hospital with recurrent pneumonia. She was losing her ability to fight off common infections. We both knew that this was her final admission to the hospital.

"That night," she said, from her hospital bed, "long ago, the summer before you graduated from high school. When your father was in the hospital. I came home, and you were moving around out in the front yard."

Of course I remembered. The night I did battle with the ghostly Hessians.

"You said you were chasing a rabid dog away with that bat."

"Yes, Mom," I said, not sure where she was going with this.

"I saw them," she said. "I saw those things you were fighting. Those—creatures."

"You—you *saw them*?"

"Yes, Stevie. Your father knew more than he let on, too. He saw that man on the horse in the field behind our house. The man with no head."

I realized now what I had missed out on. If only my parents had confided in me, I might not have been forced to confront those horrors alone.

But I suppose that I wasn't truly alone. Diane and Harry had been with me, after all. They hadn't been with me the whole time, but they had been there when it counted. That night out on Goshen Hill Road.

And they were both long, long gone now.

What my mother had just said, though: Now it made sense. That night in the driveway, my mother had denied seeing anything, but she hadn't interrogated me about my actions, either.

My dad, too, had been unexpectedly compliant that night when I'd told him to go into the house.

"Can you forgive me, Stevie?" my mother asked. "Can you forgive both of us? Your father wanted to talk to you about it. But he—we—simply couldn't accept it. It all seemed too—unlikely. Something out of a horror movie, more or less."

"Yes, Mom. It *was* like something out of a horror movie."

"Can you forgive us?"

"There is nothing to forgive. Both of you raised me with love and compassion. That summer—I'm just glad it's over—I'm glad we all made it out alive."

Oh, and my brother, Jack. There is more to his story, as well; but it isn't strictly necessary to the therapeutic intent of this narrative. Moreover, this document has grown far longer than I originally anticipated. It is time to draw things to a close.

So now you know, Dr. Beckman, what happened to me in 1976.

This is the end of the story. Make of it what you will.

. . .

STEVE WAGNER
November 2018

AND THAT WAS the end of the written account that I prepared for my family physician. But that wasn't the end of the whole story.

Not quite yet.

121

Adam and Amy finished up their weekend visit with their grandparents. Mark and Laura were appropriately grateful for the time alone as a couple.

The following Tuesday, though, I was interrupted during a meeting at Covington Foods with an emergency call from Peggy.

I knew that it was something urgent, because—as I've noted—Peggy prefers to text. She only calls me at work when it's something truly urgent.

"It's Adam," she said gravely. "They think he's gone into heart failure."

"Oh, no," I said. (My colleagues would later tell me that my face had turned white as a sheet.) "Where is he?"

"Children's Hospital. Mark and Laura are already there. I'm going to head over. Can you—"

"Go," I said. "I'll meet you there."

THERE WAS A NEW, previously undetected problem with one of the valves in Adam's heart. The doctors had no choice but to perform an emergency surgery.

That meant a waiting game.

I sat in one of the hospital waiting rooms with Mark, Laura, and Peggy. (A babysitter had been summoned for Amy. This experience was stressful enough for the adults.) Laura's parents were there, too.

We sat there together, beginning the interminable wait for some word from the operating room. Then we had yet another visitor.

It was Jack. Peggy had called him shortly after she called me.

He was wearing a three-piece suit. Jack now owns his own real estate brokerage. He explained that he had been in the middle of a closing, or he would have been here sooner. As soon as he got the news, though, he arranged for one of his trusted subordinates to take over for him.

I stood to greet him. "That's okay, Jack," I said. "You got here as soon as you could. Thanks for coming.

"Of course," Jack said. "There's no need to thank me. Adam is my nephew, after all. My grand nephew, that is."

Jack is now sixty-nine years old. He is still a tall, broad-shouldered man; and even at his age, he has retained something of the dark good looks and charm that so captivated Leslie Griffin and her friends more than forty years ago.

Oh, yes: What else happened to Jack that summer? I'll be brief.

A few weeks after those events out on Goshen Hill Road, Jack stopped by the house one night. He was sober. He said that he wanted to talk to Mom, and Dad—and me.

Sitting there in the living room, Jack basically apologized, for everything that he'd put Mom and Dad through.

He made an apology to me, too—albeit a somewhat grudging one. (When you're twenty-seven, I suppose that it isn't easy to apologize to your seventeen year-old brother, is it?)

To make a long story short, Jack turned himself around. He is nothing like the man he was in 1976.

What precipitated the change? Guilt over our father's brush with death? My rebuke of him out on Goshen Hill Road? A new seriousness brought on by fear over the dark things that were lurking about that summer?

Or did Jack simply grow out of his old self?

I can't say for sure.

"How's the little guy doing?" Jack asked now.

"Can't say yet," I said. "He's in surgery."

Jack laid a hand on my shoulder. "He'll be all right. Let's just believe that until we know otherwise—which we don't yet."

I nodded.

"I called Kelsie," Jack said. "She's on her way here from the UC campus. Susan will be here, too."

Kelsie is Jack's nineteen year-old daughter. She's currently a student at the University of Cincinnati. Jack married late, to a woman (the aforementioned Susan) twenty years his junior. Jack became a father for the first (and so far) only time at the age of fifty.

"Our prayers are with all of you," Jack said. "Hang in there, little brother."

And when Jack called me "little brother" this time, there was no irony, no meanness in it. Only compassion and brotherly love.

122

About two hours after Jack's arrival, the doctor came out and told us that Adam was out of the woods.

"We'll need another hour to finish up," the doctor said. "But he's going to make it."

"Thank God," Peggy said.

Laura leaned onto Mark's shoulder and cried with relief.

I told Jack and his family that they should go home now. Adam had survived, but there was still a long night of waiting ahead.

Jack, Susan, and Kelsie reluctantly agreed to go. Only Mark, Laura, and both sets of grandparents remained.

The tentative good news delivered, I felt a sudden need for a break from the waiting room.

"I'm going down to the hospital cafeteria for a cup of coffee," I announced. "Would any of you like to join me?"

To my surprise, no one took me up on my invitation. That was okay, I could use the time alone to clear my head.

But I wasn't to be alone in the cafeteria. I had another visitor—though not a welcome one.

. . .

It being late in the evening, the cafeteria was mostly deserted. That was okay with me. I had no desire to engage in small talk with any random strangers. I paid for my cup of coffee, and took a seat at a long table on the far side of the room.

I sipped my coffee and thought about all my previous hospital visits. For a man of fifty-nine, I had been very lucky where my own health was concerned. I had never been hospitalized. But in my many trips to the hospital for others, I'd lost both of my parents, and both of Peggy's parents. I'd nearly lost my grandson—twice.

And, of course, I'd lost Diane. Although I loved my Peggy without reservation, I still thought of Diane from time to time. What might have been.

My thoughts were suddenly and rudely interrupted by a nearby voice.

"There you are, you bloody bastard. Saw me the other day, didn't you? Well, I saw you, too. But you turned away before we could get reacquainted, all proper like."

Those words, which were delivered with an antiquated British accent, chilled me to my core.

I looked up, and Banny was sitting across the table from me, a few seats down. He was wearing a nondescript Oxford dress shirt and tie. He was still pretending to belong in this century—versus the one he had come from.

But it was him. There could be no doubt. And even though I had aged so much over the past forty-two years, Banny looked exactly as he had that long-ago summer. Exactly has he had when he was the Butcher of Waxhaws, more than two hundred years ago.

He shot me a familiar sneer. A sneer that I had tried to forget over the past forty-two years.

"What's the matter? Cat got your tongue?" he asked.

"Go away," I said in a dry voice that didn't seem to be my own.

Please God, I thought. I can't face this now. I am no longer a young man. I am no longer strong and pliable, like I was back then. My dad isn't here anymore, either. Nor are Diane and Harry. I'm on my own—the only one I have to fall back on.

"I see you got yourself a new doxy," Banny said. This was an obvious reference to Peggy, my wife.

"You stay away from her," I said.

Banny chuckled malevolently. "That's what you said about the last one."

I was stung by the depth of Banny's cruelty. But then, what else could be expected from Bloody Ban?

"Tell me, Steve: Does that sugar stick of yours still work, eh? Because my sugar stick still works just fine."

Until this point, I had avoided looking directly at Banny—as if willing him to go away. Now I took a closer look.

And I noticed that something about Banny was different.

An entire section of Banny's cheek was missing flesh. Through the opening, I could see into a dry mouth that was nothing but skull.

I recalled what Harry Bailey had told me, as he bade me farewell, for the first and the last time, in the parking lot of the McDonald's:

"AND IF THEY *do ever come back, they'll be shadows of their former selves, phantoms that you can disperse with a strong word or mere intention.*"

"YOU CAN'T STAY HERE," I said suddenly.

"What?" he shot back.

For a moment he looked as ridiculous as he did macabre, talking through that ruined mouth.

"You came back for a short while," I said, "because of my weakness—my stress of late. But you can't stay here for any amount of time, because when you came back before, it was at his behest—the Hessian horseman. He was the source of your power. But he's gone now, and so your power is gone, too."

"Oh," Banny countered. Now one of his eye sockets was rotted out, too. "Is that what you think? He's come back, too, I tell you."

"No," I said. "He hasn't come back—because he can't. I might have thought that I heard him the other night. But that was you, wasn't it? You were behind those hallucinations of mine, too."

"You bloody bastard!" he shouted. His words were faint and barely perceptible, like a voice on a distant, static-choked radio station.

"You're fading, Banny," I said. "Look at you."

Banny looked down at his hand. It was no longer a hand. It was a twisted, skeletal claw.

Banny cried out at the sight of his rotted appendage.

He didn't want to manifest as something dead and rotten. Now I saw a pattern that I hadn't clearly identified before: While Marie Trumbull had appeared in the form of a hideous ghoul, Banny had always preferred to appear as lifelike as possible. He was possessed by a certain vanity in death—just as he had been in life.

"You're rotting, Banny. You're turning back to some ugly, scaly thing. That's what you are. That's all you are."

"Noooooo!"

The rotting continued. Banny's arms fell off, and his body slumped against his chair.

The shirt and tie he was wearing dissolved into tatters—then into dust.

I caught a whiff of something foul and putrid. The air was filled with septic, particulate matter.

Banny's head—what was left of it—toppled forward onto the cafeteria table.

SUDDENLY WE WEREN'T ALONE. A kid of about nineteen sat down near my end of the table. He had a slice of pizza and a fountain soft drink.

The kid was about to pick up the pizza and take a bite. Then he sniffed at the air.

He stood up from the table.

"Dammit! Smells like somebody died in here!" the kid said.

He looked at me accusingly. I was the only one in this section of the cafeteria, after all.

123

I returned to the waiting room.

Adam was out of surgery now, but it would be a few more hours until he would be out of post-op, and we could see him.

The doctor came out, however, and told us that Adam was stabilized and doing fine.

"Do you and Mom want to go home?" Mark asked. Laura's parents had departed a little while ago, with promises to return first thing in the morning.

I looked at Peggy, and our unspoken decision was immediate and unanimous

"No," I said. "We'll stay until we can go in and see him."

"It might be a few more hours, Dad. And it's getting late."

Mark was right about that: It *was* getting late.

I remembered that night, long ago, when I had driven to the hospital after my father's heart attack.

"So it's getting late," I said. "Don't worry about us, son. Your mother and I are still young. And Adam is our only grandson."

"We called the sitter," Mark said. "She's going to stay with Amy for the night."

"All right, then. We'll wait with you and Laura."

"Thank you," Laura said. She looked exhausted. She hugged Peggy and me.

"Your mother and I are going to go for a little walk, though," I said. "We won't leave the hospital. If something changes, call my cell phone, okay?"

"Okay," Mark said. He put his arm around his wife, and they picked out a spot on one of the nearby waiting room couches. "Laura and I will try to catch a quick catnap."

After they walked away, Peggy said: "We're going for a walk, Steve? *Why? Where to?*"

I took her hand. "You and I need to have a talk," I said. "A talk that's long overdue."

124

I walked with Peggy to another waiting area, one that was down a side hallway, where we could be alone. The hour had grown so late that the hospital was practically deserted, anyway.

We sat down in two comfortable chairs that faced each other.

Peggy looked at me with a worried expression.

"Steve," she said, "you're scaring me. And it's been a scary day already. What is this about?"

"I—I have something to tell you," I said. "Something I've never told you before."

"Steve?" she asked. "Are you...*sick*?"

I shook my head. "No."

"You aren't—leaving me, are you?"

"No," I said emphatically. "You're my life, Peggy. You know that, don't you?"

She smiled. Then she placed her hand on mine. "Yes, I suppose I do know that. And you're my life, too." She took a deep breath. "What is it, then, Steady Steve? Did you have a dalliance with one of those young women at the office? Is that what you're wanting to tell me? Because if you are, I'd rather not know about it in detail. Just tell me that it's over, that you had a stupid, late midlife crisis moment of weakness, and that you'll never do anything like that again."

"Peggy, I didn't sleep with anyone. I've never been unfaithful to you. I've never even been tempted."

"Then what is all this about?"

"There's something in my past. From before I knew you."

"Steve, we were just kids when we met at UC. How much of a past could you have had?"

I let out a long sigh. "Peggy, I need to tell you a story. And this is going to take a while, I'm afraid."

She looked around the empty waiting area.

"We've got two hours until Adam gets out of post-op," Peggy said, "and we have this space to ourselves." She tensed up a little, as she braced herself. "So tell me, whatever it is."

"It all started one afternoon in the summer of nineteen seventy-six," I told her. "My last summer of high school. I had just bought my first car. I went to a local market to buy a copy of *Car and Driver*...."

We sat there in the lonely waiting room of the hospital, and I told her everything.

FINALLY I FINISHED. It had taken the better part of two hours.

"Do you believe me?" I asked.

"I wouldn't be telling you the truth, if I didn't acknowledge that what you've just told me is a little hard to believe, by any rational standard. But I also know that in all our years together, you've never lied to me."

"No," I said. "I haven't. Like you always say, I am Steady Steve, for better or worse."

She sighed. "I believe you, then. But I'm going to need some time to get my arms around this."

"That's fine," I told her. "It's taken me forty-two years to get my arms around it. And to tell you the truth, I'm still not there yet. I don't know if I ever will be."

"And that girl, Diane," Peggy said. "That was so sad. She was good to you. Wasn't she?"

"Yes," I said. "She was."

ADAM GOT OUT OF POST-OP, though he would spend a few more days in the hospital. We went into his room and he held my hand.

Just like my father had held my hand from his hospital bed, all those years ago.

I HAD **plenty** of vacation time banked, so I called Loretta and informed her that I would be taking a few days off from Covington Foods. She had heard the news about Adam, and expressed her concern.

"Take all the time you need," she said, as if she were my boss and not my administrative assistant. I smiled and thanked her.

The next night Peggy reached across the space of our marital bed, and touched me in that familiar, pleasantly shocking way.

And this time, I had absolutely no trouble.

No trouble at all.

125

There was only one task left to me. I had to report for my follow-up appointment with Dr. Beckman.

As we sat there in his examination room, Dr. Beckman began by inquiring about the condition of my grandson.

"He's home from the hospital and doing fine," I said.

"That's good," Dr. Beckman said. "I'm glad to hear it. Now—about you."

"Did you read the document I sent you?"

"You mean the Mead notebook? Filled from beginning to end? Yes, I read it, Steve."

"And what did you think?"

"I found it quite disturbing," Dr. Beckman said.

I thought I knew where the doctor might be going with this. I cut him off at the proverbial pass.

"Listen, Doc, if you're going to recommend that I seek psychiatric care, I appreciate your diagnosis; but no thanks. I've been able to work this out on my own. I'm quite certain that I won't have any more —problems.

At least—I thought but did not say—for maybe another thirty

years. I now knew that old problems, both supernatural and otherwise, have a way of popping back up when you least expect them.

I couldn't be absolutely sure that I'd seen the last of the revolutionary ghosts. But I was reasonably sure that I'd seen the last of them for a while.

"Steve," he said. "I'm not going to recommend you seek psychiatric care. But after reading your account, *I* might need to."

This surprised me. I didn't have any desire to pry into Dr. Beckman's mental state, any more than I wanted him to pry into mine. So I changed the subject.

"Tell me, Dr. Beckman: Did the quarter I gave you fetch a good price on eBay?"

I could see Dr. Beckman squirm a little on his stool. "To be honest with you, Steve, I never did get around to selling the quarter."

"Oh? You still have it, then?"

Dr. Beckman took a deep breath. "No. Not exactly."

Now I was the one who was playing the role of inquisitor.

"Really? Do tell, Doc."

Dr. Beckman took another deep breath before beginning. "Okay. If you must know: When I left the office that day, I had the quarter in my pocket. I had the quarter when I returned home."

"All right," I said. "Then what?"

"I placed the quarter in my sock drawer. For safe keeping"

"Of course. For safe keeping."

The doctor said nothing, hesitating.

"And?" I pressed.

"Oh for goodness sake, Steve. You already know the answer, don't you? The quarter disappeared. When I checked a few days later, it was no longer at the bottom of my sock drawer."

"Maybe your wife took it," I suggested, trying to be helpful, "when she was putting your clean socks away."

Dr. Beckman shook his head. "Steve, gender roles have changed somewhat since you got married. And my wife is a pediatrician. She's as busy as I am. I put my own socks away. But I did ask my wife if she had happened to get into my sock drawer and take the quarter. She told me that no, absolutely, she hadn't been in the drawer. And I believe her."

"Of course," I said.

"And we don't have any kids yet," he added. "And no maid or housekeeper. Although my wife keeps saying we should hire one."

I couldn't resist smiling. Just a little. "So the quarter just disappeared into thin air, is what you're telling me?"

"Yes, I suppose that is what I'm telling you!" Dr. Beckman said. "But there must be a logical explanation."

"Of course," I said. "There must be. There is no way that logic can explain what happened. But there must be a logical explanation, which science will provide. Someday."

Dr. Beckman folded his arms. "Steve Wagner, I do believe you have an ornery streak."

I laughed. "And Dr. Beckman, I do believe we've just challenged your relentless, scientific skepticism."

Dr. Beckman waved his hand dismissively. "Let's just say you have a clean bill of health, okay—in mind as well as body."

I stood to go. "I'll see you in two years. For my next biennial exam."

"Steve," he said. "I have to ask you this once—and I'll only ask it once. Tell me honestly. Is everything you wrote in that notebook the truth, as you remember it?"

"It's the truth," I said.

"Oh, Dear God," he said, slowly shaking his head. "Are you going to be all right?"

"I'm going to be all right," I said.

I MADE my exit from Dr. Beckman's office. I had to make haste in order to be on time for a meeting back at Covington Foods.

I stepped out into the air. It was an unusually mild early winter day.

I thought about what I had given Dr. Beckman—my Bicentennial quarter and my story.

I realized that I had given Dr. Beckman a burden as well as a gift—the knowledge that the world is full of both curses and miracles.

He will likely need some time to reconcile that with his rigidly scientific worldview.

But he had asked, hadn't he?...And so I had told him.

I had also told him that I was going to be all right.

And somehow—I think that's true.

THE END

(Turn the page for author's notes, and information on additional titles.)

AFTERWORD

Revolutionary Ghosts is a story that brings together a handful of my interests: "The Legend of Sleepy Hollow" (one of the great, original American ghost stories), the 1970s, and the American Revolution.

Many of the "revolutionary ghosts" depicted in this book are based on actual historical personages. Others are made up.

This naturally brings forth the question: Which of them are real, and which aren't?

Banastre Tarleton, also known as "the Butcher of Waxhaws" was an actual officer in the British Army. The details revealed about him in this book—including his later service in the British Parliament—are more or less true.

At the time of the American Revolution, Tarleton was young, ambitious, and more than willing to bend the rules of civilized warfare in the fulfillment of his mission. Although I am the first author (to the best of my knowledge) to depict Tarleton as a vengeful ghost, I am not the first storyteller to cast him as a dramatic villain. He has appeared in various novels and movies about the American Revolution.

John André, the executed British spymaster, was also an actual historical figure. Urbane, dashing, and intelligent, he was indeed admired by men-of-arms on both sides. In a 1780 letter, George Washington described John André as "an accomplished man and gallant officer." André is portrayed by the actor JJ Field in the television series *Turn: Washington's Spies*—which I highly recommend.

Marie Trumbull, the condemned Loyalist spy who committed suicide with a blade smuggled into her cell, is completely fictitious. Nevertheless, there were more than a few Loyalists (called "Tories" at the time) who sided with the British. Many of them suffered acts of violence, both official and unofficial. (And, needless to say, the Loyalists carried out violence of their own.)

For a detailed nonfiction account of this often underreported side of the American Revolution, I recommend the book, *Scars of Independence: America's Violent Birth* by Holger Hoock (Crown, 2017).

"The Legend of Sleepy Hollow" (1820) is a short story by Washington Irving. Although the language and style are somewhat dated, the story is still very much worth reading.

The 1949 Disney adaptation of the story mentioned in the book is also real. Clips of it are available on YouTube.

As mentioned in several chapters of *Revolutionary Ghosts*, the Headless Horseman of legend was a Hessian officer killed at the Battle of White Plains on October 28, 1776. According to the legend, he was killed by a shot from a Continental cannonball. His execution by sword is completely my invention.

America did celebrate its Bicentennial in 1976. As anyone old enough to remember that year will attest, the phrase, "the Spirit of '76" was everywhere. The celebrations of America's 200th birthday provided a welcome air of festivity to the otherwise gloomy 1970s, a decade known for Vietnam, energy crises, violent underground revolutionary activities, Watergate, and stagflation.

The Bicentennial quarters that play a key role in the prologue and epilogue of this story are also real. I was eight years old in 1976, and coin collecting was one of my childhood hobbies. Somewhere among the forgotten boxes in my basement, I still have a cigar box full of circulated Bicentennial quarters.

And each of them is still worth twenty-five cents.

Clermont County, Ohio is a real place—just east of Cincinnati, along the Ohio River. The county exists more or less as described herein: a semi-rural area between the country and the eastern suburbs of Cincinnati.

For the purposes of this book, however, I have taken significant liberties with the county's history, institutions, and geography.

If you enjoyed this book, I would recommend checking out my horror/dark fantasy novels *12 Hours of Halloween* and *Eleven Miles of Night*.

Information about my current and upcoming books can be found at my website, EdwardTrimnellBooks.com.

Made in the USA
Coppell, TX
22 September 2022